ECHOES OF AVALON

A TALE OF AVALON
BOOK I

Adam Copeland

For Mom and Dad

Other Works by Adam Copeland

Ripples in the Chalice: A Tale of Avalon Book II

Midnight in Silverton: American Gothic

Chapter One

The boat rose and fell on the swells of water. The pattern was unrelenting and eternal. Placid waters had gone with the sun and the water was gray now. Only the different shades of gray differentiated the sky from the ocean at the steely horizon. White lined the swells of water. A light, constant drizzle seemed to conspire with the ocean spray to soak everything onboard. It was not a particularly large vessel, which made it all the worse for everyone.

For the crew of hardened fishermen, Cornishmen all, this posed no great discomfort. The crewmen at their work looked like gray mice scurrying over a large, wet, wheat barrel. For the lone passenger on board, however, the matter was altogether different. A single, still figure sat huddled on a bench in the aft of the boat. He was wrapped in a great-cloak, eyes transfixed on nothing. Only when the boat heaved to one side or the other would he move to brace himself.

One of the crewmen leaned over to his elder shipmate and asked, "Eh, Ebert, what is the matter with the man? Is he seasick?"

Ebert looked at their passenger. The sweat on the man's face was not from the ever-present moisture of rain and ocean.

Ebert knew this because the sweat was there long before the weather had turned bad. The passenger's gaze focused on one point only, as though attempting to minimize the pitching of the boat and make it appear steady. The shipmate shook his head.

"He looked like that when we picked him up in Cornwall. Exceptin' he were not starin' so much."

"Who is he anyway? Where we takin' him?"

"His name is Patrick Gawain. I hear talk that he is an Irish nobleman, come back from the Crusades." Ebert did his share of pulling the heavy netting from the side of the boat while still carrying on a conversation with his mate.

Peter, the younger crewman also pulling on the net, exclaimed under his breath to Ebert, "Gawain!"

Ebert put up a halting hand. "I know what you be thinking, an' you be wrong. Different Gawain, no relation to *the* Gawaine that were in Arthur's court. But he is knighted, I believe, because he carries a mighty sword with him under that great-cloak."

"Well, bugger me! A Crusader!" Peter shook his head. Peter paused momentarily while pulling on the net, but then resumed. "We not be takin' him home are we, I mean to Eire an' all, because if we are, we be heading in the wrong direction."

Ebert laughed at the younger fisherman. Peter was relatively new to the crew and not accustomed to the occasional practice of taking on passengers for transport to a certain locale. "No, he will not be going to Eire, we be taking him west, into the Misty Isles. To Avalon."

"Avalon! We be goin' there?"

"Of course not, ya bloomin' fool. Nobody goes into Avalon except the folk of Avalon and those invited like the young Sir over there. We just be taking him to the edge of the mist and wait for a dinghy to come out for him. That is how it's always been done."

Peter dropped the last of the netting onto the deck and shook his hands violently to be rid of the seaweed that clung to him. This went on for a good minute before he looked around frantically and decided to rub his hands on the edge of the boat instead. "Why do we have to do it then? Why do they not send for him themselves, the folk of Avalon I mean? Why do they have fishermen like us doin' it? 'Tis not exactly the entrance a nobleman merits. You'd think they would send out one of their own nice boats."

Ebert shrugged, not entirely sure if Peter's agitation was due to the slime on his hands or the fact that they had the added duty of dropping off a passenger before they could return home. "I think most traffic between here and there happens in groups, almost seasonal. He be traveling out of season. Could na' tell ya why, though."

Peter smirked. "Well, I hope he makes it. He looks none too good."

The aft of the boat came to a point where a seat was situated halfway between the railing and deck. Patrick Gawain was now pushed as far back into this nook as one could go. He held out his two long, sinewy arms on either side to brace himself. His hands gripped the railing so fiercely that all the blood drained out of them and they were more pale than his complexion. The railings creaked under the stress of his grip. Patrick's face was just as tight as his body. It looked as if he was trying to withdraw upon himself. His eyes were fearful, with that same transfixed gaze. He was breathing in quick, short gasps now. This was an improvement over his earlier appearance, when it was hard to determine if he was breathing at all.

"Are yea well, m'lord?" Ebert cautiously approached the Irishman. "Is there anything I can do for yea?"

Patrick didn't reply.

"M'lord?" Ebert turned and looked at Peter and shrugged, then turned once again on Patrick. "If yea be needing anything, just let..."

Patrick's head jerked up and he looked at Ebert. Sweat poured down his face and his breath quickened. He just now seemed to realize that another human being was present. He glanced at Ebert, and then turned his gaze away, once again maintaining the same stare into nothingness. The young nobleman said nothing to disturb the fisherman, nor had he looked upon him in anger, but his eyes were frightening.

Ebert stepped away towards Peter.

He had looked into the eyes of Patrick Gawain. They were a strange blend of brown and green with a hint of dusk at the core. Peculiar, yes, but no more extraordinary than Ebert's own.

It was what lay behind the eyes that frightened him. Though they had looked straight at him, they didn't even register Ebert in Patrick's mind. Patrick had a fearful look, like a caged wild animal, yet at the same time he was thoughtful as if pondering some great mystery. He looked as if he were going to explode into a frenzy, and like he was waiting for the chance to do just that. The man was not trying to keep from being seasick. He was wrestling with something inside himself. He was haunted.

Truth be told, Patrick was staring at something in particular. Before him, at a distance about half the length of the boat, stood a creature of nightmare that returned his stare. Though Patrick could not see the thing's face, he knew it was looking right at him. That was how it always was. No face. No identity. Even the hands were gloved. But it was obvious that the robed and hooded figure had come to haunt him like some hellish visitation.

As the fisherman returned to work, he passed right through the robed thing without even knowing it. He penetrated the Apparition like a ship passing through fog and continued on about his business. The fisherman disappeared on the other side of the specter. For all its misty translucence, it was not transparent.

He tried pushing himself into the back of the boat to put even more distance between himself and the thing, but he was already as far as he could go. The Apparition did not advance nor did it threaten to. It just stood there and stared as it had always done. This did not comfort Patrick much. If he thought for one instant that he could jump overboard in his armor and swim, he would, despite the fact that he did not know how far he was from the nearest land: Cornwall or Avalon.

And anyway, he had tried running from the Apparition before. It was always there, wherever he turned. It stayed with him, gazing at him, until it decided it was time to leave, and not a moment before. He tried calling to it and pleading, but it never responded. It stayed just long enough to unnerve him, and then disappeared. Patrick never saw it vanish. It only disappeared after he had squeezed his eyes shut tight.

Others had thought him mad. The first time it came to him, it had come to the Mont St. Michel and harried him through the maze-like corridors. Patrick had run like a madman, begging the thing to leave him.

"Who are you? What do you want?" he had cried.

It had not harmed him. It appeared and disappeared in silence, first over him in his bedchamber, pointing an accusing finger at him with a black–gloved hand.

The presence itself was a shock, as the monks who nursed him back to health usually left him alone. They came in the morning, at noon, and twice in the evenings: at the evening meal and after vespers. And other than that, he was supposed to rest, unless he had energy for a walk. He was still quite sick from the fever he had picked up on his journey through France, on route home from the Holy Land. The weather had been miserable in Lyon, and a few hours after he arrived he fell sick. At first it was only a slight fever and chill. They said it was probably from the rats on board the barge that brought him and the other travelers up the Rhône from the Mediterranean. But on the overland journey to Troyes, trudging through the rain and mud, his fever became so bad that others swore they could see steam rising off his face as the cool rain touched it. He was incoherent, babbling about cutting his arms off at the elbows to rid himself of the pain. He had even tried drawing his sword to do so, but the other veterans held him down and took his weapons. They carried him to an inn to stay until he was well enough to travel again, though it became clear he needed much more rest. He, like the others, had been traveling a long time since Jerusalem.

Patrick agreed, but he would not travel by boat again, not with the seasickness and rats. Therefore that ruled out the Paris and Seine River route, so it must be by horseback to the West—towards Angers. Many of the veterans headed for Paris anyway, because they were healthy and eager to be home after three years away. Only his friend, David of York, went with him.

At Rennes he fell sick again. It was the same fever–induced delirium that had caught him just before Troyes—and in the same dismal weather. David did not know what to do with him. Neither had much money and neither had family in the region, so David decided that perhaps the Church would help. He soon discovered that the only parish in the vicinity that could administer the medical attention Patrick needed was nearby. Actually, it was off the shore of France itself, and that was where David of York took him.

The journey from Rennes, seemed a part of the delirium. He recalled being led on horseback, strapped to his saddle so

that he would not fall, by many robed monks down a long, straight road. On either side of the road was the sea, boiling at the edges like a cauldron that might at any moment froth over and wash all away. He could not understand why it had not happened already; the turbulent water seemed a mere arm's length away. He could almost see the faces of demons in the frothy water, reaching up to pull him off his horse. David was with the monks. He walked straight ahead, mindless of the demons in the water reaching for him too.

At the end of the road was an island in this boiling cauldron. Directly out of the tumultuous waters rose a fortress, built tier upon tier, an island city rather than a castle. It was indeed an island, for there was a break between the lower fortifications and the uppermost structure, which looked like an acropolis of granite. In this break was steep, rocky land with trees. The tallest structure, at the middle of the acropolis, had a spire reaching high into the sky. The horizon behind the fortress stretched to infinity. As far as the eye could see was the demon filled ocean. The sky was much akin to the water, a swirling mass of black, endlessly twisting and turning. Occasionally it would light up with incredible bursts of lightning, followed by deafening thunderclaps.

The monks chanted, exclaimed in French, a language now familiar, "Le Tonnerre!" and "l'éclair!"

#

When he awoke, he was in a stone chamber with golden sunlight streaming in from a high window. He was lying in a bed and somebody was tugging on his exposed undergarments, obviously trying to remove them.

Patrick panicked.

He grabbed a metal pitcher full of water from a nearby bed stand and struck at the robed man who pulled at his clothing.

The man cried out in surprise and ran for the door. Patrick followed him, swinging the pitcher.

He chased the man out into the hall, but stopped when he heard a familiar voice, "Patrick! For the love of God! Stop! The poor soul was just trying to help."

It was David. He was standing with a load of fresh linens in his arms, and he began to laugh like Patrick had never seen him laugh before.

The journey to the island-fortress had been no dream, David explained. It was the monastery at Mont St. Michel, just walking distance off the coast of France. David said "walking distance" because at low tide the waters completely pulled away, leaving a sandy flood-plain between the mainland and the island. It was possible then to walk to the abbey. But, at high tide, the ocean came rushing in at half a man's height every second.

The monks were charitable enough, and agreed to nurse Patrick back to health. He and David stayed until they lost count of the days. When Patrick awakened, he felt better, but was still hot to the touch, disoriented, headache-ridden, and congested. And, of course, he was incredibly tired. He slept most of the time.

When he was feeling up to it, he and David would go for walks.

Patrick was surprised to find in the light of day, and when not veiled in a fever-dream, that the complex looked very different from what he remembered from his journey. The abbey was not as tall, nor as elaborate, and there were no battlements that circled the lower portions of the island near the water's edge.

"Perhaps you somehow glimpsed the future of this place. It would make an excellent fortress," David said whimsically when Patrick commented on it.

Patrick only shook his head.

In any case, the abbey was no less interesting, housing many paintings and other works of art, not to mention how the monks' chants filled its empty spaces; all of which pleased Patrick, especially the chanting. He stopped whatever he was doing during the various prayer hours, and listened with his eyes closed.

Outside the abbey proper, the village was a maze of winding narrow streets which dipped and rose all around the island. Patrick was glad that the weather was turning to spring, a pleasant change from the cold and miserable rains which had fallen without respite since he arrived in Europe. Leaning on David, he would take deep breaths of the spring air as he hobbled along the cobblestone paths.

One day, they leaned on a waist-high wall at the edge of a cliff. From here he could see much of the land surrounding the island monastery. The tide was out and below was nothing but flat, wet sand. The sun was rising in the east and, as it struck the earth, the moist sand sparkled in such a way that he had to shield his eyes. Seagulls drifted lazily on the wind. It was beautiful.

Another riddle was puzzling Patrick as he frowned in the direction of the mainland. There was a natural land-bridge that connected the mainland to the island, but it was only a series of disjointed outcroppings—not at all the straight and well engineered causeway of his feverish memories. When he commented on this as well, David insisted that they had crossed the sand in a hurry the night of their arrival to avoid the approaching tide.

"I guess I was truly out of my mind," Patrick mused.

"What do you mean 'was'?" David said laughing.

Patrick laughed as well, then closed his eyes and drew in another breath of fresh air, savoring it.

"Why did you join the Crusade?" David asked.

Patrick was slow to respond. He shrugged, saying, "It seemed like a good idea at the time."

David could not get much more out of him after that. Patrick really did not want to talk about it. They had both come out of the experience somewhat disenchanted; many had. Yet they had survived, though this did not comfort him much.

"I want to thank you for coming with me," he told David. "I mean taking this route instead of going to Paris like the others. Who knows, maybe I would be dead by now if I had gone that way too."

David shrugged. "It was a good idea at the time."

They laughed.

"I am surprised that you are still with me after all this time," Patrick said. "Most of my friends usually part with me by now."

David frowned. "What do you mean?"

"Most people I come to know usually tire of me or something and they drift away. You saw what happened a long time ago when we started our march from Flanders with those men I used to ride with, before I really came to know you. I have heard no word from them in over a year. And the ones who left to go back home, have sent no word of how they are doing, as they had promised to do."

"Patrick, that is a normal thing," David said.

Patrick shook his head. "But everyone? Always? A curse is on me, I tell you, and I know not why."

"Maybe it is your wonderfully optimistic attitude," said David, giving Patrick a playful punch to the stomach and grabbing his head in a wrestler's hold.

They were both grown men in their early twenties, and soldiers to boot, but they wrestled around for a few moments like boys.

"Stop it," Patrick gave a muffled cry from under David's arm. "Or I'll get sick on you."

David backed off. He had seen Patrick get sick before.

The Irishman made a face when he was released and suddenly lunged at David, cupping his hands over his mouth. David cried and jumped back. Patrick's face beamed and he began to laugh.

David smiled also. "Bastard."

They walked back arm in arm.

"Well, Irishman, you do not have to worry about me leaving you. I have too much pleasure beating you," David said.

"You can only say that because I am sick, otherwise I would thrash you." They laughed together.

#

In the following days, Patrick got increasingly better, and David grew steadily more restless. He talked increasingly of his family and friends in York and complained that there was little to do on the island.

One morning, he was simply gone.

He hadn't said anything to Patrick or anyone. Just left. He hadn't even left a message or a way of how he could be reached in York.

For days Patrick just looked out windows onto the wind swept expanse of wet sands. He couldn't understand what happened. He thought perhaps he had done something wrong. But he knew that he hadn't. David was just eager to be home and didn't know how to say goodbye, so he made it easier on himself by saying nothing. Could Patrick blame him? Or could he? All that he knew was that it hurt.

"Why the long face, Patrick? It's not like this is the first time," he lamented to a mirror. Shortly afterwards, he had a relapse. Not a serious one, but serious enough to discourage him from traveling.

His throat became so sore he could barely eat. The evil-looking phlegm it produced woke him prematurely in the mornings with racking coughs, but at least it didn't choke him to death.

And that is when the Apparition first came to him.

It just stood there, pointing, though Patrick could not fathom what he was accused of. At first he thought it was one of the monks in strange garb. But then it turned, moved away toward the door, and then faded right *through* the door.

The thing, which he named "Apparition," appeared to him in the mornings, in the evenings before he went to bed, and on his walks in broad daylight down the cobblestone streets. It never approached, but watched coldly.

One night, Patrick awoke and knew the creature was in his room. He could neither hear it nor see it in the darkness, but he knew it was there, peering over him. He knew that it was leaning closer and closer to put its face near his own. He had never seen the face. He had a feeling that he did not want to. He pressed his body into his mattress as much as possible and began to shake and sweat with the effort. He tried convincing himself that it was not there; it had never harmed him, so why should it do so now? But a yell escaped his throat and he bolted for the door. He ran down the corridors screaming in a panic. Monks came from all directions, blocked his path, and wrestled him to the ground. They demanded to know what was wrong. Patrick stammered an explanation, but they seemed incredulous. His room was checked and there was nothing there.

"There!" Patrick shouted. "It comes! Can you not see it?"

The ghostly Apparition moved down the hall, walking slowly, taking deliberate steps toward the gathering of monks. It passed through objects and bodies in its path, and the living monks took no notice. The elder monk, who was closest to Patrick, shook his head.

"Mon seigneur, je ne vois rien." I see nothing, my lord.

As the thing approached, Patrick cowered on the flagstones with his eyes closed and held on to the nearest monk.

"Monseigneur? Monseigneur?" The monk shook Patrick. The Irishman opened his eyes and the robed figure was gone.

"It is only the fever," the monk said. "You will be fine. We will take care of you."

#

For the following nights, Patrick slept fitfully. He was still feeling unwell.

Patrick was from the green hills of Eire and his Celtic heritage was strong. He believed that he was sicker than he thought and the monks would not tell him. He thought that a *Bain Sidhe*, a banshee, had come to herald his death. He had never heard of a banshee that was utterly silent; they were supposed to wail terribly. Patrick imagined footsteps around his bed.

He began to accept his fate as the haunting became more frequent. He became resigned to the fact that he was going to die and no longer gave notice to the creature. He mostly lay in bed, wondering what he should write to his family. After a while, it seemed to lose interest in him and came less and less frequently. Remarkably, he started to feel better as well, and the haunting almost ceased completely. Patrick thought perhaps that was the secret to defeating death: to accept death for what it is and embrace it.

Or perhaps it really all had been a fever-dream. Patrick did not care. The Apparition appeared to be gone.

Once again his health was improving, and this time he meant to keep it that way. He made sure that he had plenty of sleep, ate regularly and well, and kept warm. He had become pale and thin since his illness, but he knew that would change with his renewed appetite and increased activity. The monks commended his improvement and commitment to health. Patrick sensed they were eager to be done with him, being the nuisance that he was, although they never said anything to him and were always polite.

To tell the truth, Patrick wished to leave. He had stayed at the monastery for almost two months now, and it was closing in on him. He was incredibly bored and could not stand to feel useless. He did not feel he deserved the hospitality bestowed upon him. And worse, he did not know where to go once he felt well enough to travel again. He had only been traveling with David and the other veterans in the first place because David was going in the same direction, and it was in the general direction of his homeland. But, now that he was here, he had no idea where he wanted to go. He had been moving toward Eire, but he knew that he would not be happy there, that the series of events which caused him to leave in the first place would resurface and he would leave again. So why go there now?

In a sense, he felt trapped in the Mont Saint-Michel monastery. Nothing kept him there but his own indecisiveness. He could go in search of David of York, but he questioned the wisdom of that. Perhaps David did not want to be found. Or maybe Patrick felt it would damage his pride to chase after him, no matter how good friends he believed they had been. In any case, he did not think that was an option and he again felt depressed.

As it turned out, he needed only wait a while longer for chance to step in and offer a choice to him.

Travelers had come to rest at Mont St. Michel to break their journey, and Patrick met them in the Common Hall for a meal. Such events were common. The abbot was always hosting visitors and temporary guests and thought it quaint to have them dine together. News from abroad could be exchanged this way, and mutual traveling arrangements could be made. Even friendships, too.

At the meal, Patrick was conversing with a young lady from Alsace and her male escort when he noticed a gentleman sitting across from him. He was unabashedly staring.

"You are not French or Norman," the man said in Latin, the lingua universal.

"Is my accent that bad?" Patrick had always been conscientious of his French, even after being a long time among Franks during the Crusade.

The man smiled. "No, that was not my meaning. I could not help but notice that you are not from these parts."

"Neither are you," the Irishman pointed out. The man was tall and lanky, even taller than Patrick. His face was long and pale, not with the pallor of illness, but a natural lightness of complexion common among the Anglo people. He had brown, whimsical eyes with smile lines around them. He was dressed in a plain surcoat with a broad leather sword belt wrapped around his waist. Although he saw no scabbard, Patrick could tell from the man's hands and mannerisms that he was a knight, if not some other kind of soldier.

"My name is Marcus Ionus." The man extended a hand.

"Patrick Gawain." Patrick took his hand. Marcus's eyes narrowed. "Gawain? The name seems familiar to me."

Patrick laughed. He was used to it. "You are doubtless thinking of *the* Sir Gawaine, nephew of King Arthur and Knight of the Round Table."

"Perhaps a relation?" he inquired.

"No relationship of which I am aware," returned Patrick. They talked for a while about current news. Patrick had been cut off from the world by his illness and geography. He found that he had missed much, but nothing that really interested him.

"So tell me, sir, how is it that an Irishman comes to the coast of Normandy?" Marcus asked.

"By way of the Holy Land," Patrick replied.

"Do you fight in the Crusade?"

"I did. It is a very long tale."

Marcus seemed intrigued. "I plan to stay in the abbey for a few days, and I would be interested to hear it."

Patrick gave a slight, almost tired smile. "It is not exactly the stuff of ballads and epics. I really do not think you would want to hear it. And what is an Englishman doing at Mont St. Michel?"

"I am completing certain research. You might say that I am on a crusade myself." Marcus replied. The woman from Alsace was now talking to others at the table, allowing the two men to talk.

Now Patrick was intrigued. "How is that?"

"I belong to a certain order of knights," Marcus explained. "And we must occasionally replenish our number, as many in our order move on to other missions in life. That is what I have been doing this year past, searching for new candidates. I am close to finding all that I need to complete our regiment, as well as six reserves. I came here because I have heard that in Les Salles Des Chevaliers there are documents describing the whereabouts of knights throughout the kingdoms."

Patrick leaned forward, pushing his plate aside. "What is this order?"

"It is very select," said Marcus. "Many of us go on to become royal or elite guards for the nobility. We are called the Avangarde."

Patrick frowned. "I never heard of it."

"Of course not," Ionus said. "It is a small, private, and almost secret group."

"Is it a Holy Order?" Patrick asked.

"Religious? No, not at all. It is quite secular. We guard knowledge and guests who seek safety and learning, most of whom are the children of nobility, sent for an education away from possible harm in their homelands."

"I have heard of such schools in Paris and in Rome, but I have never heard of them using an order of knights to protect them," Patrick said.

Marcus Ionus bobbed his head from side to side as if thinking carefully in choosing his next words. "It is not just a school per se, but a way of life—an environment, if you will. And since there is such a large concentration of noble lineage present, the great houses of the world have insisted, quite reasonably, that their noble offspring be protected."

Patrick stroked his chin as he sat back on the bench. The concept was confusing. He was not sure if he understood, but he liked the idea of being a part of an order of knights given such a responsibility. A secular order. He had had his fill of fighting for religious reasons. And by the sound of it, it could lead to good references for a life afterwards.

"You say you still look for men?" Patrick asked.

"Yes," Marcus replied.

"What must one do to become an Avangarde?"

"One need only take audience with me for a while, answer many questions and, of course, demonstrate some amount of fighting skill," Marcus explained. "That is but a small portion, in any case. It is much more complex than that," Marcus paused for a moment while swirling wine around in his goblet. While sipping from the cup, he looked at the Irishman over its rim. "Are you interested?"

Patrick didn't respond right away. He was afraid of looking to eager.

"I should warn you, however," Marcus continued, "not to get your hopes up. I have found all that we need in the main regiment. Now I am but looking for reserves."

Patrick's brow furrowed. "And the difference between the two?"

Marcus replied, "The main regiment of Avangarde receive room, board, clothing, equipment, and a stipend each month. Nothing to make them rich, mind you, but enough to make them comfortable. And of course, there is the prestige and other intangible benefits that go with the station."

"And the reserves?"

"They," continued Marcus, raising again his goblet, "receive room and board and get the opportunity to work and function side-by-side with the other Avangarde."

Patrick rubbed a hand over his face. Of course there had to be some kind of caveat; he was never so lucky.

"Make no mistake," Marcus offered quickly. "The reserves are essential to the existence of the Garde. Without them, we would have no guarantee of maintaining our numbers in the event that some of the main corps of men fall. They hold high position and are respected."

I wonder about that, Patrick thought.

"It is not at all uncommon for reserves to become Avangarde within a short amount of time," Marcus continued. "Avangarde are always being offered positions which are closer to normal civilization and their positions must be filled."

This last point caught his attention. "What do you mean 'normal civilization?'"

Marcus's smile deepened the lines around his mouth and eyes. It was a light smile, which made Patrick feel as if Marcus knew something in particular that the other did not. Patrick tried imagining disliking him and found it impossible.

"Our holding is in Avalon, on the Misty Isle in the Western Sea," he said simply. "It is far from any city of the known world."

The room was nearly quiet now. Candle light flickered shadows along the floor as monks began clearing the table. He and Marcus sat almost alone.

"How do you expect me to believe that?" the Irishman asked after a moment of silence. "First you ramble on about this order of knights that I have never heard of, and now you tell me it is located on a mythical island." He felt stupid. Worse, he felt gullible to have listened to the tale all along. He expected Marcus and his men sitting nearby to erupt in laughter.

Marcus continued to smile, as if expecting this outburst. "How do you know it is mythical? Have you ever been there to prove that it does not exist? How much faith and belief did you put into the tomb of Christ and the other Holy Relics until you actually saw them in Jerusalem?"

Patrick did not reply.

"I tell you, young sir, that we exist, the island exists, and if you like and if you meet the standards, you are invited to be an Avangarde reserve."

Patrick wiped his mouth one last time and threw his napkin on the table. "If you will excuse me, sir." He rose from the table and turned to depart. As he left, Marcus began to laugh, not a malicious laugh, but a slight humorous one.

"If you change your mind," he called after Patrick's back, "you can find me in the apartments by Les Salles des Chevaliers."

Patrick Gawain did not see the knight Marcus Ionus all the next day. Patrick stayed in his room, mostly stretched out on his bed staring up at the vaulted ceiling. He had not bothered getting dressed. He felt more depressed than ever.

Probably waiting to see if I come to him. Then he will laugh, thought Patrick.

This made the Irishman all the unhappier, because for a moment, one moment, he believed that perhaps he had found somewhere to go. Somewhere that was not home and was not York. A place where he could feel useful, unlike this damned huge abbey where the monks constantly asked if he was feeling well enough to travel yet, and then looked at him askance.

"Besides," Patrick muttered to himself. "A reserve? What's that all about? "

Avalon? It was a legend. It was as endearing as the legend of King Arthur; but many believed the legend of King Arthur to be true. Why else would so many inquire if he were related to Arthur's Gawaine? In the back of his mind, Patrick believed in such things, just like he believed in his own Celtic legends, such as those of Cu Chulainn. He had seen faerie circles in Eire, and heard the stories of changelings.

Have you ever been there to prove it does not exist?

He shot up from his bed and threw the metal pitcher of water against the wall. He then began to pace back and forth in the stone chamber.

It is not true. He was making jest at your expense. He walked back and forth, rubbing his temple.

His agitated wandering came to a stop before the water stand. He stooped over and placed his hands on either side of it and looked into the mirror on the wall behind it.

"Where are you going to go?" He demanded of the pale and sullen-eyed individual in the polished copper. "What are you going to do?"

He stared at his reflection until the already-low candle burned itself out and he no longer could see in the darkness.

#

Marcus Ionus answered the knock at his chamber door and was not surprised to see the Irish knight.

"I..." Patrick did not know how to say what he wanted to say. He did not know what he wanted to say. "...Need..." his sighed angrily. "If these are stories to amuse yourself, I do not find..."

"Sir Gawain." Marcus grabbed Patrick with both hands by the shoulders and looked into his eyes. "As Almighty God is my witness, I do not lie to you."

Patrick relaxed. He still did not know what to say.

"Be warned though. I still must test you. I have been a year now searching for people. I do not choose lightly. It is not just a matter of swinging a sword."

Patrick nodded.

#

The following days were strange ones for Patrick. Marcus was correct when he said he would ask all manner of questions. And strange questions they were. At first Patrick did not see the point in them. Then he came to realize that they were a form of evaluation of his character by way of example. These often took place while on long walks around the outer wall. The weather was improving, and outdoor activity was becoming the norm.

One such question: "Gawain, if you were walking down the street one day and you came across a young girl whose kitten was stuck in a tree, would you stop to help?"

"Of course."

"But you are in a hurry, the king awaits your audience."

"Is the girl crying?"

"Yes."

"I would stop to help."

Another time, while Marcus accompanied the Irishman on walks with steeper paths to challenge his health, the Englishman asked; "Gawain, you catch a man robbing your house, but he is not stealing valuables, only food, for he is poor and his family is starving. What do you do with the man?"

"I let him take the food."

"But you are poor yourself."

"But I have food, and he does not. I am not as poor as he."

And then; "Gawain, you are in combat and you see your liege fall under the attack of many. What do you do?"

"I ride to his side."

"You have no hope of survival."

"Better dead than a failure."

Marcus looked at Patrick curiously. The answer was quick and the Irishman looked sternly forward, deep in thought, saying no more.

And so the questions went on for days. Patrick felt that he answered most of them wisely. The ones he had doubts about, he wagered that it was best to tell the truth, what he would really do in such a situation. He also answered many questions about his family, his reasons for leaving home, his travels in the Holy Land, and his general point of view on life. Marcus seemed to find him interesting, and once, he said, a little difficult to follow.

"An Avangarde must have stability, a strong grasp on reality," the tall knight emphasized.

Patrick did not mention the robed Apparition that had paid him visits.

His fighting ability was tested the day after the questioning. This took place at the base of the walls that formed the inner battlements, higher up on the island where there were trees and rocks, and not so many people about. There was much sunshine now. The demonstration of fighting skills was much easier than the questioning. Marcus only demanded simple demonstrations of the different defensive, offensive, and passive use of the weapons with which Patrick was already familiar. The two men fenced. Patrick found Marcus a capable fighter.

"Your methods are unorthodox but effective," Marcus pointed out.

Patrick gave a light smile, while stroking away at his sword with a sharpening stone when the sparring was complete. "I have seven brothers and three sisters, remember? They were a quarrelsome brood."

The third day began with Marcus bringing Patrick to the location where they had fenced and placed a rather large rock on Patrick's head. He told him to balance it there until he said otherwise. Then he went and laid down under the shade of a tree, stretching out his arms and putting them behind his head.

After an hour of sweating in the sun and listening to the sound of insects buzzing in the sparse grass among the rocks, Patrick tossed the rock.

"You know what I think?" the Irishman asked.

Marcus opened his eyes. "No, what might that be?"

"I think you have no intention whatsoever of telling me when to put the rock down. You want to keep me guessing. To perdition with that." Patrick folded his arms, as if to challenge any response Marcus might have.

Marcus clapped his hands. "Very good, my Celtic warrior."

And that was the end of that.

#

The following day Marcus told Patrick that he did not want to see him. He wanted to confer with his entourage about the matter.

The morning after that, however, Patrick awoke to find the knight standing over his bed. "Congratulations. You are an Avangarde reserve now." He then poured the pitcher of water over the Irishman. "Get dressed. Let us break our fast." And then he went out the door, laughing.

Patrick sat there pulling at the soaked sheets, shocked by the total irreverence of it all.

After they broke their fast, there was somewhat of a ceremony. Patrick was asked to recite the oath of the station and was touched on both shoulders by Marcus's blade.

"I pronounce you a reservist of the Avangarde," Marcus said, and followed it with something in Latin that Patrick did not hear clearly.

And finally it was time for Marcus Ionus to leave.

"I must be getting back to my duties," he said. "I consider myself very fortunate that I came across you here. You have cut my journey in half."

He gave Patrick a small leather volume with incredibly small print. "Read this. It is the basis for all the Garde as well as the establishment that it protects. All Garde and reservists alike must know it thoroughly. You should have enough time to finish it before you arrive at Avalon. As for getting to Avalon, take this." He handed Patrick a rolled scroll of waxed parchment with a seal on it. The seal was of a swan. "Show it to any fisherman of Cornwall. It will be recognized."

"Fisherman?"

"Yes, fisherman. Whatever you do, do not break the seal. It is your only way through the mist."

"What if I accidentally break it?"

"Take care that you do not. The fisherman will take you to where you need to go. From there, you will meet a man named Wolfgang von Fiescher. With him you will finish your journey." Marcus mounted his horse. "Good luck, young Sir Irishman."

"Will I see you at Avalon?" Patrick asked. Marcus gave that now-familiar smile.

"No, my days in Avalon are done. I work for it on the outside now. My next destination is London, then finally Rome where I maintain certain correspondence for the Misty Isle. Someone has to do it. Do not worry, I will send word of your arrival."

With that, he gave a salute and a farewell, and rode away with his men. That was the last time that Patrick Gawain saw him.

#

Patrick stayed a few more days at Mont St. Michel. He started to read the volume that Marcus had left. Although small, it proved to be long and tedious reading and though he was fortunate that his mother had sent him to the parish school, he was not a proficient reader. Before putting it down out of frustration, he got a better glimpse of what was in store for him: The pages reiterated the Avangarde's singularity, but he was unsure if his duty was to guard the inhabitants or to keep them happy. The little book mentioned again and again the Avangarde's presence with the guests as well as the maintenance and protection of the establishment. Patrick expected that all would be made clear when he arrived. With that, he put the little book down.

When it was time for him to leave, the monks gave him a hearty farewell.

"I will really miss you, too," he said under his breath as he rode out the front gate. It was easy to find passage to England, although he detested the sea journey. It seemed he would now and forever hate water.

He landed on the coast of Land's End in Cornwall and wasted no time getting on with the journey.

At Cornwall he sold his horse. From what he understood, he would not be able to transport it on the fisherman's boat, but he kept the saddle, tack and harness. He went down to the docks, introduced himself at the first boat he found, and showed the sealed scroll to the captain.

"Do you understand what this means?" Patrick asked.

"Why, yes, m'lord," the man replied. "I would be happy to oblige yea." He gestured for Patrick to get onboard. Before

Patrick stepped on, he turned and looked to the direction from whence he came. He was about to make another life changing decision. He could feel it, just like he felt it when he decided to leave home so long ago, and again when he decided to join the Crusade. What was going to happen this time? When was the wandering going to end? Was he making the right choice?

He had no answers. He seldom, if ever, did.

"Do you have a problem with rats on board?" the Irishman asked.

"M'lord?"

"Never mind." And Patrick stepped down onto the deck of the single-masted fishing vessel. He sat on a bench in the aft of the boat and stayed out of the way so the fishermen could go about their business.

And then suddenly, as he turned to watch the port slip away behind, he thought about the ghostly Apparition that had been appearing to him during his sickness. He mused that if the thing was indeed a spirit, then it could not follow him, because legend said that evil spirits could not cross large bodies of water.

#

He was wrong.

For there it was. Staring at him. The thing suddenly stepped forward and smoothly made its way to Patrick's position. The knight gave a start, closed his eyes, and curled up on the bench, stricken with fear. Although still a little weak, Patrick knew he was mostly recovered and had been for quite a while now. Therefore, he no longer had any reason for the visions. He could no longer blame it on fever. He was haunted—a dead man.

And then suddenly, miraculously, the boat stopped its violent pitching and the clouds broke.

"All clear, Sir!" one of the crew members cried.

"And thar be the mist!" another yelled. There was scurrying about the vessel.

Patrick looked up tentatively and saw that the Apparition was gone. When he saw this, he stumbled to his feet and leaned over the railing, and vomited violently into the water.

"Where is the Sir?" the captain called.

Somebody responded, "He be over here, feeding the fish."

"Best tell him to get ready. His ride is here."

Patrick looked up and saw that the fishing boat was now traveling in a placid ocean under a crystal-blue sky. A wall of pearly mist stretched as far as he could see in either direction.

A small rowboat with a single oarsman was coming out of the mist.

"M'lord, yea best be gathering yourself," somebody suggested. The man sounded eager to be seeing him gone.

I will really miss you, too.

Patrick wiped his chin and picked up his belongings and headed to the front of the boat. As he did, the crew cleared a path for him as if they were afraid. Patrick could see it in their eyes. He handed his belongings to the ferryman and then climbed in. The ferryman threw a small leather bag to the captain of the fishing boat, who caught it and gave a slight nod. The dinghy pulled steadily away from the fishermen.

Just before the mist obscured the sight of the fishing boat, Patrick Gawain could see the crew making the sign of the Holy Cross.

Chapter Two

Traveling through the pearly, wet mist took some time. During the journey, Patrick's only company was the sound of the creaking oars splashing into the water over and over again.

He tried making conversation with the boatman, but the man, garbed in the same simple wool and leather clothing as the fisherman he just left behind, did not speak much and only made curt responses to Patrick's questions.

"Are you Wolfgang von Fiescher?" the Irishman asked. The man gave a quick bemused shake of the head, as if to say of course not.

And so the journey went, long enough for Patrick to go over and over in his head what he would say to von Fiescher after meeting him.

Eventually the mist gave way to bright sunlight and crystal-blue sky. Ahead was land, a rolling mass of green that rose only slightly above the sea. Whether it indeed was an island was difficult to ascertain because the shore extended for some length to either side. In any case, it was large. Patrick found it difficult to believe that such an extensive mass of land could go undetected for so long, so close to the lands of Britain. He looked around. The mist on this side was not as wall-like as it had been when he arrived on the fishing boat. In fact, it was now hardly discernible, giving way to a glassy ocean.

"So this is Avalon." Patrick meant it more as a statement rather than a question. The boatman bobbed his head with a smile. They moved on steadily, long enough for Patrick to take in the scenery some more until reaching the shore. Here was a sandy beach, which separated from the water sheer cliffs not unlike those at Cornwall. Several docks stretched from the land like fingers extending from a hand. They seemed sturdy enough and could accommodate a larger vessel than the simple boat in which the Irishman had arrived.

The boat was moored at a ladder and the rower offered to help Patrick and his belongings up onto the dock. He accepted the help, and when he was well established on dry land, the rower climbed back into the dingy, unmoored it, and started to row away.

"Wait! Where are you going?" the Irishman called. The man waved farewell. Patrick cursed. This was all very unusual indeed. Everything from the manner of Marcus Ionus' introduction to his arrival on Avalon was strange.

"Sir Gawain."

He turned in the direction of the voice. Just at the end of the dock was a man sitting astride a great horse with a second horse and a pony in tow. The man dismounted and approached. Patrick made his way towards the man, struggling with his gear.

As the two drew nearer to one another, Patrick noted that the man was taller and stood ramrod straight. He walked with natural authority, and his gaze suggested that he had every right to. He was dressed as a knight with silvery mail, a dark surcoat with a border of white, and an equally white swan symbol emblazoned on the surcoat. Girded about his waist by a thick belt was a broadsword, held in a scabbard criss-crossed by strips of leather. His face was lined, and he had a large, silvery-grey drooping mustache the same color as his full, bushy head of hair.

"You need not have brought your saddle, young sir," the man said as he clasped hands with Patrick. He had a Teutonic accent. "One will be provided for you as well as a horse."

Patrick looked at his saddle with displeasure. Carrying the saddle had been annoying, all the more so now.

"I had not asked Marcus Ionus about the matter. Perhaps I should have," Patrick pointed out.

"It is of no consequence," the man said.

"You must be von Fiescher," Patrick stated.

The man nodded. "That I am. And you are Sir Patrick Gawain of Galway, in Eire."

Patrick gave a courtly bow.

"Do you have the invitation that Marcus Ionus gave you?"

"Sir?" Patrick was puzzled for a moment, and then he remembered the scroll with the swan seal. He placed some of his belongings on the ground in order to search through his bag. After a moment, he retrieved the scroll and handed it to von Fiescher.

Patrick's jaw dropped when the seal glowed and made an audible pop when opened by Wolfgang. Von Fiescher looked over the parchment, seemed satisfied, and stuffed it in his surcoat while exclaiming "Welcome to Avalon, Sir Patrick."

#

The other horse that Wolfgang von Fiescher had brought was for Patrick. It was a warhorse, a powerful chestnut stallion at least seventeen hands high. Von Fiescher called the animal Siegfried after the hero of the Volsung saga.

Patrick felt undeserving of such a fine beast, though von Fiescher told him not to feel indebted. All Avangardesmen and reservists got a good horse. "But do not become too attached," he warned. "They belong to the Order and are only yours during your service." The pony was to carry any of Patrick's belongings. In addition to his traveling bag, there was the old saddle with its tack, his bedroll, shield, helm, and few other miscellaneous things. He was wearing his own suit of mail covered by his family's surcoat of green on which was sewn a gold dragon. His long sword was at his hip. Draped over his shoulders was the great-cloak, still damp from his sea journey.

Patrick placed the bulk of his equipment on the pony and then climbed into Siegfried's saddle. He then followed von Fiescher's lead. The horse was fearsome looking, but was actually friendly and had wanted to nuzzle his hands before he mounted.

"He seems to have taken a liking to you, young sir," Wolfgang pointed out. Patrick was happy. It was the first truly nice gesture anyone had made towards him in quite a while, and he could not help but wonder how long it would be before Siegfried decided not to be his friend, like David and the others. He tried to banish the thought from his mind. Instead, he made conversation and asked questions.

"So, please tell me, Sir von Fiescher, what is your function with the Avangarde?"

They were trotting up a dirt path from what Patrick now realized was a sort of tiny harbor. This path ascended to the point where it was level with the top of the cliffs.

"You might say that I am the Grand Master of the Order, yet that is a rather crude description, for there is no one Grand Master. The control of the Avangarde is divided amongst myself, the staff of the Keep at Greensprings and, of course, the Patrons on the outside. I am mostly charged with training the members of the Order."

Von Fiescher rode straight in his saddle and looked ahead from beneath bushy brows with an ever-searching gaze. He looked very serious, and Patrick surmised that this was his usual posture.

"What is the Keep at Greensprings?"

Wolfgang seemed somewhat puzzled by this question. "Did Marcus Ionus not tell you of it?"

Patrick replied, "No, he was somewhat ambiguous about the whole nature of the Order. It appeared to me to be somewhat of a secret and was to remain so until I arrived. Therefore I did not question much. I was just happy to be accepted."

Now Wolfgang was amused and muttered something about his protégé slacking off. "The Keep at Greensprings," he explained, "is the stronghold for the Avangarde as well as the establishment that accepts and houses our charges, our Guests if you will."

They left the sea cliffs behind and passed through fields of tall sword grass that swayed in the wind. Off to the left near the cliffs were several long rows of standing stones. The arrangement suggested that they had been placed there deliberately. The stones were of a black, crude rock that was different from the neighboring rock. In his lifetime, Patrick had seen many such arrangements in his homeland in Eire and had heard of others in Britain, Brittany, and Normandy. Some were set by men of Patrick's own ancestry a few generations back, but others were incredibly ancient. Indeed they were often called the bones of the earth, and no one was quite sure who placed them or for what purpose. Some said they were not placed by human hands at all but by the Fey, the Fair Folk, before the coming of man. Others maintained that they were created by magic. The great circle of Salisbury called Stonehenge was thought by many to have been erected by the magic of Merlin. The standing stones on the western shores of Gaul were thought to be the remnants of an army turned to stone by magic.

Patrick did not know what to believe. He could almost believe anything now, for was he not on the fabled Isle of

Avalon? Could the erectors of the stones have come from this Misty Isle, or perhaps it was where they went and faded into antiquity. Or maybe they were still here.

With this thought, Patrick looked around and took in the scenery. He thought again, this is Avalon.

The sky was cerulean blue, with a hint of green or aquamarine. The climate was warm and springlike, with none of the summer mugginess that wrapped up Cornwall and Mont St. Michel like a blanket. It was a comfortable place. Indeed, everything seemed dreamlike. The colors of the countryside, which would have been mundane anyplace else, seemed more vibrant here. The horizon shimmered.

Or perhaps it was all what he wanted to see and feel.

"I must admit that I am still terribly confused about the nature of the Avangarde and this whole business about what they are protecting and why at the keep,"

Wolfgang put up a halting hand.

"I will do my best to answer your inquiries, but please, one at a time, if you will. What would you like to know first?"

Patrick was silent for a moment, considering all he wanted to know and what order to say it in.

"To begin," Patrick began, "I understand that this place, the Keep at Greensprings, is a sort of school. Correct?"

Wolfgang von Fiescher seemed to muddle over the description much as Marcus Ionus had, and then replied, "After a fashion. It is more like a..." he searched for a proper word. "A sanctuary." He seemed most pleased by the word. "Yes, that is it, a sanctuary. Many people, mostly younger people of noble houses, come from near and far to be our charges, or our Guests as we prefer to call them. The fact that most of them are younger and that they spend a great amount of time here has obligated us to continue their education during their sojourn. So, yes, we have many scholars and educators among our staff and do not deprive our Guests of the enlightenment they would have in their home courts. In addition, we like to take the opportunity to give them a special education due to the diversity of the Guests."

"How is that?"

Von Fiescher was now a little bent over in the direction of the Irishman and was gesturing emphatically as he spoke. "As I pointed out," Wolfgang continued, "our Guests come from near and far. They come from families whose houses are at war with each other, have been in the past, or will be in the future. Just look at the state of the kingdoms alone. Just recently the throne of England has fallen into the hands of Henry, whose older brother, Richard, returning from the Crusades like you, gathers his forces in Normandy to invade the British Isle and claim what he feels is rightfully his. Meanwhile, King Phillipe of France watches, looking for an opportunity to accost Normandy while Richard is distracted. It is a never-ending story.

"If we can invite enough Guests here from many and varied houses of the world, we can make them live and work together like brothers and sisters. That is what we do at the Keep at Greensprings. We put them in situations where they collaborate together. It may only be organizing a feast, or acting in a Greek drama, or singing together in a choir, or dancing. But the point is, when they leave this place, they leave as friends, and further down the road, it will be difficult to make war on your friend. We hope to accomplish more than any arranged marriage ever did."

"That is a very noble concept, but as you pointed out, Henry and Richard are brothers, yet they make war on each other. Pope Urban has declared a sort of Holy Truce among the princes of the Christian kingdoms during the Crusade, yet the fighting continues," Patrick pointed out, not wishing to be the devil's advocate but feeling that it needed to be said.

Von Fiescher sighed. "This is true. However, we will endeavor to make a better world anyway. Look at Christianity itself. Its doctrines run counter to human nature and strive to make people better, despite the obvious obstacles. It certainly does not stop from a lack of trying. Do you have any misgivings with the office now that you have a better understanding of it?"

Patrick shook his head. He was just happy to be accepted, and therefore did not wish to push his luck by pointing out to von Fiescher what role he saw Christianity play in the Crusade, and what impact it had on him. "No, not at all. I would be pleased to be part of such an undertaking."

The road meandered through the countryside. Sword grass changed to oak forests, ponds laced with cattails and reeds, gurgling brooks, and the occasional standing stone.

"Why here in Avalon? And how on earth did it come about?" Patrick asked next.

"That is a bit of a story in itself," Wolfgang said. "Let us rest here for a while, eat, and I will tell it to you. You must be hungry."

Patrick was indeed hungry. He had not eaten much before leaving Cornwall, and now hunger had caught up with him. He was once again thankful for the man's foresight as he watched the older knight dismount and hand him a wedge of cheese, some bread, and uncork a flask of wine. They sat on the grass and ate.

While attempting to fend off Siegfried's nuzzling, Patrick listened to the tale von Fiescher spun.

#

"Long ago, as many stories go, there were those who sought the Holy Grail, not unlike the Knights of the Round Table. This took place after the time of Arthur. Latter-day knights quested for it still, as it was the symbol of the ultimate achievement in chivalry. Indeed, to but lay eyes on it was an honor and was considered a successful quest. Many considered that such a quest would bring wisdom and enlightenment. It was for this reason that a band of knights set sail into the Western Sea in search of Avalon. They believed that, since it was Arthur who last possessed the holy object, he would naturally have brought it to Avalon, where it was carried after his last battle.

"Some versions of the tale say that the fortunate knights came upon an enchanted boat in the shape of a swan on one of the tributaries near the Tor at Canterbury. As all stories had the heroes boarding such a magical craft, they did not hesitate to do likewise. They were then subsequently borne to the Misty Isle, where the boat turned into an actual swan and led them inland to a bubbling spring among whispering green willows.

"There they drank from the waters and had a vision of the Grail. They fell to their knees and praised the Lord. After that, they commenced to pile stone upon stone and built a fortress about the spring. They called the fortress the Keep at Greensprings and resided there, keeping vigil for another vision of the Grail."

Von Fiescher was silent for a moment. "That is the tale. A shortened and unromantic version in any case. I am sorry for that, for I am no great storyteller, and we do not have all day."

"I have not heard this tale," Patrick said.

The older knight shrugged. "That is not surprising. I had not heard it myself until I joined the Order. "Anyway, the story does not end there. Not long ago, fishermen of Cornwall, the Scilly Isles, and southern Eire reported a mist that came and went on the Western Sea. Occasionally their boats would drift into this mist and become lost, sometimes for days. During this time, the crew men would see an island fading in and out of the mist from time to time. All attempts to reach this land were futile. It was like chasing a mirage. They guessed, and correctly so, that this was the fabled realm of Avalon, unattainable by mortal man by ordinary means. After a while, all fishing vessels stayed clear of the mist.

"One day, however, after there had been hunger among the common folk of England and their nets had caught next to nothing in the seas, a poor fisherman came across a large white swan on the ocean. He thought it extremely strange that such a creature was so far from land and out of its element, but he did not ponder the matter much, for he was hungry and so was his family back home. He was set on capturing the bird.

"'If I cannot catch fish,' the fisherman said, 'then my family shall dine on roast swan.' The fisherman cast his net over the fowl and dragged it into his boat. But lo and behold, the bird spoke and begged the man not to kill it. Although the fisherman was frightened, he was also very hungry, and that soon won out over fear.

"'I am sorry,' the fisherman said, 'but my family goes hungry and they must eat.'

"The swan pleaded more. 'Please sir,' the swan said, 'I can see in your heart that you are a good man and would not bring harm to a defenseless creature such as myself, for as you can see, I am no ordinary swan.' The fisherman began to weep, for it was true that he was good in his heart and felt that it would be a sin to kill the swan. He released the bird and told it to go.

"'I shall not forget this,' the swan said, and left behind two of its feathers. 'Take these as a remembrance of this occasion so that you will never forget that you have a place in Heaven.' With that the bird flew from the boat into the mist that was collecting on the water.

"In his despair the fisherman almost threw the feathers into the water, but decided to do as the swan suggested, and he kept them. When the fisherman returned home to his family empty-handed once again, he was filled anew with despair and began to weep. But, as a tear alighted on one of the feathers, it turned into an egg of solid gold, and the fisherman and his family were never hungry again.

"Many years later, the second feather was given to a priest as a gift. The priest, not fully appreciating or believing the tale of the swan, used the feather as a quill for writing. This priest wished to commune with God, so he set off on a pilgrimage in search of the Holy Grail. He, too, knew of the legends of King Arthur and of the Keep at Greensprings and decided to seek the Grail at Avalon. He knew also the reports that the fisherman made of the Isle in the mist that could not be reached. But he suspected that if his pilgrimage was pure enough, he would be granted access to the Isle. To assist in his endeavors, he wrote out on parchment a long list of prayers that he would chant through the mist on his journey. He did this with the swan quill.

"He commissioned a fishing boat and set sail into the Western Sea. And soon, he came across the mist and headed straight into it, chanting the entire way. As he had hoped, he penetrated the mist and came to land on the shores of Avalon. He discovered the land to be wild and the Keep at Greensprings abandoned, the knights having ascended into Heaven much like the prophet Elijah. But he also found the spring from whence the knights drank, and whose water gave them visions of the Grail. The priest did likewise, and he, too, had a vision of the Grail. But with the vision was a message. It told him that it was not the prayers alone that had brought him through the mist but the feather of the Avalon Swan. And only the feather, or an invitation written with the quill, would provide conduct through the mist.

"The vision also showed him a new order in the Keep at Greensprings, and the peoples of the world united there. We are that legacy, Sir Gawain, and so are you now."

Patrick sat with his knees pulled up to his chest and his arms wrapped about them as he listened. Now that the story was finished, he pondered silently. Siegfried had stopped nuzzling him and was now noisily munching on grass nearby.

"How did this priest know what to do? I mean, today you have the Guests working together to know one another. Was it always this way?" Patrick asked.

"At first he did not know what to do. All he knew was that he had an isolated island, a vacant fortress, and a mission," von Fiescher responded. "He returned to his parish and asked advice of all manner of people: first other clergymen, then nobility, and then the scholars. Many needed to be convinced since they did not believe the priest's story. The priest invited several representatives to the Isle before it was widely accepted. The priest still had trouble convincing others of his vision, of the possibility to unite people. In the end, he could only persuade the richer lords to send their representatives, their children, their heirs to Avalon under the guise of a sanctuary. A place where they would be safe from troubles in their homelands."

Von Fiescher was silent a moment, as if pondering something himself. "Like you, others came to see the Keep at Greensprings as an école privée. Under that pretense, Greensprings received sanctions and funding from several great houses in Europe. Representatives of those who had interests at stake in the idea gathered in Rome, and there they set up a council. It is through them that nobility and merchant class alike petition to have their children attend Greensprings. It is they who handle the funds. It is they who issue the invitations written with the swan quill. It is they who are answerable to the families and the Pope. It is they who demanded that Greensprings be protected by an order of knights. And thus, we were created: the Avangarde."

"Marcus Ionus is on the council," Patrick said.

"Correct," Wolfgang answered. "He is the Greensprings and Avangarde Advocate. He reports to the council. We like to say that he is our man on the outside, since he was once an Avangarde himself. Last year many of our Guests finished their studies, and many were called home. And because of the wars, right now we are in an interlude of sorts. A number of our Avangarde have gone to follow other banners. Marcus Ionus was charged with finding new members. He has completed his mission none too soon, for as we speak, shiploads of new Guests embark for Avalon with swan-sealed scrolls like the one you brought me. I have recently received word that the last of the Reservists will be arriving soon from London. Much work must be done before the new Guests arrive. The fortress must be prepared and the new Avangarde trained. It is a never-ending process." Wolfgang sighed heavily, but he was smiling as if experiencing fond memories.

"Just how long has this been going on?" Patrick asked.

Von Fiescher took some time to remove himself from his reverie to reply. "The original founder, the priest in the story Father Dominique Chanceroy, passed away some twenty years ago. So it has been going on for that long and another, I would guess, four years. We have had around seven or eight interludes like the one we are experiencing now. As for myself, I have been part of it only for the past ten years, and Marcus Ionus for five."

Patrick was astounded. "It is a wonder that I have never heard of any of this."

Wolfgang shrugged. "The Council likes it that way. I imagine they would like it kept that way. Marcus is usually a good judge of character and evidently saw in you the potential to make a good Avangarde someday, as well as one who would believe enough in Greensprings to maintain its secrecy."

Patrick nodded. "Of course. But what if I decided this was not for me, and wanted to leave?"

The old man smiled in a way that reminded Patrick of Marcus Ionus. Both men could have a twinkle in their eye as if they had made a remarkably witty statement and were waiting for the listener to catch on. "Then you would be free to go your own way. And if you should tell the world of Avalon and Greensprings, would anyone believe it? Did you when you were first told? In any case, it would just feed the legend."

There was good reasoning in this.

They sat for a while after finishing their meal, Patrick digesting the story, along with the cheese and bread. Siegfried was still nosing through the green grass.

"And what is your story?" He asked. "How did you become part of the Avangarde?"

Another Ionian smile. "You will find, Sir Gawain, that many of us, Guests and Avangarde alike, have our own 'stories' and wish to keep them private." He leaned closer to the Irishman, becoming more serious, but still maintaining a smile. "You may understand that. Many come here for a while as a retreat from reality. To reorganize themselves. And during that time, they like to be known only for their valor. Do not misunderstand me; this is not an island full of criminals and shady characters." The seriousness left von Fiescher, and his own, bigger smile took control of his face as he looked away. "And there are those who will talk your ears off."

Patrick concluded that privacy was to be respected here. Because he was in no hurry to tell others of the robed specter that hounded him, nor anything else, he was content to mind his own business.

"Shall we be going?" Wolfgang asked. Patrick nodded and helped gather up their mess. They then mounted and continued on their way.

The final leg of the trip was short. The entire journey from the harbor totaled perhaps two hours, not including their lunch. The path entered a forest and mounted a hill, and then broke out over a small, gently sloping wooded valley.

Here, von Fiescher pointed across the valley while saying, "The Keep at Greensprings. Welcome, bienvenue, and willkommen. I hope you enjoy your stay."

A gray fortress on the opposite side from the hill was built into the far valley wall. One got the impression of cylinders and cubes held together by a wall, but it was not an unpleasant sight. It evoked a feeling of safety.

From von Fiescher's story, Patrick imagined a rudimentary place, a kind of pile of broken stones on a hilltop. Patrick was impressed.

"Let us get you home, Sir Gawain," Wolfgang said.

#

A crevasse stopped them short of the main gate. They drew their horses up, and a hail from Wolfgang brought the drawbridge down and the portcullis up.

The heavy sound of the horses' hooves on the wood bridge became the resounding noise of metal on cobblestone once they reached the courtyard. Inside was the rounded face of the large central keep. A stairway fanned out from two massive iron-studded doors. On either side of the doorway was a set of craftily shaped columns in the shape of trees. Great pains went into making the columns appear as if they had been live trees taken from the forest, so detailed were they. To the right of the keep entrance was a large fountain. A spring flowed from the living rock, which made up this portion of the wall and bubbled into a pool at the foot of the stone. The stone where the water originated was carved into the image of a bearded man with water gurgling forth from its open mouth.

Currently, there were many women washing clothes in the pool, and several more were taking buckets full of water away.

There were also many men dressed in Avangarde surcoats and many who appeared to be some sort of cleric. Many of them hailed von Fiescher as the horses plodded past, around the keep to the stables.

"You will keep Siegfried here," von Fiescher said. "Here in Greensprings, everything you need for him can be found inside. The animals, especially the horses, are treated almost like royalty." Siegfried neighed as if in agreement.

A boy came out of the wood-gabled building and gathered the reins. Patrick gave Siegfried a friendly goodbye pat on the hindquarters. Siegfried bucked and tossed his head, but finally relented to being led away.

"Do not worry about your belongings. Someone will bring them to your chamber. Right now, you will need to see the rest of the keep."

#

Inside the central keep was a steep staircase, and they climbed for several minutes. Then they came out on top of the structure.

Wolfgang led him to the back so they could look out over the other side of the fortress. They leaned on the defensive wall and Wolfgang pointed to various buildings and named them.

"We are now on top of the keep itself, where almost all functions of importance take place. The throne room, which is also the ballroom and dining hall, is below our feet as well as the library, class auditoriums, personal chambers of the staff..." Wolfgang rattled off the names of the structures. There was the spartan Avangarde bunkhouse, the smithy, the armorer pouring out sooty smoke, elaborate gardens just behind the keep, and the chapel with its impressive dual stained-glass domes.

"What is that?" Patrick asked, extending his finger. Beyond, opposite the Avangarde building, was a much larger structure with a more elaborate architecture.

"That is where our Lady Guests stay," Wolfgang replied, and then added in a fatherly fashion. "Do not go there unless you have a chaperone. The powers that be like it that way. And as you can see, beyond the garden and between the Hall for the Ladies and the Avangarde bunkhouse is the training ground for the Avangarde. We hold all kinds of drills there. Past that is what we call the 'Back Door,' which is the rear gate that leads into the apple orchard."

Patrick looked past the dusty training grounds and the rear gate and could see the long rows of lush apple trees. Beyond was green wilderness.

"They produce some very good hard cider there," Wolfgang added.

"They?" Patrick asked.

"Yon village," von Fiescher replied, gesturing towards the front of the stronghold.

"I did not know that there was anything here other than the Keep at Greensprings."

"Why yes, there is a small village that takes care of our foods and supplies. The villagers have been here almost as long as the keep. They were originally pilgrims who came with Father Chanceroy so long ago. Most of the servants at Greensprings are from there, although some come from across the sea like the Guests and the Avangarde."

Von Fiescher gave Patrick a moment to take in the sight.

He then was led back down the stairs and through the various rooms. By now, Patrick was lost and did not bother keeping track of all the places he went, how to find them, and all the people he met briefly as von Fiescher introduced him as "Sir Gawain, our new Reservist." Patrick was discovering that he was very tired and that he had a lot to learn about Avalon.

At last they exited the keep and gardens, and they headed for the Guest Hall for men.

"Why are we going here?" Patrick asked.

"The Reservists are housed here as well," Von Fiescher was curt. This did not please Patrick at all.

They entered into a stone hall with many wood tables and chairs and a large fireplace. They went up a stairwell to the second floor, where there was a long hallway with many doors on both sides. Many of the doors were slightly ajar, and it was fairly evident that the place was empty.

Von Fiescher led Patrick to the end of the hallway to the last door on the left. A scrubbing sound reached them as they drew near. Von Fiescher knocked on the door and gently pushed it open.

Inside, and right before them on the floor, was what Patrick at first thought was a pile of white linen rags. Then it moved and proved to be a woman. She had her back to the door and had been on all fours scrubbing with a brush, but, as von Fiescher and Patrick entered, she stood up with a gasp.

"Oh, m'lords! Forgive me, I did not know you would be here so soon!"

The woman before them, or girl, came up to Patrick's chest in height. She had the strong build of a peasant, broad shoulders, muscular limbs, and a thick midsection.

"Mademoiselle, Sir Gawain's room was to be prepared quite a while ago," Wolfgang, said.

The maidservant moved forward with a rustle of clothing. Her hair was blond and full, and was not encased in a bonnet. Strands of hair fell across her cheeks. She was dressed in typical servant fashion, a floor-length white linen skirt and a wool under-tunic with short sleeves for free movement. She was buxom, and to ease the weight, she wore a laced bodice over her tunic. The thick yarny laces were undone at the top for comfort's sake, but the next set of laces still strained, and she was almost bursting out of her clothing.

"I am sorry, Herr von Fiescher," she said. She had a strong French accent, though it was different than that of the Mont St.

Michel's monks. "But we were not quite sure as to what room the monsieur would be staying in," she continued. "I have just finished scrubbing the floor."

Von Fiescher still did not seem pleased. "You still should have been gone once you saw that Sir Patrick's belongings had arrived." Patrick saw that his belongings were indeed in the room, piled at the foot of a large bed that took up most of the room.

"Yes, m'lord," the maidservant said. Yet despite her admission, von Fiescher continued to berate her with the protocol of the keep.

Patrick did not like having people chastised in front of him, especially because of him. "It is all right, I do not mind at all," he said. Von Fiescher turned to look at Patrick. "As I see it, it is a fortuitous opportunity to meet another personage of Greensprings. Do you not agree, Sir von Fiescher?"

Wolfgang raised an eyebrow. "Yes, of course, how thoughtless of me. Sir Gawain, this is one of our many servants here at the keep: Aimeé. Mademoiselle, this is Sir Patrick Gawain of Eire. He is to be a Reservist with us here in Avalon."

Aimeé, who had been sheepishly looking at the floor up to this point, dared to look up and smiled. She curtsied, looked into Patrick's eyes with appreciation, and then looked down again. Her eyes were light green, not unlike the color of the hills of his homeland.

"I am pleased to meet you," Patrick said.

"Well, Sir Gawain," said Wolfgang. "I hope your lodgings are satisfactory. Later this evening, around sundown, there will be a gathering in the dining hall, that is the throne room, and your presence is required. You will have the opportunity to meet most everyone here in Greensprings. In the meantime, you can situate yourself. I will see you then."

Patrick nodded and expressed his gratitude.

"You best be going as well, Aimeé," von Fiescher said to the maid. Aimeé's eyes had found their way back to the Irishman, and she started at the verbal prodding from the old knight.

The gaze had not gone unnoticed by Patrick, who also noted that Aimeé's chest was heaving ever so slightly and that there was a distracting beauty mark above the globe of her left breast. Despite these enticing visual pleasures, Patrick averted his eyes as he bid good afternoon to his guests.

#

After Wolfgang and Aimeé left, Patrick went about putting away his things. What earlier seemed an inordinate load for one man to carry now appeared paltry as Patrick tried to fill his room with his personal items out of the saddle bags that held his possessions. It was impossible. The room was lonelier and had nothing to adorn it. The chamber was perhaps four paces by five paces, with a simple wood armoire, a bench with a washbasin, the large bed that took up most of the room, and a wood rack for accommodating a fighting man's gear.

When seeing this, he unclasped his sword belt and hung it over one arm of the roughly man-shaped rack, with the sheathed sword dangling. This was followed by draping his armor over it after the laborious process of shedding himself of the mail. After digging his helm out of one of the bags, he placed the bowl-shaped item on top of the rack's center beam, nose guard facing the center of the room. He hung his great-cloak on a hook in the armoire and was thankful to be rid of it. It was warmer here in Avalon, much more agreeable than it had been at sea, and the heavy garment was damp and smelled of sweat.

Next he washed his hands and face in the washbasin, wanting to sink his entire body into it. Afterwards, he removed his old garments and put on a fresh tunic and leggings. At this point, he realized that he had plenty of time before going to the dining hall, yet he had no desire to explore the new environment in which he found himself. He sat on his bed. It was awkward being here. Von Fiescher had clarified a great deal about the nature of Greensprings and the Avangarde, but Patrick still was not clear as to what *he* would be doing. What were his responsibilities and duties? Were they different from those of the regular Avangardesmen? If not, then why was he not given full compensation or the right to live in the same hall as the others? What if he wanted to leave? Would that be dishonorable?

Would anyone believe him on the outside if he told them that he had been part of an order of knights of Avalon? Patrick shook his head sadly.

He no longer felt sleepy, though he was still exhausted. He tried to lie down and sleep, but could not. He stood up and paced between the bed and armoire. His heart was beating fast with the prospect of having to start all over in some place that was neither Eire nor in the company of Crusaders.

He stopped. Something had distracted him, and he remained motionless to catch the sound again. After a brief moment, he did. It was a short, strange whining noise that came from outside his window, followed by an even longer one. This became a full-blown, eerie, harmonious wail. It was not unpleasant. Somebody was playing the bagpipes.

Patrick went to the window, leaned out the stone portal, and looked about. From this vantage he could see the Avangarde Hall, the practice field, the Back Door, and a portion of the Hall for Ladies, yet he could not locate the source. He sat on the windowsill and listened.

The sound was relaxing and comforting, much as the monastic chants at Mont St. Michel. He closed his eyes and leaned his head on the stone. The music moved through and into his soul; and he let it. He let it wrap around his tense muscles and stressed nerves and drown out the voices that teased him with doubts. Even the robed Apparition could not harm him. The bagpipes rose and fell in gentle, undulating pitches. The sound washed away everything, leaving only itself. Patrick's back fell against the windowsill, his chin fell to his chest, and he was riding a horse for an interminable amount of time. Thirsty, he trudged on. He saw armed and armored men chasing children. He saw green hills along a big, slow flowing river. Sword drawn, he dismounted and ran in his chain mail. His white surcoat with the red cross was smudged with soot and blood. He ran across a field, jumped a low-built stonewall, and raced up a path to a manor house. He entered a gate topped by the Holy Cross. Beyond the gate was a veiled woman in green and blue wool. He ran to her and embraced her, starting to cry.

"Oh Kellie," he sobbed. Patrick relaxed his embrace and looked into the face of the woman as she removed her veil.

"I've missed you, too, Patrick. I've been waiting for you," she replied. Her face was Aimeé's.

And he woke. There was a scuffing noise, and his neck ached.

The noise from across the hall, he realized, had awakened him. Still rubbing his neck, he got up from the windowsill, went to the door to investigate, and poked his head outside. Across the hall and to the right, it sounded like someone was moving furniture in a room. A shadow moved back and forth across the wedge of light at the foot of the door, which was ajar.

He knocked on the door, and it swung open.

Inside in the doorway stood a heavy-looking man. His mane of shaggy blond hair crowned a beaming moon face.

"Good afternoon," Patrick said, extending a hand. "I am Patrick Gawain, and I am new. I guess we are neighbors."

The man took the Irishman's hand and pumped it, smiling all the while. "Most pleased to meet you. Jonathan of Northumbria, but you can just call me Jon. I am a Reservist."

Jonathan wore a simple tunic similar to Patrick's. Had he not mentioned that he was a Reservist, Patrick would not have guessed him to be the knightly type. He seemed more like the happy baker type.

"Sir Jon..." Patrick said, smiling.

"Yes?"

"You can stop shaking my hand now if you like."

Jon looked down and stopped pumping Patrick's hand and withdrew his in a hurry, smiled even more broadly, and bobbed his head. "Sorry."

"That is all right," Patrick said. "I am glad to know that you are happy to meet me."

Jon invited Patrick inside a room that was not all that different from his. They talked for a while, first about nothing in particular, then about what brought Jon to the Misty Isle. "My uncle was an Avangarde. He did not really tell anybody about it. He just kind of disappeared one year and was gone for a while. He came back a little bit richer and went on to be a guardsman for an earl in Manchester. It was then that he put in a good word for me with the Avangarde. A man named Marcus Ionus came to the family estate asking for me."

"How long ago was that?" Patrick asked.

"About six months ago, but he told me that I was not to come to Avalon until later. I arrived about two weeks ago. I was one of the last to be picked. I guess there is you and then another who has not yet arrived."

Patrick nodded. "I remember Marcus Ionus saying something about going to London."

And so the conversation continued. Jon fussed with his room, moving what little furniture there was, straightening out a framed icon, and rearranging his belongings. He seemed to take great pride in his new dwelling. After a while, Patrick apologized and left, as he was tired. The little nap had only primed him for more sleep. Jon promised to rouse him when it was time to go to the gathering, and this pleased Patrick. He had made a friend.

He slept soundly, but after some long seeming amount of time had passed, his subconscious began warning him that perhaps it was getting late. The notion that he should be at the gathering plagued him. What if he was missed? That would hardly be a proper first impression.

After some tossing and turning, he got out of bed and saw that the sun hovered over the horizon, and the shadows in the room had become much longer.

Patrick went to Jon's room and knocked. *Probably fell asleep himself*, Patrick mused.

Several moments passed and no one answered. It was evident that no one was home. A little peeved, Patrick stalked off in the direction of the stairwell and the exit of the Hall.

#

Patrick left the Hall for Guests, crossed a dusty corner of the training grounds and found his way into the keep via the gardens. That much he remembered. Upon entering the keep, however, he became instantly lost. He could not find his way to the dining hall but managed to find the front entrance with the ornate tree-shaped columns. From there, he decided to go to the stables and visit Siegfried.

He had no trouble finding either the stables or the horse. At the sight of the Irishman, the horse shook its mane, pawed at the ground and then trotted over to the side of the stall.

"What do you think, boy? Was it a mistake to come here?" Patrick asked. Siegfried neighed and shook his head in a flurry of black mane. Patrick smiled. "I will take your word for it."

It was getting dark. Straightening his tunic and cloak, he resolutely walked back to the keep's entrance.

In the courtyard, he came across a dark-haired knight in the black cape and swan-emblazoned surcoat of the Avangarde. Patrick asked where the dining hall was, and the knight offered to show him the way, explaining that he was going there himself. The knight introduced himself as Geoffrey.

He found the dining hall easily. It was just a matter of being familiar with the keep—main entrance, down the hall, left, right, left. The room was two stories tall. The next level had columned openings so that spectators could gather on the higher floor, convenient for court affairs, since the hall was narrow and already crowded.

The hall was filled with all kinds of people: servants, priests and nuns, scholars, and of course Avangardesmen. Patrick noted almost immediately that the knights all sported the same black-and-white surcoat as Wolfgang von Fiescher. They looked professional. They looked like a unit. Perusing the room some more, Patrick saw there were also several men wearing their own family tabards or garbed in common dress like his. Patrick guessed that they were the other Reservists, and maybe did not receive the uniform.

"Would you care for a drink, monsieur?"

Patrick looked down and saw Aimeé holding a tray full of flagons, which she extended toward him. Her smile complemented her eyes and other considerable attributes.

"Thank you." Patrick said, taking one of the cups. Aimeé did not move, but stood there smiling at Patrick. An awkward moment passed, one he did not know how to fill, so he moved away and just as quickly bumped into someone else.

"Hello, Gawain," Jon said.

Patrick started to apologize for bumping into him, but then remembered something. "I thought you were coming to find me," Patrick said.

Jon's eyes widened, and he slapped his hand over his forehead. "I completely forgot. I left to take care of another matter, and did not think to go back to the Guest Hall." Jon was all smiles again. "Oh my, there is McFowler, I have been looking all over for him! I must go. Enjoy the morsels, and I will see you about." Jon waved a hand as if to catch someone's attention and left.

The knight Geoffrey had made off, too. Patrick looked around. There was a wide circle of space around him in the sea of people. After an indecisive moment, he made an effort to bridge this gap between himself and the other guests by stepping over to the nearest group and throwing out an innocuous comment. He was unsuccessful. Even after mild initial success, they seemed to lose interest in him quickly. He spied Wolfgang von Fiescher in a small group of people deep in conversation. He tried getting close to be a part of the talk, or at least listen. But after long, awkward moments, the Irishman concluded that he probably just looked obvious and pathetic and moved on.

There was a long table at the side of the room and he sat down. He stared for a long time into his flagon of wine, pretending that it held something of great interest. Someone bumped into him while seating himself and a lady at Patrick's table, which was rapidly becoming crowded. The man, a Reservist by his appearance, apologized politely.

Patrick pounced on the chance and introduced himself, and started to ask the usual get-acquainted questions. He didn't get very far before the conversation dwindled off to nothing. The man seemed more interested in his lady friend. All Patrick learned was that the man was a Reservist named Jeremiah.

Patrick watched the people. They all looked so happy. They were laughing, and the noise in the hall was almost deafening. They all seemed to know one another, all old friends. Jon was across the room talking with a burly man in a kilt who had a shock of red hair and a mischievous smile. People surrounded him, listening and laughing at his jokes. Patrick went into another fascinating study of his wine cup. Something drew up beside him and waited. He turned.

There was the Apparition.

Patrick's blood froze, and the hair on his body prickled. He did not move, just stared. An indeterminate amount of time passed before he moved his eyes to see if anyone else had seen the Apparition. Nobody acknowledged its presence. They carried on, merry, unaware of the creature in their midst. Patrick slowly rose from his seat.

The thing did not move.

Patrick moved ever so slightly toward an exit.

The Apparition glided toward him, passing through people in the hall as if they were mist.

Patrick bolted. He slammed into people and knocked a tray of drinks out of a servant's arms. He cleared the door and ran helter-skelter down the corridor. He found the garden, then the Hall for Guests, and then his room. He slammed the door and placed the wooden bar across it. He then sat in the nearest corner, gathered his knees to his chest, and let his body shake. His heart beat in his brain and pounded in his ears.

Heavy, booted footsteps slowly approached down the hallway. The Apparition was coming, and with every step it took, Patrick's heart beat faster and louder. He had nowhere to go. There was nothing he could do. How can you hide from something that passes through walls?

Patrick cupped his face in his hands. His hair was limp and wet against his brow.

The steps stopped before the door, and the Apparition pounded heavily on it, causing the wooden crossbar to shake. Patrick cowered in his corner, crying out and scraping his boots on the floor. All he could hear was his own deafening heartbeat.

The door stopped shaking.

Patrick paused in his thrashing and spread his fingers enough to see a blade appear between the door and frame which knocked the wooden crossbar off its pegs. It clattered on the floor. And then, the door opened.

"Gawain?" a voice said.

Patrick looked up. It was Jon, holding a long dagger. "Are you well? Forgive me for breaking in, but I was worried."

He propped his elbows on his knees and gazed at the other knight.

"I am fine," Patrick said. He ran his hand through his hair

"Are you sure? I can..."

"I am fine!" He said. "I became sick in France. I had a fever and I am just now recovering, that is all. Now go please, and let me be."

Sir Jon hesitated, and then obeyed. He closed the door behind him as he left, and Patrick collapsed in a heap on the bed.

#

The following morning, Patrick did not bother getting up. He knew of no engagement that committed him to be anywhere and had no special desire to go anywhere or see anybody, so he just lay there. And thought.

There was a knock. Patrick got up from the bed to answer it. It was the servant Aimeé with a tray of food.

"Sir Jon said that you were not feeling well, and I did not see you at breakfast this morning, so I thought that I would bring you something to eat," she said, starting to enter the room.

Patrick hesitated behind the door. "I am not dressed. I am only in a nightgown."

"Oh, don't be silly. You are not on your horse at the moment and besides, I have many brothers and there is no one around to care." Her voice flattened a bit. "Not that any one would care what a knight does with a servant anyway."

She forced her way inside and set the tray on the bureau, after which she took Patrick by the hand and led him back to his bed. Patrick, shocked by her bluntness, did not protest. "Now, get in. There is a draft and you are sick. How do you expect to get better?"

Patrick crawled under the blankets while Aimeé retrieved the tray and brought it to him.

"I am fine, really. I exaggerated last night when I left the banquet."

"You could not have exaggerated too much. You did not come back. Everyone thought you had fallen in the throne."

"Excuse me?"

"The throne. You know, *la toilette*."

"Oh." Patrick smiled. "Yes, well, once I was rid of my foul spirits, I thought it best to sleep. In any case, I did not think anyone would notice me missing."

"I did," she said, smiling.

Patrick began to slowly pick at the morsels of food on the tray. He felt self-conscious while she stood by watching him eat. He said nothing, as he expected her to depart.

After several more moments during which Aimeé intertwined her fingers before her and twiddled her thumbs, she cleared her throat and said, "Well, I must be going, I guess. We have so many linens to wash. The new Guests will be here shortly." She turned toward the door, and then turned back, a look of mock-sternness on her face accompanied by a wagging finger. "Now eat up; you need to get your strength back."

Patrick smiled wanly. "Of course."

Aimeé's mock-sternness turned to a meek smile. "Will I see you soon?"

Patrick nodded.

Aimeé's smile broadened. "Très bien." She skipped away down the hallway. As soon as she left, Jon knocked on the open door.

"Hello," he said. "How are you feeling today?"

"Fine, thank you. Sorry for my behavior last night," Patrick replied.

Jon shrugged. "Do not worry about it. And to change the subject," he said, "it looks like you have made a new friend." He jerked his head in the direction of the departing servant girl.

Patrick sighed heavily, which caused Jon's brow to furrow in curiosity.

"I try to avoid women. I have not had much luck with them, lady or not," Patrick explained.

Jon smiled. "I am sure we all have had the same trouble at some time."

#

A group of Avangarde immersed in a raucous conversation rounded the corridor. They were gesturing wildly and laughing, but managed just in time to avoid a collision with Jon and Patrick. As they passed, the emblem of the Avalon swan crest shone on their well-kept surcoats, and their capes danced behind them.

"Do you think we will ever be Avangardesmen?" Patrick asked.

"They say it is quite possible. There are Gardesmen leaving all the time, from what I understand. I have been talking a lot with the men here. You know, getting to know them and getting myself known so that when the time comes, maybe they will take me into consideration before the rest."

Tricky fellow, Patrick thought. "So how do they choose from among the Reservists when an Avangardesman leaves?" Patrick asked.

Jon shrugged. "I believe they just vote on it."

As they continued their journey through the keep, Patrick found the Englishman to be a great source of information. With Sir Jon's help, Patrick found out where to have his travel-stained, smelly clothes washed and his arms and armor mended. He also received a thorough tour of Greensprings. Before the end of the day, he felt he had his bearings.

Upon entering the main hall, he followed Jon to locate a place to sit in order to avoid a faux pas. Sir Jon took a seat among the men in the swan-embroidered surcoats, and Patrick sat beside him. There were nods in his direction. He ate the plentiful food and was silent, looking on occasion for a hooded figure lurking in the shadows.

#

After dinner, he took his leave of Sir Jon and decided to test his knowledge of the grounds. Not only that, he wanted time to reflect.

He thought of David of York and his sudden departure, and whether or not he would see him again. He thought about the Apparition. He wondered if he would ever have a neat Avangarde surcoat. Then, deciding that he was brooding too much, he turned his thoughts to his time in the Crusade. As much as a trial the experience was, there were good times as well; the taste of a new spicy food, the sight of the veiled women, the high-pitched ululations the Muslims made before they attacked, the sheer heat of the day. There was the camaraderie among the knights; tasting the same dust, getting bitten by the same insects, feeling the same fear and feeling the same thrill of victory. Sharing experiences with men he could relate to. He missed that here in Avalon, but it would probably change once the Guests arrived. He had heard at dinner tonight that they would arrive in less than a month. The last of the Reservists had come, and training would commence tomorrow. Once a routine was set, he would begin to fit in, feel comfortable.

He leaned against one of the battlements and felt its coolness. Stone. Solid. Unmovable. Ah, to be a rock. What worries does stone have? He let his hand linger on the grainy surface and imagined it conducting the heartbeats of the inhabitants of the keep. Yes, soon there would be hundreds of new such heartbeats. New people who didn't know him. People he could have a fresh start with. This new season would be better than the previous one. Anything would be better than what he had experienced. It had to be.

#

Von Fiescher stood at a lectern in the amphitheater.

"Those of you, who cannot read, please listen carefully as we go over the Creed of Greensprings. Please refer to your text that should already be in your possession or that was recently given to you by Sir Marcus Ionus."

Patrick opened the book that he had meant to read so many times but never did. He felt a pang of guilt and hoped that it was not all that important.

There were all manners of men in the amphitheater. They sat on the stone benches that formed ever rising levels in semi circles around the stage at which Wolfgang stood. There were close to a hundred in all. They came from many and varied backgrounds: English, Norman, Scottish, Flemish, and Bulgarians. As far as Patrick knew he was the only Irishman. It was a hodgepodge, not unlike his experience in the Middle

East. Knights who might have been enemies elsewhere were friends here.

He and Sir Jon sat with the other Reservists, Jeremiah and Gregory, a short blond, blue-eyed Londonite who had just arrived the previous day with a swan-sealed invitation. He had come through the gates much the same way Patrick had: in the company of Wolfgang von Fiescher and atop a new horse. There were two others. They sat together, but not because anyone had told them that they were supposed to.

"Page xi, introduction, preface..." began Wolfgang, reading out loud the mission statement of Greensprings in a long dry manner. He turned the page, and without looking up, continued in monotone a verbalization of the next verse of the Creed. Page after page this continued, and the fighting men gathered in the amphitheater began to fidget.

Just when von Fiescher was starting to show some sign of animation (he was starting to delve into the exciting topic of Avangarde being soldiers of the spirit...or some such) he paused for a moment and looked out from underneath his bushy eyebrows into the audience of assembled men. Patrick, as well as everyone else, looked in the same direction. The red headed Highlander, Jason McFowler, sat with his hand in the air.

"Yes, McFowler. You have a question?"

"I did not quite get all that. Could you repeat it?" he said. Laughter erupted in the auditorium, and the place was alive.

When the noise had died down, Wolfgang looked sternly at the Highlander. "We will have none of that. You have been through this many times, but we must all go through the same experiences to form a kinship that bonds this order together. And I mean *all* experiences."

With that, McFowler rolled his eyes, grabbed up his kilt, chewed on it, and leaned his head on the neighboring knight's shoulder.

Laughter erupted in the room again.

#

None of his mother's churchgoing or schooling had prepared him for the Greensprings sense of discipline. When there was no study, there was mass to attend. They listened for hours to Father Hugh Constant give homilies that illustrated the necessity to not only defend the Guests from worldly harm, but from spiritual danger as well. To truly be soldiers of God.

Patrick shook his head over the notion. He had seen first hand in the Holy Lands what "soldiers of God" were capable of doing. He still believed in God, but he no longer claimed to understand Him.

In two weeks, he did a lot of sitting and listening, and it was driving him mad. By the look of it, he was not alone. At each day's end, the group of stalwart knights was edgy and exhausted. The veterans, taking it blow by blow like everyone else, slept in the auditorium. Most were startled into wakefulness by von Fiescher and a long wooden pole, but many, like Jason McFowler, were left undisturbed. It seemed that Wolfgang had his favorites.

#

"Humility!" shouted Wolfgang von Fiescher one morning from the battlement walls surrounding the courtyard. "Humble before God and each other. This will make you a better knight as well as a person. Trust me!" Wolfgang laughed wickedly.

The Avangardesmen were on their hands and knees, dressed in simple clothing, washing the courtyard cobblestones with hand brushes. They were performing all manner of menial labor unbecoming to noblemen. They were roused early every morning and herded like cattle into the dining hall where they ate a quick meal prepared by the servants. Then it was their turn in the kitchens to cook under the servants' supervision. Then, to the great dismay of the Greensprings staff, they were served half-burnt or undercooked meals by Avangardesmen who were covered in flour and soot.

Avangardesmen painted, pounded nails, piled and mortared stones, and washed linens in the fountain with their pant legs rolled up while maidservants pointed and giggled.

Each night the men went to bed exhausted, wondering what they had gotten themselves into, and were roused what seemed only moments later to do it all over again.

Despite the hours, the knights rarely went to bed right away but stayed up and recounted their "war" stories about the chores that they had to perform that day, and complained pitifully about the ones they were to do the next. But social or personal differences began to melt away in the torrent of labor, as Wolfgang von Fiescher looked on.

#

"Heave-ho, boys!" the portly Father Hugh Constant cried. His voice echoed in the building. He was the spiritual leader of the Greensprings community and caretaker of the church, and von Fiescher had sent the Avangarde to help him with manual labor. Patrick was one of many pulling on a chain that hoisted a huge stone crucifix skyward into the stained-glass dome above the pulpit.

Father Hugh thought that it would be spiritually inspiring to suspend the massive piece of art at an angle in the colorful dome, high above the pews. The knights heaved and groaned as they pulled on the thick chain.

"Why don't you come over and give us a hand, Father," somebody grunted.

"I'm busy myself, lads. I must clean the chalices for communion, not to mention my own cup here." With that, he lifted a goblet full of wine. "Here's to your health, laddies!"

The Avangarde thought it could get no worse, but they were wrong. The day when the labor ceased, the lessons in manners began. "Manners?" somebody cried. "What the hell is that for?"

Von Fiescher tsked. "We are not barbarians here in the Avangarde. Some of you, perhaps all, may be cultured, but we are going to make sure." So commenced the training in bowing, greeting, eating in the presence of women, and dancing. "You will be expected to rub shoulders with the nobility of the world. You will not set a bad example."

Patrick found this extremely amusing, if not annoying. Polite behaviors seemed no more than a series of antics. He, like most knights present, was used to eating with his hands at dinner and throwing the bones to the dogs on the floor. On the other hand, it was almost worth it to see the big, masculine lads being taught to hold the cutlery "correctly" at a meal.

The dancing proved most difficult. Patrick could not dance to save his life. And worse, when it came time to be paired up with a female partner, there was none for him.

Female staff, maidservants, even nuns were brought in for the occasion but still, Greensprings suffered from a steep shortage of women.

"Well, gentleman, it seems that I have to sit this one out." Patrick bowed an adieu and sat down in order to become a relieved spectator.

"Not so fast, Sir Patrick," von Fiescher said among the protests of the other Avangardesmen. He was towing Sir Jon behind him. "It seems that Sir Jon is also without a partner." The knights burst into laughter, and then cheering. There was no arguing the matter, either. Von Fiescher had made up his mind, and the Avangarde would settle for no less. So Sir Patrick and Sir Jon danced.

At first it was a joke, but as the dances became more intricate and the hours wore on, the jeering knights became too engrossed to notice the paired men. When it was certain that they had learned all the steps, von Fiescher announced that there would be a contest to see who was the best dancer.

The knights, who had become invested in their newfound skill after so much work, were all for it. "Let us show these ruffians what we have in us, my darling," Jon said to Patrick, which was met with much laughter. The contest began as several staff members played musical instruments and others judged the contestants. When a couple was obviously out of step with the music, a judge asked them to leave. Some knights made quite a spectacle out of themselves when they were eliminated.

"We have been robbed! We were doing much better than them!"

The contest came down to two couples, Sir Geoffrey and his maidservant, and Jon and Patrick. The music became quicker and more complex, and the contestants whirled at a dizzying rate. The sidelined knights and staff were clapping and cheering their favorites.

And as the music speeded up again, and the cheers swelled, Jon and Patrick cried out almost simultaneously, "What are we doing?" They stepped back from each other and let Geoffrey and his partner continue. "You win," they shouted, and stepped off the dance floor. Patrick leaned toward Jon and whispered. "I cannot believe we almost won."

Jon grinned. "I cannot believe we were actually trying to."

The hall still buzzed with laughter.

#

At last came the drilling of arms. The knights spent the next portion of the final week on a dusty practice field, with padded faux armor, wooden swords, large bucket helms, and jousting dummies. From sunup to sundown, the Avangardesmen thumped on each other under the skillful guidance of the Teutonic knight and several older veteran warriors. They learned new skills and honed their old ones, and all the pent-up frustrations of the previous weeks were released on the drilling grounds. From von Fiescher's beaming smile, it would appear that he had planned it that way.

Wolfgang was a harsh teacher when it came to jousting with the lances. In the beginning, just about everybody was unhorsed by the jousting dummy. The simple mechanism consisted of a target to be struck by the lance, and, if not correctly hit, it caused a counter-weight to swing around and strike the rider with a sack of dirt.

"That is terrible!" von Fiescher would shout. "Idiots! You are all idiots! My grandmother can joust better than that! And she is dead!"

But at the end, all had mastered it to some degree.

Patrick and Jon found vengeance on those knights who had chastised them for their dancing exploits. The Irishman and the Englishman proved to be formidable opponents in melée practice. They could best all but a handful, which included a robust knight named Mark and his friend, Jason McFowler, who was a veritable demon with his huge claymore sword.

#

Finally the training was over, and another banquet was in order.

Patrick was in high spirits. He knew his way around Greensprings as well as he knew his own hometown. He now knew, or at least was acquainted with, all the Avangarde and most of the staff and servants. Unfortunately, however, he was still without friends other than Sir Jon, who held himself somewhat aloof from the Irishman.

And Patrick made it a point to avoid the energetic Aimeé, who came to his room less and less often now.

At the banquet, he sat and talked with many and did not feel too terribly out of place, and nobody treated him or the other Reservists any differently—but he still felt different. *Patience, Patrick, be patient*, he told himself. He was happy enough, if only because there was no ghostly Apparition.

#

The following day, news arrived that several ships were approaching, laden with Guests. The knights shined and oiled their armor, and donned the ceremonial pieces with bright surcoats and long swords. Horses were saddled, polished helms were crowned, and flags unfurled. Patrick's green and gold surcoat was well mended and washed, and, astride Siegfried, he felt proud to be there, even if he and the other Reservists made up the rear of the long procession of mounted knights as they headed for the sea to meet the Guests.

"Well," said Jeremiah. "Let us hope that the coming year is a favorable one for us all."

The knights rode forward.

Chapter Three

Wolfgang von Fiescher raised a gloved hand to halt the regal procession of mounted knights. Up to this moment Patrick and the other Reservists had been ribbing one another; or mostly it was the other Reservists ribbing the Irishman for having actually gone through the effort of bathing and fastidiously combing his hair for the occasion.

"The Guests won't be able to see your hair underneath your helmet and mail," Sir Jeremiah pointed out, smiling. "And besides, we probably won't be close enough for them to notice how pretty you smell now." The Reservists laughed.

"Better safe than sorry," Patrick returned, not really minding the attention.

The multitude of horses was restless now that the column had paused. Their tack and harness jingled noisily, and the beasts snorted as if to question why they had stopped.

The harbor in which Patrick had arrived several weeks before lay below them, at the end of the road. The day's bright new sun, which had sparkled on the polished armor and made the colored banners glisten, had grown hazy behind a mist that engulfed the island shore. A strong breeze carried the smell of salt and seaweed. Sand blew about in whispers, and seagulls drifted in the air, crying down at the horses. Farthest away was the ever-present crash of the waves rolling into the surf, just beyond the harbor. Inside the harbor the waters were calmer, lapping against barnacle-covered piers.

On the dock stood three men. Patrick did not recognize them. They were all dressed in some sort of uniform which consisted of a red tunic with black border and a matching sash that hung over their shoulders and down their backs. On their heads were black caps. These men stood near a ladder—the one Patrick had ascended from the ferryman's dinghy. Three similar such vessels were moored there now. Von Fiescher motioned for the Avangarde to remain while he galloped down to the dock and greeted the men. From their vantage point, Patrick and the Reservists could not hear the conversation, but watched their exchange.

The strangers pointed out into the misty sea and made gestures as if demonstrating something quite large. They also enumerated on their fingers, adding up some quantity. After some more brief words, they all nodded in assent, and Wolfgang abruptly turned and galloped back while the men descended the ladder and entered the boats—one in each. Once leaving the noisy wood of the dock, the hooves of Wolfgang's horse became muffled in the sand, and he was not long rejoining the Avangarde.

"Men, make way for the wagons and keep servants," Wolfgang shouted. "When they have passed, I want you to evenly split up and position yourselves on either side of the roadway." Von Fiescher's horse was restless beneath him and he struggled with the reins in one hand, while gesturing with the other. "Put up your lances so that you form an arch. Space yourselves far enough apart that you allow plenty of room for the Guests to pass underneath on their way to the carriages, but not so far apart that the banners hang too low to the ground." With that, Wolfgang was again off, this time to the rear of the procession where the keep staff made up the rest of the colorful caravan.

"You heard the man," Sir Mark shouted. "Let's get moving."

The knights parted to different sides of the road and let the wagons rumble by. Once they had passed, the knights arranged themselves as von Fiescher had commanded. Patrick had to admit, it was an impressive sight; some hundred knights to a side forming a corridor of draped banners fluttering in the breeze.

As they were taking up their positions, the Irishman noticed the three rowboats pass the harbor mouth and then take divergent paths. He expected the boats to gradually fade into the mist, becoming ghost-like, and disappear altogether. But they just blinked out of existence.

"Hey, did you see..." Patrick started to say, but everyone was too busy jockeying about. He paused and stared out into the waters with his disbelieving eyes until mist started to collect on his eyelashes. Finally, someone grumbled for him to get in line and he complied. The banner-streaming lances began to lift like an undulating wave to allow the returning Wolfgang to pass. Evidently he had finished giving instructions to the carriages, which were to transport the Guests back to the keep.

"Well done, handsomely done, lads," he said. His mount kicked up sand as he rode past. The lances fell back into place behind him, only to lift again in another undulation. This time Father Hugh Constant galloped wildly by on a braying donkey. The Avangarde laughed as the portly man struggled to slow the beast down. Eventually he did, and joined von Fiescher on the dock. The two elder statesmen of Greensprings dismounted and waited, looking out to sea.

The conversation among the knights died, and they held vigil in the same direction. The gulls quieted as if sensing the anticipation, but the breeze gusted and threw whispering sand along the shore. Waves crashed against rocks outside the harbor, then pulled back in a bubbling hiss, marking time as the procession waited. How many cycles of waves, Patrick could not say, but it seemed many. He started to wonder if anything was going to happen at all, let alone the arrival of Guests. Then, just as the little rowboats had blinked out of existence, three enormous galleys appeared out of nowhere.

They were fat-bodied wooden vessels with a single billowing sail. Men moved quickly about the decks of the ships, pulling on ropes and working winches that caused the sails to be gathered into the mast, effectively slowing the ships down as they approached the docks. Patrick could see now that the strangers' clothing was a sailor's uniform. Many of the active figures on deck wore them, but there were many more people gathered around the railings gawking at the island, and none of them wore a uniform. These appeared to be richly dressed civilians.

The galleys took little time mooring to the docks. With precision, the large vessels gently bumped sideways into the wooden structures and almost simultaneously dropped iron anchors into the water with a loud splash, chains rattling behind them. The sailors threw ropes to the waiting Greensprings servants, who tied them to the dock pilings. The servants then hurried back to their wagons and positioned them closer to the boats so that chattering hoists could lower luggage, supplies, and crated items onto them. There, the diligent servants disengaged the items from the hoists and lashed them down.

Wolfgang von Fiescher approached one of the gangplanks lowered from a ship, and Father Constant another, and Patrick saw that Mother Superior had been among the keep servants all along. She too positioned herself near the third galley gangway. Though Patrick still could not hear from this distance, he saw them welcome the passengers as they descended from the ships. First usually came a man in a sailor's uniform, but with a more elaborate sash and cap, followed by a parade of young men and women, finely dressed but with rather blank looks on their faces. Wolfgang, Father Constant, and Mother Superior directed the Guests towards shore.

They tottered on the wooden dock with uneasy steps, which became almost outright stumbling when they came onto the sand that approached the Avangarde, but by the time they reached the mounted knights and their bannered archway, they had found their land-legs.

As they passed by on their way to the waiting carriages, Patrick and the others got a good look at them. They were all young—ranging from eleven years of age to their mid-twenties. None were older than that. Many wore rich clothing and jewelry. The Crusades had done these clothes service: once-rare silk from the Far East now fluttered abundantly among the Guests, and the variety of colors dazzled the eyes. It wasn't just the spectrum that was startling, but their brightness and newness. And even more astonishing than the variety of colors in cloth was that of jewels and gems. Gold was common, even at Greensprings, but here, gold was inset with rubies, emeralds, and sapphires. Even the misty air could not deaden their sparkle.

The Guests themselves were almost as varied and intriguing in appearance. Most were female. Patrick saw the black hair of the East, the brown of middle Europe, strawberry blonde among some of the younger children, and all manner of blondes—straw-gold to snow-white. There were strong-built boys and lanky ones, young ladies ample and willowy. Most of their complexions were the milky tones of Western Europe, but some had darker complexions common to Moorish Spain or the Southern Italian states, yet these Guests had eyes that glittered like the jewels they wore about their necks and on their fingers. They numbered several hundred; a handsome bunch, the lot of them. Not just nobility, but royalty. They chattered to each other as they gawked and looked around with innocent abandon at the soldiers and the Isle of Avalon.

#

Patrick's first duty after the arrival of the Guests at the keep was to make rounds and welcome them. He was assigned to the Scottish knight, Jason McFowler, who led the charge in this diplomatic mission. Patrick and the Reservists met Jason and several Avangarde outside the Hall for Guests, as they were already residents there.

Jason McFowler like Marcus Ionus, was a long time veteran. And because of that, Jon had almost completely stopped talking to Patrick so he could spend all his time trying to win McFowler's favor.

Jason cavorted about like a child and was joking around. With his mane of red hair braided into tails and his prominent blue-tattooed arms, he looked more a Viking than a Highlander. He fought more like a berserker with his claymore on the drilling ground than a rule-abiding knight. There was a rumor that he had actually spent a stint as an ocean going raider among those Vikings and was now a fugitive in hiding.

McFowler led his band to the first floor of the Hall for Guests. As the Avangarde split up on the floor to introduce themselves and offer their assistance to the still-arriving Guests, McFowler and Patrick meandered through the crowd. Servants were busy with trunks, boxes, bags, and other assorted luggage. McFowler led Patrick toward Patrick's chamber, but they did not go in. Their destination was the room next to his and across from Sir Jon's.

Jason rapped on the door loudly so that it could be heard over the din in the corridor, which was a tremendous change in the Hall compared to the previous weeks' cavernous silence. The door readily opened and inside stood a short, strong boy of perhaps fifteen years.

"Greetings. We are Sir Jason McFowler and Sir Patrick Gawain," the Scotsman said cheerily. "We are Avangarde, and we would like to personally welcome you to the Keep at Greensprings upon the Isle of Avalon. We would like you to know that we are at your service. You see, we are not just protectors, but also a veritable well of aid."

The boy straightened and visibly blinked at the sight of the knights on his doorstep.

"Pleased to meet you," he stammered. "I am William of Monmouth." By now the tone in the corridor was changing from the sounds of toil and moving, to that of raucous conversation with the Avangarde. William just stood there with big eyes. Jason leaned forward a little with an expectant look on his face.

"Well boy, you're in a new place," he said. "Isn't there anything you are dying to know?"

William shrugged. "Where can I get something to eat around here?"

McFowler shook his head and laughed at the boy's nervousness and gave him quick directions to the keep kitchen.

Over the course of the next several minutes, Patrick watched the Scotsman expertly soothe the boy's discomfort and slowly draw him into conversation. Patrick felt like he should be doing something other than just watching, but every attempt to jump in and join the discussion was rebuffed by the charismatic McFowler.

"So, if I need help of any sort, I can find you where?" William asked.

"If not around and about the keep, then I would try the Avangarde Hall," McFowler replied.

"Or you can find me right next door to you," Patrick offered, finally finding an opportunity to say something. He gestured to his door.

William looked confused. "Right there? Why are you not also in the Avangarde Hall?"

Patrick did not like William's tone, but did his best to smile as he explained the difference between him and Jason, Avangarde and Reservist. William did not seem to understand or care.

"So, William of Monmouth." Jason inquired. "Who are you? And what brings you to Avalon?"

"I am from Monmouth," William said, puffing out his chest as if the place was important. "My father is very rich. Several other houses are jealous of his power, and they threatened my family. So my father decided to ship me off here, out of harm's way, wherever here is." He sniffed. "I doubt it is really Avalon. If there ever was a real Avalon, it sank beneath the waves along with Lyonesse." William crossed his arms.

Jason's eyes went round and his smile broadened. "So tell me then, where are you if this is not *the* Avalon?"

William shrugged. "Some uncharted island, I guess."

"So you are rich, are you?"

William puffed up. "Why yes, I suppose you could say that. My father is powerful enough to incur the jealousy of his peers and influential enough to send me here, and at no small price."

McFowler leaned against the doorframe and withdrew a long dagger from his belt, with which he began to clean his nails.

"So tell me, Willy boy, does your father care for yea?"

William backed up a step. "I suppose so. Why yes, of course he does."

"Does he care enough for yea that he would be willing to pay a ransom for your worthless hide?" Jason blew on his nails and held them out to inspect them.

William finally looked to Patrick as if he could help him. But Patrick played along with McFowler.

"Well, you know, my father is not that rich, and he probably does not care that much for me. I mean after all..." William's forehead grew shiny with moisture and he clutched at his chest as his breath grew short.

Jason burst into laughter. He put away his dagger as he gathered William up into a single-armed embrace. William tried to step away but then began to laugh himself.

"You had me fooled there for a moment," he said.

"Oh, we are still going to kill you, Willy."

Jason was all seriousness again. William's face turned pale, which caused Jason to begin to laugh anew.

The door next to William's opened, and a tall, lanky boy younger than William strode out.

"What is all the commotion about?"

"Oh, do not worry, Trent, I am just about to be murdered, that is all," William said calmly. Trent frowned. William explained the situation, and Trent smiled at McFowler.

"My uncle warned me about the Avangarde's sense of humor," Trent said.

"Your uncle has been here?" Patrick asked.

Trent noticed Patrick. "Yes, it was he who suggested I come here for a while. He said that the experience would be invaluable," he replied. William put an arm around Trent.

"Trent's father is also a rich merchant in Jersey. Maybe you want to ransom him off also?"

McFowler snapped his fingers and looked at Patrick. "That is a fabulous idea! Do you not think so, Sir Gawain?"

"Quite," Patrick answered, smiling with eyebrows raised.

They laughed and stayed to talk for a while, and then Jason gathered up his group of Avangarde and moved on to meet more Guests. They spent much of the day in this fashion.

#

The following evening was cause for yet another banquet, this time as a formal reception for the Guests. Unlike the first gathering, this was a full-blown gala. The dining hall's throne room was decorated with sweet-smelling evergreen sprigs, mistletoe, and forest flowers. The food was rich and abundant. Everyone was colorfully dressed, and the candle and lantern lights reflected off the white plaster walls to brightly illuminate the hall. Patrick sat among the knights. He pulled at his collar and swallowed hard as he remembered how that first gathering went. He was only mildly more comfortable, and again feared an inopportune appearance from the Apparition. He tapped his foot nervously.

On the upper balconies, the servant women rested for a few minutes. They leaned out the windows overlooking the dining hall, watching with wonder and some measure of envy the beautifully dressed people below.

"Tis the life down there," one of the servants said. Her name was Anna. "Ah, to be a noblewoman with nothing better to do than to wear jewels and eat fancy food all day!"

"Sounds boring to me," said another servant, whose name was Claire. "And you would get fat and unattractive besides."

"Well, it is better than hauling this thing about," replied Anna, hefting a bucket of leftover food. "Besides, you are already fat and unattractive. Why not be bored as well?"

Claire made a face at Anna, and they both giggled. "The only reason the pretty lasses down there are so skinny is because they are still young and have not squeezed out a few babes."

"True, true. Time will catch up even with them." Anna nodded to herself. "Don't you agree, Aimeé?"

Aimeé leaned out the window on her elbows. Her thoughts seemed to be elsewhere.

"Yoo-hoo, Aimeé. Are yea there, lass?" Anna waved a hand in front of the younger servant girl's face. Aimeé blinked.

"Taken away by the noblesse down below, are you?" Claire asked

Aimeé smiled. "It is not the women I am looking at most."

Anna and Claire crowded into the balcony opening to get a better look over the hall.

"So you are right." Claire giggled. "Much more interesting view from this angle. Handsome knights we have here, no?" Anna maneuvered for a better view of the long table where the Avangarde sat noisily before their trenchers.

"Which ones do you think are the most handsome?" Claire asked.

"Tis a simple question, that," Anna said. "Sir Geoffrey is by far the most handsome."

Claire scoffed. "That poppin-jay? A beau, yes, but I would wager that he spends more time gazing in a looking glass than he does at women."

Anna chuckled. "You know who I think is worthy of a girl's attention?"

Claire placed both hands to her breast and swooned. "Oh, do tell!"

"Jason McFowler."

Claire's hands went to her hips. "I can see the reasoning behind that. Though he is an odd-looking fellow, he can make a girl laugh, and he is handsome in a scruffy sort of way."

Anna's mouth made a sudden O, and she placed a hand to her cheek. "My goodness, how could we have forgotten the most generous prize of them all! Why Sir Mark is the greatest catch."

"Oh my, yes," Claire leaned on the wall. "And there he is, sitting among the knights." She and Anna were practically climbing over each other order to see better. They swooned over the golden-haired image of the knight sitting among his comrades in arms. Aimeé retreated, arms crossed.

"A modern-day Lancelot, do you not think, Aimeé?" Claire asked.

"Oh, I know who she has a fancy for," Anna teased. "'Tis yonder knight from the Green Isle."

Claire giggled. "Smitten by this one, are we? He is a handsome lad, Sir Gawain, especially since he got some food in his stomach and some sun on his face. I dare say he looked like a ghost when he first arrived here, being so pale and all."

"He still looks like he has *seen* a ghost from the looks of him. You know they call him Sir Silence because he does not talk much," Anna said.

"He is a strange fellow, all right, but who cares. Aimeé approves of him enough."

"Would you silly wenches stop talking about me like I was not here?" Aimeé's French accent sounded out of place among Anna and Claire's English, though not too out of place in relation to the keep, for the court at Greensprings was a veritable hodge-podge of accents and languages.

Claire smiled with one side of her mouth. "You have had eyes on that one for a while. Though it is the same story every year. Tell us, does this one even know you exist?" Claire inquired.

Aimeé rolled her eyes. "Of course he knows I exist."

"But does he have eyes for you?"

Aimeé did not reply right away. "Not yet, but I wager that I can make him."

Anna and Claire tsked. "Careful, girl," Anna said, "it is a simple matter of going for a roll in the hay, but that can lead to trouble. And I doubt that he would be so noble as to marry you for it, let alone admit it. He is noble born, and you are not."

"Thank you, 'mother,'" Aimeé said, "but I was not talking about that. I meant only a little harmless attention."

"I think you would have as much luck as you have had in the past," Claire said.

"Now that sounds like a challenge," Aimeé said gaily, hoisting up her tray of food. "But why not watch and let us see whose head I can turn?"

She sauntered past the giggling Anna and Claire toward the stairwell. When she disappeared from sight, the two servants leaned out the window again to watch her reappear below on the hall floor. They watched her work her way through the crowd toward the long table where the Avangarde sat. Upon reaching the table, she placed the tray in the center of the table, even though there was already an abundance of food. She went out of her way to be near Patrick, who was sitting with the knights Jeremiah, Jon, and Gregory. She leaned heavily against the Irishman's shoulder. Anna and Claire's knowing eyes watched her stick her bosom in his face. Patrick averted his eyes and made room for her to work. Aimeé made some trite apology, to which Patrick courteously replied, but then he returned his attention to the knights.

Anna and Claire laughed. Aimeé placed one hand on her hip and shook her fist at the back of Patrick's head with the other, but no one noticed except the other servants. Largely unnoticed. Aimeé stalked back up the stairs.

"I told you, lass, but do not worry," Claire laughed. "Either he is incredibly pious, or likes young lads."

"Or he finds me vulgar and obvious," Aimeé said, her face red. Anna and Claire took her in their arms and walked her away from the balcony.

"You will get over it," Anna said. "You always do."

"For now, we best be getting back to the kitchens. Rosa Maria will be wondering where we are. And you know how those Italian kitchen madames can be," Claire said.

#

"Good evening, gentlemen," Sir Geoffrey said. He sat himself at the table near Patrick, Jon, Jeremiah, and Gregory. They greeted him with handshakes all around.

"We were just speculating on how this year will go," Jeremiah said, brushing back a dark curl of hair from his eyes. "All of us are Reservists, and this is our first year."

Geoffrey took a long draft of wine from his goblet. "Well, lads, my best advice to you all is to just take it day by day. There will be plenty of drilling of arms, horsemanship, and night watches." He drank from the cup again and then made a swooping gesture, which encompassed all four junior knights. "But if it is adventure you are looking for, there is little enough of it. This is my third year, and there have been few calls to arms. Once to handle pirates and raiders who blundered through the mist, and another to rid the woods of critters."

"Critters in the woods?" Gregory asked. His sharp blue eyes sparkled like a child's.

Geoffrey gently pulled off his expensive velvet gloves and placed them on the table. "Why, yes. This is Avalon, the fabulous realm where creatures of legend truly exist. You know, ogres, trolls, and witches." The four listeners put their cups down and silently stared in Geoffrey's direction. He laughed, and it became evident they had again fallen victim to the unusual sense of humor typical of all the Avangarde.

"Seriously," Geoffrey said, "once a year we beat the bushes to appease the villagers. The folks here are terribly superstitious, and they claim that all kinds of fairy folk beset the woods, making their cows dry up, scaring their chickens and dogs and so forth."

"Is there any basis for their fears?" Sir Jon asked. Geoffrey shrugged and ran his hand through his thick brown hair before replying. It was full and soft as if he had just bathed.

"The milk in the cows' udders often mysteriously dries up. Dogs sometimes bark until all hours of the night for no apparent reason. We can hear them even up here on the hill. Fairy rings of toad stools and stones come and go, just like good old grandma used to talk about," Geoffrey took another drink of wine. "When we do our annual bush–beating, some of us catch fleeting glimpses of something from the corners of our eyes. Occasionally, although I have only heard rumors, an Avangarde will come back alone, sword drawn and eyes the size of this goblet, gibbering like a madman." He took another drink. "Such knights often pack up and leave Avalon. Which is good..." Geoffrey shook his head and slapped Gregory on the back,"for you gentlemen, for then you can take their places and become full-fledged Avangardesmen." He took yet another drink from the goblet. His cheeks were turning pink now.

"Is it really all that eerie around the isle?" Patrick asked.

Geoffrey laughed. "A forest is a forest is a forest. I would rather not go galloping about in search of adventure. I prefer to stay inside the walls of Greensprings and do my civic duty of protecting the Guests, particularly the more attractive ones." He winked at Patrick. "And there is plenty of adventure there for the taking."

The Irishman frowned. "I thought we were discouraged from having romantic liaisons with the Lady Guests."

Geoffrey smiled into his wine. "Details, details. There is no harm in a little fun every now and again. Just be discreet about it, or those women in habits will have you saying the rosary until Kingdom come." He jerked his head in the direction of the table where the nuns of Greensprings sat at their dinner.

Jeremiah smirked. "Sounds like trouble to me."

"Nonsense," Geoffrey rolled his eyes at Jeremiah. "Why, I am engaged to be married to a former Guest."

"Really?" Jon asked.

"Why, yes, a lovely young woman by the name of Amy du Lac."

"Where is she now?"

"At her father's court in Normandy, but she will be returning here later this season before the sailing gets bad." Geoffrey drained his cup, filled it again, gathered up his gloves, and bowed to the Reservists.

"Now if you will excuse me, gentlemen, I think I will go apply myself to my civic duties." He turned and walked up to a table full of attractive Guests in colorful gowns.

"What a scoundrel," Gregory said. Jon nodded. "But he does have the right idea. We ought to be mingling and not hiding in a corner like this."

"Hear, hear," Jeremiah added, and they departed together. Patrick had no intention of leaving the safety of his table, and fortunately, Jon stayed with him. Patrick was glad for that, because he did not want to be alone at this banquet.

#

Patrick awoke to the sound of bagpipes. Time and time again he had heard the sound outside his window at dawn, but he was unable to pinpoint its origin. He lay back and stared at the ceiling. Pity he was not capable of creating his own peace of mind, as a disciplined man should.

That sound was soon lost over the noise in the corridor. Boy Guests were waking up. Laughter, shouting, and roughhousing had become the norm every morning.

Patrick groaned and folded his pillow around his head. The raucous Guests cavorted about like students in a boys' school. This was basically it—the dormitory of a fancy school. And he was their glamorized guardian. Or at least, one of them. The Guests were attending classes with the resident scholars and priests. They collaborated in religious plays and choir concerts, although it was too early yet to see the fruits of their work.

Patrick groaned again and threw his pillow at the wall that separated his chamber from that of William of Monmouth. The stocky merchant's son had entirely too much energy and liked to rise early every morning to vent it. Patrick could hear the boy moving noisily around his room as if he were moving heavy wood furniture. Patrick found that he liked the Hall for Guests much better when it was empty. The Avangarde didn't have to put up with such indignities every morning.

He was supposed to take his turn on the keep walls. There was nothing to guard against, as far as he could tell. But then again, you could not exactly have walls and knights who did not use them. The Benefactors on the outside would probably be at a loss were they to find out that the keep and all its important inhabitants were needlessly invaded because the knights sworn to protect it decided to sleep in an extra hour.

Still, Patrick had to force himself to get dressed. Halfway through putting on his surcoat, he just sat on his bed with the garment hanging over his head, blanketing his face.

The Irishman was painfully aware of the fact that he was performing only the minimum of what was expected of him as an Avangarde Reservist. He did not mix with the Guests or even with the Avangarde. He spent much of his time with the other Reservists. Patrick mused that if this behavior continued, it would be entirely possible that he would be asked to leave Avalon. And where would he go then? Not home, not yet. He had nothing to show for his journeys except stories. With that thought, the image of himself on his knees staring at bloody hands came to mind. He squeezed his eyes shut and shook his head. No, this place was his chance to make his life normal again. He could not leave. He certainly could not leave in dishonor. He needed this.

He knew something needed to be done, but didn't know what. He found it difficult to be the carefree knight ready to settle the disputes, disruptions, or just plain homesickness of the Guests. Dealing with challenges of the social realm did not come to him easily. Worldly dangers, however, did not pose a problem.

Patrick smiled. It was too bad that the keep really was not being attacked from outside. Now t*hat* he could handle; *that* he had experience with.

Perhaps wishing for such a thing is not so wise, he thought.

A noise from his door brought him back. He pulled the surcoat all the way over his head, brushed his hair out of his eyes, and stared at a corner of paper someone was trying to force under his door.

He walked over to the door and opened it.

A young woman was bent over and holding the rest of the paper in her hand. She jumped up and gasped. She was stout and wore a servant's veil and shapeless gown. She was not one of the Greensprings' servants.

"Can I help you, mademoiselle?" Patrick asked.

The woman just stood there, wide-eyed, and began to make funny noises. At first Patrick thought that she was perhaps in pain, even though she wore a bit of a smile, but then he realized that she was laughing. Her laughs were contorted, and Patrick further decided that she was perhaps a mute. Not knowing what to do or say, Patrick said, "Is there something that I can do?"

The woman looked about, making her laugh-grunt sounds, and held the piece of paper up for him to see. It was addressed to William of Monmouth.

"Oh," Patrick exclaimed, finally understanding. "You had the wrong door. Here, I believe he is home. Let us knock and see..." He started towards the door, but the woman shoved the paper into Patrick's hand and ran down the corridor, laughing.

The letter was scented with a woman's perfume. The door to William's room opened and he came out.

"What's all the noise about?" William snatched the letter out of Patrick's outstretched hand.

Patrick's frown deepened. "What?" he said, snatching the letter back. It was his turn to read it. It was an anonymous, brief love letter announcing someone's amorous intentions. "It is not from me," Patrick protested, getting red in the face.

William raised his eyebrows.

"It was from a short servant woman," Patrick said, "with big brown eyes and cherubic cheeks who couldn't talk. Just sort of grunted and laughed." William's expression was getting more receptive. "She was trying to force it underneath my door. She thought it was your chamber." William turned and beat his head against his door.

"She is such a nuisance!"

Patrick smiled. "It seems you have a lady admirer."

"No, you do not understand." William explained, scrunching up his shoulders and clenching his hands into fists. "The message is not from her mistress. It is from her, the servant herself. We were on the same boat coming to Avalon. For some reason, she fell in love with me. She has been a nuisance ever since."

Patrick laughed. "If this is all the trouble you have, you are a lucky man. If you will forgive me, I must attend to my duties. I will see you later, and I trust you will wake me up again tomorrow morning as you have faithfully done since you arrived. Good day, Willy."

#

At the end of his shift on the wall, Patrick descended the battlements and made his way across the training grounds toward the keep. He was cold, tired, and hungry. A long day's vigilance usually did that to him, and he was looking forward to a hot meal.

But as he was entering the chamber adjacent to the gardens a French noblewoman stopped him.

"Mon Seigneur Gawain?" she asked. Patrick nodded, and then realized that he should bow or at least say something polite despite his foul mood.

"I was wondering if you could help me with a matter?" the woman said.

She was as tall as his shoulders, and had long, dark, silky hair, expressive eyes, and beautifully arched thick eyebrows. Patrick did not know what sort of matter he could possibly help her with that demanded that she seek him out in particular. She was a Lady Guest, from Vichy, but he was unable to recall her name.

"How may I help you, m'lady?" he said. His French was crude compared to her flowery formality. She began to pace before him, wringing her hands.

"It is quite silly, actually," she said. "My maidservant seems to be terribly taken by one of the other Guests. I know that he does not requite her feelings, and though he has held his temper, I can see in his face that someday he will berate her, which will devastate her. Can you see my problem, Sir Gawain?"

Patrick's mouth moved involuntarily, striving to form words that would seem appropriate, but none came.

"Oh, I have disturbed you with this ridiculous drama, have I not?" She stepped up to him and laid a hand on his forearm. "I am sure you Avangarde have better things to do, but we have been told that you knights are like family, and this is not a matter one can bring up to Father Hugh at confession, let alone seek out his advice."

Patrick shrugged. "Mademoiselle, perhaps it would help if you told me who we are talking about and why you think I can help. And, I am terribly sorry, but I am afraid I cannot recall your name. Forgive my memory."

The woman gasped. "Oh my manners, forgive *me* Sir Gawain. My name is Christianne Morneau, from Vichy. I am newly arrived in Avalon with my maidservant, Melwyn. She told me of the incident in the Hall for Guests, where you reside, while attempting to send a letter to William of

Monmouth, the man with whom she is in love. That is why I am asking your advice, because you are an Avangarde, a neighbor, and perhaps a friend of William's."

Patrick laughed. "I see now," he said. "So it is your maidservant who is in love with Willy." He stopped laughing once he saw that Christianne did not join him. "I am pleased that you came to me, of all people, to ask advice, but the best that I can offer is to let the drama unfold by itself. She is obviously infatuated, and with time, she will get over it."

"I know that, but as I said, I am afraid William might lose his temper and hurt her. She may be only a maidservant, but we grew up together, I have known her all my life, and she is very much like a sister." Lady Morneau's eyes were beseeching. "Please, Sir Gawain, it is a simple matter. Speak to William. Father Hugh and Mother Superior tell us that you Avangarde are not only soldiers of arms, but also soldiers of the spirit. Can you use your position to keep her from being harmed? However silly this may sound to you, it is important to me."

Patrick drew in a deep breath. The girl had a point. That was just what the Creed stated.

Patrick said, "You are obviously distraught over this, and it is my duty to do my best to remedy it. I will talk to William and straighten the whole matter out. You need not worry about it." An easy promise, but he did not have the slightest idea how to fulfill it.

Christianne embraced him and thanked him. Patrick held the French noblewoman awkwardly in his arms. The form of contact was alien to him.

She was absolutely beaming. She must indeed be close to her maidservant, he thought.

"One question, though," he asked. "Melwyn? That's her name? Does she talk?"

Lady Morneau smiled and leaned back from him, hands on his shoulders. "When it suits her. I would not say that she is touched..." she gestured to her head. "...but she is a unique girl. She laughs nonstop, though I have no problem communicating with her. Actually, I find her very refreshing."

"That's sweet," said Patrick.

Jason McFowler came striding into the chamber.

"What is this? Fraternizing among the Guests and Avangarde?" Patrick eased out of Christanne's arms. He remembered the rules but also remembered Sir Geoffrey's view on the matter and wondered if Jason felt the same way.

"Sir McFowler, you devil in a kilt, how are you today?" the Frenchwoman asked. The conversation was now in Latin. Christianne went to the Highlander and gave him a warm hug. "Sir Gawain has just agreed to help me with a diplomatic matter of great importance. I am eternally indebted to him."

"Well, then, it seems he has won himself a lovely treasure. Though I hope it can wait until later, for he is just the man I am looking for."

"What on earth for? I have already done my duties for the day," he started, but McFowler put up a hand. His other arm was around Lady Mourneau's waist.

"I am sure you have worked hard and diligently and are a credit to the Reservists, as well as the Avangarde, but I just wanted to invite you and some others to the village for supper and some ale."

"I will leave you two to go to your entertainment," Lady Morneau said, once again coming up to Patrick and taking his hand in hers. "I do wish to know as soon as possible what comes of your 'diplomatic mission.' And, of course, I would not mind spending some time with you, Patrick. Perhaps we can sup together in the dining hall sometime? I would love to hear about your homeland."

She walked away and waving goodbye, all smiles. But halfway through the doorway she stopped and turned. "Oh Patrick, there is one thing I have been meaning to ask you.

Who is that hooded man that I sometimes see following you around?"

#

They walked to the village. Patrick was quiet. Any questions he might have had concerning McFowler's motives were forgotten in the mental clamor of Lady Mourneau's inquiry about the Apparition

"Why so glum, Irishman? I thought everyone from the Green Isle was a cheerful drunk."

Patrick half-smiled. "Long day."

They entered the village of Aesclinn, and the dust under their boots gave way to cobblestone. This was Patrick's first time in the village, and he found it tidy with its stone fences and gabled earthen buildings. They found the inn, which looked small from the outside but seated many. Someone at the corner of the room hailed them.

"Look it's McFowler and Sir Sil..." He got a sharp jab to the abdomen by the knight seated next to him.

Jason led Patrick to a circular wooden table in the corner. Patrick recognized them all and noted that they were all veterans. There was Sir Mark, Sir Brian, Sir Waylan, who looked more like a warrior hermit than a knight, Sir Corbin, and Sir Eirech Bischoff, a hulking long-haired German who spoke neither Latin nor French very well. He always managed to make himself understood even though the only thing that he ever said was "Good! Good!" with a toothy grin. They called him "Bisch."

Room was made for Patrick and Jason.

"What will you be drinking?" Sir Corbin asked.

Patrick shrugged. "What is there?" The inn brewed its own and smelled of barley oats and malt and something else even stronger. Every time the barkeep passed between the swinging door that led out of the common room, Patrick caught a glimpse of huge wooden fermenting vats.

"Oh, ale and beer, flavored with fruit or not, and dark or light ones. If you have a craving for wine, there is..."

Sir Waylan cut Sir Brian off. "Fool, it is his first time here, not to mention his first time in Avalon." There were murmurs of assent. "Frederique, a pint of Aphelon for our companion."

Patrick sat with back rigid and hands at his sides, waiting for the spindly old Norman barkeep to bring his drink. How to act among veterans? He had not spent much time with them, and he definitely had not expected to be among them in this manner.

Frederique brought the earthenware goblet and placed it before Patrick. It smelled of apples and alcohol—hard cider. Patrick reached for his coins, but Corbin waved him off.

"My pleasure, Sir Gawain," he said.

The drink was tasty and potent. They told Patrick that it was made from the local apples and harvested by the villagers. The apple trees were native to the Misty Isle and had the unlikely trait of blooming year round, therefore providing an endless supply of apples, and hard cider.

Food was ordered, and they ate a splendid meal of roasts, hams, chicken, stews and soups, fresh bread, and cheese. It was different, more pleasant, in comparison to the meals served at Greensprings. Though the Keep meals were fine, they lacked a certain personal quality, most likely because they were made often and in volume.

After the meal, more drinks went around. Patrick smiled more, relaxed, and began to see the men around him as companions rather than superiors. He wondered if this had been their intention all along. Or maybe it was only Jason's.

They talked long into the night, mostly reminiscing about the old times they had shared as Avangarde. Patrick politely sat by and listened, as the stories did not involve him or anything with which he could really relate. But between stories, they asked him questions, mostly about his journeys through the Holy Land and what the Crusade had really been like. Unfortunately, he did not feel that he was much of a storyteller, and it was evident that he could not hold their attention for very long. That made him sad, for these knights of the Avangarde were allowing him the opportunity to become better acquainted, to prove his mettle, so to speak, and he was ruining it.

It should be Sir Jon sitting here, not me, he thought ruefully. He was glad that he was, for the most part, pleasantly drunk.

"So, Sir Gawain, what do you think of our little island with our little castle?" Mark asked rather suddenly. He, too, was drunk, and his blue eyes were glassy. His speech was slurred in an almost-comical way, and his finely chiseled face was flushed. Patrick hoped that he did not look half that bad. The Irishman was happy to see that the barrel-chested Mark was susceptible to something. Patrick recalled that he was one of the few people who could best him at swordplay during training.

"I am enjoying my stay very much," Patrick replied.

"Well, it is hard to tell that from your behavior," Brian said, pouring more hard cider into all the cups.

Patrick shifted uneasily. "How do you mean?"

Brian gestured with his hands as if this would enable him to speak better. "You do not talk much, you know, and tonight is the first time that I have seen you smile," he said.

"That is not true," Waylan said. "He smiled plenty during the dance contest." The recollection of the event caused all to laugh, Patrick included.

"You see!" Waylan pointed at the Irish knight. "He smiles yet again."

Patrick waved them off. "I am not in jeopardy of taking my own life. I'm just getting used to this new place. It is different here, that's all." *And I am being haunted by a robed specter.*

"Well, I say you fit in just fine," McFowler said, turning to the others at the table. "Why, just today before coming here, I saw him leaping to the aid of a damsel in distress. He performed like a true Avangarde."

"Damsel?" Corbin exclaimed, arching an eyebrow. "Which one would that be?"

"None other than the fair Christianne Morneau of Vichy," McFowler replied. Brian whistled and Bisch exclaimed "Good! Good!"

"Caught the fancy of quite a little woman," Waylan pointed out.

Patrick blushed. "I am just helping her with a personal matter concerning her lady-in-waiting."

"Oh, do not belittle it, Patrick," McFowler said. "She is not the only girl whose attention you have caught. Many a lassie, from maidservant to noblewoman, has an eye for you."

"Surely you jest," Patrick said. He looked from face to face for a laugh to give them away. But they persisted.

"It must be that Celtic heritage of yours," McFowler said. "This would also explain why the women fall at my feet as well." Jason puffed up his burly chest. Now the table erupted in laughter.

"The women feel sorry for you, is all, you old pirate," Corbin laughed. "Besides, Waylan and I here are just as much Celtic in our Briton heritage, and women could care less."

"Aye," Brian added, "I'm as Scottish as yea, and I have no luck."

"That's because you are a city dweller from Edinburgh, hardly Scottish at all if you ask me," Jason replied. "You have to be from the Highlands to be considered truly Scottish."

Brian took a swig from his drink with one hand and dismissed Jason with a wave of the other.

"So the idea of being sort of a Lancelot troubles you, Patrick?" Mark asked.

Patrick shrugged, moving his finger around in a pool of hard cider on the table. "I just have not had much luck in the past with women, that is all."

"Perhaps your luck will change here in Avalon," Mark said. "Avalon has a way of changing you. I would say that it could either make your future or be your undoing."

This reminded Patrick of an interesting point. He told the knights at the table about the conversation with Sir Geoffrey, particularly about the bush beatings that sometimes hastened Avangardesmen's departure.

Those at the table listened to the stories and had several of their own. Sir Brian saw the shade of his father in the woods, Sir Corbin a skeletal knight and horse by a river. Sir Waylan heard voices as if at a party but coming from the bottom of a lake, and so on. A shiver crept down Patrick's spine. And he also noticed that it became awfully quiet at the table.

"What does it all mean?" Patrick asked.

"It really is Avalon," Waylan answered. "But what that means, exactly, I could not say. It is a place of legend. Even though it seems empty and abandoned, who is to say that it *is*? Who knows what happened to the original Knights of Greensprings."

"If it is so mysterious, and possibly dangerous, then why have an école privée here with the children of some of the most powerful and richest men in the world?" the Irishman went on.

Corbin shrugged, saying, "Because that is what the Holy Duck told Father Chanceroy when he found the springs on his pilgrimage." This brought on huge guffaws of laughter from the drunken knights.

"It was a swan, you idiot," Brian said.

Corbin took another swig from his drink. "Details." Once the laughter died down, Patrick pointed out that he was not looking forward to the bush-beating and was then informed that he and the other Reservists would not be participating in the excursion, some weeks hence.

"Somebody has to stay behind and watch the keep while we are out thrashing in the woods," Waylan pointed out. Patrick did not know whether to be flattered or offended: Tending to the Guests once again while the Avangarde did the real work.

"Is it always going to be like that?" he asked. "The Reservists always being left behind to play diplomat and mediator?"

"Adventure is what we are looking for, is it, laddie?" Jason slurred.

"Yes, I suppose so," he replied to Jason's taunt.

"Well, even Camelot at its zenith had its dull moments," Brian said.

"That is what prompted the Knights of the Round Table to quest for the Holy Grail," Waylan remarked.

Corbin's brow furrowed. "They were bored off their arses?"

"They had defeated all their worldly adversaries, you unromantic fool," Waylan said. "They had to turn to spiritual quests to fulfill themselves. You are obviously not a learned man, Corbin."

"I shall drink to that!" Corbin shouted, once again raising the cup to his mouth.

Waylan slapped his hand on the table. "I have it!" he cried. "We are in need of a quest. Just look at us. Sir Patrick is right, we need an adventure. Why, we are sitting at a round table," he gestured at the table, which was indeed round, "and we have a Lancelot." He gestured at Patrick.

"No, no, you infidel. He cannot be Lancelot," Brian protested, standing to address Waylan who had himself risen up in his excitement.

"Why not?"

"Because his name is Gawain, so he must be Gawaine."

"Very well then, he will be Gawaine, and Mark shall be Lancelot."

"That will not work either," Corbin said, also standing up. "Mark is likely to be chosen as successor to the Stewardship of Greensprings, so he must be Arthur."

"Very well. You, Lancelot; Patrick, Gawaine; Mark, Arthur; and I..."

"Merlin," Corbin said.

"Why Merlin?" Waylan asked.

Corbin was very drunk and leaned into Waylan. "Because you are a long-bearded bastard."

"You're drunk," Waylan said.

"I'll drink to that." All were standing now, arguing about who should be whom. Eventually they worked it out and then asked Waylan/Merlin what his quest was.

"Follow me, men! But first, a toast to the Knights of the Round Table!"

The patrons, as well as Frederique the barkeep, grinned at the drunken knights as they clashed cider cups like swords and then followed Waylan out the door on their quest.

#

"Did you find it?" Waylan asked of the still-panting Corbin. Though it was technically mid-autumn, Avalon had the unique characteristic of staying springlike the year round. Perhaps there was a warm ocean current near the island. Maybe it was magic after all. In any case, Corbin was sweating heavily as he ran up to the group and huddled with them under a bush.

"Yes, we did, but we found it at the smithies, and not at the stables like you said it was, Horse Face," Corbin replied. Behind him came Bisch huffing and puffing and carrying a large ladder. The German grinned.

"Good! Good!"

"We were wondering what took you so long, Sir Chaser of Sheep," Waylan said.

Corbin's eyes went wide, "That is a lie, I was only helping the sheep over the fence, honest."

"What do we do now, 'Merlin'?" Brian asked.

Waylan thought for a moment then said, "First we need somebody to go on a reconnaissance. Any volunteers?"

McFowler mimicked Patrick's Irish accent, saying, "Me! Me!" and lifted Patrick's arm.

"Wonderful!" Waylan exclaimed. "Go then, and quickly." They pushed Patrick out of the bush. Patrick had no idea what was going on. He was very drunk, and his last clear recollection was that he was being pulled out the door of the inn in Aesclinn. Now he found himself staggering across a well-groomed lawn in front of what appeared to be the Hall for Lady Guests.

"No, Patrick, like this!" Waylan shouted, though considering the way he said it, he probably thought he was being quiet about it. He and the others were standing next to the bush, making hunkering down gestures. Patrick saluted them in acknowledgment, hunkered himself down, and made his way across the lawn. He went through the entrance into the small courtyard and tried to remember why he was there. As he searched his memory, someone opened a ground-floor window.

"Who is there?" a young feminine voice asked. "I thought men were not supposed to be in here, especially at night."

Patrick suddenly remembered. "Uhm, I am the gardener."

"At night?"

"Well, you see, slugs come out only at night. That is the only time I can get them."

"Oh, well, goodnight then." The window closed and Patrick wiped his brow. He then went to the entrance and motioned for the other knights to come in.

The knights extricated themselves from the bush and staggered across the lawn. Patrick shook his head. It was a wonder that Western Christians ever captured Jerusalem at all.

The knights set the ladder against the building while six of them held it steady, and Mark climbed up until he could peer into a window. After a moment, and without looking back down, he waved at the assembled men below to move the ladder to the next window. This was accomplished again and again with some grunting and cursing until Mark made a halting signal. He then waited motionless for some time before coming down.

"Next," he said.

They fought for a while to decide who would climb first, and McFowler took advantage of the confusion to climb up. He, too, sat for a while, chewing on his kilt as he was apt to do when excited, and then came down. This went on until it was Patrick's turn, though he was sitting with his back against the wall, feeling very woozy. They pushed him up the ladder until he reached the illuminated window. Once there, he peered in to see what all the commotion was about.

This was definitely the Hall for Lady Guests, for before him was a Lady Guest all but naked, preparing for bed with the aid of her lady-in-waiting, who was also all but naked in a half-open shift.

Patrick was shocked. He could hardly believe that these Avangardesmen, these veterans, would sink to pranks. These were the ladies they were entrusted to protect and who looked up to them as confidants and role models. He gestured to the knights below to move him so he could get a better view.

Five of the six of the knights no longer held the ladder. Only Bisch was holding it. They figured the hulking German could manage it while they talked and snickered amongst themselves. With a grunt, he lifted the ladder, Irishman and all, and teeter-tottered it to his left where Patrick was gesturing. He didn't make it very far before his eyes went wide and he exclaimed, "Bad! Bad!"

Rather than moving left, the ladder started to slowly sway back into the courtyard. Bisch over-compensated to stop it from wobbling, only to have to over-compensate in the opposite direction. This happened several times and the other knights fell over themselves trying to aid Bisch, which ended up making matters worse. The hapless Irishman on top of the ladder held on for dear life, but to no avail as the travesty finally came unhinged. There was a loud crash as Patrick fell on top of Brian and Mark and the ladder broke into pieces.

Seven seasoned knights retreated from the Hall for Lady Guests in complete disarray, carrying portions of ladder with them.

#

"What was that noise?" the lady that was preparing for bed asked.

"I believe that was the gardener," her lady-in-waiting snickered.

"Gardener?"

#

The following morning, during Church services, many of the knights present had trouble fighting off fatigue and headaches. And when Father Constant had finished Mass, Mother Superior had a special announcement to make: boy hooligans searching for excitement after curfew at the Hall for

Lady Guests would not be tolerated, and any offenders caught would be dealt with by the Avangarde.

#

The following weeks brought a marked change in Sir Gawain. Though Siegfried was still his best friend, he saw more and more of the Avangarde and the Guests. He could not say that he was the best of friends with them, but he no longer shied away or felt as uncomfortable around them. He would occasionally join them in Aesclinn, but only when invited.

Once, upon entering the main door of the keep, he came across something that had not been there before. He saw a dour-looking stranger coming at him, walking briskly. The sight so took him off guard that he reached for his sword, only to realize that it was no stranger. Somebody had placed a mirror in the entrance's vestibule. It was a good mirror of glass backed by silver. Patrick suspected that it was a tribute gift to Greensprings from the family of one of the Guests.

The stranger was his own reflection. He had never seen his own image with such clarity. He stepped closer to the mirror and ran his hand across the image. His face was now blank, rather than hard, and he noted his high, sharp cheek bones, shoulder-length black hair, and the moist swirl of greens, browns and orange hues in his eyes. Long ago, he had considered himself a handsome man, but then he thought that his experiences in the Holy Land had robbed him of his youth and vigor. Now as he gazed upon his reflection, he saw that they had not left him but had only been forced into submission. He was older, yes, and a little more worn. Perhaps there was some truth in what the Knights of the Round Table had told him. He slowly backed away from the mirror and left.

#

It seemed as though yet another banquet was in order. Patrick was beginning to think that all that ever happened at the keep was one banquet after another. However, it was the Guests who organized them now. This particular banquet was to announce the new Steward of the keep, the man who would take over the administrative affairs of Greensprings once Wolfgang von Fiescher left to meet the Council in Rome for the year.

Lady Christianne Morneau invited Sir Gawain to be her escort, and, of course, he accepted. Sitting nearby were an uncomfortable-looking William of Monmouth and a fawning Melwyn. Also close at hand was Trent of Jersey, who found his friend's predicament a constant source of amusement.

"Have you talked to him yet?" Christianne asked.

Patrick pulled at his collar uncomfortably. "I intend to do so soon."

The banquet proceeded like most others, except that many of the Guests performed songs, dances, and skills native to their homelands. Patrick was amazed at the artistic talent among the young folk assembled in the hall. And also, a great mystery was resolved.

Sir McFowler stepped before the assembled crowd and performed music from his native Highlands, utilizing an instrument also native to those mist shrouded regions. He carried a worn, baggy instrument with smooth wooden pipes sticking in all directions. The bag was made of a multi-colored cloth similar to that which made his kilt. This he carried under one arm, and with the other he put one of the pipes in his mouth, drew in a deep breath, and blew. The bag inflated, and while maintaining it trapped underneath his elbow he gingerly grasped the one pipe with both hands and strategically placed fingers over holes in the hollow tube. Squeezing the bag, an eerie, yet beautiful wail issued forth followed by a melody Patrick had heard time and time again from his chamber window. A hush fell upon the hall as all, obviously moved by the sound, listened intently. McFowler's fingers expertly flew up and down the pipe, covering and uncovering the holes as they went. Occasionally he would draw a quick, yet deep breath and replenish the air in the bag under his arm. Doing so did not cause him to miss a note.

The music lasted perhaps five minutes but seemed much longer. When finished, Jason bowed deeply to acknowledge the ovation that greeted him.

"Did you hear that?" Willy exclaimed, very much taken by the spectacle. Patrick nodded.

Wolfgang stood clapping as he made his way over to the dais where the performance took place. He shook McFowler's hand as the Highlander made his exit.

To wrap up the evening, Wolfgang made his announcement as to who would take over his administrative duties. It was to be Sir Mark, the unofficial captain of the Avangarde. From then on, he would be known as Steward Mark, which everybody would eventually change to "King" Mark anyway. It was all in good humor, Greensprings fashion. The choice came as no surprise to anyone. Mark was a veteran, one of von Fiescher's favorites and well loved.

As Mark approached for the simple ceremony, Wolfgang held out a ceremonial circlet and placed it on his brow.

Brian leaned over to Patrick and murmured, "So much for our nightly excursions." Patrick had trouble keeping a straight face.

#

After the banquet Christianne led Patrick into the gardens behind the keep. There, they sat on stone benches surrounded by vine covered trellises. The moon shone down on them, full and bright.

"You know, Sir Gawain," Lady Morneau said, "you talk enough when you have your mind on it." She sat on one of the many marble benches surrounding the central fountain piece. Patrick sat beside her, though at a distance.

"I believe that is more of a credit to you than to me, Lady Morneau," he replied.

"How is that?"

"I generally do not talk, unless spoken to. In case you have not noticed, you have done most of the talking, and I have simply answered your questions."

Christianne thought on this last point. "Not really. You have contributed many interesting things on your own accord."

"If you say so."

Christianne smiled mischievously. "You know, they used to call you 'Sir Silence' because you were so quiet."

Patrick rolled his eyes, not surprised. "What else have they said about me?"

The Frenchwoman looked away, biting her lip. She toyed with a lock of hair for a moment before responding, "That you like boys."

Patrick sat up. "That is complete nonsense! Who said such things! Why, I will…" He almost started to draw his sword. Christianne laughed and urged him to sit back down. There were others in the garden taking a late night's walk, and Patrick had attracted their attention. She was laughing so hard, she had difficulty speaking. She gently grabbed him by the wrist and guided him back to his seat.

Christianne said at last, "It was just a silly rumor started by some women whose affections I am sure you spurned."

Patrick became calm again. "I really do not like boys," he insisted.

"I have seen your gaze wander to the ladies, or above their necklines," she said, "but it is odd that you do not do anything about it. You avoid girls as if they were a plague. Why, until a moment ago, you were leagues away from me on this bench, in mind and body." Patrick looked down. His hands were now cradled in her milky white ones. "Why is that? Please tell me. I am your friend, Sir Gawain."

Patrick stood and let his hands fall to his sides. He paced for a while, then said, "I was hurt terribly by a woman once." He cut the air with his hands. "I do not care to have it happen again. Being in love is wonderful, but losing it can hurt worse than any physical pain. I wish to say no more."

Christianne came to him and slipped into his arms despite his protests.

"I would never imagine trying to force any painful memories out of you. You can tell me when the time is right."

The Irishman awkwardly held her. "Is that why you enjoyed my company at first, because you thought I liked boys and thought I would not be a threat to you?"

Christianne smiled. "No. I can tell that you are a nice man. To me, you are more like Sir Sensitive than Sir Silence. Melwyn, however, is absolutely convinced that you do like boys."

Patrick smiled, feeling devilish. "Why, that gives me a wonderful idea."

#

On his way back to the Hall for Guests, Patrick came across the person he was looking for. With him was the other person he was looking for.

"Willy," he said, briskly approaching the merchant's son. Melwyn was attached to the boy's arm, though he held it stiffly and at a distance from himself, doing his best to be on his best behavior as Patrick had asked until he could think of a way to free Willy from her affections.

"Sir Gawain, I am happy to see you," William said, his stiff posture relaxing and his eyes brightening.

"It is late, my handsome young darling, and we should be getting back." Patrick put his arm around William.

Willy stiffened again. "Beg your pardon?"

"Come, come, we must be going. Say good night to the mademoiselle." Melwyn blinked and looked between the knight and the merchant's son, and when Patrick kissed Willy on top of his head and then winked at her she made a noise like a curious kitten. Patrick hooked his arm through Willy's and dragged the stunned boy off. "Good night, Melwyn! Say good night, Willy."

And they left.

#

They had a good laugh about it all the way back to the Hall for Guests once William understood the trick.

"Thank you, Sir Gawain. I imagine she will leave me alone now that she thinks that I am spoken for."

"Yes, but how come I have the feeling that we will be having a talk with either Mother Superior or Father Hugh tomorrow concerning our 'unholy union'?" Patrick replied.

William shrugged. "We will explain the situation, and they will understand."

"I hope so."

"You Avangarde certainly are a strange lot."

"Reservist, actually..."

"Whatever. Good night, Gawain, and thank you again." With that, Willy entered his chamber, and shut the door tight behind him.

#

Patrick's room was quiet and dark. Still energized from his performance, he moved to a chair over by the window and sat down, foregoing a lantern.

He opened the wooden shutters, let fresh, spring-like air in, and leaned back in his chair. The moon lit up a silvery shaft across the room. The sky was clear, and many stars twinkled with Avalon's surreal quality. They appeared larger and brighter than on the "outside."

Were there more stars over Avalon? Did they really shine brighter here? Patrick could not remember, he had been out of the world for so long now. He rested his chin on his fists, and after some time realized that he was only half awake, lost in that state where dreams mingle with reality. For some reason that state, too, seemed more acute and frequent here on Avalon.

He began to see his home, a gabled manor, in Galway. But it was not really his home, for there, in the background, was the Keep at Greensprings. He was fitting his horse for a long journey.

"Why must you go, my son? You do not have to go," Patrick's mother was saying. Her face was looking up into his, twisted into a mask of sorrow as tears rolled down her cheeks.

"I do not belong here anymore, Mother. I will never be happy here like this. I have to go." His turned his back to her as he pulled tight the last strap on the saddle.

She suddenly spun him around and hugged him. She barely came up to the middle of his chest. "I know why you are running, and I know you are hurting, but why the Holy Land? Why the Crusades? It is for the Franks, not for us."

"I need to find my salvation, mother. I do not know what I possibly could have done to deserve what has befallen me here. Maybe I will find answers along the way." Patrick mounted the horse, holding his mother for a long time in his gaze, and rode off.

Sitting in the chair in his chamber, it seemed to him that his mother was still there with him. She stood behind him stroking the hair that was so much like hers.

"I hope you find your answers, little one, and I hope you come home someday soon," she said, and then she, too, was gone.

#

At dawn Patrick awoke to a noise like a cow being slaughtered in William of Monmouth's chamber.

He jumped from his bed, stormed out into the hall and burst into the boy's room.

"What in God's name are you doing? Every morning you insist on incurring my wrath! What could you...!" Patrick stopped his ranting. This was his first time inside Willy's room, and he was surprised at its décor; half-finished paintings, charcoal drawings, dancing figurines carved from bits of wood, books and papers.

Willy lowered a baggy apparatus to his knees, it bristled with pipes.

"How course of you, Sir Gawain, to barge into my room, shouting. And still in your nightshirt."

"Willy, most people are just waking up now. Not everyone rises as early as you..."

"Well, they ought to."

"...and I have put up with your hobbies long enough, and I must tell you that you must be quieter about them! Particularly in the mornings!"

Willy looked startled. "Trent does not mind."

"I'm not Trent! And what in perdition are you doing anyway? It sounds like an agonized cow!"

Willy brightened and presented the baggy leather thing that he held. "I liked the music Sir McFowler made at the banquet last night. I had him show me how to work it. He even loaned me an old one of his to practice with. What do you think?" He began to wail on the instrument. It was dreadful, an affront to the memory of the sounds that crept into his room on occasion. Patrick ripped the thing away from Willy and threw it on the bed. It made a dying sound when it landed.

"Sir Gawain, I am not letting you bully me, knight or no. I will continue practicing with it whether you like it or not. Sir McFowler says I show promise. I intend on playing every morning."

"No!" Patrick cried as Willy moved towards the bed to retrieve the instrument. Patrick grabbed the back of Willy's shirt and struggled to keep the boy from the object of his torture. They tumbled onto the bed and the bagpipe honked as they fought over it.

"What are you doing? Are you mad?" Willy exclaimed.

"I am going to destroy it!"

"But it is not even mine. It is McFowler's, and he will be angry with you."

"He will understand!" Again, the bag honked.

The two were intertwined, not only with each other, but with the bed sheet and the bagpipes as they wrestled for control over them. They stopped when they heard a nervous laugh coming from the doorway.

There stood Melwyn, wide-eyed. She hurriedly made the sign of the cross and fled, laughing madly.

#

Patrick spent the next week in the company of Lady Christianne Morneau. Nobody asked any questions about their relationship, which was not much of one insofar as Patrick was concerned. He kept his distance for a number of reasons. Melwyn left Willy alone and did not seem too crestfallen over the matter, which was exactly what Christianne had hoped for. Most other people understood that Patrick and Willy's "relationship" had been a ruse. In any case, word had not reached the stern Mother Superior. Patrick was less concerned about the more liberal Father Hugh finding out, but the Priest gave him a start just the same one evening when Patrick was late to dinner, which also led to one of the longer conversations he had with the man:

He was one of the last to enter the great hall for dinner. His usual table was full, and the only space he could find was among the keep's clerics. He approached the brown robed men. "May I join you?" he asked nobody in particular, standing at an opening on the bench.

"Of course dear boy, have a seat," said Father Hugh Constant himself. Patrick settled into the seat across from the priest. There was still much food on the common platter, despite his tardiness and Hugh's presence (if the rumor of the priest's appetite was true). "How are you this evening, Sir Gawain?" he asked.

"Well enough," Patrick replied and reached for a bowl of greens. He tossed some cabbage leaves and carrot sticks on the clay plate before him, and then asked for one of the brothers to pass bread. If Patrick felt out of sorts sitting among the veteran Avangarde, he was feeling especially so now.

"A bit late to sup this evening, aren't we?" Father Hugh made eye contact, making him feel uncomfortable.

"Aye, I couldn't find the stable boy, so had to put Siegfried to bed myself."

"Siegfried?"

"My horse."

Father Hugh nodded. "Not afraid to take matters into your own hands and get them dirty. A noble quality."

Patrick made a slight shrug and an attempt at a smile, then reached for the remnants of chicken at the center of the table. This he pulled apart, and placed the edible portions on his plate. He was about to dig into the food when he noticed Father Hugh watching him.

Though Patrick normally dispensed with the ritual, he thought it wise to cross himself and say grace tonight. When he had finished, he reached for his food and ate hungrily. As he took his first bites, Hugh placed a cup before his plate and filled it with wine from the pitcher on the table.

"Thank you, Father," Patrick said through a mouthful of chicken.

"*In vino veritas.*"

"Pardon?" Patrick asked, not quite hearing the Latin idiom over the din.

Father Hugh smiled and made a dismissing gesture. "So how are you finding your tenure here on the island?"

"Good, good," Patrick replied, followed by an awkward silence in which the priest kept his eyes on the Irishman. The priest momentarily looked away to fill his own wine cup. His cheeks were flushed. Then again, Patrick thought, he kind of always looks intoxicated. He was a portly man, though stout. His cheeks were ruddy and round, though you couldn't quite call them jowls. His shaved pate, ringed by brown hair, was often ruddy as well.

"I've been hearing things about you," Hugh said, watery blue eyes returning to gaze at the knight.

Patrick stopped in mid-chew. With the large piece of cabbage hanging from his mouth and wide eyes, he looked more like a deer caught in a garden then a nobleman at dinner. He quickly pulled the morsel from his mouth and swallowed hard.

"It was a merely a ruse, I swear, William's behavior and mine," he stammered.

Father Hugh frowned. "I haven't heard anything about you and William." He took a drink, and added, "I'm not sure I want to."

Patrick let his shoulders sag, relieved. "So, what have you heard?"

"I was about to say that Mother Superior has commented that she has overheard some of the Lady Guests talk about you."

Patrick placed a hand over his chest, a look of genuine surprise on his face.

"What a gentle fellow you are, how easy it is to talk to you," said Hugh, answering the question Patrick did not ask. "That you are a good listener."

"Well, that is not hard to accomplish," Patrick said. "I am not much of a conversationalist. They do most of the talking."

"They say that too. They call you 'Sir Silence.'"

Patrick bobbed his head, already aware of that moniker. He still didn't like the sound of it.

"They also call you 'Sir Sensitive' and 'Sir-Can-Keep-a-Secret,'" Hugh continued. "They confide in you, and in this gossip-prone environment, you respect their privacy."

Patrick smiled wearily, not sure he liked these names any better. "Perhaps it's just that I don't have anyone to gossip with."

Hugh chuckled. "I doubt that. Keeping confidence is a good trait to have. You'd make a fine priest in the confessional."

"Perhaps I should set up my own booth."

They both chuckled at the image. Father Hugh let Patrick finish his meal, and drink his wine, which he refilled. It looked as if the priest intended on keeping him captive for a while. The hall was starting to empty and the servants set out to clean the tables.

"Speaking of confession," Hugh said nonchalantly. "I understand you have not been yet, since coming to Greensprings."

Patrick swirled the wine in his cup. He stared at the points of light floating in the dark red liquid, reflections from the candle and torchlight in the room.

"I guess I haven't much to confess," he said at last. "No mortal sins, in any case."

"You realize all Avangarde, Reservists as well, are meant to set an example," Hugh pointed out. "To be good Christians."

Patrick took a gulp of wine, and then asked, "Is this a question of my faith?"

"No, no." Father Hugh took a drink himself. "Marcus Ionus chose adroitly when he chose you in that regard. And the fact that you were a Crusader makes the question of your faith unimpeachable."

Patrick frowned. "Not that I want to cast doubt on my own faith, but I can tell you from experience that many a Crusader had little to do with anything Holy. From our leaders on down to the women who washed the lice from our clothes." His voice rose in pitch as he finished his sentence. He told himself it was the wine. His cheeks felt hot.

"I can imagine," Hugh said, upending the empty wine pitcher, shaking it as if the action would miraculously cause more wine to gush forth. He got the attention of a passing maidservant. She took the empty pitcher with the promise of bringing back another. Hugh turned back to Patrick. "Sin infiltrates all peoples at every level, in every circumstance. Even when trying to do the work of God. I was speaking more on *you* being a Crusader. I'm sure your intentions were Holy, or at least well meant. You see, Marcus is not the only good judge of character."

Patrick sat silently, having no desire to question what the priest saw in him, let alone debate it one way or the other. But the conversation did raise a burning question in his mind. He drained his cup.

"If people commit sin—create suffering—when they believe they are doing the work of God, why does God allow it to happen? Especially if it's in His name? I mean, to defeat your enemies is one thing, but to commit unholy savagery while doing it?"

"Just as I said, sin," Hugh replied. The maidservant returned with a new pitcher of wine. The priest filled their cups, and then stared off into space, face pensive. Finally he drew a deep breath and said in monotone, "They crush your people, Lord, torment your own. They kill the widow and the alien; the fatherless they murder. They say, The Lord does not see; the God of Jacob takes no notice."

"That is from the Bible?" Patrick asked.

"Yes, and many verses like it," he replied. "You see, yours is a very common question, which has been asked many a time, for many an age. King Solomon himself asked it."

"So there is an answer?"

The priest smiled wryly. "There is, but most are dissatisfied by it: Suffering is so God's mercy and love can be known."

"You mean, suffering is just a backdrop for God to display His work? So it can be seen more clearly?"

"Yes, but it is much more complex than that."

"I think *I'm* dissatisfied with that answer," Patrick said, taking a drink.

Hugh smiled. "You're not alone in the world with that sentiment. The book of Job addresses such matters. There, God himself tells Job's nay-saying companions, 'Where were you when I founded the earth? Who determined its size; do you know? Into what were its pedestals sunk, and who laid the cornerstone, while the morning stars sang in chorus and all the sons of God shouted for joy?'"

"Like a parent says to a child, 'Don't question my judgment,' and 'Because I said so.'" Patrick frowned.

The priest's jovial, yet sympathetic smile did not waver. "That is the nature of faith. We just have to believe that the wicked will be punished and the just rewarded. Even if it is to happen in the hereafter. All the more reason to walk the straight and narrow in the here and now. And consider this; what do redemption, forgiveness, compassion, charity, sacrifice and mercy have in common?"

Patrick mulled that one over, finally answering with a shrug, "They're all good things?"

"Precisely. And they exist only because there is suffering in the world. You see, it was man who let sin into the world, and suffering because of it, not God. But God took a hopeless situation and made some good out of it."

Patrick was nonplussed by that statement.

Still not entirely satisfied, Patrick asked, "But what if you honestly believe what you are doing is the work of God, but in the eyes of God it is evil? Will you still be held accountable?"

"I assume you are speaking of your experiences as a soldier in the Crusade?" Father Hugh raised his eyebrows.

"Well, not so much myself," Patrick confided. "I was thinking more on the behavior of others. I have no doubt they thought *they* were doing the work of God, but *how* they went about it..."

Father Hugh's eyes were sad and downcast. "Yes, religious fervor can cause one to...overreact. Sometimes the fire of the Holy Spirit in some individuals can burn out of control. If such an individual is not reined in by his fellow man, then I must trust that he will be set straight when he stands before God and is repentant. His actions in life, in some way, actually furthered God's plans. If he is not repentant when facing God on the matter...then it will be better for him that he had not been born at all."

Patrick chewed on his lower lip mulling this over. Knight and priest took another drink from their cups.

"If it is your actions you are concerned about," Father Hugh said, leaning over and touching Patrick's forearm, "the very fact that you ponder such things, are concerned about them, goes to show that you are a good person, or at the very least, repentant. It is the blind man who should worry."

The priest polished off another glass and belched. His watery blue eyes were becoming glassier. Patrick was thoughtfully silent again. His tongue probed the inside of his cheek as Hugh filled their cups. "And there is always the possibility," Hugh said, his jovial demeanor returning, "that atrocities committed during the crusading campaign really are the will of God. All soldiers functioning as His instruments of divine justice."

"Does it say that in the Bible?" Patrick asked, though he said it distantly, as if thinking out loud.

"Why, yes," Hugh replied. "Psalm 149 states: 'To bring retribution to the nations, punishments on peoples, to bind their kings with chains, shackle their nobles with irons. To execute the judgment decreed for them—such is the Glory of all God's faithful. Hallelujah!'"

This last was exclaimed out loud and punctuated by the priest raising his cup in the air and spilling a bit of wine. Others in the hall looked up from their conversations to see what all the commotion was about.

Patrick smiled in spite of his somber mood. He took a drink and suspected that his own eyes were looking pretty glassy. If he were late to his morning duties, who would believe that it was because he had been up late drinking with the keep's head clergyman?

"It all comes down to a matter of faith," Hugh said after recovering from his outburst. He pounded his chest. "What does your heart say?"

Though this had been a statement, Patrick replied, "What if you do not know? What if your heart is silent?"

Father Hugh's expression took on that sympathetic cast. "Then once again you are not alone. Few of us receive clear words from our Lord, as the prophets do. God's intentions for us are difficult to discern by listening to our hearts, however intently we try. And for yet others of us, for whatever reason, we are altogether ignorant of the language of the soul."

Patrick smiled wanly, raising the cup to his mouth. "I believe I fall under the latter category."

Though the priest's words were wise and his speech still clear, he now swayed on the bench. "Fear not!" he said, a little loudly. "There is always hope. Through time and effort, God's will for us all will be made known."

Patrick was silent for a time, tracing imaginary shapes on the table. The maidservant who had brought them wine was clearing away the plates and cutlery, leaving them their cups and pitcher. They were all alone at the table now. The other clergy had left some time ago.

"If you say so, Father," he said. "Though I believe the waiting is killing me. I care not much for stumbling in the dark when it comes to the will of God."

Father Hugh smiled deeply. He stood, teetering a bit as he did. "As I said earlier, you are not alone. Take some comfort in that. Now, if you will excuse me, I believe my bed is calling me."

Patrick said good night, and thanked him for his conversation.

Hugh turned to walk away, but then turned back around. "You know, all this talk reminds me of a story...a fisherman drowned recently."

"That's terrible, I hadn't heard," Patrick said, concern on his face.

"Yes, yes, terrible all that," the priest continued. "As I understand it, as the man was floundering in the water he prayed loudly to God. He cried out, 'Lord, have mercy on your poor servant, save me from drowning!' About then another fisherman in a boat came by and said, 'Hold still, and I will extend my oar to you!' The drowning man replied, 'No thank you, my Lord God will save me.' The fisherman in the boat, somewhat taken aback said, 'All right then,' and rowed away. Another boat came by, and the fisherman in that boat said, 'Hold still, and I will throw you this rope!' to which the drowning man replied, 'No thank you, my Lord God will save me.'"

Hugh's face was very animated as he told the story, making flamboyant gestures, pantomiming the actions of each character. It was about then that Patrick realized that this was exactly what it was; a story. No fisherman of Avalon had drowned. Patrick smiled despite having been lured into believing otherwise.

The priest continued. "'All right then,' the man in the boat said, then rowed away. A third fisherman came by and said, 'Hold still, and I will pull you into my boat!' to which the drowning man replied, 'No thank you, my Lord God will save me.' This fisherman left him as well. Eventually, the man succumbed to the waters and drowned. He went to heaven and met God face to face. He said, 'Lord, why did you not answer my prayers? Why did you let me drown?' To which God responded, rather indignantly, 'Well, I sent you three boats. What more did you want from me?'"

With that, Father Hugh winked, and left.

#

The following evening, Patrick was escorting Lady Morneau to dinner when Sir Geoffrey approached them in the keep corridor.

"Ah, Lady Morneau, may I have a word with you?" He asked all smiles.

"Why, of course, Sir Geoffrey," she replied.

"Alone, perhaps?" He looked askance at Sir Gawain. Christianne was puzzled but nodded.

"I will not be but a moment, Patrick," she said, and moved off to one side with Geoffrey. While she did so, Patrick merely frowned at the abruptness of the well-manicured knight and leaned against a window ledge to watch the dazzling sunset over the garden. As beautiful as the vista was, however, Patrick found himself glancing over his shoulder at the conversing pair.

Christianne and Geoffrey talked for a few moments, during which time Christianne's demeanor changed from cheerfulness to concern. She also looked twice in Patrick's direction toward whom Geoffrey gestured once, subtly. Finally, Geoffrey shrugged as if to say, "Sorry," and Christianne shook her head as if saying, "No, no. That is quite all right, I understand." Geoffrey then departed without a glance to either her or Patrick, and she returned to Patrick's side.

"What was that all about?" Patrick asked. Lady Morneau did not answer for a moment, lost in thought.

"Oh, nothing, he was just giving me some...brotherly advice," she replied.

"Is there anything that I can...?"

"No. I'm fine."

She was quiet and aloof the rest of the evening and did not wish to go for their usual evening walk. The following day, Patrick could not find her, and Melwyn claimed she did not know where she was. This went on for a few days until finally Patrick saw her sitting with Sir Geoffrey at dinner, and from then on, they were always together. All attempts to find out what happened met with resistance or indifference. Patrick had no idea what Geoffrey had said that convinced her to suddenly lavish her attentions upon the foppish knight instead of himself.

Patrick sulked in his chamber. He would not approach Lady Morneau or Sir Geoffrey about the matter. It was an unfortunate affair, one not worth talking about. There were those who looked down their nose at Sir Geoffrey's actions, but those same people did not offer Patrick any sympathy. And Patrick had decided that he had spent too much time with the stupid girl anyway. The Knights of the Round Table no longer asked him to go to Aesclinn, Sir Mark was now too busy being King Mark, and it had been a mistake to think that McFowler had been his good friend. McFowler was good friends with everyone, not just with the Irishman. And no one came to him anymore to tell him their stories or secrets. Had he spent more time with the Avangarde and not Christianne, he would still be closer to them, and they would be slapping him on the back, chiding him to forget her.

Patrick sighed deeply, and it seemed that once again his mother was there, hand resting on his shoulder as he gazed out upon the stars.

"I am cursed, mother," he lamented. "Why can I not hang on to anyone, be it companion, or lover, or whatever the case may be, even when I try to be cautious about it?" He took her hand in his.

"You are not cursed, little one, that is just the way it is," she said softly, sadly.

"It has to be a curse. It is too much of a coincidence."

She was beautiful in her simplicity, and all the more beautiful with tears in her eyes, like the many Madonna statues in the county churches. She bent over and kissed him. "Come home when you are ready, but not until then. I understand your quest, but come home. You are missed." She faded away, and from the corner of his eye, Patrick could see the hooded Apparition pointing at him accusingly.

Chapter Four

Patrick returned from his guard post as the sun was setting behind the keep. The Back Door cast a long shadow across the practice field. Most days in Avalon were springlike, but there were occasional days, sometimes several weeks, when the island mirrored the outer world. It was during these times that the true weather showed through. It was late autumn outside the isle and today the leaves and petals of the trees and flowers fell to the ground. On this particular evening the air was cold and crisp and his breath rose in front of him like an escaping soul. On the battlements Patrick had seen and smelled burning the of leaves down in the village. The smell of burning oak leaves reminded him of home.

As he meandered through the keep on his way to supper, familiar voices approached his way. The Irishman chose another path, and was out of sight by the time Lady Morneau and Sir Geoffrey rounded the corner. He walked briskly away from the laughter and idle talk, great-cloak flapping in his wake.

#

Patrick spent most of his days in this manner. He once again fell into his old pattern of rising in the morning, performing his guard duties, then spending the remainder of his day shining his armor, practicing swordplay with a willing partner, and then avoiding certain persons he had no desire to see. He no longer had Guests coming to him to talk of their personal problems and tragedies, and he didn't go out of his way to find them. Instead, he sulked about with a bitter look on his face.

So it came as no surprise when one day Jason McFowler approached and informed him that King Mark wanted to play chess with the Irishman the evening after the annual Bush Beating.

Such an event could only mean that Mark wanted to talk to Patrick, and likely not about chess. It was just like McFowler's request he join him that one night in Aesclinn. That was an attempt to help the young knight. Unfortunately, Patrick felt that this was not a meeting to give him another chance to change his antisocial behavior, but to ask him to resign from the Avangarde Reserves and leave the island.

At the news, Patrick sighed. Although he had known this day would come, it still didn't stop the sting of humiliation.

Jason smiled and gave him a friendly slap on the shoulder. "Don't worry, I hear he's not as good a chess player as he is a swordsman."

Jason left him then. Sunlight streamed through a window and cast Patrick's shadow in a manner much the same way he felt; long and dark. A second shadow appeared next to his, but when he turned to find its source, he found nothing.

#

The morning of the Bush Beating, Patrick stood atop the main gate with Sir Jon, Gregory, Jeremiah and the other Reservists. They were armed and armored head to foot as if they too were to sally forth with the Avangarde and stir up trouble. The Reservists were expected to stay behind, alert, as if expecting a siege. It was wise practice.

Wolfgang Von Fiescher was with them, and more and more Guests were mounting the walls to wave farewell to the assembled Avangarde as they rode beneath the gate and across the drawbridge. The men were all smiles, in better humor to be leaving the walls of Greensprings to do something for once. As the last of the heavy horses plodded off the bridge and onto the dusty road, Wolfgang ordered the bridge up and the gate closed then said, "All right then, everyone man your posts, stay alert, and sound your horn if you see trouble or if for any reason some of the Avangarde return."

The Reservists sounded a "Yes, sir" and split up in different directions. Von Fiescher motioned at the Guests still milling about the battlements.

"Let's go, boys and girls, we have classes to attend and things to do, don't we?"

#

The rest of the day was uneventful. Patrick stood at his lonely corner of the keep wall, standing watch. It was lonelier than regular guard duty. Then, somebody always came by eventually to talk a bit. Today there were none of the Avangarde, and the other Reservists could not leave their posts. Wolfgang, who was managing the keep as his last duty before he left for the outside and handed over all responsibilities to Mark, brought the Reservists their meals. He could have sent a maidservant to do the job, but he wanted to make the men feel somewhat special since they could not go beating around the forest like the rest.

Occasionally, Patrick spotted patrols of Avangarde riding near the village or at the head of the valley of apple orchards, almost beyond eyesight. Sometimes they appeared to be at a run, as if in a hurry.

#

By nightfall, the Avangarde had not returned as they should have. He cursed as the last bit of daylight disappeared and he blew into his hands to keep them warm.

No sooner had he done so than he heard the main gate opened followed by the drawbridge lowered with a thud. Then came the unmistakable sound of a horseman entering the courtyard. There was some commotion and the sound of the gate closing again.

Gregory had let someone in.

An Avangardesman came running along the catwalk towards the Irishman. Patrick had seen the man numerous times but was not all that familiar with him. He thought perhaps his name was Parador. He was dirty and flustered, eyes wide. The man paused before Patrick to catch his breath and gasped, "Something's afoot! Sir Mark sent me back to tell you to light the battlement fires and be on the lookout. I have to go tell the others now. Von Fiescher knows..." The man ran past Patrick and towards Jeremiah's post.

"What's afoot?" Patrick shouted after the man, curious and excited.

"There's something in the woods," the Gardesman called back and ran on.

Patrick frowned. *Something?*

He lit a torch in a nearby censer filled with coal, then ran along the wall lighting more torches as he went. He met up with Sir Gregory.

"Did you hear the news?" the shorter knight asked.

Patrick nodded. "Do you know what happened?"

"I just let Parador in and saw him talking with Von Fiescher, who told me to start lighting the fires."

More fires were illuminating the far wall. Evidently word had reached Sir Jon and the others. Gregory departed, and Patrick went back to his post. The next several hours were tense. The Irishman expected something to happen, but nothing did. The fact that Wolfgang repeatedly came by with a grim face didn't help matters. He would survey Patrick's line of sight, then depart without an explanation of what was happening.

Around midnight something finally did happen. Dogs yelped in the village and a long procession of torch lights appeared in that direction. One long blast from a horn drowned out the dogs and then faded. Judging from the speed and the fashion in which they bobbed, they were borne by horse men. A similar procession was approaching from the opposite direction, from the valley of apple orchards.

The torches were borne by Avangarde and the group coming from the village appeared to be chasing something. They bypassed the main gate of Greensprings and took the trail that passed before Patrick's wall. That's when he had a good look at the Avangarde's quarry.

First came the dogs. They were large, like wolfhounds. One leapt above the pack, and when it landed he got a glimpse of its eyes-fierce and glowing with an otherworldly light.

There was no way to count them. They raced each other, and in the shadowy torchlight they seemed to meld and separate like a flowing river of mud. They barked and brayed to make the soul shudder.

Following them came a rider whipping them on. This man was no Avangarde, as he was garbed from head to foot in dark animal hides and was crowned with a helm adorned with a stag's pair of horns. The latter masked his face. A light brighter than any torch hovered over him, and lit his path. He blew on a hunting horn.

Sir Jon and Sir Gregory were at Patrick's side. "The torches coming from the valley are borne by a second group of Avangarde who intend to cut off the rider and his pack of dogs," one of them said.

Just when the trap was about to snap shut, the rider sounded his horn again. He and the dogs broke away into the forest, passing through the brush as if it were smoke. The mounted knights shot into one another's ranks and had trouble regrouping to pursue their prey into the woods. They jumped brambles and were unhorsed by tree limbs. From behind, the huntsman and his pack of shadowy dogs seemed almost transparent; the brilliant will-o-the-wisp that followed them dimmed and dimmed until it was completely out of sight. The only thing visible or audible now were the normal lights and sounds of the Avangarde stumbling in the woods.

"Oh my God," Sir Jon said in a raspy voice. Patrick saw that all the Reservists were gathered around in shock. "What on earth was that?"

It was a good question. But they had to wait until after the Avangarde returned to find out. Von Fiescher came striding up the stairs in a foul mood, ordering everybody back to their posts.

#

The Avangarde did eventually return. They were tired, dirty, and white as ghosts. It was hard to obtain any information from them. They seemed in a daze, and many had stopped off at the pub in Aesclinn to get drunk before returning home.

Wolfgang spoke to some of the other veterans, but was long in talking with Mark and Jason. After the conversation was over, Von Fiescher nodded, and clapped the men on the back.

As usual, Sir Jon was the clever one and acquired most of the story, which he brought back to the Reservists. He told the story of how the Avangarde sighted a lone rider who was no villager and no knight. All attempts to approach the rider ended in frustration. Soon the rider was seen traveling at a gallop with a pack of hounds as if on a hunt. Villagers claimed sightings too, but no tracks or any other signs were ever found, thus making it impossible to give chase once the pack moved out of sight. They decided to set a trap and the result was what transpired before Greensprings.

At the end of his story, Wolfgang Von Fiescher approached them. "I see Sir Jon has done much of my job." He planted one foot on the edge of the fountain in the courtyard where they had gathered to watch the Avangarde return and dismount. He leaned heavily on his knee as he spoke with the junior Gardesmen. "What has happened here tonight, believe it or not, is not uncommon. I personally haven't witnessed a manifestation this fantastic since before the oldest veteran here came to Avalon. These hauntings are harmless. I'm sure you all have heard the stories, and now, you have one of your own." He winked at them. "Carry on, and good job. Goodnight, gentlemen." He started to depart, but then turned as if struck by an afterthought. "Oh, Sir Patrick, Mark would still like to see you tomorrow evening."

Patrick's heart sank a little bit, and he pretended not to notice the other Reservists' curiosity.

#

Patrick approached King Mark's quarters just in time to see the door open. Von Fiescher exited, followed by King Mark. The two clasped hands and the Irishman heard Wolfgang say, "Don't worry, you'll do fine. Take care."

After Wolfgang nodded at Patrick on his way out and turned the corner, Mark spotted Patrick and smiled. "Sir Gawain, how good of you to come." The door into the apartment was open still and McFowler sat in a chair, toying with a chess piece. "Could you wait a moment before we begin?" Mark said. "I have some unfinished keep business I must go over with Jason first."

Patrick shrugged. "Certainly."

King Mark's smile did not waver as he backed into his quarters and shut the door.

Patrick paced for a while, his stomach twisting and turning. There were no seats in the corridor, and judging from the tones of the conversation coming from inside, Mark was going to be more than a moment. Patrick decided to wander down the hall, taking stock of the tapestries, no doubt gifts from benefactors to the keep, same as the mirror in the Greensprings entrance.

His wanderings took him out of the corridor and to a room, the library. He decided to enter. Though he could read, he didn't much enjoy it. He meandered about, through the tall aisles, running his fingers along the dusty leather-bound tomes. He chose one arbitrarily, looked at it disinterestedly upon seeing a language with which he was not familiar, placed it back, and continued to roam.

He put his hands behind his back as he penetrated further into the collection, letting his eyes gaze move from one side of the aisle to the other. Reaching the end of the row, he turned the corner and came across a robed man bent over a table, who suddenly turned about. Patrick jumped back. One of the man's eyes was monstrously big.

"Oh, hello," said the man genially. "It's only glass." He plucked out a glass disc from under his brow. "I use it to read things up close. My eyes aren't all that good, you know." He pocketed the thing and extended his hand to the Irishman. "I'm Father Benis. Or the librarian, as everyone calls me. And you are?"

Patrick took his hand. "Patrick Gawain, of Galway."

The librarian's mouth turned to an O and he shuffled closer. "Why yes, the man from the Green Isle. The only one among us, I believe. And what a lovely accent you have. Definitely of Gaelic blood you are..." He gently took hold of Patrick's jaw. "What sharp cheekbones you have. Tell me; are both your parents native Irish?"

Patrick, though surprised at being handled, didn't budge. Father Benis didn't seem dangerous. "Yes, of course. Why are you holding my head?"

"There are several Celtic tribes in the isles. Eire in particular. Milesians, Firbolgs, Picts, and Britons to name a few. I'm trying to place your ancestry by looking at the slope of your skull."

Patrick guffawed like he hadn't for quite some time and grabbed at the librarians wrists. "You're jesting. You can do that? Can you also tell my fortune by reading tea leaves?" Patrick ribbed with a smile.

The librarian also laughed. "Yes to the former and no to the latter. It would be heresy to divine the future through the arcane arts that don't apply to the Holy Father. I may be a learned and inquisitive man, but I shan't incur the wrath of the Lord." He made the sign of the Holy Cross, but in a lax manner and with a smile. "Though from what I understand, there are such arcane tomes hidden among these books." The short, affable man took Patrick by the arm and led him among the bookshelves.

Patrick liked this man. "How do you know that?" He asked.

"My predecessor told me of several among these books. When Father Chanceroy arrived, he discovered that the former denizens of Greensprings had amassed a significant collection. Some of those works dealt with topics of the supernatural bent. Naturally, Father Chanceroy had all such items removed. But in spite of that, due to the sheer size of the library, some questionable material was overlooked. My predecessor said to remain vigilant, lest they fall into the hands of audacious children who might be led down the wrong path."

"Have you found any?"

The priest sighed. "No. I've been over every single book and scroll. I know this library like my own room. After all, I am the Librarian. Nothing out of the ordinary here. My predecessor locked up all the material that concerned mysticism and the Island of Avalon."

"Why didn't he destroy them if he was so concerned about them?"

"Because, I imagine, he was like me. Inquisitive. He seemed to think that they were the works of Morgana Le Fey, sister of King Arthur. He felt them to be of too much historical importance to destroy, whatever they may be. This was her island you know, Avalon."

"Have you seen these books?"

"No," replied the librarian. "Though I have the key to the vault that houses them, I respect wishes to let them be."

"These books concern Avalon?"

"Yes."

"Well, I have no desire for books, but I do wish to know more about this island that I find myself on," Patrick said.

Father Benis nodded and gave him a whimsical smile. "You must be referring to the Bush Beating that stirred up the Huntsman."

Patrick was surprised at the man's nonchalance. "It doesn't amaze you?"

"On the contrary, I find it very, very fascinating. But you must understand, I've been here for a while and have seen a thing or two." Father Benis shrugged. "There are many such manifestations. You must have heard as much from your Avangarde friends who venture outside these walls more than I."

"But what are they?"

The priest was thoughtful. "I believe that they are images of days gone by. Echoes of ancient events." At Patrick's confused look, the librarian said, "Metaphysically speaking, they are like the ripples on the surface of a pond. Though you can no longer see the stone that dropped into the water, you can still see the movement that it caused."

"I can almost believe that. But images of goblins and legendary figures? Does that mean that they actually existed, then? What happened to them?"

The priest withdrew a Bible from his robe pocket. He thumbed through it until he came to the verse he sought. "Genesis, Chapter Six, Verse 1. 'When men began to increase in number on the earth and daughters were born to them, the sons of God saw that the daughters of men were beautiful, and they married any of them they chose.'" Benis lowered the Book. "That could be interpreted as the servants of God—angels perhaps—marrying mortal women." He raised the book and began to read again. "'Now it mentions that there were *Nephilim* or giants in those days. And during these days when the sons of God went to the daughters of men and bore children by them, they were the heroes of old, the men of legend.'" The librarian raised his thumb to his mouth, chewed thoughtfully on the nail, then continued. "In the myths and pantheons of ancient civilizations, the giants are always the antagonists. Even in the Old Testament, there is the mention of David fighting Goliath. Were giants once otherworldly servants of God who lost their faith and were cast from Heaven, much like Lucifer? Were they doomed to roam the earth for their impudence? Or were they misbegotten hybrids?"

"If so, where are they now?" Patrick interjected.

Benis shrugged. "There are many references to them sleeping beneath the earth, their movements causing the earth to shake as it does in some regions.

"If the daughters of men bore children to the Sons of God, I'd imagine they would be men of legend indeed. That would explain the likes of Samson, his incredible strength. That would also explain Hercules and Thor in their respective myths. Perhaps eons ago, these men were viewed as gods by us mortals. Especially to those mortals who had not yet heard the word of God, who turned to anyone or anything that would protect them. But these men, calling themselves Zeus, or Odin, or Marduk lacked the wisdom of God, and still were ultimately human, however powerful they may have been. They were subject to the vanities and passions of mortals. They did terrible things and demanded tributes and offerings from their mortal worshippers. The temptation must have been incredible."

The Irishman put up his hand. "But I was speaking of goblins and ogres, not gods."

The librarian smiled. "Don't you see my meaning? Goblins and ogres could have been lesser offspring, or a different form. Creatures turned twisted and ugly as they hid from the light and grace of God, living in caves and under bridges." He chuckled. "Perhaps some children's stories are more than they seem."

"But what of fairies and elves? I thought they were supposed to be fair," Patrick said.

"They, too, could be lesser offspring. The product of a loving union between mortal and immortal. Perhaps God took pity on these creatures that did not belong in either world, and created an intermediate world for them on earth, which was later called 'Faerie' by common folk."

This seemed to make sense. Patrick had never thought much on the subject. Being a scholar had its advantages, he guessed. "Then what has become of them? Do they, too, sleep beneath the earth?"

Father Benis was thoughtful once again. "I'm not sure. It seems to me that the giants were waylaid souls who chose unwisely not to follow the Lord, but as for the Fair Folk, perhaps they were innocent offspring. Who knows what became, or is becoming," he raised his eyebrows, "of them. It seems their realm of Faerie is diminishing with the advent of man. I think Avalon is a surviving portion of their world. I think that Morgana did dwell here. After all she was called Le Fey—the Fairy—because of her ancestry. I think this isle is full of ghosts that show us a glimpse of what life must have been like before man and the one true God came along and drove them into hiding." Benis was silent for a moment, looking down with a sad and vacant stare. "Or maybe, I'm just a silly old man with some crazy stories. In any case, I wouldn't worry about the manifestations. They are harmless. The worst that they can do is frighten."

It was Patrick's turn to be thoughtful. He surmised he was as safe here as anywhere in Avalon.

"There you are," McFowler's voice came from the library entrance. "I've been looking for you. Mark is eager to play chess with you."

I'll wager he is, Patrick thought gloomily. The appearance of the Highlander suddenly reminded Patrick that he may not have to worry about Avalon much longer anyhow. Regardless of how he felt, he put on a smile and strode forward to meet King Mark. He met Jason at the door and Father Benis spoke to the Scotsman. "McFowler, I haven't seen you in a while. You know, I still think it would do you good to learn how to read." Jason grunted and crossed his fingers at the librarian as if to ward off evil spirits. The priest smiled and waved to Patrick as the two withdrew. "Come again, Irishman, and let me look at your skull."

\#

Mark sat across from the Irishman at the game board, silently. After the initial greeting and other pleasantries that commenced the game, conversation ceased. Even the normally quiet Patrick tried reviving it, the silence was so pervasive. He asked simple questions of the golden haired-knight, mundane things. When did he become a knight? What kind of accent is that? How did he come to Avalon?

Mark tactfully declined to respond to almost all of them. Especially those that revealed anything about his past. In Patrick's mind, this bolstered the rumors that Sir Mark was actually a prince in exile from Constantinople.

When Patrick took the hint that he was traveling a dead-end path, he fell silent again and waited for the barrel-chested king to make his next move. The game had commenced quickly enough, with both of them maneuvering pawns, but once the infantrymen took up their forward positions; the two players took their time in moving the noble pieces.

Mark cleared his throat several times and seemed extremely tense or nervous. Perhaps this was going to be just as hard on his superior.

"There has been talk," Mark commenced, "that you are unhappy here in Avalon. But you don't say anything." He didn't look up, but rather continued to scrutinize the board.

Another silent moment passed. Patrick choked down a swallow. "I imagine it would appear that way."

"You know then?" Mark looked up.

"If the rumors don't reach me directly, then I can surmise from the behavior of others."

"Are you unhappy? There certainly have been no complaints about your basic duties, but naturally, as you know from your training with Wolfgang, there is more to being an Avangarde than meets the eye."

Patrick sighed heavily and sat back in his chair, mirror image of Mark's posture. He then explained how he felt, or at least, did the best he could do.

He told Mark about the feeling of alienation and the sensation of lesser status that came along with being a Reservist. He felt useless not knowing exactly what he was meant to do. He felt like he didn't have the right or the authority to impose his will on the Guests, let alone the other staff and residents. He was an outsider looking in.

"...or maybe I'm just not meant for this. Maybe Ionus made a mistake in choosing me," Patrick finished.

Mark leaned forward and moved a knight in a non-linear move, his brow furrowed in concern. "I can understand much you are saying, but I tell you this: you are only different in status by name alone. I'm sorry you feel otherwise. As for Ionus, he is an incredibly good judge of character, which is why he is charged with the task that he has. He saw something in you..."

"...which you don't see," Patrick offered.

Mark shrugged. "I see something in you. I'm not sure what and I don't want you to leave, but I admit that something has to be done."

Patrick nodded gravely while positioning a bishop to discourage Mark's knight. "Do you have any suggestions? I can't think of anything."

Mark stood up, stretched and went to gaze out the window. After a moment he said, "It seems you are happiest when you are actually doing something specific, accomplishing something. Routine life among the men in peacetime is difficult for you..."

"Yes."

"You need a task that will satisfy this need and at the same time give you some recognition that will, in your eyes, elevate your position." Mark turned around. "You need a quest."

Patrick laughed. "As I recall, the last 'quest' I went on resulted with me landing on top of your head, a piece of broken ladder in my hands."

They both laughed for a moment, maybe harder than the memory deserved. "Well, I was thinking a bit more on the serious side," Mark said. "The villagers in Aesclinn were mightily disturbed after the last Bush Beating. They are claiming that more occurrences are troubling them. That they are afraid of something more dangerous than just some spooked chickens. They say a wolf prowls the hills and takes some of their sheep. They would be happier if one of the soldiers from Greensprings did something about it." Patrick leaned forward, intrigued. "I know you are no huntsman, but I think that the presence of one of the Avangarde would make them feel more secure. All you need do is patrol the area. Stay about a week, then come back with a report and we'll see what else we can do. I don't know, perhaps set up some sort of rotation among the Reservists to sheriff the region. That will give you all something to feel useful and proud about. But I want you to be the first to pioneer the situation. Is that acceptable to you, Patrick?"

Patrick was absolutely jubilant inside, but kept his composure. "Why, yes, quite."

"Good then. This may not solve your problem altogether, but I believe it will make you a happier person, thus strengthening you to becoming a more effective Avangarde. Let's have you come back tomorrow evening after supper, and we'll go over it in more detail. The following morning you will depart. Agreed?"

The Irishman nodded.

Mark smiled. "Oh, by the way, checkmate."

#

The following evening there was cause for a special dinner. It seemed that any occasion was a good occasion for the denizens of Greensprings to outdo the gala before. Mark's announcement of the Irishman's quest was one. Another was the arrival of a special Guest, the Mademoiselle Amy du Lac of Normandy, Sir Geoffrey's fiancée.

Patrick sat on one side of the doe-eyed woman and Sir Geoffrey on her other. Patrick couldn't help but notice that the Lady Christianne Morneau sat nowhere near the trio.

"So, tell me Sir Gawain," asked the new Guest, "are you any relation to the Sir Gawaine of King Arthur's court?"

The question usually annoyed him, but tonight, little could get his spirits down. He wasn't sure which was bolstering him more, his upcoming mission, or the sight of Christianne sitting across the hall, her mouth set in a grim line and toying with her food. In any case, the Norman noblewoman had a charm about her that made him not mind talking.

He laughed. "No, not at all. And you? Are you of any relation to Sir Lancelot? His name, if I recall, was also du Lac."

"Of course," she replied, laughing.

Watching the chamber lights glisten off her silky hair made Patrick wonder what she could possibly see in the rogue Geoffrey. Does she know? He wondered, sneaking another glance at Christianne from across the room, her head now down. He decided not to worry about it and drank his wine. Life was a fickle woman that traveled down strange paths. And besides, at this time tomorrow he would be away from the court, away from its intrigues and its silliness.

#

The following morning, Patrick trotted up the muddy path from the stables atop Siegfried. The weather was drizzly, but he didn't mind. Some people had actually come to see him off. Sir Jon and Aimeé were among them. He waived. Aimeé came to the front of the group and threw a couple of flowers at him, like the throngs of Guests who had thrown flowers at the Avangarde when they departed for the Bush Beating.

"Maybe it will be a tradition that will catch on some day," she said.

Sir Jon had helped the Irish knight saddle and supply Siegfried, and now slapped the horse's hindquarters. "Patrick, you're a lucky dog. What did you do to convince King Mark?"

Patrick shrugged, "It's a surprise to me too." He could see Christianne Morneau in the courtyard, though she hadn't come down to the crowd. Jon noticed this and remarked, "She seems somewhat put out now that the Lady du Lac is here."

"Serves her right," Patrick chided, and then urged the black horse forward. He waved goodbye and clopped noisily across the drawbridge, out of Greensprings. The air felt fresh, and the sun peeked out every now and again to produce some fantastic rainbows. He wondered if there were any treasures at the end of them.

#

He spent much of the day trotting down the road that meandered between the harbor and Aesclinn. When he came to a fork in the road, he read the simple wooden sign post with its accompanying pictures graven in wood. To his left a sign pointed with the words "Inland road", with a picture of an evergreen tree, and to his right (though actually more straight ahead than anything) a sign below the first pointed with the words "Cliff Side" and a picture of a sea cliff. He took a deep breath. There was the smell of salt in the air and the sound of ocean waves crashing against rocks. Siegfried snorted and shook his mane as if questioning.

"No, not there yet, friend." Patrick said, noting that there were sheep grazing in the grass on the hillside. The springlike showers made this side of the island very green; perfect for putting sheep to pasture.

He urged Siegfried forward to the right and followed the ocean sounds. It wasn't too much longer that the road veered left as it approached the edge of the isle, and then paralleled a cliff overlooking a gray sea. The very same body of water that had borne him to this fabled land.

That seemed like an age ago.

Patrick roamed up and down this stretch of land, noting the sheep on the inland side and how the road seemed to go on forever along the water side. When he was satisfied that he was in the right place, he decided to dismount and make camp.

Patrick removed Siegfried's saddle and let him loose, not bothering to hobble the beast. Siegfried was as loyal as they came and would not wander too far off. Patrick wished he could say as much for others in his life. He made a simple lean-to with a length of wax treated canvas and set his saddle, saddle bags and travel purse in it. Wrapping his great-cloak tighter about him, he decided to survey the area by foot while in search of firewood.

It was sloping hills on one side, which in itself was nothing more than moorland coming to an end and finishing at high cliffs above the Western Sea. Patrick walked along this cliff, throwing sticks and rocks over the edge. The sea gulls hovered above him, crying plaintively, as if he was invading their kingdom. The entire scene reminded him a little of his own island home, but the sheer cliffs reminded him more of the shores of Cornwall. There was plenty of wood about from scraggly old evergreen trees that were wind-bent and sparse in needles. They seemed to have willingly and frequently parted with their branches which littered the short grass that had been well manicured by hungry sheep. Once he had a sufficient amount of wood, he returned to his camp, finding nothing better to do. As he set about to making a fire, it began to drizzle again, but he didn't mind the dampness; he had been through worse on his journeys to the Holy Lands. Much worse.

#

He spent the next couple of days in this manner. Other than the constant sea breeze whispering through the sword grass, the land was silent. He sat up nights waiting for the signs of predators, but found none. Only in his dreams did he hear the howl of a wolf.

When his food rations started getting low, and he thought he might die of boredom, he decided he would stay one more night and return to Greensprings.

It was about then that a farmer and his boy paid him a visit. He was sitting against the tree that made the focal point of his camp, whittling a piece of wood that was slowly taking on the shape of a horse's head. This he hurriedly put under his horse blanket with a couple of other carvings—a castle tower and roughly person shaped figure. He didn't want to give the man the impression that he had only been making chess pieces this whole time.

"Bon après-midi," the man said in Norman-accented French. Patrick was familiar with it from the Crusade. He approached with broad smile and hand in the air as a greeting. Then remembering his manners, he removed his hat, which had a long pointed bill, and bowed deeply.

"Good afternoon to you," Patrick replied in French.

The boy, perhaps the age of eight or nine years, peeked shyly from behind the man. When noting this, the man grabbed the boy by both shoulders and gently moved him before the Irishman.

The boy bowed as well and mumbled, "M'lord."

The man looked familiar, though Patrick couldn't place his face.

"My name is Gustave, and this is my son Frederique," the man said.

"Fred," the boy corrected.

Gustave rolled his eyes, but put an arm around the boy just the same. "Frederique, named for his uncle, my brother."

Patrick then made the connection. "Frederique, the inn keeper in Aesclinn."

"Oui," Gustave responded. They then clasped hands in a more informal manner. Fred returned to his position behind his father.

"I am Sir Patrick Gawain, Reservist of the Avangarde of Greensprings. What can I do for you today?" Patrick said.

"The wolf," Gustave said as the smile left his face. "It was near my farm last night. I heard you would be here, so I came as soon as possible to tell you."

"I'll pack my things," Patrick said, and did just that.

A short while later he was walking alongside Gustave, leading Siegfried by the reins. Astride the saddle sat Freddy, who had a smile going from ear to ear. Putting the boy atop the giant warhorse went a long way in removing his shyness.

As they walked, they discussed the wolf. "What makes you think it will be there again tonight?" Patrick asked.

"All the farmers and herdsmen who have been victims of the creature say that it comes at least twice. Sometimes as many as three times. Always after dark. Last night was the first that I saw it."

"Did it kill any of your animals?" Patrick believed that one could never have too much information about an enemy or prey.

Gustave shook his head. "All my animals were indoors last night. The milk cows in the barn. The pigs and sheep inside the cottage with us. I saw the beast prowling the edge of the woods near our land, sniffing the air in our direction." Gustave shivered. "Even though it was at some distance, I could still see that it is quite large, this wolf. But that is not what concerns me most, nor what made me seek you out so quickly."

Patrick raised an eyebrow. "What is the reason, then?"

Gustave was a moment in responding. "This thing is truly a monster. The other farmers have described the carcasses of the thing's kills. Only some are eaten, fewer are dragged off. Most are..." he paused, as if searching for the proper word. "Mutilated."

Patrick raised both eyebrows this time. "Mutilated?"

Gustave nodded gravely. "Sometimes the head is missing, and the body left untouched. Sometimes the animals have been gutted, slit down the center of their bellies as if by the sharpest of blades. All the innards gone, but the meat of the carcass intact, and not a drop of blood on the ground. And still other times, the entire carcass is intact but for puncture wounds about the neck and throat, and the poor creature has been sucked dry of blood. It is unnatural."

"But it sounds as if you have learned from your neighbors' misfortunes and placed your animals indoors at night, which thwarted the wolf from attacking them last night," Patrick pointed out.

"That's what I'm getting at," Gustave continued. "A creature that kills in such an unholy manner may not be put off by walls and thatching for long. Attacking the cows in the barn is one thing, but what if it should come into the cottage? I have bigger concerns." He glanced back at Freddy who was cheerfully stroking Siegfried's mane.

Patrick nodded, also glancing back at the freckle-faced boy.

They did not talk much more as the sun made its way towards the horizon and they turned down a side path that led away from the ocean. Not much further on was a modest farmstead. The living quarters were contained in a simple stone cottage. Smoke drifted upward from the chimney, and blew slantwise across the thatch. All around was lush green grass, grazed short by Gustave's many sheep, which drifted around the establishment like puffy low-lying clouds. A brook gurgled nearby under an arched bridge; the bridge was more decorative than functional, as most anyone could easily step over the water. A bit further off was a larger structure made of gabled earth and wood. It too had a thatched roof, but not in quite as good repair as the cottage. This, Patrick surmised, was the barn. Just beyond it were two cows, moving languidly through the grass and shrubs. They were burdened with pendulous udders. Bells about their necks made occasional dinging noises. Still further out was the edge of a thick forest of evergreens and oaks.

"Bienvenue à notre maison," Gustave welcomed. "It may not be Greensprings, but it is home."

"Thank you, Gustave." Patrick replied as they approached the doorway of the homestead. Gustave reached up to Freddy and brought him earthbound. "Frederique, take Monsieur Gawain's horse to stable." He looked to Patrick for his approval. Patrick nodded. "Then round up the cows and milk them. Supper will be ready when you have returned."

"Ah, papa," Freddy said, disappointed.

"Don't 'ah, papa' me. Move along now, Frederique."

"Fred." The boy insisted, scowling as he stomped off with Siegfried in tow.

Gustave sighed heavily and rolled his eyes. "My apologies, Monsieur Gawain. My boy is a willful sort."

Patrick grinned. "I'm sure my father would have said the same about me."

Still shaking his head, he led the Irishman into the cottage. Inside it was dark, despite a single open window. Patrick stood still and allowed his eyes to adjust to the dark while Gustave busied himself at the hearth; some embers yet lived among the ashes. To these Gustave held a taper, which quickly caught fire, and this he put to an oil lantern that lit up the room.

The building was divided into two rooms. A simple dining table took up most of the one in which they stood. It was made of three large planks of wood on top a single lateral plank. Four cylindrical legs, tree branches really, held it up. All held together by wood pegs. Three similarly fashioned chairs sat around it. To Patrick's left was a bench that held many clay jars and sacks. To his right was the hearth. The floor of the cottage was earth; though he could not see any animal droppings, Patrick could smell the rich smell of manure, and the musky smell of fur—yet also the more pleasant odors of baked bread, thyme, and dill. Straight ahead, through a narrow doorway, was the other room. A bed took up most of the space.

Gustave looked around, fidgeting. "Like I said, not much to look at, but it is home." He moved across the room to the bench and picked up one of the sacks. White powder puffed off its surface as he handled it. He paused, looked at it, and smiled meekly. "Suppose it would help if I made a fire first before I tried to make us some fresh bread, eh?" He looked at the hearth.

"You go ahead and make the dough; I'll make the fire," Patrick offered.

"No, no monsieur. You are a guest, and a nobleman," Gustave protested.

Patrick waved him off. "I'm going to feel very awkward just sitting here doing nothing otherwise."

"If you insist, monsieur."

\#

By the time Fred returned, it was almost completely dark. He brought with him a wet sack that he placed on the bench. From this he withdrew a wedge of cheese and a clay jug, both of which he placed on the table. These now accompanied clay plates, goblets, and a wooden bowl full of vegetables from a fenced garden behind the cottage. Gustave was just then pulling a breadboard out of an oven cleverly incorporated into the hearth's chimney. A pleasing odor preceded the loaf to the table.

Gustave joined his son and Patrick at the table. They crossed themselves, said the mealtime prayer, and dug straight into the food. "Forgive me for not having any meat, monsieur," Gustave said as he filled the goblets from the jug brought in by Fred. It contained milk, probably chilled in the brook. "We should hurry with our meal; there is no telling when the wolf might come. Frederique, are the cows in the barn?"

"Fred. Yes, papa."

They ate hurriedly and in silence. By the time they were done with the vegetables, milk and cheese, the bread had cooled enough to eat. It tasted very good.

#

Patrick watched the farmer and his son herd the last of the sheep inside the house. Once inside, Gustave shut the door behind them and urged Patrick and Freddy towards the field, pulling his cloak tight about him.

"As much as I value my stock, it is they the wolf wants most. Therefore, I do not want to be anywhere near them when it comes."

"So why not leave them out, and stay safely inside?" Patrick asked.

"That is where you and your sword come in, monsieur," Gustave replied. "If I left them out, they will be too spread apart and there will be no telling which animal to watch. If we round them up into a smaller location, the wolf will have no choice but to approach all of them at once, and then you can attack it."

Patrick had to smile. He did not know if his poor hunting skills were so obvious that Gustave knew he needed all the help he could get, or if the man just wanted to achieve the quickest kill possible. He stopped a fair distance away from the cottage and barn on a knoll. To their left was the forest; to their right was the farmstead; and in between, green pasture gave way to the brown stubble of a harvested wheat field. The three of them hunkered down.

It was a dark night, with only the stars to light the landscape. This turned out to be adequate, though, once their eyes adjusted. The air grew chilly as the night progressed. After several hours, Freddy gave up any pretense of trying to be one of the "men" and crawled inside his father's cloak to stay warm. Patrick moved himself closer so that the boy was between them, which drew a beaming smile from the boy.

"Monsieur, if I may be so bold," Gustave said in a barely audible whisper, "may I ask where it is you are from? I notice an accent in your language. You are not native Norman or Frank, nor do you sound like any of the Anglos I know."

Patrick smiled. "I am Irish, from Eire."

Gustave blinked. "Where did you learn our tongue?"

This time, Patrick did not smile. "The Crusade. There were few other Irishmen. I spent most of my days among the Franks of Gaul and Bouillon."

Gustave's eyes widened and Freddy drew a gasp.

"A cru—" Freddy started to exclaim, but Gustave elbowed the boy.

"Shh! Mind your voice, boy; we mustn't frighten the wolf off."

Patrick hung his head. He did not want to be the cause for excitement, nor the cause for consternation between the man and his son. Certainly not over the Crusades. Perhaps sensing this, or perhaps knowing the nature of some fighting men's hearts, Gustave did not ask the usual questions.

Freddy, however, alive with a boy's spirit, asked in an excited whisper, "What was it like?"

Even from the opposite side of the boy, Patrick could feel Gustave giving his son a harsh elbow. Patrick shrugged. "It was nothing that I would ever want my son to do."

Maybe it was the sadness in his voice, but Freddy no longer seemed keen on asking questions about glorious battles. Instead, he asked, "You have a son?"

"No. But if I did, I'd want him to be just like you." Patrick winked at him.

Before Freddy could fix that beaming smile on him for too long, Gustave shot an arm forward and hissed, "Look!"

Patrick looked out into the darkness. He stared for a while, but saw nothing. Gustave grabbed at his sleeve and pointed, instructing the Irishman to look down his arm. Patrick did so.

There, past Gustave's outstretched index finger Patrick could see a dark blob moving in the distant shadows. It moved along the edge of the forest on the field side, coming closer as it traveled. At first it was indistinct, but then turned into a four-legged beast. It was very large.

The trio on the knoll held their breaths. The creature no longer moved towards them, but now took a tentative step towards the cottage and barn. It paused, and the sound of its sniffing carried on the breeze—a deep, huffing noise. It took another tentative step and bobbed its head, taking another sniff. Patrick's heart started to pound in his ears, and he fought the urge to exhale loudly after holding his breath for so long. He thought the lack of air was causing his eyes to play tricks on him. What was a fairly distinct four-legged creature a moment ago now looked like a shapeless mass again. Patrick slowly put his mouth down to his shoulder and with his hand inside his cloak, covered his mouth with the cloth and exhaled quietly. It was a trick he had learned during the Crusade. He then forced himself to breathe slowly and deliberately. He looked up to resume his vigil. It was once again a four-legged creature and on the move again.

About then both Gustave and Freddy breathed heavily, probably neither realizing they had been holding their breaths until it was too late, as Patrick had. The wolf stopped in its tracks and snapped its head in their direction. Despite his earlier efforts to control his breathing, Patrick once again found himself holding his breath, as he was sure the others were. A few torturous long moments crept by, their hearts racing, and then the wolf bolted for the forest. In the blink of an eye the creature melted into the shadows of the woods. It moved as fluidly as the Huntsman's hounds.

Patrick cursed. He grabbed his sword in its scabbard that lay on the ground next to him and he stood up to give chase.

Gustave jumped up and grabbed him by the arm. "The forest is dangerous enough at night, let alone when pursuing that thing."

Patrick took a deep breath, legs and arms aching to run after the wolf anyway, but under Gustave's staying hand, he nodded and sheathed his sword.

#

The following morning they returned to the site of the creature's appearance. A mist engulfed the landscape, cloaking it with a stifling pallor. The men needed a while to find evidence that the creature had existed anywhere outside their imaginations. The field of stubble was hard packed and did not lend itself well to footprints. But at the forest edge, there was some soft earth, and it bore a few very large tracks.

Patrick spread his hand over a print. It was nearly as large as his hand, from wrist to the tip of his index finger.

Gustave bent down next to him and whistled through his teeth. "Most of my life I've been on this island, and I've never seen or heard of a wolf ever being here." He tipped his hat back. "When I first started to hear people talk about the sightings, I thought they were at most seeing ghosts like we do from time to time, like during the Bush Beatings. But then the mutilations started."

Once Patrick realized Gustave was thinking out loud, he started to pace back and forth along the tracks they had found. "Does it seem to you, as it seems to me from these tracks, that the beast sometimes appears to walk upright? I didn't see it do that last night. Did you?"

Gustave reseated his hat. "I could not say, monsieur. I am a farmer, not a huntsman." But he made the sign of the Holy Cross just the same.

Patrick took a deep breath and called Freddy over. The boy had been standing at a distance, holding on to Siegfried to keep the large horse from disturbing the tracks. It was clear now where the wolf reentered the forest.

"You will be going now? After the wolf?" Gustave asked.

Patrick nodded solemnly. "To give it a good try, anyway." He took the reins from Freddy. "At the very least I hope to find where the thing has its den."

Gustave smiled. "I hope what little food I gave you will help in the cause."

Patrick returned the smile. "More than enough. I must be going now."

Before Patrick could turn to leave with Siegfried in tow, Freddy rushed forward and wrapped his arms about the Irishman's waist. He clung for a moment, and then rushed back to his father, who was smiling bemusedly.

Patrick winked at them, and then entered the forest to follow the trail of the wolf. Gustave and his boy waved, wishing him luck.

#

Following the tracks was no difficult task for the first hour, but then they became sparse and hard to discern among the rocks and moss. Patrick was now deep in the forest, farther from the keep than he had ever been on Avalon. He knew the rough layout of the island, having discussed it much with the Avangardesmen and villagers, but he now found himself much disoriented.

Eventually, as he had feared, he came to realize he had lost the trail of the wolf. It angered him a little, but then he reasoned, *what would you do if you found it anyway*? The sun was low and the forest dimming and he decided to return to its edge. Gustave's warning about being there alone at night repeated in his head.

Patrick surmised that it would be better to wait once again for the wolf to attack the livestock, and attempt to slay the creature then. Following it into the woods would be a mistake. The wolf would be in more familiar territory, and thus would have even more of an advantage against a poor hunter like Patrick.

The knight turned in the direction he had come from and made the best time he could. But after a while, his stomach sank. Nothing looked at all familiar, and he should have long ago reached the edge of the forest. Siegfried snorted.

"I'm sorry, old boy, but I think I've gotten us into quite a mess."

Siegfried neighed.

"I said I was sorry."

#

Patrick traveled farther, and the oak trees become more and more immense. They had huge tangles of mistletoe in their branches as well as long beards of lichen. It was growing truly dark now and his imagination began to play tricks on him.

He thought he saw movement in the corner of his eye. Steps came from behind him, the old gnarled trees had faces of sorts, faces that leered at him. Avangarde stories of past Bush

Beatings came to him against his will. The stories about how stalwart knights' hair turned white from fear.

Patrick unsaddled Siegfried and made a fire just before the last light was gone. He huddled by the yellow flames with the large horse near and his sword drawn. And as night drew on, he did see and hear things.

Off in the distance, through the trees, he saw lights bobbing. They reminded him of no lantern or torch he had ever seen. They flickered in and out at random, and even turned colors.

> *"Will-'o-wisp, will-'o-wisp*
> *what secrets do you whisp?"*

Patrick sang softly, recalling an old fairly tale from Galway. These lights, though, never came near the camp.

Then he could hear a wolf, the wolf, baying in the distance. He listened. Eventually he fell into a fitful sleep, with half wakeful dreams of trees with faces gazing at him scornfully, and the occasional mournful howl of the wolf.

#

He didn't waste any time breaking camp once light began to show. Patrick oriented himself to the rising sun and headed in the direction he knew to be Aesclinn and Greensprings.

But after what he deemed to be a half hour's journey he emerged onto a cliff that overlooked a misty valley.

"What the hell?" He said out loud. Siegfried whinnied as if to say the same.

Patrick knew of no such valley. He hadn't heard of this valley from anyone who knew the geography of Avalon. He then thought that perhaps he had unwittingly traveled to the other side of the island. He dismounted Siegfried and led the horse up the slope of the cliff. Achieving higher ground was difficult as the undergrowth was thick here, and maneuvering the large horse through it was even harder. But Patrick reached what he thought was the highest point. Here there was little undergrowth and the few trees were wind twisted evergreens.

In the direction of the valley, there was indeed an ocean, but it seemed far off and the land appeared to continue as if it were a peninsula attached to a greater landmass. Patrick shook his head. If he didn't know better, he would say it was Cornwall somehow forested over.

He looked in the opposite direction, expecting to see the familiar sight of Greensprings in the distance or at least the hills that harbored it, but he saw only forest.

"No, this can't be," he murmured. "This doesn't even look like Avalon anymore, Siegfried." He began to pace back and forth, running his hands through his hair.

"Now," he said, emphatically stopping before the horse. "This is still an island. The mist or the heights or both is distorting the view. Or maybe it's the Avalon glamour, but regardless, this is still an island, right?" Siegfried tossed his mane. "So, what we have to do is go straight downhill, come to the coast and find our way to a homestead, or even the port, and then we'll find our way back to the keep and then tell nobody we were ever lost. Agreed?" Siegfried had nothing to say on the manner.

They set off. He rode where he could, and led Siegfried through the brush where he had to. But before long he felt he was not making any progress again. Though midday had come and gone, there was still mist about, and it obscured his view. For all he knew, he was making circles. He stopped to eat, and then realized his supply of food and water was becoming low. This was no longer a silly inconvenience, but serious. He imagined that he could survive off the land if it came to that, but it would be difficult considering he had not seen any sign of deer or other large game. That struck him as curious. How could a wolf survive on this island for so long without big game animals, only recently feeding off domesticated livestock?

Darkness started to fall once again, so Patrick made camp for the second night in the forest.

That night he saw no eerie lights, heard no howls, and the trees were friendly, faceless willows, though he could swear he actually heard them weeping.

#

The following day he staggered about even more. Siegfried was becoming agitated and difficult to handle. Patrick found himself arguing with the beast as if he were another person.

Patrick came to glades, lakes, hills and dales, none of which looked familiar. Not once did he come across the ocean no matter how many times he picked a compass direction and attempted to travel in a straight line. The land was misty in the mornings and hazy in the afternoons to the point that the trees seemed to shift and move of their own accord. Patrick's face was now stubbly and his clothes were filthy. Siegfried was faring no better. His mane was matted with twigs, moss and bark. His saddle was scuffed, torn and chafing. They were both tired and disoriented. Patrick didn't bother camping down for the evenings. He just unsaddled Siegfried and leaned his back against a tree to catch some sleep before resuming his search.

Patrick ate the last of the hard bread. "Well, it looks like it's grass for the both of us."

One night, while sleeping against a tree stump next to a lake, Patrick dreamed of the sounds of a banquet coming from beneath the water. He could smell the food being served and hear the clink of wine glasses and silverware. He longed to eat the food and be in a warm banquet hall. But how could it be warm at the bottom of a lake?

"It's warm everywhere we are," said a voice. Patrick opened his eyes. There was a fellow standing between him and the lake. He held a wine glass.

"Are you thirsty? Would you like a drink? It's the best tasting nectar this side of the Pillars of Heracles." The little man with sharp features beckoned. "Come, come. There is food aplenty. Come with me to the bottom of the lake. You are expected."

Patrick stood up. A warm meal sounded good. He stepped forward, reaching for the glass. The little man didn't make any efforts to put it in Patrick's hand, but seemed impatient for him to take it.

"Take it!" The little man leered. "Come with me to the bottom of the lake!"

Patrick stretched out his hand but wavered. He wished he could wake up so he could think straight. There was something he was supposed to know. Something every Celtic person was supposed to know.

"Take it! Before I change my mind!"

Fairy Folk, he remembered. *You aren't supposed to take their food. If you do, you will sleep for a hundred years.*

Patrick snapped out of the trance, and drew his sword. Something was splashing in the water. Siegfried was going wild, rearing and striking the air. It was then that Patrick realized Siegfried had been trying to get his attention.

Patrick backed away from the now quiet water.

"*Each-uisge!*" he spat, calling the evil water sprite by its Gaelic name.

#

Patrick made sure not to sleep near large bodies of water again. He continued to wander his way through the forest, following animal trails in hopes they would lead somewhere familiar.

Then one day, or thereabouts, he came across a small clearing and a man-made stone well. He was delighted at first, finding a sign of civilization, but then could find no path that came to or left the clearing.

"What look yea for, Sir Knight?" rasped a voice behind him. Patrick spun around. Any voice was alien to his ears after having heard only his own for so long. There, leaning against the well with a wooden bucket in her hand, was a crone in dirty and torn peasant clothing.

She cackled "Oh, my! I didn't mean to startle yea, my good lord."

Patrick staggered forward. "Are you from the village? Is it near?"

The crone, whose eyes were black as night yet flickered with a vibrant life, put a hand to her cheek. "Poor creature, you're lost aren't yea?"

Patrick no longer cared to soothe his pride. He just wanted to go home and have a warm meal. "Yes, I am. Very lost," he said.

The old woman put the bucket into the well by means of a rope and smiled good naturedly. "How comes it that yea are lost, good sir?"

Patrick had no patience, yet he tried to be polite. "Good woman, I am in somewhat of a hurry. I really need to return to the keep. Could you please tell me how to find it?"

The old woman seemed oblivious to Patrick's inquiry as she pulled heavily on the rope. "I never thought knights, with their airs and all, went around becoming lost," she rasped. "I thought they were supposed to be saving maidens from dragons and helping old ladies cross rivers and such."

Patrick took the hint. In his hunger and fatigue he had forgotten his manners. He stepped forward and offered to take the rope from the woman.

"May I?" he asked. The woman acquiesced.

The Irishman pulled on the rope until the bucket came into view and he could withdraw it from the well. It was empty. Patrick looked down into the well itself. It was filled in with earth, dry earth that sprouted weeds.

The crone took the bucket from the knight and carried it as if it were brimming with water. "Yea never did tell me why yea are lost," she pointed out.

Patrick stepped back from the well. "I was, um, looking for a wolf that has been terrorizing the island."

"Oh, that wolf. What a nuisance it has been."

"You know of it?" Patrick's interest was renewed.

"Know of it? I know where that devil hides."

"Can you tell me?

The crone stood up as straight as she could and put her fists on her hips. "Well, which one is it yea are looking for? The keep or the wolf?"

"The wolf. No, I mean the keep. Well, actually right now I need to find my way to the keep, and then I'll find the wolf later." Patrick's face had grown hot.

The crone frowned. "I thought yea were to slay this beast to keep it from terrorizing the isle, Sir Knight? Why would yea be wanting to prolong the terror? What if it eats a child while yea are riding home?"

"Well, I can hardly be fighting a wolf in the condition I'm in now." Patrick pulled at his torn and dirty surcoat.

She wrapped her shawl around her elbows and started toward her bucket. "Like no knight I ever heard of."

"Fine, all right, tell me where I can find the wolf! I'll slay it, and then the whole isle will be safe. Then could you tell me how to find my way back to Greensprings?"

The old woman looked shocked at the Irishman's outburst. "Well, yes. Yea didn't have to become cross with me."

"My apologies. Now, where may I find the wolf?"

"Down that path." The crone pointed past his head. Patrick turned in the direction she was pointing and saw a clearly marked path where he was sure there had been none before. He shook his head, thanked the crone, and started in that direction.

As he approached he noticed there were really two paths, not just one, traveling in diverging directions.

He turned again towards the old woman and called back, "Which path, good woman?"

She wore a mischievous smile. "One leads to your wolf, and the other to your castle."

"Yes, quite, but which one is which?"

"What's it worth yea, this information?"

Patrick placed his hand on his forehead and leaned heavily on Siegfried. He would never have thought that this mission would hinge on a madwoman.

"What's it worth to you?" he asked.

"A kiss," she replied simply. Patrick backed up in disgust. "What's wrong? Kissing an old woman is too much to ask when greatness could be yours." She thrust out her skinny arms and puckered her lips.

Patrick was horrified. He didn't want to touch the woman. But then he began to think: this is Avalon. Those paths hadn't been there before. He had seen strange lights and sounds. Perhaps this was such another fairy tale coming true.

"Alright then," he said and bent over to kiss the hag. He squelched his feelings and thanked God that she had her eyes closed so that she couldn't see his expression. As he touched her lips, she grabbed a firm hold of him and kissed him back deeply. She tasted like rotting potatoes. After a moment's struggle, she relinquished her hold and braced herself on the well. Patrick backed up, fighting the urge to retch in front of her.

"Well done, Sir Knight. It's the left path," she sighed. Patrick stood there watching her. "What's wrong? I said it was the left."

Patrick fidgeted. "I was hoping—well, I was hoping you would turn into a beautiful maiden. Like in the stories."

The crone cackled wildly. "No, you ninny, I'm just a lonely old bag." The woman went into spasms of laughter. Patrick turned around brusquely and spat violently. His mouth felt full of hair. He stumbled towards the left path with Siegfried in tow. It then occurred to him that he didn't know which destination the path led to: The wolf or the keep. He turned to ask one last question, but saw that she was gone. He ran to the well. There was no bucket, no crone and no way could she have gotten by him without him knowing it. He looked down into the well itself and a huge white swan flew out of it honking irritably as it disappeared into the sky.

#

Riding down the path atop Siegfried was an improvement on pulling him through the brush. And at least Patrick had the comfort of knowing that the crone was possibly supernatural after all. He intermittently leaned over Siegfried's side to spit. *For the love of God, she could have at least done me the favor of turning into a beautiful swan-maiden or Valkyrie.* Maybe he wouldn't tell this part of the story when he finally returned to Greensprings. *If* he returned to Greensprings.

He couldn't remember when he had been at the well. He couldn't remember how long he had been away from the court. He wondered if he was missed. How on earth do you become lost on an island? He wasn't sure he really wanted to be found.

Siegfried reared and bellowed. The horse bucked; Patrick caught the glimpse of a large shadowy creature on the path.

It was difficult to discern all that happened in the next few moments. His heart was racing and he tried to reach his sword and control the horse at the same time. The creature on the road snarled, causing the normally stalwart warhorse to go into another frenzy that threw Patrick out of his saddle.

He hit the ground rolling, right through ferns, branches, and underbrush, finally stopping against a mound of dirt on the slope of a hill. He stood up quickly, dirty and scratched, and drew his sword. He looked up the hill, but saw only trees. The muddy ravine was moist with loamy brown earth, filled with ferns and evergreens. The only light offered was from the milky sky above, peeking through the dark canopy.

He thought he heard something to his left and spun in that direction, then to his right. He kept his sword above his head in a strike pose, free arm outstretched as a counterbalance, and turned slowly in circles. He favored one foot, realizing he wasn't entirely injury free from his descent down the hill.

A snarl from behind sent shivers through him. He whirled, there was the wolf.

It was a huge creature, perhaps four feet at the shoulder. Its giant paws ended in strange hooked claws. It was all black, but grizzled. Its eyes were the color crimson, not just the feral glow of a predator, but otherworldly. The face of the beast had the play of intelligence. It snarled again, displaying a fierce set of teeth that seemed impossibly sharp. A steady, viscous stream of saliva dripped from its mouth.

It pressed back its ears and gave a ghastly howl. The sound made Patrick's ears ring, and made his hairs stand on end. He leveled the sword between the creature and himself, figuring that that would be the best defense should it attack.

When the wolf ceased its howl, it again stared intelligently at the Irishman. This very sight immobilized him, and he could only imagine what his own face looked like at that moment. There was a peculiar noise, once, then again. Patrick realized that the wolf was laughing. Laughing wickedly like a human.

"What's wrong, manling? Surprised?" it hissed. The thing pawed at the ground, as if testing the earth for the foothold that would offer the best leap. "Never have you seen a creature speak? I was hunting and devouring your kind before they could speak. Did you know that?"

"What are you?" Patrick stammered.

"Why, I am a wolf, fool."

"No, wolves don't talk."

The wolf began to circle Patrick at a distance; the knight kept the sword between him and it. "I'm not just any wolf," the creature said. "I am kin to Fenris and Cerberus. Eater of flesh, drinker of souls. I am a god compared to you. You and your kind are but hairless monkeys. Just because you use tools of iron to tear up the earth and throw down the trees does not make you special." The wolf stopped his circling. "But your kind is everywhere nowadays. You are prevalent like pond scum. A disease. I can find no peace, even on this isolated island." The wolf laughed scornfully. "You however, little manling, cannot stop me. Don't think that your iron can hinder me for long. You are alone."

Patrick did understand that he was alone. And the wolf lunged with such agility that Patrick almost did not see it. If his sword had not been between them he could not have struck a blow in time to save his life. Patrick thrust the weapon once, the only chance he had, but the point of the blade connected with the wolf. It snarled, and then was on top of him. Against the onslaught of teeth and claw, Patrick held the blade in both gloved hands and attempted to use it as a barrier between the savage teeth and himself. The wolf's claws were tearing into his torso and thighs, and he knew it was only a matter of time before his armor gave way, or the wolf worked his way around the sword blade to Patrick's throat.

But, the wolf was cast aside, yelping. The gigantic mass of Siegfried appeared above him, huge shod hooves kicking in all directions. The wolf came for another assault, but was once again struck by the warhorse's hind legs. It flew into the ferns as if struck by a thunderbolt, and then scrambled off into the forest.

Patrick staggered to his feet, grabbing hold of the saddle for support. "Thank you, old boy. You're my best friend that ever lived. I love you like you wouldn't believe." He fell to his knees and retched. He stayed on the ground for some time, but came to when Siegfried nuzzled him. After he had cast out as much as his empty stomach could produce, he stood and mounted the horse. His disorientation was almost as total as it had been on the isle of the Mont Saint-Michel. His wounds weren't so bad; yes, he was bleeding, but not profusely and it hadn't been long enough for infection to set in. He wondered if perhaps the claws of the wolf were somehow venomous.

Patrick held up his sword and noted that it was blood stained to the middle of the blade. The creature was hurting just as bad, if not worse. Possibly it was dying. *Maybe* I'm *dying at this moment. Such a pleasant thought.*

He tried to re-sheath his sword, but couldn't manage it, so he laid it across his lap. Siegfried trotted in a random direction when Patrick slumped over in the saddle.

#

When he awoke next, he was lying on moss and the sun was just rising. Wherever he was now, the trees were thinner and mostly saplings. He rose stiffly.

Siegfried was nearby, unsaddled, and grazing on grass. There was a broad leaf with mushrooms on it at his side. He held up one of the fleshy fungi and sniffed it. He then gulped it down hungrily, not caring whether it was edible or not. His stomach demanded it. After he had finished all of them, he limped over to a gurgling brook and drank. When he sat up, he was confronted with a large swan.

The fowl and knight stared at each other. After some moments had passed, Patrick said, "Are you a magic or holy swan like in all the stories that concern Avalon?" The swan only rooted around in the mossy patches for food. "Well, if you are, I'd appreciate some help." The swan started to wander off. When it had waddled so far, it stopped as if waiting for the knight, bobbed its head and began to waddle away again. "Do you want me to follow?" It kept waddling. Patrick saddled Siegfried as fast as he could manage and followed the bird.

It waddled further into the woods, in the direction the Irishman didn't want to go, but he followed it anyway, feeling that the plan was just as good as any. After a short journey, the swan stopped on a trail and pecked at some moss. Patrick approached it and saw blood on the ground and wolf tracks.

"No, no. No more wolves. I want to go home now. Do you understand? Home. I want to go home." Patrick began to pace back and forth. "I'm talking to a swan," he murmured. *Why not, yesterday you were talking to a wolf, and the day before that you were arguing with your horse.*

"It's not finished, yea know," rasped a voice.

Patrick looked up. The bird was gone and in its place was the crone.

"Why can't I just go back? The wolf assuredly is done for. Can't I just leave now?" Patrick no longer knew what was real or fantasy. He had spent years in the Crusade's hard realities. Now he was living in a child's tale. Nightmare, more like it. He didn't know which was worse.

"Yea can't run away from everything all your life, Patrick Gawain of Galway. If yea start something, yea must throw yourself wholeheartedly into it and finish it. Yea must face your fears."

"I do!" Patrick threw up his hands. "I've never run away from anything in my life!"

"You are whining, Sir Knight."

Patrick turned in frustration, but the crone was gone. He was left alone on the trail with Siegfried. He almost wanted to cry. Not knowing what else to do, or what other direction to go in, he decided to pursue the wolf.

#

The blood spots became more frequent as the trail drew closer to a cave, the wolf's lair.

Patrick dismounted and left the warhorse untied, lest he not return. He removed his flint and tinder box from the saddlebags to fashion a makeshift torch from branches and his ragged surcoat. He lit this, said a quick prayer and entered the mouth of the cave. All was still dreamlike. He swayed to and fro and braced himself with a steadying hand to the walls. It was then that he noticed that they were covered with crude paintings. He hadn't looked long at these pictographs when a howl, followed by a burst of wind, came down the cave. The gust caused the cobwebs to flutter in the wind like phantoms, and another howl caused Patrick to stop in his tracks for a long pause. Nevertheless, he proceeded, torch in one hand, sword in the other.

The cave came to an end around a corner, and there, lying on a glorious mound of coins, jewelry, arms and armor of exquisite craftsmanship, was the wolf. The monster looked sick, and mixed with its slaver was blood.

It turned its gaze upon the Irishman. Patrick thanked the Lord that he was feverish after all, for it numbed his senses and eliminated the fear he normally would have felt.

"So, you have come to finish the fight, have you?" it taunted. "You can't beat me. You can damage me, but you can't defeat me. I've survived far worse at the hands of greater than you." The wolf labored to its feet, and crouched. "Was it worth it, manling? To throw away your pitiful life without anybody knowing your fate, here in the darkness that is not even your world?" It leapt.

The wolf was slowed by its wounds. Patrick struck out with sword and torch, fighting as if in a nightmare. The mind would not obey the will no matter how hard he tried. The wolf tore and bit, but he bludgeoned back with the torch, and the cavern was stifling with the stench of burnt hair. Patrick stabbed at the creature with his sword, wearing it down until one final stab penetrated deep into the chest cavity and the beast shuddered and went limp

Patrick slumped, and then cast himself away from the carcass with what strength he had left. The wolf was dead but he knew that he was not far behind. The thing had bit deep into his leg, and he was positive that it was venomous after all, for now he had no control of his body. He lay there listening to his breath wheeze slower and slower in tandem with the dying torchlight. He was dying, and the only thing going through his mind was the wolf's last words; *was it worth it?*

When the light had died out, Patrick was sure that he was dead. But a light began to fill the cavern. It was no torch. It was far more brilliant and pure than any worldly light. The paintings danced on the walls—images of battles and warriors, a sword, a cup, a boat, and swans. These images blurred, and a golden haired woman appeared before him. She was tall and lithe with skin whiter than bone. Her cheekbones were high, her brows arched, and her eyes at first seemed dark, but were a green so luxuriant they matched the darkest evergreen, and at their centers they bore brilliant sunbursts.

"Well done, Gawain of Galway," she said. Her voice was music.

"Who are you? Are you an angel come to take me away?"

The cavern filled with laughter that sounded like chimes on the breeze. "No, not at all. I am no more angelic than thou and I will let thou decide just how angelic that is." Her smile was genuinely caring, as she brushed a damp cloth against his forehead. "I am your kinswoman."

"My kinswoman?"

"We are of the *Tuatha De Danann*, the children of Dana, the Hill Folk. Do you not see it in your own eyes?"

Patrick shook his head.

"The blood pulsing in your heart still sings, though softly, of the Old Ones. You are special among men."

Patrick frowned in puzzlement, but decided not to dwell too much on the strange revelation. His vision had begun to swim even more and chill wracked his body.

The woman sighed. "Your wounds are great. They will be mortal soon." She turned and Patrick could hear the clink of treasure. But when she returned, she bore a simple wooden cup. Its base was convex and as wide as its open mouth; its stem was almost non-existent, giving the goblet an hourglass shape. She also produced an earthenware jug, which she used to pour water into the cup. She poured the water from the cup over his wounds, and when she did, the cup turned into a golden chalice. His pains melted away. Then she made him drink. The water tasted sweet and clean, and all his internal pains vanished, leaving him feeling warm and drowsy. Now his vision really was swimming, and all was becoming dark again.

"We thank thee, Gawain of Galway. We no longer reside in this existence as we once did, and could not banish the wolf. That it claimed this sacred place as its own is an abomination. You are still of the world, and could, and did, destroy it. We thank you. Take care, and remember to face thy fears, kinsman."

Patrick drifted off into the sweet arms of sleep like he never had before. He dreamed of white swans.

#

Sir Corbin brought his mount to a halt and held up his hand, to signal the other Avangarde in his patrol to do likewise. He turned to the others, pushed up his helm by his nose guard and asked, "Is that who I think it is?"

"It sure looks like it," Sir Waylan said.

Coming down the valley of apple orchards was Sir Patrick trotting at a leisurely pace atop his great black warhorse. He wore a blank gaze. What was left of his armor, surcoat and other gear was filthy and tattered. Rolled and slung across the back of his mount was a giant wolf's pelt.

Sir Bisch exclaimed, "Good! Good!"

The patrol of Avangarde hailed him and waited for him to approach. He didn't seem to take any notice of them and the knights looked at each other quizzically. Sir Corbin trotted up to Patrick's mount and took it by the harness, for Patrick was in the process of passing them by.

"Whoa, Siegfried," he said. "Patrick, how do you fare? Are you wounded?"

Patrick did not respond.

Bisch scowled. "Bad. Bad."

Patrick stared ahead. The Englishman waved his hand in front of the Irish knight's face. "Hello, hello? Are yea there, Sir Patrick?" No reply. Corbin resorted to shaking Patrick. The Avangarde circled.

Patrick finally shook his head and blinked as if waking. He looked upon Corbin as if seeing him for the first time. "Corbin! How are you?" he almost shouted. "Waylan! Bisch!" Patrick was smiling now. The knights looked at one another once again with renewed curiosity.

"We'd better get you back to Greensprings," Corbin said, a smile forming at the corners of his mouth. "Though I see no injuries on you, you don't seem to be altogether well, Patrick."

"Looks to me like he ran right out and killed the wolf, then spent the next few days shacked up in some cottage with the farmer's daughter instead," Waylan declared. The Avangarde laughed. They all started back to the Greensprings.

Patrick's brow furrowed. "Days? I thought that I was gone for weeks."

Waylan laughed. "Must have been some farmer's daughter!" There was more laughter and good natured jeering.

"Well, the way things have changed since you left, one might think that it has been weeks," Corbin said.

"How's that?"

"Well, the Lady du Lac found out about Sir Geoffrey's extra efforts, packed up and left, and Geoffrey has been in a confessional booth ever since. And you'll never guess who has been spotted holding the Lady Morneau's dainty little hand out in the gardens at night." Corbin had one arm thrown over Patrick's shoulder as he recounted the current gossip. When did his return commence? He couldn't quite remember the last few events that led to his arrival.

He was nonetheless curious. "Who?" he asked.

"Why our very own King Mark! Do you believe it?" He didn't. Corbin changed subjects. "But enough of idle talk, it looks as if you have a tale to tell." He tugged on the rolled pelt. "What shall we do? Go to the pub at Aesclinn first? Or would you rather go straight to your room and clean up?"

Patrick smiled. "I think I would like to see the librarian."

"Eh?"

"I'd like him to take a look at the slope of my skull."

Chapter Five

Of course there was a celebration banquet, but it was not long before it became old news and he was once again just Sir Patrick Gawain, Reservist. But somehow he didn't mind as much. He couldn't entirely remember what happened, but something told him that it had been overwhelmingly good. He was unofficially relieved of his duties in order to recuperate.

Patrick now sat in the window of his room overlooking the keep grounds. He had his eyes closed and a cool breeze washed over his face. Off in the distance he could hear the laughter of Guests and the sound of paper kites diving and shuddering in the wind.

The day was a perfectly clear Avalon day, with its aquamarine skies.

No sooner had he begun to truly relax, however, than the weathercock atop the watchtower turned suddenly in the wind.

#

Aimeé rolled the fluffy dough with skill and care. Once it was exactly twice as thick as pie crust, she began to cut expert little shapes out of it with a paring knife. The portly maidservant Anna approached her from behind and placed her chin on Aimeé's shoulder.

"What are we making, lass? That doesn't look like what Rosa Maria assigned to ya to be making for tonight's supper."

Aimeé shrugged. "What fun is working in the kitchen if you can't make it fun?"

"Well, if I were you, I wouldn't wear my heart on my sleeve so much," Anna said holding up the heart shaped dough. "...Or in my dough. Still lovesick, are yea?"

Aimeé threw more flour on the dough and rolling pin listlessly. She also took back the heart. "I'm just sad, that is all, Anna. The men around here are either young weakling servants, uppity knights and noblemen who don't know I exist or care if I do, or old married villagers. It's not fair."

Anna shook her head sadly. "I wouldn't worry about it, girl. It will pass. There is somebody for everybody out there...uh-oh!" She suddenly grabbed for the heart shaped dough while looking over Aimeé's shoulder, but Aimeé pulled the heart away.

"Hey! What are you doing?" she cried.

Before Anna could reply, the kitchen Madame Rosa Maria walked up and snatched away the heart. "What this?" she exclaimed in her barely understandable Italian accent. "This is not breadstick."

Aimeé hung her head. "I'm sorry, Rosa Maria, I have been distracted from my duties."

Anna was giggling, and the other servants looked up from their tasks. Rosa Maria held up the heart so that she could look at it better. Her face lightened. "Ah, the girl is in love!" She placed the heart over her own breast and danced around. All in the kitchen laughed.

Aimeé's face turned bright red, but she was smiling. She was glad that Rosa was not terribly angry with her, otherwise she wouldn't be poking fun at her like this.

When her dance was finished, Rosa Maria placed the heart back on the counter. "I know we would all rather be making love right now, and not breadstick, but we must make breadstick. Back to work you," Rosa looked into Aimeé's flour bowl. "You need more flour, get more off the shelf, and close that window while you're at it. My joints are aching; I think a storm is coming."

Anna laughed. "Don't be silly, it's beautiful out there."

#

Outside the keep, even the Guests on the verge of adulthood played like children. Jason McFowler dozed at the edge of the kite-flying throng, sleeping through his own history lesson on how kites had been used at the Battle of Hastings as communication devices. This was one of the many reasons he was favored among the Guests; he was lax and more fun than the scholars and priests who gave the majority of lessons.

Jason snored heavily. Two of the youngest Guests tickled his nose with a cattail just to watch him swat at it in his sleep.

"He is so adorable when he's asleep, isn't he? He looks like a big furry bear in hibernation," commented Lady Clarice, who was several years older than the two girls.

"And his feet are stinky," said one of the girls, and giggled.

"Well, look what I made for you two," said Clarice. She held up a delicate kite of reed and parchment paper. In the center of the kite she had painted a stick figure in water colors. The figure was of a smiling man with bright red bushy hair and beard, and who carried a sword. "Who do you suppose he is?"

"Jason!" They exclaimed. "Let's fly him!"

They stood and ran up the hill, waving the kite overhead until the wind caught it. Yarn unspooled behind it, and it soared higher, flapping merrily in the air.

They giggled as Elaine, one of the younger students, pulled on the string to make the kite dive and swirl.

"Let me try," said Rachel, the other younger student.

As Elaine started to hand it over and Rachel reached for it, the yarn pulled through Elaine's hand viciously. She cried out as she snatched her hand back and looked at it as if it had been bitten. Rachel caught the string just before it disappeared into the heavens with the kite which was now thrashing in the air.

"I can't hang on!" she cried, a quiver in her voice.

Clarice reached over to control the device, but was soon struggling herself as she pulled with both hands and leaned back on her rear foot. With a scream of surprise she lost hold of the kite and fell backwards, knocking her comrades over and landing on top of them.

Heavy dark clouds roiled into existence like ink drops as on the clear sky, and the sun vanished. Fat droplets smacked the ground and left large wet spots on the Lady Guests' gowns. The rolling mass of clouds flickered with lightning.

Guests were crying out and laughing as the rain and wind came down harder.

"Alright everybody, back into Greensprings," McFowler called, stumbling to his feet.

"But why, Sir Jason? It's only rain," said a little boy who was standing on Jason's foot and clutching his leg.

The Highlander reached down and picked him up. "The rain is fine, but I don't think Father Hugh or King Mark would be too happy with me if you were suddenly fried by lightning. Though I'm sure you would make a tasty treat." Jason tasseled his hair and the boy laughed. Jason once again called for all Guests to go inside.

As they rushed in through the Back Door, one kite remained behind. It was Clarice's, which caught in a tree. A branch had impaled the stick figure, and the figure's smile was now blotted by the rain. The paint that made its red beard was running like blood.

#

Father Benis, the librarian, put down a tome he was reading and looked up at the window shutters. They had been chattering in a strong breeze. He moved to close them, and when he did he noticed a marked difference in the weather. Rain was pelting the tiles on the buildings and towers, and the entire courtyard below was shoe-deep in water. He shook his head sadly, closed the shutters, and turned from the window.

But he had accidently caught his prayer beads between the shutters. When he turned, the beads snapped and broke from their string, falling all over the floor in a noisy shower.

"Oh, my."

#

The violent wind guided a black ship towards the isle. The ship was a great longboat, with the effigy of a flame-tongued dragon at its bow. Black sails were fat with wind.

Whereas seafarers on longboats normally enjoy the windy elements offered by most such open-aired vessels, this particular craft seemed more designed for concealment and separation from the world. This was evidenced by a single ark-like structure that occupied the majority of the deck. Monstrous oars bristled from its sides and beat the water, moving effortlessly to a drum beat somewhere within the belly of the ship.

The same wind that propelled the vessel cut the mist surrounding Avalon, and admitted the ship to the enchanted isle. Lightning flashed.

The black ship slipped into the harbor. The huge oars dragged in the water, then suddenly lifted skyward to accommodate the vessel near the dock.

Within moments of reaching the isle, a wide section of the ship between oars collapsed neatly inwards, revealing an opening. Horses could be heard from within just as a ramp extended forth from the darkness onto the dock like a protruding tongue.

The sound of thundering hooves on wood could be heard as the beasts galloped forth. They were six great black creatures with flaring nostrils and wild eyes, harnessed to an elegant carriage as black as their glossy coats.

This vehicle clattered across the ramp without hesitation and continued on its way along the now muddy road to Greensprings. The ramp was withdrawn, the opening closed up, and the strange ship slid into the mist that had collected around it, and disappeared without a trace.

#

Just as suddenly as the storm came, it left. The dark billowing clouds rolled on, taking with them the pelting rain and driving wind.

The gutters and rain spouts rattled and gushed. Gargoyles all about the keep disgorged water at such a rate that it spurted out horizontally, but within minutes the streams faltered and sunshine glittered on the puddles.

Guests ran about the corridors, shouting and excited.

Patrick stepped out of his room. "What's going on?" William and Trent were drenched.

"Somebody is approaching the keep in a rich wagon. It's a new Guest," Trent said. Patrick followed the two up onto the castle walls where a crowd was gathering, some soaked, some dry. They looked over the wall and watched the sleek black carriage approach the keep.

"Who is it? I didn't know any new Guests were coming," Trent said to Patrick.

Patrick shrugged. "You're asking the wrong person. I didn't even know that Amy du Lac was coming, let alone leaving so soon. Well, actually, now that I think about it, I could have guessed she would have left that quickly." A few people within hearing distance chuckled.

The carriage reached the gate and waited for the drawbridge to be lowered. Mark was standing at the forefront, legs apart and fists on hips. He was in Avangarde garb, with a huge broadsword belted at his side. He looked very kingly. Gathered around him was a retinue of knights, and behind them were milling Guests and staff trying to get a better view of the new arrival. There were murmurs in the crowd, and many questions. The drawbridge was down, and the horses pulled the carriage across and stopped in the courtyard before the assembled greeting party.

"Does anybody have any idea who this is?" King Mark asked from the corner of his mouth. McFowler at his side shook his head.

A stocky driver scurried down from the carriage and approached the coach door. He was a pale looking creature with narrow slitted eyes and a shorn head. He looked more a toad than human. He lowered a stepladder from the side of the coach by a metal hinge and then opened the door for the passenger.

First came his glossy leather boots, followed by kidskin leggings. The man who stood upon these tall legs was thin with a craggy face and a well-groomed beard and mustache. His hair was dark to the point of having a blue sheen. His eyes were an indiscernible color and were situated perfectly between razor sharp cheekbones and finely arched brows. In short, he was all angles and edges. Even his ears were oddly elongated, slightly pointed, and he wore a golden ring in one of them.

The man stood momentarily gazing upon Greensprings. Then he threw back his cape and leaned forward on a silver-tipped walking stick. His entire wardrobe was composed of fine dark fabric with a rare lavender lining.

He stepped forward, motioning to his dwarfish servant to retrieve something from the carriage, and walked up to King Mark and his entourage.

"Greetings," said Mark. "Welcome to the Keep at Greensprings. I am its Steward. And whom do I have the pleasure of meeting?" He extended a hand in friendship. The man took Mark's hand and smiled. His teeth were extremely long, but perfectly straight and white.

"I am the Viscount Loki, of Jotunheim. I am delighted to make your acquaintance." The sun was back out and shone radiantly on Loki. A sweet perfume surrounded him. The servant returned with a scroll, and handed this to his master who in turn handed it to Mark. "I believe this is for you."

Mark took it, looked it over then popped the seal on it. It glowed for a moment as all the swan-sealed invitations did. Mark unrolled it and read silently. His brow furrowed, then cleared. He folded the document and placed it inside his surcoat. He shook hands again with the newcomer, and then turned to all assembled.

"Welcome our new Guest, the Viscount Loki."

Chapter Six

The Viscount Loki was an enigma.

He did not at first interact with the other denizens, and he did not make many appearances. His first many days at the Keep at Greensprings he stayed concealed in his room, sending out his dwarfish valet, Minion, to fetch his meals and do his errands.

In the process, Minion was into everything. His odd squeaky voice was everywhere as he asked directions or for assistance—anything to make his master more comfortable. Minion's spikey haired head was seen in the kitchens, the stables, the vestuary, the library and even managed to be kicked out of the Hall for Lady Guests, having wandered there, so he claimed, on accident.

Loki's arrival may have been a surprise, but he bore an invitation, so he was given all the hospitality afforded to any other.

"What does he look like up close?" Sir Jeremiah asked McFowler at the dinner table one night.

Between large bites of food, Sir Jason answered, "He's a thinnish fellow, all bones and edges. And his face, Mother of Joseph, it's all pock marked as if he tripped and fell face down in an alchemist's vat. His ears aren't all that easy to look at either; all stretched out and chewed on looking, and they say I'm strange looking?" Jason shoveled more noodles into his face and caught many of them on his beard.

"Who invited him anyway? I hadn't heard of his coming. Who's his Patron on the outside?" asked Sir Waylan.

Sir Geoffrey shrugged. "I was right there when Mark read the invitation. It was signed by Marcus Ionus himself, but it didn't mention who recommended he come here."

"Where's he from anyhow? What's his reason for being here?" Sir Jon asked, reaching for bread in the middle of the table.

"He said Jotunheim. Where's that?" asked Sir Corbin.

"He has a funny accent, like those people from the far north..." McFowler began, but Sir Brian shouted; "You would know!" His smile suddenly turned painful and he jumped in his seat, as if he'd been kicked underneath the table. McFowler finished, "...but his mannerism and dress are completely unlike them. His speaks eloquently. I can't place him."

"Perhaps you all should let it be. He is not obligated to tell us about his origins," King Mark said. He was in hearing distance of the knights from his large chair at the center of the table. Christianne Morneau, who was ever at his side now, ate quietly while pretending not to listen.

"But we do have the right to know why he showed up on such short notice," Sir Geoffrey said. Patrick could not discern if there was awkwardness or animosity between the two noblemen because of Christianne, and if there had been originally, he missed it during his mission in the woods.

King Mark shrugged. "His invitation bore the seal, and it was signed by Marcus. That should be all we need to know."

"But it can't hurt to ask him," said McFowler. "If he so wishes to divulge all, he will. Correct?" There was a mischievous glint in his eye. Mark conceded.

"Good then," Jason said, standing. "Lord Viscount, how timely. Won't you join us here at our table?"

There in the doorway was the black clad Viscount, having just arrived with his servant Minion.

Mark groaned.

"Why thank you, Sir McFowler, I would be delighted to join your company." Loki's words were almost musical. He approached the table and the knights made room for him before the feast. Minion dutifully stood behind him. Sir Jon called for a maidservant to bring more food and drink.

"Viscount, I'm afraid you have me at a disadvantage. It seems you know my name, though I have not been properly introduced to you."

"That is quite alright," the nobleman returned. "I'm familiar with all of you: Sir Mark, the keep Stewart, Sir McFowler, the Captain of the Guard; Sir Corbin, Waylan, and Brian, senior Avangardesmen; Sir Jon, Jeremiah, and Patrick, Reservists and..." he raised his goblet, "...assorted lovely Ladies."

All around the table there were surprised and flattered murmurs. He was very informed for somebody who spent most of his days in his chamber.

Talk was easy for much of the meal. The Viscount, who insisted on being addressed as just "Loki" was very interested in the Isle of Avalon, and those at the table were very interested in him. But McFowler, who was usually very good at the talking game, found his inquiries rebuked.

"Where exactly is Jotunheim?" the Highlander finally asked.

"Why that is difficult to explain."

"Try me; I'm a very traveled and learned person despite my brutish appearance." Jason flexed his tattooed arms.

"Well, if you insist on knowing," Loki commenced. Mark was frowning at the Scotsman. Loki turned to one of the Ladies present and stroked the underside of her chin. She smiled with kitten-like pleasure. The eyes of the other Ladies present widened and they giggled. "It is a wonderful land beyond the Northern Wind, where dwarves with magical silver beards weave the finest clothing from them. It is a place where a giant tree that sings holds the sky together with its boughs and keeps it close to earth. It is a land where terrible giants roam the hills and it is a land where," he stopped and tweaked yet another girl's nose, "every girl is a princess."

The Ladies sighed. Sir Geoffrey rolled his eyes.

Loki turned to his glass and swirled his wine while dabbing at the corner of his mouth with his napkin.

"But I am more interested in this land," he said losing interest in Lady Guests. "This...this Isle of Avalon. It intrigues me. As a matter of fact, I plan on venturing out into it and learning more about it."

This caught Mark's attention. "We would be more than happy to provide a chaperone to show you around the island."

"I wouldn't dream of inconveniencing anybody. I can travel about myself, with my man Minion of course. You see, I wish to spend an evening or two underneath the stars and explore the out of the way places. I am an adventurer of the truest sort."

"It is no inconvenience, and I'm afraid that it is a matter of keep policy that all Guests be escorted by Avangarde when out of sight of the walls."

Loki chuckled. "Why really, Sir Mark, I am an adult and I can take care of myself." He touched the slim sword at his side.

"Believe me, Viscount, I mean no disrespect, but the keep rules apply to everyone. It would be difficult to explain to the Benefactors that I let one of their Guests fall afoul of some misfortune. It is for the best."

"Come now, it can't be that dangerous. Unless there is something to hide," Mark's eyes narrowed at the comment.

Loki changed his stance. "Perhaps you are right. I am the one being childish. I should follow the rules like everyone else. After all, I am a guest and should be a polite one. My apologies."

"None needed, Lord Loki," Mark said, saluting him with a drink.

#

Sir Jason McFowler swaggered into the kitchen, surveyed the treats arrayed on the preparation table as if surveying a kingdom, and began to reach for a tart as he walked by.

The Kitchen Madame, Rosa Maria, swooped in from another doorway and gave the would-be thief the eye. Jason, not even skipping a beat, withdrew his hand and bypassed the table whistling to himself and continued on his way.

His swagger turned into a saunter as he passed into the corridor and came across one of the maidservants bent over a basket of laundry. He approached, all smiles, grabbed the lass by the wrist, spun her around and reeled her back into his arms. The young girl squealed in surprise and McFowler grabbed her gently around the waist and dipped her in a dancing maneuver. The maidservant didn't seem to mind once she recognized her assailant.

Just the same, Jason twirled her away and gave her a slap on the behind before he moved on down the corridor where he came across his next victims. They too were maidservants, bent over their task. Which in this case happened to be picking through baskets of apples from the orchards. Jason tapped one on the shoulder, jumped to her opposite side, stole an apple while she was distracted and kissed her on the cheek when she turned in the opposite direction.

"Sir McFowler!" The maidservant Claire exclaimed. "You are worse than a child."

"If you are saying that I am young at heart, I gladly accept your compliment." Jason bowed. "And how are you lovely ladies on this lovely day?"

"If you are trying to make up for stealing apples, flattery will get you everywhere," said Anna, the other maidservant.

"We are fine, Sir Scoundrel, and you?" Claire replied.

Jason merrily ate his apple. "I'm bored, underpaid, surrounded by beautiful women whose virtues I am sworn to protect, and must be on my way to give a lesson in Gaelic song. That is how I am."

"My, aren't we the busy little bee. Well, go then, and teach your music before I spank you for being naughty. I'd hate to do that." Anna shooed him away.

"Spank me? I think I might rather like that."

"That's why I'd hate to do it."

McFowler laughed and skipped away to the auditorium.

#

When Jason entered the chapel, a previous class was just leaving. Many, probably all, of the youngest Greensprings Guests were scattering like a flock of birds to go play now that lessons were done. Several stopped by McFowler to say hello and hug his legs.

"Why Sir McFowler, what a pleasant surprise. What brings you here?"

Jason turned to be confronted by the Mother Superior and her entourage of young nuns. He surmised that it had been they who administered the singing lessons.

"Would you believe me if I said I came to be in your charming presence?" he offered. Mother Superior's icy blank stare told him that she would not. The woman never smiled.

"No, hardly," she said. "But I would be delighted to direct you to a confessional, should that be the reason for your visit."

Jason's grin widened. "I wager you would," he whispered under his breath, and then said quickly, "Mother Superior you know that you would be the first person that I would come to *if* I had any sins of major consequences to confess."

"Ha!" she exclaimed with a straight face. "I wasn't born yesterday—"Jason fought hard to suppress a comment. "—and your roguish behavior hasn't gone unnoticed. If only I knew the extent of it."

Jason looked to the nuns. "If only you knew." The nuns snickered and blushed behind Mother Superior's back. Jason placed his hands together and said, "Actually, seriously, I am here to teach lyrics of Gaelic song to the Lady Katherina. She is a remarkable musician and was very much taken by my bagpipe playing and wished to know if there were any words that accompanied the music. I told her that there were, but I never sang them because I can only carry the tune of a bulrush in rut." He winked at the Mother Superior.

"And?" She said, refusing to let Jason's antics perturb her.

"...and she said she wished to learn them. So I offered to teach them."

"That was mighty kind of you. And I suppose it will be just the two of you, all alone in here?"

Jason feigned shock. "Why Mother Superior, I am just aghast at what you might be suggesting."

"But I am right in assuming it will be just the two of you?" she said, eyes narrowing.

"No, no, not at all. Ah, Sir Gawain!" Jason's face brightened with relief. The other knight, who seemed to be in the process of passing through the chamber, furrowed his brow at the sound of his name.

"Yes?" he said.

Mother Superior seemed incredulous. "And just how is he supposed to help you?"

Patrick had approached after being addressed, and was now encircled by Jason's one-armed embrace. "He also speaks Gaelic."

The nun glared. "I thought Irish Gaelic and Scottish Gaelic were different?"

Jason shrugged. "Details, details."

"So, you're going to help McFowler, Gawain?"

Patrick had been standing with a blank look on his face. "Actually, I was just passing thr...ouch!"

Jason pulled on his ear. "What a funny one this one is!"

"Yes, help! I'm going to help!" Patrick cupped his ear tenderly.

Mother Superior was silent as she stared at the nervous looking pair of knights. "Hmph!" she said, with what might have been the slightest hint of a smile, and departed with her nuns.

Once gone, Jason relaxed as if dropping a weight from his shoulders. He wiped his brow. "Lucky thing that you came by when you did."

"What am I supposed to be doing?" Patrick asked.

"I'm teaching lyrics to the Lady Katherina, and for a moment I thought the Mother Superior was going to insist on staying."

"Ah, I see..." Patrick smiled.

"No, you fool. Seriously, I'm teaching lyrics and that's all. My music has words to it, and for once I would like to do it justice by having it heard by a voice that conveys the true meaning of it. Surely you must understand, coming from Eire. The ballads are similar, right?"

The Irishman nodded. He wasn't sure if he entirely believed it, but he would give Jason the benefit of a doubt. Why else would he play his pipes at all hours of the day?

"Ah, and here she is," Jason said. "Sir Gawain, the Lady Katherina of, of...how do you say it again?"

The girl was approximately the same age as the Lady Christianne Morneau. She was slight of build and stature with dove colored skin. Her hair shined like platinum tied in plaits that ran down her back, though rogue bangs hung in her eyes. Her most striking feature was her eyes. They reminded Patrick of clear ice and were almost ghostlike in their infinite depth. Patrick had seen her many times, but she remained one of the few Guests that he had not been introduced to.

She smiled at McFowler and said a strange sounding word that Patrick did not catch. Jason tried to repeat it but found himself at a loss to do so.

"I'm sorry," Jason said shrugging. "I can't pronounce her homeland."

Patrick smiled and held out his hand. "That's quite all right, I probably couldn't either." She placed her hand in Patrick's, and he kissed it gently.

"Lady Katherina, this is Sir Patrick Gawain, of Eire."

She returned the smile. "Pleased to meet you, Sir Gawain." Her accent was odd and heavy. "I heard that only barbarians came from Eire," she said to the Irishman. McFowler laughed. Patrick maintained his smile, though he was a little peeved at the comment. "No, not really. At least you have heard of my country, I haven't heard of yours at all." He slapped her lightly on the shoulder as if she were a boy. This action surprised her, and didn't seem to please her too much. Patrick's smile turned to one of mischief; he derived a certain pleasure from angering the girl. It was the least he could do after being essentially called a barbarian. "I will let you two get to work, good day, and nice meeting you Lady Katherina."

As Patrick headed for the exit, McFowler thought of something else and rushed after him. "Patrick, old pal, could you possibly do me another favor?"

Patrick rolled his eyes. "Sure. But you owe me, Highlander."

Jason grinned. "It's simple. Sir Corbin and I were to escort the Viscount Loki around the Isle. Would you be so kind as to take my place?"

"Certainly, but like I said, you owe me one."

"But of course! All the beer you can drink!"

#

The following morning Patrick sat idly on Siegfried, waiting next to Corbin and his horse. The day was misty yet bright as the rising sun turned the vapor in the air pearlescent. Patrick and Corbin had originally tried talking Loki out of his scheduled tour of the isle, since there wasn't much to see in the fog, but the Viscount had insisted. Now, though the landscape was veiled, the sun sent wonderful rays through the trees and undergrowth. Patrick also mused about Mark's consent to the nobleman's unprecedented request for an adventure.

A lone duck squawked as it flew over, headed inland.

Patrick stretched his lengthy arms to full span and yawned loudly.

"Didn't sleep much last night?" Sir Corbin asked, between bites of a carrot.

Patrick grunted, "Of course not. Not with Willy playing those damned pipes to all hours."

"I thought you liked those damned pipes."

"In Willy's hands they sound like a dying cow—say, where did you get that carrot?"

Corbin grinned. "From your saddlebag."

"It must be one of the carrots that Siegfried spit out after I gave it to him," Patrick said, straight faced. "I can't figure it out, some days he can't get enough of them, others he acts as if he couldn't care for another." Corbin spat out the vegetable and wiped his tongue with his hand.

"What do you suppose he is looking at?" Patrick shaded his eyes and studied Loki and his valet. The Viscount stood on the shore of a lake, gazing at a mass of rocks that formed an island of sorts in the middle. His valet, Minion, seemed just as curious. It wasn't much of a lake really, but still bigger than a pond.

"Beats me," Sir Corbin, and spat one more time. "If it were a nicer day, I would say he was looking at the scenery, but with all this mist—you can't even see the bushes, let alone the lake."

A carpet of mist rolled in, obscuring their charges. Although visible, their forms became elongated and warped. Their voices too were distorted, bouncing around the register of sound and made unintelligible. Corbin and Patrick made no moves, as the Guests seemed in no danger and it was certain the mist would soon part again.

"Ah, that's better," Loki said as he gestured with his left hand. The mist seemed to gather ever thicker with each wave of his hand. "We can't have people listening in on *everything* I do."

Minion scratched his head as he looked back and forth between Loki and the mounted knights. The Viscount began to pace back and forth along the lakeshore. He alternated between pacing with his head down and hands on hips, as if deeply pondering something and pausing to gaze out into the center of the lake at the stones. He became increasingly agitated. Minion followed his every footstep.

"What is it, Master?" Minion's odd voice was especially annoying at this particular moment. Loki stopped suddenly and grabbed the little man by his garments.

"I know this is the place!" He hissed. Minion's eyes were the size of wagon wheels. "The textbooks, the legends, even the winds blew in this direction. But where the hell is it!" Loki dropped Minion and continued to pace, running hands through his hair.

Finally he stopped and gazed at the rocks in the lake. "Maybe..." he whispered. He stood up straight as an arrow, tilted his head back and closed his eyes. He took in a deep breath, and began to hum.

"Master?" Minion said timidly.

Loki said from the side of his mouth, "Minion, assume the position."

"Yes, Master." Minion removed his cap and bowed his head and Loki quickly slapped it, eyes still shut.

"Bad Minion. Now be a good fellow and don't disturb me."

"Yes, Master, bad Minion."

The Viscount began to hum again. This time, uninterrupted, the hum evolved into more complex noises that originated in his sternum, forming into a song of sorts. He concentrated on this effort for some time, becoming lost to his environment, forgetting the presence of his valet.

After a moment, he exhaled long through his nostrils, lowered his head, opened his eyes and once again looked out into the lake.

"Ah, yes. That's a little better," he purred. He now saw the rocks as part of a structure, and there even appeared to be more of them. It seemed truly to be an island in the lake now. And if he squinted hard enough, he could almost perceive ivy-covered walls, windows and other structures. But then he blinked and it was all gone. Before him now was only a pile of stones protruding out of a shallow lake. "Not exactly what I had in mind, but better."

Loki was now smiling, ugly ear to ugly ear. He gathered Minion up in an embrace and kissed his head. From a distance, it was an odd little show.

"He certainly is an unusual fellow," Corbin commented. Patrick grunted, but said nothing because Loki and Minion were hurrying away from the shore toward the trail.

"Let us go gentlemen, I've seen enough for today!" Loki exclaimed, walking back to his carriage. Minion was climbing up to the driver's seat.

"But Viscount, there is plenty of daylight left..."

"No, no. This is plenty for the day," Loki stepped into his carriage. "I so wish that there were maps and literature and such that I could read about this fabulous island. That way I could plan my outings in advance..."

"Oh, but there is, Lord Loki," Patrick pointed out.

Loki seemed incredibly interested. "You don't say? And where might I find such tidbits?"

"In the keep library, of course."

#

Sir Corbin parried, jumped back, and made his own attack. He made several blows with his sword to Bisch's one. Bisch grunted and stepped out for a wide-arcing swing. Corbin anticipated the blow and held off, even though it rang in his bones.

"Damn, Eirech," Corbin grunted, though a smile managed to escape his lips. He recovered and brought his sword up, intertwined the guard with Bisch's, and twisted violently. Bisch's sword was ripped from his meaty hands.

The assembled knights cheered and congratulated Corbin. Bisch laughed and exclaimed "Good! Good!" and slapped Sir Corbin on the back so hard the smaller man staggered forward a step.

From beyond the crowd of gathered men came a slow repetitious clap. The Avangardesmen turned in the direction to see the Viscount Loki sitting casually on a wall, putting hand to hand. He smiled and raised his eyebrows, then removed the book he had underneath his arm and began to read.

Sir Corbin, who had been struck silent as had everyone else, stepped forward. "Did you have something to comment on perhaps, Lord Loki?"

Loki looked up from his book as if just realizing he was being addressed. "No, not really."

Corbin smirked, and turned to take his place on the bench.

"...except that it seems to me that you boys would have better things to do."

Sir Corbin turned suddenly and gestured with his sword. "You don't approve of our leisure and exercise. Is reading books more admirable?"

"That's all relative to the individual," he shrugged. "I suppose we exert ourselves where our abilities lie."

The Englishman's face gained a little color. "I see you fancy yourself a swordsman," he said, gesturing at the weapon hanging from the Viscount's belt. "Would you care to join me in an exercise to see whether you find sword play or reading more to your liking...as an 'individual'?"

Loki pondered the invitation. He then said, "Why, that would be splendid. This particular tome is rather dull and not quite what I was expecting in any case. I could use a diversion." Loki jumped from the wall and removed his dark cape to reveal a clean white shirt and black vest. His cape he threw over the wall next to the book and he strolled over to the circle of men. Cheers and catcalls went up from the Avangarde.

Sir McFowler leaned over from the crowd, squeezed Loki's thin upper arm, and shouted, "Careful Corby, go easy on the old fellow, he is a Guest after all."

Loki brushed the place on his arm where Jason's hand had rested. Then he pulled free his sword and took a defensive stance. Sir Corbin circled him; a moment later, he made the first attack by lunging with blade straight. Loki struck the opposing blade with a clang. Corbin used the momentum gained from the counter blow and spun around and bore down on the Viscount.

Loki countered, then the next blow, and then the next. Corbin attacked in a flurry but all was deflected. His face was bright red, and perspiration slicked his brow. Loki seemed relaxed and calm.

Finally, Loki took the offensive. His blade was a silvery blur and Corbin was backing up and clumsily holding his sword in both gloved hands. Corbin attempted a counter blow, but he lost his balance and turned his back to his opponent. In that brief moment Loki poked the knight in the buttocks with the point of his sword. The Avangarde laughed and Sir Corbin's face flushed to purple.

The Englishman raged forward and took a wild swing at the Viscount, missed, and his sword was violently knocked away by a flash of gleaming blade.

Loki lowered his blade to Corbin's throat. The two men stood squared, Corbin's chest heaving. Loki didn't appear to be removing his blade anytime soon and Corbin didn't appear to be lowering his defiant gaze. A hush fell on the Avangarde.

There was a flash of movement and a clang, and Loki's sword was knocked from Sir Corbin's throat. Sir McFowler stood between Loki and Corbin, claymore drawn. "Well done, Lord Loki. Would you care to go at it again? With *moi*, perhaps?"

Loki grinned. "I'd be delighted."

Without further preamble, the two exchanged blows in such a manner Corbin barely had time to back pedal out of their way. McFowler gripped his great weapon at both ends of the hilt for better leverage and whirled the weapon in wide, fast circles. Loki dodged and parried. Though the Viscount was swift, he could not match McFowler's reach and strength, and the burly Highlander wore Loki down quickly. It was just a few minutes before his weapon was wrenched from his grasp. It was now Loki who stood with a point at his throat.

He pulled the collar from his neck and grinned sheepishly. "Well, it seems I stand humbled. I salute you, Sir McFowler. And you too Sir Corbin: I agree that swordplay is much more exciting than reading."

McFowler lowered his claymore and shook hands with the Viscount. The Avangarde gathered around to pat all swordsmen on the back and they mobbed Loki, requesting that he show them some of his maneuvers.

#

Loki stormed into the stables and kicked over a bucket full of water; the closest thing he could find. He threw his cape down and commenced to kick everything in sight. After a moment, he calmed himself by stopping, closing his eyes and taking several deep breaths.

"Boy!" He called. The stable hand came running. "Go fetch my man Minion, tell him to meet me in our chamber, because I know he is not there; no doubt trying to poke around some woman's dress. And if you delay, I will find you and beat the skin off your back!" The stable hand scurried off.

Loki went to a bucket that had escaped his wrath and put his head into it. He pulled it out, and whipped the dark, heavy strands of hair from his eyes.

Damn those goody-goody knights, he thought. Who do they think they are? Wait until they meet the real me! His ears still burned from the humiliation.

Several stalls down, his carriage-horses became agitated. They reared their heads, snorted and pawed at the ground. His ears perked up like a rabbit's at this development. Somebody had entered the stables to disturb the beasts. He silently stalked along the stalls in the shadows and watched the newcomer.

A maidservant, a buxom blonde with green eyes, carried in her pulled-up apron a load of carrots; which she almost dropped when the carriage horses startled her. She stood with wide eyes against the wall as the horses wildly kicked and cried in their stalls. She made several attempts to move by the fiery eyed creatures, but fell back against the wall each time.

189

"They won't hurt you," Loki said, coming out of the shadows. The maidservant cried out in surprise. "And neither will I." Loki gestured slightly with one hand and the horses were suddenly calm. "You see. Harmless. Come, touch them if you like." Loki approached his horses and stroked their muzzles. The maidservant smiled meekly and shook her head. The Viscount approached her and offered his hand. She took it timidly, and when she did, he escorted her by the dark animals. "There you go, now that wasn't so bad, now was it? I'm Loki. And you?"

"Aimeé de la Chasse, my lord."

"Do they have you working doubly so, as maidservant and stable hand?"

Aimeé smiled and shook her head. "No, I just come here after my duties and do a favor for a friend."

"What might that be?"

"I feed his horse carrots."

Loki smiled. "Why that is admirable of a friend. Your friend must appreciate it very much."

Aimeé looked abashed. "Actually, he doesn't know that I do it."

Loki looked puzzled. "Then why do you do it? Wait, don't tell me," he paused, thoughtfully tugging at his goatee "You are soft on this particular friend and he is a nobleman, and you are afraid of what he, or others for that matter, might think, correct? Don't be shy, you can tell me. I won't tell." Loki placed a finger to his lips.

"Yes," Aimeé said shyly.

Loki bent forward, looked around as if there might be listeners, and whispered. "May I ask who it is? I might be of assistance someday."

Aimeé smiled coyly and dug her slipper into the straw. "I don't know..."

"Oh come now, I just rescued you from yonder fierce beasts." Loki stroked her cheek.

"Sir Gawain," she said at last.

The Viscount feigned surprise. "The Irishman! Well, If the opportunity ever arises, I will certainly steer him in your direction. A lovely young lass like yourself is certainly deserving of such a catch."

Aimeé smirked as if Loki's melodramatic tone suddenly became too much. "I must be going. Thank you Lord Loki." She skipped off to feed Siegfried.

The Viscount watched her leave. He stored the information he had just learned for future possible use, and went to meet Minion.

#

He found the ugly little man waiting inside their chamber. Loki stormed in and commenced to beat Minion with his wadded up cape.

"Master, why are you angry?" Minion said, cowering.

Loki laughed. "I'm not angry, fool! If I was angry I would have placed a rock inside the cape, and then beat you with it!" He pummeled Minion a few more times and then handed him the cape along with his shirt and vest. "Wash these, they are soiled." He sighed deeply. He always felt better after beating Minion.

The Viscount went to the window, opened the wooden shutters and gazed upon the scene below his window; a servant pushing a wheel barrow, two Lady Guests sitting on a bench deep in gossip, and the many knights leaving the practice field.

"Soon, Minion, I will not have to pretend any longer. I will find that which I seek and all will be like the days of old. I will be my former self, as powerful as I was before The Deluge. And these—these *people* will bow before me as of old." Loki spied the knight McFowler crossing his view below. The Viscount put up his thumb and forefinger and caught the sight of Jason between them. He squeezed his fingers together repeatedly as if crushing the Highlander between the digits.

"Ooh, ouch, it hurts, stop it..." Loki squeaked.

"What's left for us to do, Master?" Minion piped.

Loki finished his virtual attack on the Scotsman. "First, we must find alternate means of coming and going from this fortress. It just won't do constantly begging permission to leave." He paused, smiling. "Next, and more importantly, I need to pay a little visit to the librarian to find valuable information. The discovery at the lake the other day shows that we are on the right track, but we must be certain."

Minion rubbed his hands together impishly.

#

Patrick sat motionless while Father Benis wrapped a measuring tape around his head. "You really think you can discern anything about me by doing this?" he asked, head still, eyes up.

Father Benis removed the strip from Patrick's head, pursed his lips and read the graduations.

He hmm'ed and jotted a note on a piece of paper. He then consulted a very large tome resting open on the table. Patrick's skepticism grew.

"My origins, my relations to other peoples? You said that you may be able to tell me what sort of people I come from by looking at the size and shape of my head. Is that true?"

Benis perused the pages and chewed on his thumbnail. "Perhaps."

Patrick leaned over and examined the book that held Benis' attention. It was a monstrously huge instance of leather bound workmanship, reinforced by what looked like copper or brass strips and studs. The pages were covered in Latin characters, though in an unfamiliar calligraphy. Instead of the usual flowery script, the characters were rigid and pointy. What little he could understand of it had to do with the Roman conquest of Germania hundreds of years ago. A charcoal image on the page depicted a heavily bearded man with a stern appearance.

"Looks nothing like me," Patrick smiled.

The priest also smiled. "No, but it does look a good bit like our own resident Teutons, Wolfgang von Fiescher and Eirech Bischoff."

"Then why are you consulting this?"

"Because," Benis said, turning the page of the book. "Julius Caesar was a meticulous note-taker and often commented on the similarities and differences of the cultures he fought—which was virtually all of them. That, and their histories, culture, religions, et cetera. 'Know thy enemy,' I suppose."

Benis plucked from the table an instrument composed of two metal sticks held together at their ends. This he manipulated such that they moved on a hinge where they joined, spreading the sticks further apart. The hinge was an arc of metal with many slashes and some writing on it. Patrick had seen such devices used by generals in their campaign tents. At first he couldn't fathom what the priest was going to do with such a thing with regard to his head, but Benis held an arm of the instrument to each of his temples, noted the position of the central arc, and then performed the same procedure on his cheekbones.

While Benis wrote some more notes on his paper, Patrick gestured at the book. "This was written by Julius Caesar?"

"Not exactly," Benis moved back to the open book and placed the metal instrument on another charcoal image. "It is a copy of the works of the Caesar, as well as the Roman historian Tacitus and some works of unnamed authors. It is a fascinating piece. I know not of any other such work outside of Avalon. Its craftsmanship almost rivals that of the Book of Columba at the

Abbey of Kells in your own Eire. So I've heard." He recorded a line of numbers. "So tell me more of this vision you experienced in the den of the wolf. What did this maiden look like? Are you certain she said you were like her?"

"I'm not certain of anything anymore. I'm not sure if it even happened. I don't remember how I got there, and I certainly don't remember how I returned. The last thing I remember was that I was hopelessly lost."

"But her appearance?"

Patrick shrugged, hands held out open. "Beautiful, full of light...?"

Benis smiled. "I suppose if one asked Mary and the Magdalene to describe the appearance of the man they met at the open tomb of Christ, they too would be hard pressed to recall."

"Are you saying this woman was an angel?"

Father Benis placed a gentle hand on Patrick's shoulder and gazed upon him with his warm grey eyes. "If anybody asks, especially Father Hugh, that is the story I would stick with. The official Church stance on the sightings here on Avalon is that they are demons. Father Hugh is not particularly fond of the practice by the locals of putting out saucers of milk at night to appease the Fair Folk."

"But you're a priest of the Church."

"I hope I've been a priest and on Avalon long enough to know the difference between good, evil, and indifferent creatures. Mostly so, anyway. And it seems to me the majority of the fantastical sightings, such as the Huntsman, are harmless ghosts. Or the poor lost children of God. Even more lost than we humans, but not necessarily any more good or evil. I hear from the villagers that for every prank played on them by a mischievous fey, a lost object turns up or a wayward child brought home safely." Benis shrugged.

"So the Fair Folk are like us; some good, some bad."

"Precisely."

"So, is that true also of the giants you spoke of earlier? Or the god-beings?"

"I would imagine, though I can't think of too many instances where the character in question was 'good,'" Benis replied. "More often than not they are depicted as hostile, as with Goliath. Even the 'gods' appear petty and cruel, using their powers to exploit mankind rather than aid them. Which is strange, really, because you'd think that immortal creatures would be full of wisdom after long years of living." Benis sighed and turned several pages of the tome. "I guess I shouldn't be surprised. Even the long-lived patriarchs of the Bible often displayed less-than-perfect behavior."

"Like Moses," Patrick said. "Not being allowed to enter the Promised Land because of his transgressions."

Benis smiled. "Very good. I see somebody wasn't entirely asleep during Mass. Noah is a good example as well; becoming drunk on wine and passing out naked in front of his family."

"That was a common occurrence in my household," Patrick said, and they laughed. "But not all mighty men of legend were wicked," he added. "Finn McCool was a hero, a protector of his people who fought Buganes."

The priest raised his eyebrows. "Who? Against what?"

Patrick smiled. "Finn McCool, legendary warrior of Eire, leader of the Fianna, mighty warriors all. It was said they too were giants."

"And these 'Buganes?'"

"They definitely were giants, ogres rather. Covered in hair and sharp teeth."

"Hmph, sounds fascinating."

Patrick leaned over and regarded the book's pages. "Does the slope of my skull, or whatever, give you any thoughts about what the maiden might have meant?"

"I'm afraid not," Benis said. "My theory of comparing what I know of your country folk, and the pictures associated with the legends of these historical writings, has yielded very little. It certainly would be nice if I could convince McFowler and McCabe to submit to the same procedure—then I could at least start building a catalog of Gaelic folk such as yourself. But they seem awfully superstitious and wary of my intentions."

Patrick laughed. "They're probably afraid you will try to make them wash and comb their hair as part of the process."

Benis turned another page or two. "So, Sir Gawain, is there anything else I can help you with? Are you having visions of anything else?" Something in Patrick's face must have caught the priest's attention, for he raised an eyebrow. "Is there something you wish to tell me?"

"No, not really," Patrick responded too quickly.

Benis made a face as if Patrick were a child who had just told a fib. "Come now, Sir Knight, if I can take your confessions in confidence as a priest, I can hear whatever else may be going on in that sloped skull of yours. Besides, what could be more shocking than the tale of the maiden in the wolf's den?"

Patrick smiled sheepishly. "Oh, you'd be surprised."

Father Benis smiled warmly. "So surprise me."

So, in so many words, Patrick told Father Benis about the Apparition—when it first appeared, and how it hounded him. He felt his face heat as he did so. The priest listened thoughtfully, and took a seat at the table. He was silent for a while.

"And you say this has been going on since before you came to Avalon?"

Patrick nodded.

"My first thought would be that it is a demon or evil spirit. It has not harmed you? Said anything? Done anything?"

Patrick shook his head. "Only follows, points at me, and shows up at the most inconvenient of times." Benis was deep in thought, and rubbed his jaw. Patrick had visions of being cast out of the Avangarde for having hid such visions. "What am I to do?" he said finally.

"It doesn't sound like any demon I've heard of, or portent or omen for that matter," the priest responded. "And since it hasn't harmed you or anyone else, I don't think any immediate action is necessary—but if it gives any indication of true harm, something must be done."

"What might that be?"

Benis took a deep breath. "Exorcism."

Patrick leaned over and placed his head in his hands, elbows on knees. He said through his hands, "And, I'm sure that will mean letting Father Hugh and Sir Mark know."

"Yes," Father Benis said. "I understand your concern—that they might think you are a liability to the safety of the Guests. I don't think that you are. As you have pointed out, the thing has done no harm. Perhaps with a lot of prayer, it will go away on its own. No need for extraordinary measures that will involve others."

Patrick sat back in his chair and leaned on his elbow on the table. "Prayer," he said distantly, chewing his thumbnail. "God and I haven't spoken much lately."

"Perhaps it's time again." Father Benis fixed sympathetic eyes on the Irishman.

A snapping noise indicated that a piece of thumbnail had come off in Patrick's mouth. "I was hoping God would have revealed some mysteries to me by now, not thrown more at me."

"Nothing will be revealed if you don't talk about it." A silence hung between them. "Give it some thought," Benis finally said. "And if this apparition proves dangerous, let me know immediately. For your sake, we will have to approach Father Hugh. In the meantime, your secret is safe with me."

"Thank you, Father."

The sound of approaching footsteps drew their attention away from their table. The Viscount Loki approached, cloaked in his dark cape, framed by the outer hallway's darkness as he passed through the doorway. The shadows, his dark cape, his black hair, made it seem as if a pale face were floating towards them. This illusion vanished as the nobleman stepped into the pool of candlelight surrounding their table.

"Good evening." Loki greeted, baring perfectly straight teeth. Like the rest of the man's features, they seemed a bit sharp and elongated.

Sir Gawain and Father Benis returned the greeting.

"Are you, perchance, the keep librarian?" Loki addressed the robed priest.

"I am," Benis replied, bowing slightly. "At your service."

"Excellent. I was told by...well, by this fine gentleman here," Loki reacted as if he had just noticed that Patrick was present, "that I could find documents, writings and such about the Isle of Avalon here."

Benis smiled. "Why yes, just over there on that shelf is a lovely copy of The Creed of Greensprings, some records of commerce with the village, journals of keep affairs since the time Wolfgang von Fiescher has been Grand Master, and some drawings of the keep itself, which look to me rather like construction plans..."

Loki waved off these descriptions. "I was thinking more along the lines of maps, descriptions of locations, even local stories."

Allowing the two to discuss library business, Patrick turned his attention to the book he and Father Benis had been studying.

"No, no we don't have much in the way of that sort of thing. You're more than welcome to..." the priest was saying, but was distracted when Loki abruptly reached over and snagged one corner of the book and dragged it to his side of the table.

"What do we have here?" he said, turning the pages of the book, oblivious to Patrick's indignant stare and Benis' shock.

"That's a work of historical matters outside of Avalon," Benis said.

"And not at all what you are looking for," Patrick added, snagging the book back. When he did their eyes met. The oily depths of Loki's gaze announced his resentment of the act. He held Patrick in his stare—it was as if a shutter on a lamp had opened, and rather than let light out, it radiated a cold ray of extreme discomfort. A barely perceptible sneer formed on his mouth. Patrick's cheeks flushed, and he dropped his gaze back to the book, feeling foolish for being upset at losing a juvenile test of wills.

No sooner had he done so than Loki was again all smiles and cheerfulness, addressing Father Benis. "Construction plans you say?"

"Yes."

"Well, I suppose I can entertain myself with those for a while. Thank you, Father, and good evening."

With that, in a brisk flash of black and lavender lined cape, Loki headed for the shelves pointed out by the priest. His walking stick clicked on the flagstones.

"What a disagreeable fellow," Father Benis mumbled.

"He gives me an uneasy feeling every time he comes around, too."

"Oh, I'm sure you are just intimidated by his overbearing personality, as I am."

"No, more than that," Patrick insisted, sounding slightly offended, or perhaps embarrassed, at having his discomfort openly pointed out. "When he is around, it makes my skin literally crawl. It feels like..." He struggled for descriptive words. "Like the room is out of sorts when he is in it."

Father Benis raised is eyebrows. "I'm not sure what to make of that. But I do know we should endeavor to do as Jesus suggested: love our neighbors, as we do ourselves."

#

"Now my darling," Loki said sweetly to the young female Guest. Her name was Beatrice, or some such. She was the sort of girl who talked about inane things, but she was nice to look at. "Hold the stick thusly..." He maneuvered behind the girl, reached his arms around her, and gently pushed up on her elbows so that her outstretched arms rose a little. He took his time in doing so, allowing his arms to rub against her sides and to inhale her sweet smell. He leaned in closer and put his mouth close to her ear and whispered softly, "Keep it just like that." He slid away from her.

The girl stood smiling, back straight, arms held out. She held in her hands a tree branch that had been stripped of leaves and bark. It forked in two, forming a Y. Each dainty hand held a fork as if they were handles. The pointing end drooped towards the earth, weighed down by a string and bronze weight.

Loki approached three other Lady Guests, who were standing by watching the proceedings, whose chatter sounded like the clucking of hens. Loki retrieved a handkerchief from one of them and returned to the girl with the stick and bob. He stood behind her and placed the cloth across her eyes, fixing it neatly behind her head.

"Let's see if you fare better than your companions." He took a step away from her. "And remember, the whole time you must picture in your mind the hidden object. Focus in the idea of something *hidden*."

Minion stood next to Loki, frowning. "Master, I don't understand why we're going through the trouble of having the ladies do this. We could do a much quicker and more accurate job ourselves."

Loki smiled. "Subterfuge, my dear Minion, subterfuge. We would look suspicious carrying out this activity, especially here." Loki gestured around with only his chin. They stood on the cobblestones of the main courtyard just inside the gate, near the fountain. Many people were going about their business. Some, like the guards on the wall, occasionally stopped to watch the peculiar goings-on. The girl with the stick walked blindfolded, arms held out almost like a sleepwalker. "With the young ladies involved, it's just an innocent game. Nobody would ever suspect we're searching for a secret door. The library has yet to yield anything of my true goal, but the construction plans gave mention to a secret door near here. Most useful!"

"Uh-oh," Minion said, looking behind them. Loki turned to see what had attracted Minion's attention. Coming toward them, walking at a leisurely pace with a diplomatic smile, was Father Hugh Constant and a retinue of acolytes trailing behind him.

"Hmph," Loki sniffed. "The God-squad approach-eth."

As he neared, Father Hugh took in the scene. "Good morning, Viscount," he said congenially, bowing.

"And to you, Father, and what a lovely morning it is."

"Yes, lovely enough to be giving lessons out o' doors. And what kind of lessons might you be giving?"

"Oh, I wouldn't call them lessons, really." Loki's smile was just as congenial and diplomatic as the priest's. He made a sweeping gesture over the gathered Ladies and their comrade who had just poked an innocent by-stander in the eye with her stick without knowing it. "More like fun and games."

"I believe it's called 'dowsing,' a technique used for finding lost or hidden objects or something generally desired to be found. Superstitious villagers, for instance, use it for finding water on their property in order to dig a well."

"Right you are!" Loki exclaimed. "Why, Father, I had no idea you were so learned a man on such a variety of topics."

"Well, yes, but unfortunately this particular practice is viewed by the Church as more akin to witchcraft than fun and games," Hugh said, his smile dissolving and his tone taking on the quality of one delivering bad news. "And since this is a Church-sanctioned establishment, I am going to have to ask you to find another game."

Loki's mouth dropped and his eyes widened. "Witchcraft? Nonsense—we were simply playing a game of find the hidden brooch, not casting spells or fashioning charms."

Hugh raised a hand to calm Loki's escalating voice. "No doubt your intentions are well-meant, but yes, if a divining process other than imploring the Almighty or requesting the intercession of one of His angels or saints is employed, then the Church must call it suspect."

"Look!" one of the Ladies cried. "She's heading straight to where I went."

"As I did, but neither of us found the brooch there," said another girl. "There must be a stone or something we did not look under."

Loki looked at the blindfolded girl. She was tentatively walking towards the fountain where it connected to the keep wall. His expression brightened and he turned back to the assembled men of the cloth. "Well, we can't be offending the Lord, now can we?" He turned and clapped his hands. "That's enough ladies; let's call it a day, shall we?"

The young lady with the dowsing rod pulled off her blindfold. "But Lord Loki, I really felt I was on to something," she said with a pouty expression.

"If we couldn't find it, then neither would have you, Beatrice," one of the observing Ladies called out. She turned to Loki. "So where is it?"

Loki fished around in his pocket, eyes widening in mock surprise, then pulled out a shiny object. "Why, here it is!"

The girls simultaneously moaned in protest at the sight of the bronze brooch. Their clucking rose to new levels as they complained about the fairness of the location of the "hidden" object. "Now Ladies," he said, voice smooth and calming. "I never said where I hid it. Besides, I'll show you another game tonight at dinner which is much more fun. It only requires three nut shells, a pea, and some of your money." He turned to Father Hugh and winked. "That's not the work of the Devil, is it?"

Father Hugh gave the slightest of sighs with a hint of a smile, or perhaps a smirk. Just the same, he shook his head and left with his retinue, their shaved pates glinting in the sun as they walked away.

"Now what, Master?" Minion squeaked at Loki's side. He had gathered the dowsing rod and bob from the girl, and returned the handkerchief to its owner.

Loki turned in the direction of the fountain. "I'm certain we've pinpointed the location of the secret door. It is up to you to figure out how to open it."

"Me?" Minion said.

Loki pinched the little man's cheek and shook it. "Of course you. I have a date with three young ladies."

#

That evening, when most everyone was at supper, Minion strode out into the cobblestone courtyard. He carried a bucket, which he swung lazily to-and-fro by its hemp handle. He whistled as he walked.

He noted the night watchman on the wall and waved a greeting. The watchman returned the gesture and continued on his patrol. Minion knew that the man would walk the length of the wall before turning around and coming back. The same was true of his colleague on the other side of the gate, walking in the opposite direction. Minion knew from long observation that it would be approximately fifteen minutes before they came this way again. If his task took longer than that, then his apparent water-fetching errand would turn into a garment-cleaning errand. All of this was a mere precaution, as the guards probably wouldn't pay him any heed. Their attention would be focused on the other side of the wall. After all, danger was supposed to come from outside.

Minion placed the bucket on the side of the fountain and quickly moved to the corner where it and the wall came together; where the bob on the dowsing rod had leaned multiple times. He began testing stones by pushing on them, then rapped on them with his knuckles and listened for hollowness. He found nothing. He leaped up and down, whacking several higher stones. After a short while of this exercise, he smartened up and retrieved the bucket. This he turned over, stood on it, and recommenced his search. But again he found nothing. He cursed as he heard the sound of the guard's spear clicking on the stones above as the watchman returned. Minion brought the bucket back to the fountain and took off his cloak. He laid it on the edge of the fountain and made scrubbing motions over it while whistling.

Some time passed, and Minion couldn't help but notice that the guards were taking their sweet time in resuming their patrol. His mouth grew dry from whistling and he tired of scrubbing. He wound up the garment length-wise and pretended to wring water from it. After a period, he ventured a glance up to see the position of the guards and cursed again when he saw that they were chatting not far from him.

Minion rolled his eyes and bobbed his head from side to side in rhythm with his whistling, which was becoming more and more strained. He unrolled his cloak and began waving it in the air as if drying it. He sneaked another peak at the guards and was pleased to see them move on. And then his cloak escaped his grasp and fell in the water, getting wet for real. He cursed his luck, and was reaching to retrieve the article of clothing when he noticed that it was floating towards the edge of the fountain. So were the bubbles, leaves, twigs and other objects floating in the water, marking a faint current.

The cloak bunched up against the edge, and some of it was getting sucked under. It never occurred to him to consider where the water went after it gushed from the bearded fountainhead against the wall. Minion ran his hand under the edge of the fountain and found that the water was spilling into a gap.

Minion maneuvered towards the corner while keeping his hand in the drain slit. His arm had to stretch further the closer he got to the corner, as the gap widened from a hand's width to a shoulder's. At the corner, Minion was on his tiptoes and flattened out over the slab. Because he was, his ear was to the stone and he could hear a large amount of water plunging, as if over a waterfall. And more, the sound echoed, as if in a cave.

His heart leapt with excitement and he reached out with his other hand and joined his first on the stone lip above the slit. He huffed and puffed as he tugged on the stone, not sure what to expect, but then almost cried out when the slab tilted in his direction. His feet were now on the ground and he could pull even stronger, though he found it unnecessary. The slab tilted easily and came to rest perpendicular to the fountain edge.

Through some neat trick of engineering, the pivot slab was hinged to the adjoining stones by the contours of their rough surfaces. The opening was just big enough to allow one person down a shaft carved into the stone, and Minion could now see that the slit just underneath the lip of the fountain edge was really a shallow gutter running along most of the fountain edge, hidden just out of sight. Water flowed down it from left to right and gradually widened as it approached the shaft where it plunged down into darkness. Opposite the falling water were rough-hewn mason stones protruding from the shaft wall to form a ladder.

Without hesitation Minion jumped into the opening, grabbing at an indentation carved into the center of the underside of the pivot slab and pulled it closed behind him. As he closed the stone, he was certain that he had not been seen, and the noise of the bubbling fountain had obscured the sound of grinding stones.

He made his way down the dank, noisy passage until his feet touched firm ground. There he stood for several minutes to listen and let his eyes adjust to the dark. Judging by the echoing sound, he was in a relatively large chamber with a pool. The air smelled of mildew, and the walls were slick with slime.

At first, this was as far as he planned on going. But then he was surprised to see two dim shafts of light penetrating the dark from above him. Rather, they were more like lighter shades of dark compared to the rest of the stygian blackness. As he stared at them, he realized that they were coming from the eyeholes of the carved bearded figure on the fountain. Evidently the fountainhead was hollow, save for the mouth where the water bubbled, and behind the effigy was this hidden cavern. The moon cast just enough light through the eyes to make navigation possible. In daytime, the place was probably very well lit.

Two bulwarks of stone framed an exit. Between them the pool drained into a stream. Minion guessed that he was directly beneath the keep walls, and these man-made bulwarks were their roots.

He slowly made his way along the wall away from the ladder and paused beside the stream, next to the bulwarks. His eyes adjusted again. As he proceeded, he stumbled and fell many times—the floor of the cave was crooked and strewn with rocks. It wasn't long before the light began to increase and he could see an opening. When he finally reached it, it was very tall, but very narrow. Even his small frame had to turn sideways in order to exit. As he struggled out of the crack, he noticed immediately the smells of the outdoors—grass, trees, flowers. The damp and rocky earth gave way to dry terrain, then a clear night sky broke overhead, seeming as bright as day.

When he was free, he turned to look where he had just come from. It was barely a crack among many boulders, marked only by the stream gurgling from it. Minion looked up and recognized instantly where he was. Above, up a craggy cliff, were the keep walls. He was in the bottom of a waterless moat, over which the drawbridge was lowered. He could just make out the tiny head of one of the guards, bobbing along the wall as he patrolled.

#

Father Benis wiped dust off the shelf then replaced the book. He grabbed the book's neighbor and repeated the ritual. He did this for the better part of a complete row at eye level until the removal of a book caused him to step back and gasp.

"Greetings," said the face that peered through the empty slot where the book had been. Somebody was standing on the other side of the bookshelf.

"My apologies, I did not mean to startle you." Loki said.

After clutching his chest as one experiencing a heart attack, Benis regained his composure and smiled. "Oh, hello. Fine day we are having, are we not?"

"Quite," Loki smiled, all teeth.

"Can I help you?"

Loki tilted his head to one side as if thinking. He walked to a nearby carrel and ran a gloved hand over its surface. He looked over the dust he had accumulated on the glove, and blew it off. "Most likely you can." He was so long in making a reply that Father Benis had recommenced to place books back on the shelves, while looking over his shoulder, waiting for a response. "In my travels I have heard much about this Isle of Avalon. That was one of the many reasons for my coming here. Now that I am here, I wish to learn more. But my search of this library has turned up rather lacking in literature concerning this *Insula Sacre*. Are there, perhaps, tomes that I have overlooked or are not..." he made a flowing gesture that encompassed the library, "...readily available to the general public?"

The Librarian turned his back to the Viscount and placed the last of the books on the shelves. When he turned, he was wringing his hands and he laughed nervously. "I am afraid this is the entire collection here. There are a few books which concern a brief hist..."

"That's peculiar," Loki's face turned quizzical. "I've heard from one of the Avangarde, Gawain I believe, mentioned that there is a private collection locked up hereabouts."

The priest shifted uneasily, but maintained his smile. "Oh, those works. Well, as the good knight pointed out," there was a bit of irony in his voice when he said good knight. "Those works are private and at the Church's order remain under lock and key until it is decided what to do with them."

Loki tsked. "Surely a fellow scholar such as you can appreciate my innocent inquiries. I only wish to expand my knowledge. Certainly no harm could come of it." The Viscount nudged the little priest with his elbow and winked. "I am sure you have felt from time to time the twinge of curiosity."

The Librarian grinned. "Maybe, maybe, but Father Constant, and certainly Mother Superior, forbid it."

"How would they..."

"They would, trust me, and certainly have the perpetrator excommunicated."

Loki raised an eyebrow. "Well, I dare say I wouldn't want that. I'm not that curious!"

"There's a fellow," said Father Benis.

The Viscount folded his arms and stroked his dark glossy goatee. "And where would such items be kept underneath lock and key? The keep dungeon? Treasure room? Or maybe the tower?"

Father Benis laughed. "Why, in the treasure room with all the keys that go to all the chastity belts of all the maidens in the keep."

Loki guffawed. "With the keys...!" He couldn't finish the sentence, he was laughing so hard. He slapped the Librarian on the shoulder in a friendly manner. Benis returned the gesture. Loki bade the Librarian good day between wheezing breaths and staggered out of the keep Library.

When Loki had left, Father Benis stood wiping tears from his eyes for a moment, smiling. "The keys..." He shook his head bemusedly and once again started to put books on the shelves. He paused for a moment, looked back in the direction that the Viscount had taken, and moved to the back of the library. There, he tugged on the edge of a wooden shelf. It swung away from the wall like a door, and behind it was a metal cabinet with a large key hole. He removed his string of prayer beads and held forward the large metal crucifix dangling at the end. He placed the end of this into the key hole and turned. The cabinet door swung open to reveal scores of ancient leather-bound volumes, scrolls and peculiar objects. After gazing upon them for a moment, he closed the metal portal, locked it, and shut the shelf. He then walked away.

Above him, unnoticed, was Minion sitting and watching from a shadowed shelf, expressing his enthusiasm with his characteristic hand rubbing.

#

Several nights later Loki hovered over a boiling cauldron in the woods. He stirred the coals in the fire with a stick and then threw some spices into the boiling liquid, which did absolutely nothing to improve the smell of the concoction. Utilizing the secret door, Loki had come to find that sneaking out of the keep was easy enough, even with all this paraphernalia (though it took several trips to ready for this evening). It was all about timing.

"Minion, fetch the chicken," he demanded. The impish servant moved to remove the hapless fowl from its wicker basket cage.

Loki pulled his hands back from the pot, and shook them with a look of disgust. "This is ridiculous. Eye of newt, tongue of snail...yish! I'm telling you, Minion, I long for the old days when one didn't need such silliness to facilitate a simple invocation. But then again, that is why I am here, isn't it? Give me that!" He snatched the struggling bird from Minion's fumbling hands. Loki adeptly wrenched the animal's neck and it stopped its squirming. He threw its carcass into the cauldron and chanted an arcane tune, half smirking.

He circled his hand over the boiling liquid, then reached down and picked up a mandrake root from his supplies. He brushed it off and then, barehanded, thrust it into the hot liquid. He squeezed his eyes shut, grunted terribly, then released a howl that at first sounded of pain, but turned to something that sounded akin to pleasure.

"Yes!" he cried. His lips grimaced into the shape of a smile around gritted teeth. He removed the dripping root and held it up, chest heaving, eyes closed.

"Master! Look!"

"I know, be calm."

Loki slowly opened his eyes and saw his servant huddled nearby. All about their little encampment there was movement. Shadowy, flowing figures that made no noise. There was a single set of blazing eyes before them in the night, as high as the tree branches just out of range of the firelight. These burning coals belonged to a hulk of a creature. Branches cracked and the earth rumbled as the beast shifted in the darkness.

"Who summons me, in an age when no one summons?" it growled. Its voice was unearthly. Minion's teeth chattered.

Loki stood. "Loki summons you."

The eyes narrowed in the dark. It snorted like a bull. "I know this name, though it means nothing to me anymore. Be gone, you have no power over me." The eyes shifted as the creature moved to depart.

"I beg to differ, ogre," Loki said, holding up the vaguely man-shaped root. This he squeezed violently, and fluid dripped from it. The creature in the woods lurched and growled fiercely.

After a long time: "What is your bidding?"

Loki sneered. "That's better. I need you and your kindred here. I need a diversion in yonder keep."

The eyes laughed. "You are mad. That place reeks of men and iron. What would our presence possibly accomplish? They already suspect our existence. They foray out into these woods from time to time to chase us. If we enter their walls, they could do us harm. Even I, who can not be harmed by their iron, would be eternally harassed. We are weak. No good could come of it."

"If you do this for me, I can make you strong again," Loki enticed.

The eyes narrowed again. "You lie, this is not possible. Our age is over. Even on this island the Light penetrates the mist that separates the worlds and is growing."

"Wrong. I can reverse that, even extend the vale!" Loki stepped forward. "I just need time, and the proper diversion inside the walls of the keep. Do this for me and I will grant you powers of your former self. I am Loki."

The eyes shook from side to side. "Half of us have little substance, the other half losing substance. We are like smoke."

Loki smiled devilishly. "Perfect. Smoke and mirrors are my specialty."

"I am listening."

#

Across the room, Sir McFowler entered the dining hall with his now-ever-present entourage of Willy and Sir Gregory. The trio had become fast friends—finding a common bond in their boyish exuberance. Jason personally tutored William in the bagpipes, and Gregory and the Highlander loved to play the riddle game. Their laughter echoed in the corridors of Greensprings. The two knights and the merchant's son bustled toward some open benches near the nuns' table.

Jason accidentally bumped into Mother Superior and he could be heard saying; "Oh, pardon me, Ma."

Mother Superior just shook her head.

Patrick smiled and shook his head as well. Soon, however, he realized after watching the trio carry on that he was sitting all alone in a sea of people enjoying each other's company; King Mark merrily talking with the Lady Christianne; Sir Geoffrey surrounded by young ladies like a cock in a coop; Sir McFowler and his companions; Patrick watched them and envied their carefree camaraderie. He sighed heavily and inspected his glass for the thousandth time: *Real crystal*, he thought, scrutinizing the cup. He was so often surprised at the wealth that turned up in the keep.

"Gawain, please." Christianne's shrill voice penetrated his thoughts. He looked at her, and she gestured with her head at his hands. He realized that he had been running his finger around the brim of the crystal, causing it to hum eerily.

"Pardon me, my Lady," he said, sounding more than a little sarcastic. He drained the last of the courage from the crystal, stood, straightened out his surcoat over his mail and walked over to the three across from him at their table.

"May I join you?" he asked. There was a brief moment of silence as the trio took in the sight of him.

"Of course, have a seat old boy," said Jason.

Sir Gregory patted Patrick on the back as he sat. "Just come from duty there?" he said, gesturing at Patrick's mail hood, which hung loose over his surcoat.

"I didn't keep you up this morning, did I?" William asked.

Patrick smiled. "No, not at all."

"That's because I've resorted to playing the pipes outside on the walls like Jason here. I dare say you shan't be woken by me anymore."

Patrick shrugged as if he didn't care, but was relieved to hear it.

The conversation turned back to the subject. Sir McFowler was agitated and even more animated than usual.

"...and I told him—again!—that he is to be escorted, that is accompanied, watched, followed, hand-held—call it what you will—anytime he is to be out of sight of the keep walls. 'But I just wanted a midnight stroll alone and away from those stuffy walls,' he says. What if he fell in a ditch and died? How would I explain that to Mark his Majesty yonder?" Jason did a wonderful impression of the Viscount, snooty accent and all.

"He is a bit sour isn't he?" Gregory conceded.

"And cruel. He beats on his valet constantly," Patrick pointed out.

"I'd be beaten too if I were that ugly," Willy said.

Jason laughed. "Abused just for being ugly? Is that what my problem has been all this time?"

The evening wore on and slowly the residents began to drift out of the dining hall. Willy bade the knights goodnight and left.

"I am not tired at all," Jason said. I am still much too moved by my confrontation with his Lokiness to go to bed. I need to vent my anger on something, or somebody..." He clenched his fists and looked around the hall.

Patrick raised his head, seeing an opportunity. "Hey Highlander, you still owe me all the beer I can drink. Let us go to Aesclinn and vent that rage on a pint?"

Jason slapped the table. "Excellent idea!"

#

The three men walked the dusty trail to Aesclinn by moonlight. Jason stopped periodically to punch the bushes or swat at tree limbs. He was in rare form.

When they entered the pub, the establishment was dead. There were a couple of villagers in the corner and the barkeep leaned against the bench, slowly cleaning a cup.

"I feel the cold clutches of boredom creeping up on me," Jason said. They ordered drinks at the bench anyway.

The more he drank, the more agitated Jason became and he drummed his fingers on the table. He looked about, couldn't find any trouble, and so decided to create it: He leaned over and punched Gregory across the jaw just for the sheer hell of it.

"Ouch!" Gregory shook his head and took another swig of ale.

#

They left late that night, finally admitting defeat. Gregory was rubbing his jaw and complaining. Jason was walking several paces behind, grumbling to himself.

"Relax Gregory, he quit after he made you call him Zeus," said Patrick.

"That's easy for you to say. It wasn't you he decided to play with," the little knight lamented. "He certainly has an odd sense of humor."

"He's Jason. That explains it all." He walked slightly ahead, whistling softly to himself.

When they approached the gate to Greensprings, two heads bobbed on top of the wall and shouted, "Who goes there?"

"It's us, idiots. You let us out, you can let us back in," Jason growled.

"What's the password?" the head demanded. There was giggling on top of the gate.

Jason placed his hands on his kilt-girdled hips. "It's: open up or I'm going to shove my foot up your asses."

There was laughter and the gate rumbled open. Jason exchanged good natured catcalls with the night watchmen and then said goodnight to them. He turned to Patrick and Gregory and gave them slaps on the back.

"Goodnight, McFowler," Sir Gregory said, and he and Patrick turned to go down the path that led to the Hall for Guests.

Clouds floated across the moon, blanketing the keep in shadow. Gregory and Patrick were now at-home enough to navigate, and they felt their way along the keep wall and searched with their hands for the place where rock gave way to ivy and the cobblestones to dirt. It would be then that they knew they had passed the keep proper and should turn left to the Hall.

Suddenly the moon broke free of the clouds, splashing the courtyard in eerie light. Gregory's hand clamped down on Patrick's arm. "Look!"

Patrick turned in the direction of the Englishman's extended arm. There was an old woman washing bloody rags in the courtyard fountain. A greenish glow engulfed her, and she was moaning silently.

"What the hell is that!" the little knight cried. The old woman turned. Her eyes were hollow sockets. And then the dark pits turned to blazing green flames and her moan turned to a hellish wail, and she rose in the air, circled the fountain, and then shot off like an arrow over the wall. The thing was gone. The night watchmen seemed oblivious to these events.

"That," said Patrick, "was a banshee. It means someone is going to die."

#

They went to Mark's apartment and reported the event. He seemed disturbed, but chose not to do anything about it.

"It is only another manifestation unique to Avalon. A walking myth. It doesn't mean anything, and if it does, what could I do to prevent the future?" He thanked Patrick and Gregory told them to go try for some sleep.

Patrick paced in his chamber, wishing his stomach could expunge the butterflies and let him rest. He decided to take Mark's advice and just forget it. He started to pull on the cords that held his chain mail together, but stopped. Instead he laid down on his bed fully clothed, put his hands behind his head and stared at the ceiling.

#

"McFowler seemed none too pleased with our joke this evening," the night watchman said to his fellow guard, who agreed. The night watch was the longest and most uneventful of duties.

Behind them, the moonlight cast a shadow on the wall. The shadow grew in size. It spread in all directions, and then started to grow upwards as well as outward like no shadow should. Soon it was a fully formed entity behind the watchmen.

One of them finally noticed it from the corner of his eye. "Eh?" he muttered, then grabbed his colleague, his eyes widening with panic. The other saw it, and when he did, the thing lunged at them.

They screamed and ran.

The shadow chased the knights who were unsuccessfully trying to draw their swords and run and sound an alarm at the same time. The three figures disappeared around a bend in the wall as the toady Minion appeared in the stairwell at the gate and made his way to the mechanism. He released the lever that brought the gate up and the bridge down. The courtyard had been filling with other shadow creatures seeping through the stone walls, but now the pound of physical feet rumbled on the drawbridge.

Minion jumped excitedly.

#

A knock at Patrick's door startled him into wakefulness, and he realized that he had fallen asleep. The knock came again, louder, and then the visitor barged in. It was Trent of Jersey followed closely by William. They were white as ghosts.

"Sir Gawain!" Trent exclaimed. "There are...*things* in the courtyard. They're attacking us!"

Patrick sat up groggily. "Really boys, I'm not in the mood for this."

"No, really, look!" William shouted, pointing to the window. Just then, cries came from the wall. He raced to the window and threw open the shutters. There were indeed dark figures running amok. He cursed. He couldn't quite make them out, but they were chasing and swinging weapons at servants and the night watchmen down on the grounds and walls.

Patrick grabbed Trent and William and pushed them out the door. "Willy, go straight down stairs and lock the door, and Trent, you go floor to floor, room to room, and tell everyone to meet in the bottom lounge. Now go!"

Next he ran to Gregory's room and found him still dressed in his mail shirt like himself. Evidently he couldn't sleep, either. After a brief explanation, they ran to Sir Jon's room and woke him and told him the news. In a few moments, the sleepy Englishman looked absolutely silly in a nightgown, sword, and shield, but was ready for a fight.

They ran for the stairs to meet their Guests, but those same Guests came hurtling down the corridor at them like a tidal wave. Willy and Trent were at their forefront.

"They already got inside! They're coming this way!" they yelled.

Patrick seized command. "Jon, lead the Guests down the stairs and out the back door. Take them to the main keep, and then the cellar where I'm sure the other Guests and servants are being taken. Gregory and I will stay here and hold them off. We'll follow as soon as we're able."

Jon called to the Guests and they followed after him. Patrick and Gregory waded through the crowd to the stairwell entrance.

It wasn't long before they came. The creatures were dark, leathery skinned things with wide mouths, slitted eyes, sharp teeth, scraggly hair and pointy ears. They were short of stature and walked upright like men. They wielded rusty old weapons and wore battered armor and bucket helm.

The Irishman remembered old folk tales. "Goblins!" he cried.

He and Gregory held them back with sword slashes and shield buffets. The clang of metal reverberated and shouts of knights and goblins alike echoed in the corridor. The things streamed up the stairwell, but couldn't advance through the door.

It became obvious that the same narrow corridor that served as a bottleneck for the goblins also prevented the two knights from optimizing their effectiveness.

"Let's go, Gawain! Jon will need us as he crosses to the main keep!"

The Irishman reluctantly pulled himself away from the melee and followed.

#

Father Benis was also restless. Late into the night, he hovered over the tome of historical writings that he had shared with Patrick Gawain. Something was nagging at his mind. Something that concerned their Guest, the Viscount Loki. Something about the man reminded Benis of an entry in the book, but he couldn't recall exactly which one or why. Not one to leave a puzzle incomplete, he had been perusing the voluminous pages since sunset. At last, he came to a series of entries, one on the land of Jotunheim.

"Jotunheim!" he mused out loud. The article entry described a place of legend, not an actual country. According to the entry, it was the home of the Jotuns, or giants—the enemies of the gods of the Norse—the Aesir.

"Now why would Lord Loki claim to hail from such a place?" Benis asked the empty room. "Is that his sense of humor, perhaps?"

Tired from long hours of hunching over the book, but not yet satisfied, Father Benis licked his fingers and paged backwards to the front of the book among the entries that commenced with the letter A.

"Asgard, Andvari, Alfheim...ah, Aesir!"

Benis was grateful that Gaius Cornelius Tacitus, author of the *Germania*, was a meticulous scholar. A pagan, albeit, but nobody was perfect.

Father Benis found a list of the Norse Gods, the Aesir, and their corresponding Roman names, and he blinked in surprise when he saw the name Loki among them. Unlike the other gods in the list, several notations were made next to Loki. There were two corresponding Roman gods for the entry, which were Dis and Bacchus, which, if Benis was not mistaken, were two gods from the opposite ends of the spectrum; Dis being the god of the gloomy underworld, and Bacchus being the god of wine and merrymaking. As if the chronicler was not sure himself, Tacitus added a question mark after each. Benis's frown deepened. Another notation pointed out that Loki was not truly a god among the Aesir...but a Jotun.

The priest squeezed his eyes shut and rubbed the bridge of his nose, feeling fatigue weighing him down. He was starting to forget why he had even started this research and was certain he was missing something. Although an amateur scholar, he was prone to letting his curiosity get the better of him, allowing one bit of information to lead him to another and then to another until he realized much of the day was gone.

"Why name a child after an ambiguous god?" Benis murmured. Perhaps, he thought, like Jotunheim, the name wasn't real, but selected.

Of course it wasn't his real name. It was an alias. He was a nobleman who had come to Greensprings, like many of the residents from nobility, in search of a safe haven from the outside world for any number of reasons—precisely one of the purposes the Benefactors had in mind when they commissioned the keep on Avalon.

He chided himself for having not respected the fellow's privacy and trying to discern his origins. Still, Benis was pleased with himself for having satisfied a nagging curiosity on his mind, and he was about to close the tome and put it back on the shelf, when on a whim, he turned the page.

"How is this possible?" Benis whispered to himself.

There on the page was an imprint of a woodcut, the central character bearing a striking resemblance to Greenspring's Loki, right down to the characteristic pointy ears and pockmarks. In the picture, Loki lay naked and bound by chains in a cave. Above him a serpent dripped venom over his face, but a woman stood over him, catching the drops in a bowl. Benis read the caption to the picture. "Giants in the earth," he breathed, recalling his conversation with the Irishman, when he had made what he thought were just fanciful speculations.

No sooner had this revelation come over him when the horns blew in the keep. He had heard them only a few times in the past. Even then, only as practice. They were alarms.

He walked over to the window, opened it, and looked out to see mayhem erupting in the courtyard. He gasped and raced to the library doors. He swung them closed and struggled with the wooden crossbar. A shadow blocked the lantern light from behind him and a black silky arm reached over his body, its hand grasping the crossbar. It belonged to the Viscount Loki.

"May I help you with that?" the Viscount asked, smiling.

#

Jon ran ahead of the Guests barefooted. The grounds were in absolute chaos. Avangarde were everywhere in varying stages of dress and armament. The gargoyle-like creatures swarmed like ants. Some seemed to be thin as shadows, and others seemed all too dangerously real. Horses cried out, a building was ablaze, and a contingent of Avangarde was circling the gates of the Hall for Lady Guests with a picket fence of lances.

One of the goblins jumped in Jon's path, slavering and howling. Jon put up his shield to ward off the thing's blow, and then slashed at it. It split in two.

Jon looked at his sword. "Wow," he said. "I did that?"

"Alright Sir Jon!" Willy shouted.

Jon smiled and kicked the next goblin that came at them. He sent it hurtling.

"Jon, let's go! Stop fooling around." Sir Gawain and the Englishman had appeared. The trio of knights led the Guests through the combat, through the gardens and into the keep. There they met up with a stream of servants running for the cellars. The Reservists escorted them all to the trap door by the kitchens and made sure they entered safely.

"Now what?" Sir Jon asked. He and Gregory looked to Patrick, who had thus far been giving the orders.

Patrick seemed just as confused, "Well, I don—ah, hell, how about you stay here, Jon, and guard the cellar while we go find some help."

They didn't argue, and Patrick and Gregory departed.

#

"Why thank you, Viscount," Benis said after the slender nobleman had helped him move the large timber onto the door mounts. There was an awkward moment while the priest and Loki stood face to face without saying anything. "Shouldn't you be with the other Guests, under the protection of the Avangarde?" Benis said at last, a trace of nervousness in his voice. Sir Gawain was right, the man made your skin crawl.

"Shouldn't you?" Loki returned.

The priest moved nervously to the opposite side of the round study table. "In times of emergency, I am required to stay here and look after the keep library. It is very important, you know."

"No doubt," Loki said, slowly making his way around the table towards the priest. Benis countered his move in the opposite direction. "Well, I was on my way to search the protection of the Avangarde when I said to myself, 'Loki, I wager that poor old librarian is probably all alone and needs some looking after.' And so, here I am."

"How thoughtful of you," Benis said.

By now Loki was standing over the book that was open on the table.

"Very interesting," he said, gazing intently at the picture. He touched the image of the woman, a thoughtful look coming into his face. "How often I'm surprised at the extent of man's memory."

Loki glanced up again—and his eyes, though only briefly, were luminescent and lavender. Benis took out his prayer beads and held the cross out as if to ward off evil.

"I know who you are."

Loki laughed at the gesture, his eyes normal again. "Indeed?"

#

Well into the keep, Gregory and Patrick approached a pair of double wooden doors. Long before they could reach to open them, however, they exploded. When the shards of wood had stopped falling, they uncovered their heads and saw a giant goblin looming in the threshold. Its eyes blazed red and it wielded a lance longer than both men put together.

It snorted, and fire shot out from its nostrils. The ground shook as it took a step towards them.

"Jesus Christ!" the two knights exclaimed simultaneously. They turned, and on the run made the Sign of the Holy Cross to repent for taking the Lord's name in vain...and for protection against the creature.

They ran through the corridors, zigzagging at every turn to lose the monster, but its footsteps thundered close behind them.

They finally reached the darkened throne room and huddled in the stairwell, which was concealed behind a hanging tapestry.

"You think it will find us?" Gregory whispered.

"I don't know," Patrick replied.

"Should we go find help?"

"Mm, let's wait a bit, shall we?"

Something grabbed them out of the darkness. They screamed and thrashed about like scared children being dragged from underneath a bed.

"Quiet you bloody fools!" McFowler hissed. He was wearing nothing but his kilt and his huge claymore. He was covered in blood and black ichor.

"Where are the rest?" he asked. They told him of the cellar. "Splendid! You are a credit to the Order, both of you. Let's go have some fun then!" He grabbed the two junior knights by their surcoats and dragged them in the direction of the fighting.

"But Jason, there is a really big one roaming about here!" Gregory protested.

"Yes lad, I've seen the beast."

"But it breathes fire…" Gregory continued.

"And it's really ugly," Patrick added.

Jason looked somewhat disappointed. "Look lads, you won't make your fame and fortune being timid. You must take the fight to the enemy. Now let's go!"

#

When McFowler, Patrick, and Gregory found the Avangarde, they were gathered in front of the church. Many Avangarde were throwing their shoulders against the church doors and King Mark shouted commands. The courtyard was a mess, but the fighting was done.

"What is going on?" Patrick said.

"It would appear that the goblins and their Goblin King have barricaded themselves inside the church. We've won the battle," Gregory said.

Jason grimaced. "We've won nothing yet. If they are indeed trapped inside there, then they are like cornered animals; all the more dangerous. They won't give up with out a fight."

A handful of knights carried in a large piece of timber and commenced to use it as a battering ram.

"Shouldn't we help?" Patrick asked. The other knights stood back and waited, weapons drawn.

"I have a better idea," McFowler said. "Do you boys want to be heroes?" McFowler asked. Patrick and Gregory nodded excitedly. "Good, then follow me."

#

"You are Loki. The same Loki in the picture," Benis said.

"Nonsense, how is that possible?" the Viscount responded lightly. He continued to approach the priest, who walked backwards, crucifix held out.

"You are Nephilim."

Loki froze and his devilish smile quickly turned to a sneer. "Don't call me that," he warned, stabbing a black-gloved finger at the priest. If he had any doubts before, Benis felt that Loki's reaction was as good as an admission.

"Would you prefer Jotun? Giant? Perhaps, demon? You certainly are not a god."

"I beg to differ."

"Even the Aesir did not count you as an equal." Benis pointed to the open book, the picture. "They banished you to a cave for your evil deeds among them. How did you escape, I wonder?"

Loki froze again in his slow pursuit of the priest across the library, a pained look crossing his face. He touched the scars on his face. "It wasn't easy, and it came at a great cost."

"The woman in the picture?" Father Benis conjectured, stalling for time, looking nervously at the library doors that he had barred. No one would rescue him.

"Yes. Sigun, my wife. Not too bright, but very devoted. She made good my escape, but lost her life in the process, and I'm never, never going back...but these things don't concern you." A calmness settled over Loki. "You know what I am here for, so I suggest you cooperate."

"It's the secret documents you've been inquiring about, isn't it?" Benis was now backed up against a shelf. "They were right to hide them. Nothing good would ever come of them. I can't imagine what you intend to use them for, but surely not for any good. No, Lord Loki, I won't be helping you."

Calmly, almost gently, Loki said, "The key to the vault of forbidden books—give it to me, or I'll pry it from your dead fingers." Loki held out his gloved hand, claw-like under Father Benis' nose.

"You'll have to do just that. Though I don't understand how you think it won't go unnoticed; me with a sword gash through me and the key missing."

"That, dear fellow, is exactly why I orchestrated this elaborate attack on the keep," Loki boasted. "Your death would be no great mystery in the event of an attack. Unfortunately, judging by how things are going outside for my accomplices, I don't think they are going to make it inside the keep to hack you to pieces as I had planned. So, I will have to improvise." The Viscount reached out and snatched the prayer beads away, crucifix and all. He fingered the beads. "No, I think in all the excitement, your old frail heart was under incredible strain and just—" he popped one of the beads off the string. A flash of light flared from it like the seal breaking on a Greensprings invitation—"plain faltered."

Father Benis doubled over, clutching his heart.

#

Jason hoisted Gregory up past the remainder of the drain pipe and onto the church roof. Now all three were crouching on the tiles. The battering ram echoed below.

"Now what?" Patrick asked. McFowler motioned for silence and gestured for them to follow.

Jason climbed to the stained glass dome and peered through it. From a distance, the colored plates formed scenes from the life of Christ. Now, in front of them and up close, what should have been an image of Jesus carrying the cross merely looked like rudimentary colors and shapes. Inside a couple dozen goblins were throwing the pews against the double doors for added protection. The Goblin King stood in the sanctuary, giving orders.

"With the doors blocked like that, they can almost stay in there indefinitely," McFowler murmured.

"We could burn them out," Gregory suggested.

The Highlander shook his head. "Not with the church attached to the keep. We run the risk of catching it all on fire. We need to open those doors."

"What manner of creature is that big one?" Patrick whispered.

Jason shrugged. "Ogre, troll, hobgoblin, take your pick. It is a remnant from a bygone age. A fairy tale. It should disappear like one. Leave that one to me."

Patrick and Gregory turned pale. "What are you suggesting?"

McFowler grinned. "We're going to surprise attack them."

"What!"

Jason stood up, planted his boot into Gregory's buttocks, and shoved the little knight through the stained glass. The heavy glass caved, rather than shattered, along the lead linings. Gregory fell through, into the throng of milling goblins.

The Irishman stood up in shock. "Are you ma...!" McFowler planted his hand in the middle of Patrick's chest and sent him after Gregory. His stomach turned over, and an instant later he found himself in the pile of goblins.

Sir McFowler whooped and jumped through the hole himself. He knocked over the goblins struggling to stand as well as the Reservists. He was the first to recover and began to wind-mill his claymore about, wreaking his brand of terror over the ugly creatures like a farmer in a wheat field. Patrick and Gregory stood and thrashed wildly at anything that was near them, sometimes each other.

Though the creatures were fearsome, they were surprisingly lightweight and easily dispatched, as Sir Jon had noticed earlier. The only problem was their number. However, in minutes, the two Reservists were organized and standing back to back to meet the onslaught.

The ogre thundered forward, leveling its lance like a javelin to hurl at the knights. Jason barreled forward, goblins hanging off him like children. He made contact with the creature and knocked it to the ground.

"Get to the door lads! Keep them from blocking it any more!" he shouted.

As Patrick and Gregory cut a swathe to the doors, McFowler distracted the ogre. The thing stabbed and swung its lance expertly, and Jason was hard pressed to battle it for the lance reached farther than his sword. Their contest was so fierce, the lesser goblins stayed clear and concentrated on the two knights at the doors.

Jason backed away from the creature and parried a thrust. "I say old fellow," he chided. "Is that you that I smell, or did you step in something?"

The ogre snorted like a bull and made a wild swing.

"No, that is definitely you," Jason continued. "Why, I'd almost say that is a womanly odor."

The monster drew back its head and breathed fire at Jason. But Jason crouched and sprung into a back flip to avoid the flames. Flagstones were blackened and some of the nearby pews caught on fire. Father Constant wasn't going to be too pleased.

Jason landed on his feet. "That most definitely is a woman's odor. Which makes perfect sense. You fight like one!"

The thing bellowed and raised its fists. Jason double gripped his claymore and brought the blade down on the ogre's chest. Its armor was cleaved in two in a shower of sparks, and the beast fell to the ground.

"I should know," Jason said with a smirk. "You remind me of a lass I used to court."

McFowler's eyes widened. The ogre was rising.

"Ah, hell."

#

Father Benis crawled towards the library doors. Loki ambled along behind him and scrutinized the crucifix, noting the intricate shapes cut into it. It was a key.

"How clever," he said. He popped yet another bead off the chain. There was another flash of light and Benis cried out in pain. "I hate cleverness in anyone other than me."

The priest's breath came in great wheezes. He prayed, "Though...I...walk through the valley of the shadow of death..."

"That's it, little man, pray to your God," Loki said. There was another flash. Benis grabbed his chest tighter. Another bead fell to the flagstones and bounced away. "He can't hear you. He's not here. He can't help you. He can't help you any more than he can stop me." Another flash, another cry. Another bead fell.

Loki placed his boot on Father Benis' back and pushed down hard. The priest's form flattened and Loki kicked him over. His eyes were now glassy, and his mouth formed silent words. Loki looked upon him contemptuously and flash after flash lit the room.

Finally, the Viscount's mouth twisted into a violent leer. He stripped the remainder of the beads from the string and held only the metal cross. He gripped it so tightly his leather gloves creaked.

Father Benis' blank stare faced heavenward.

#

The church doors burst open and burly Avangarde pushed through the portal, hurling pews aside. Knights garbed in black surcoats leapt through the gap while Gregory and Patrick held the majority of goblins at bay. King Mark was the first to their aid, and he made short work of the annoying little creatures. More and more Avangarde piled into the sanctuary.

McFowler had no rest. The ogre had forced him to the altar, where they fought underneath the stained glass dome and the stone cross that bore the image of Jesus. McFowler tired, and the monster pressed closer.

"Hang on Jason, we're coming!" Mark called.

Jason grinned and renewed his efforts. "Oh, take your time. I have things under control." Patrick and Gregory were with Mark and the rest of the knights, and the goblins had all been eliminated. "As a matter of fact, just stay there and I'll..."

Jason's voice was cut off into a sickening squelching sound. His smile froze into a look of shock, and then faded to confusion. Mark and the Avangarde stopped in their tracks. Jason looked down; the ogre's lance pierced all the way through his torso. "Well, would you look at that," he struggled to say. Thick blood welled up in his mouth and spilled in clotty strands down his beard.

He grasped the shaft of the lance firmly. The ogre tried to force it in further, but could not overcome Jason's strength. Jason raised his sword with his free hand and shattered the lance. He staggered forward with sword raised to continue his attack. The ogre fell back a step and looked afraid.

But McFowler fell to his knees. He slumped to one side, his sword fell with a loud clang to the floor, and his body was still.

The Avangarde did not move. The ogre made no immediate moves either. The moment seemed to last an eternity.

The creature stepped forward and pushed Jason's body down the dais.

"You see," it said scornfully, "you cannot defeat me. No weapon forged by man can bring me harm. No man who is subject to death can touch me. You may as well let me pass. I have toyed with you long enough, you bore me."

The ogre's eyes were blazed crimson, and its gaze passed over all the assembled knights. "I see no such hero. No person who can lay harm to this son of old. You are all weak. Let me pass or I will destroy you also."

The ogre moved to exit the church, but King Mark stepped in his path. The ogre stopped and chuckled evilly. This chuckle turned into a full blown malicious laugh.

Mark's face was pale and his eyes were wet with tears. His eyes were the color of darkest midnight and his finely chiseled face was contorted. His sword shook in his fist.

The ogre continued to point and laugh spitefully.

"No man subject to death..." Mark whispered, realization brightening his face. He turned and swung his sword at the stone pillar behind him. He struck the thick rope that was anchored there, and it broke like a string. The rope was sucked skyward and the church was filled with a hissing noise.

The ogre stopped laughing.

The stone cross supported in the dome came crashing down, dragging with it all the heavy rope that had suspended it. The last thing the ogre saw before being crushed was the mournful face of Jesus Christ.

Dust exploded into the air and with a flash of brilliant light, the stone effigy cracked in half.

When the dust had settled, the creature was pinned underneath the cross, its eyes bugged out and glazed over. Then it began to cave in on itself, melting until the entire ogre was but a smoldering grease spot underneath the rubble. It was later found that that was the fate of all the goblins in the keep. They decayed into grease stains on the ground, and even these disappeared when sunlight shone on them.

The knights gathered around the motionless figure of Jason McFowler.

#

The secret compartment was not as large, nor were there as many documents, as Loki had thought. Searching through the shelves, he was at first disappointed and thought perhaps all his work was for nothing. But among the leather-bound books and ancient vellum scrolls, he found a map of the island bearing numbers, astrological symbols, and arcane sigils. This surpassed his wildest expectations, and though a quick perusal of the remaining material showed other fascinating items, they did not concern his mission, so he let them be.

No sooner than he had closed the cabinet and locked it, than the horns went silent in Greensprings. All was quiet now. The attack was over.

He made for the library doors, but paused to drop the crucifix-key on the priest's chest. In doing so, he noted a shiny object in the folds of the man's robe, which he bent down to retrieve. He grunted and raised an eyebrow when he saw that it was a glass disk. This he held over the symbols on the map and noted how it magnified them.

"Interesting," he mused out loud, and placed it and the folded map in his vestment.

He took the crossbar off the double doors, set it on the floor, stepped over it, and exited, closing the doors behind him.

Shortly afterwards, the beam of wood shook, then rocked, and then levitated off the floor. As though guided by invisible hands, it slowly settled in the door mounts.

#

Though it rained the day of the funeral, the sun was out. Back home in Eire, Patrick mused, conditions like this were referred to as "The Devil's Rain". The two complimented each other, however, for there was an abundance of rainbows in the sky that day.

The church in the village of Aesclinn was used instead of the keep church, since it had been damaged in the attack. The seats filled up quickly, then the balcony, sides, and back, and soon the crowd spilled out the doors. Knights, farmers, keep servants, Guests, clergy, fishermen, and all the villagers. McFowler's death made them equals for a day. Father Hugh Constant couldn't remember the little church so full.

Father Benis, who had died of a heart attack behind the library's closed doors, had been laid to rest the previous day. His funeral was attended only by close friends and veteran members of Greensprings. That was the way he would have wanted it.

When all were assembled, the double doors swung open and knights entered clad in the black and white surcoats of the Avangarde, bearing the shrouded body of Jason. The pallbearers were, of course, Sir Mark, Sir Waylan, Sir Corbin, and Sir Bisch. Sir Brian marched in front, playing the bagpipes.

Jason's companions bore his body slowly down the aisle for all his friends to see. They brought it to rest before the altar, and then took places near Brian.

When Brian had finished, first Father Hugh and then King Mark gave their eulogies, which brought more laughter than tears as they spoke of the life of Sir Jason McFowler.

When they were done, the Lady Katherina stepped up to the sanctuary and said she would perform one of Jason's favorite ballads.

She cupped her dove colored hands before her, dipped her head for a moment in the silence, and then opened her mouth to form a perfect "O". Her lips did not move, nor did her chest, as the first note issued forth. Her voice projected as if by magic. McCabe joined in with the pipes. The sounds filled the church like a kind of light. People bowed their heads in private prayer.

Except for the Viscount Loki—he sat among the colorful noblemen like a great black bird. He looked to Minion and rolled his eyes. Minion snickered quietly.

#

Patrick Gawain entered his room, took off his sword and tossed it on the bed. He then sank into his usual seat before the window and propped his feet against the sill.

His emotions were running in all directions, and for all the wrong reasons.

A friend had just died, and the only thing that seemed to occupy his mind was how he was passed up for promotion to be an Avangarde. He felt deeply ashamed at his selfishness. He had wished for an opening in the Avangarde to present itself. Was his wishful thinking somehow the cause for Jason's death? As silly and unlikely as that thought may have been, he couldn't help but feel a tinge of guilt while Katherina, the songstress and Jason's companion, watched him throughout the funeral. Her beautiful icy eyes bored into him as if to condemn him: *You were his friend—why is it you live, yet he does not?*

He had distracted himself with the ritual of the mass during the funeral, especially while Father Hugh prepared communion. Something about the communion cup that he used struck him as familiar. Father Hugh held up the chalice to be blessed and to transform the wine in it to the blood of Jesus Christ, and in doing so, sunlight from an open window glinted off the gold. The beautiful craftsmanship, the hourglass shape, the reverence with which it was held, all reminded Patrick of another cup. A cup held by delicate fair hands in a cave.

A shadow enveloped the room, yet there were no clouds in the sky now. The Irishman suddenly had no desire to look behind him for fear of what he might see. He cupped his face in his hands and wished for the shadow to pass. Though he could no longer see it, he could feel its chill on his back.

Then, from outside his window, came the sound of bagpipes. The same music that Jason used to play. From the sound of it, the music wasn't McCabe. It wasn't his style. It was as if someone were carefully imitating McFowler himself.

The icy shadow faded away, just as David's harp-playing drove away the evil spirits that afflicted King Saul. Patrick looked up. He could see down the length of the wall to where William of Monmouth was standing, in Jason's old place, playing the pipes.

And for once, it sounded good.

Chapter Seven

The weeks that followed the attack, Mark ordered double the guards about the fortress, and added heavy patrols as well.

Envoys traveled from Rome and Brussels. They were serious looking old men who represented the Benefactors and Patrons of the Greensprings école, and they were gravely displeased with the news that the keep's defenses had been breached, exposing the royal progeny inside to risk and harm. They arrived anonymously and no banquet was made for them, and few were seen outside the meeting chamber in which they had cloistered themselves.

Patrick Gawain and the rest of the staff walked on eggshells for the duration of the inquest. For that is just what it was; an investigation into the misconduct of the Avangarde who allowed this to happen. Mark was their steward and leader, and thus responsible. There were rumors of the disbanding of the Garde, and the closing of Greensprings.

Sir Wolfgang Von Fiescher came back for the closed door meeting. He sought out many of the knights and asked them, one by one, to come into the meeting chamber to give their account of that night's events. Patrick was no exception.

"Sir Gawain," asked a hawk nosed and cold eyed man at the table. He had a heavy Italian accent. "From what we gather, yourself and..." he looked over some papers before him, "...Sir Gregory witnessed the demon that undoubtedly heralded the attack, correct?"

"Yes, my lord."

"You warned Sir Mark of this?"

"Yes, my lord."

"And yet he made no action that evening in preparation?"

"Well, no my lord, but you must under-"

"Thank you Sir Gawain, but that will be all." The man waved him away.

Patrick looked from the man to von Fiescher to Sir Mark, who looked tired and beaten at the table's end. Wolfgang nodded, and Patrick turned to leave.

"Oh, Sir Gawain, one more thing," another man at the table said. This man was short and portly. He had a Flemish accent. "You were in the Crusade, correct?" Patrick nodded. "What can you tell me of Sir Robert, Duke of Normandy?"

Patrick paused before answering. He was surprised at the question which seemed to have little to do with current events. "I never met the man personally. I fought under Godfrey de Bouillon's banner, whom I never really met either. Robert was a capable leader and soldier from what I understand."

"But what can you tell me of him personally, from 'what you understand'?"

Patrick struggled to keep his lips from curling in contempt, angry that they were berating Mark like this, and then had the gall to change subjects as if nothing important was going on here.

He replied flatly, "He was typical of the Frankish Princes who went to the Holy Lands. He went looking more for earthly treasures than for heavenly salvation."

The Flemish man nodded thoughtfully and motioned for Patrick to leave, who went gladly.

#

The meeting stretched on for another week, during which time it seemed the entire keep held its breath. At week's end, just as suddenly and just as unceremoniously, the visitors left. They looked just as agitated as when they arrived. Wolfgang von Fiescher also left, but only after having had close and friendly words with Mark.

Then, to everyone's surprise, Mark announced a feast. Lady Christianne was put in charge of the arrangements, but as was her way, she delegated the particulars to other Guests and servants.

The dinner was colorful and bountiful, but a hush wrapped the assembled guests and few people laughed or even smiled. King Mark sat in his central large chair. At last he stood as if to make a toast. He lifted his goblet and announced that Greensprings would continue unchanged. The silence cracked like the sound of a rope, long pulled taut, snapping in half. And though the hall was brilliantly lit by a hundred candles, it seemed to grow brighter.

Mark sat down. Some of the color returned to his face.

#

Sir Jeremiah ran down the corridor and burst into the kitchen. The other Reservists were gathered around some leftover wine and loaves of bread. Jeremiah struggled to get close to Sir Jon who sat at the head of the table.

"...so then they left for the port. Mark nearly collapsed after that," Jon was saying, gesturing wildly.

"What did I miss?" Jeremiah asked, brushing a dark curl from his eye.

"You would know if you weren't late," a Reservist near Jeremiah said, and slapped him on the back of the head.

Jeremiah winced. "I hadn't finished my bloomin' dinner."

Jon continued. "So I hear Mark and Corbin—who, incidentally, is our new Captain of the Garde—talking about how the Council is going to let Greensprings be for the time being, because of the fight that is happening on the outside between the brothers Henry and Robert of England and Normandy. Which makes sense; because Robert is the rightful heir to the English throne and who naturally we are supposed to renew our contract with. Avalon uses the ports of England as a jump-off point for the Guests and such. But since Henry usurped the throne, we don't know who we are supposed to pay allegiance to."

"That must be why they asked me about Robert," Patrick cut in. There was a murmur that ran through the crowd of assembled Reservists.

"Right," continued Jon. "So, the problems here are trivial to what's happening on the outside. Thus they are going to let Mark stay in control, and independent. Now is not a good time to have a mass exodus of young royal Guests. It's rumored that Robert, despite a current agreement, is massing an army to invade England later this year. We're safer here, and so are the Guests."

"The Council must know that, otherwise they would have done something by now," said Sir Gregory, his youthful face shining just as brightly as his new black and white Avangarde surcoat. It had been he who was chosen to fill Jason's place in the Avangarde.

The young Reservists, eager for information, talked for a while longer into the night. Until, that is, Rosa Maria came and chased them away. The knights might have had full run of the keep, but the kitchen was Rosa's.

#

The Viscount Loki squinted at the stars. He grumbled, handed the parchment roughly to Minion, and held up the shiny brass contraption in his hand. This he put to his eye and peered at the heavens. He lowered it without taking his gaze from the sky, and then raised it back to his eye. He frowned, lowered the device and angrily grabbed the parchment from Minion.

Minion had perused it himself. Of all the documents from the library's secret chamber, this was the only one Loki had brought back to their suite. At its center was the image of an island with several stars above it, shining upon the island.

Loki consulted the parchment for some time, shoved it back into Minion's grasp, then consulted the brass device once again. This he squinted at, ticked off several graduated symbols along its length with his finger, then turned one of the many gears on it. Its intricate parts moved in unison. Once satisfied with its new configuration, Loki again held it up to the sky. "Hmph," he said, and began to pace. He moved along the lakeshore, paused, and scratched his head. "This is certainly challenging."

"What is, Master?" squeaked Minion.

Loki shot him a glare. "Never you mind. Watch for Avangarde. We're not supposed to be out like this all alone." Loki stroked his goatee thoughtfully. "Goblins might get us. Imagine that." He swung about, looking up as if surveying an invisible structure.

"What will they do if they find us?" Minion asked.

"Spank us, I suppose," Loki laughed. "But it won't matter in a little bit. They will be the farthest thing from my mind if I could just figure out this damnable geoconfiguration of the temporal horizon—"

"What?"

Loki's face lit up and he shook his finger. "Ah-ha!" he cried. "I have it!" He snatched the parchment and ran to a position near the lakeshore and he looked wildly between it and the stars. Then he hunched over and placed one hand over his brow as if peering out over a brightly lit expanse. He straightened and began to inch forward like a man at the edge of a cliff, and he struggled against an invisible wall like an actor pantomiming in a play. He cursed and grunted, then finally stepped back.

He set the document and peering-device on the ground and paced a bit more. After several breaths, he threw himself forward with his hands outstretched as if to part a curtain. He grunted and struggled until his brow was covered with sweat.

Minion stood by shaking his head, sure Loki didn't notice. Minion was accustomed to his master's odd behavior, but it never ceased to amaze him.

Suddenly, Loki's head disappeared. Minion cried out and ran forward to grab at his legs and pull on them.

Loki's head suddenly appeared just as mysteriously as it had disappeared. "Stop, fool," he hissed, and he turned his head again into the air that engulfed it. Minion stood with mouth agape. The Viscount held his hands in the air as if braced against a wall, and then his head vanished all the way to his shoulders.

Loki pulled back one last time. His head slowly reappeared as if being drawn from a pool of water. "Damn, damn," he growled.

"M-master, what is it?" Minion stammered.

"It's what I came for, but it's not entirely accessible at the moment." Loki was angry, but this time not at Minion. He paced with hands on hips. "It must be the season. The moon and Venus must not be pulling on the doorway hard enough to open it wider." He suddenly brightened and smiled. "But that is acceptable. I'm lucky to have found it at all. If it weren't for that Irish knight suggesting I search out the librarian, I wouldn't even have found the information to come this far."

"Master, I don't understand..." Minion started to say, but before he could finish, Loki bent over and picked up the little man and shoved his head into the mysterious air.

Minion cried out. His head passed through something cold like water. The dark nighttime lakeshore was suddenly bright. He stopped kicking and his eyes adjusted.

Before him was a twilight landscape that was the fantastical mirror image of the old lake. This lake was flat and smooth as glass. The surface of the water reflected the fiery auburn sky and the image of an island. This island was composed of a clear and faceted rock, like quartz stone. Atop this island was a marvelous castle of solid ivory. From its tallest central tower radiated a single beam that flickered gently. The castle seemed to be drawing in light from all directions and focusing it through this tower, projecting it to the heavens like a beacon.

Suddenly, Minion was drawn away, and then he was lying on the dark shore of a dull and lifeless world.

"Wh-what was that?"

Loki bent forward, his eyes blazing with a life Minion had never seen before. "Home!" he cried. "Where I belong. What I've sought for a long, long time. We're going there as soon as that little window is big enough to allow us to pass."

"When will that be?"

"I calculate in about two, maybe three moons passing."

"What if the portal doesn't get any bigger than that?" Minion asked innocently.

Loki's eyes widened and he looked around as if someone might be overhearing. "Shssh! Shut your mouth!" Loki slapped the little man upside the head. "You mustn't say such things!" Then just as suddenly he grabbed Minion's head in a playful headlock and stroked it gently. "No matter if it shouldn't get much bigger. The important thing is that I found it. I am not without means to force it wider. However, I should still wait until the moon and Venus are properly aligned to try. I may only get one chance. Unfortunately, that will mean putting up with that nest of do-gooders, Greensprings."

Minion made a muffled concession from Loki's armpit.

Loki stopped his stroking, absent-mindedly wiped his hand on Minion's shoulder, and turned them back towards the keep. "But that is acceptable. I am a patient man. I've waited this long; I can wait a little longer. Even if I have to put up with those wretchedly happy people. They remind me so of that silly Marcus Ionus whom I beguiled into inviting me here. I'll just have to make a game of it.

#

"Is it only me, or does Sir Gregory seem a bit cockier than before?" Patrick said to Sir Jon at breakfast, gesturing for his fellow Reservist to pass him the bread. "Certainly he never swaggered like that before."

"Gregory has never been, nor is he now, cocky. You're just angry that it was he who made Avangarde, and not you." Jon passed him the loaf. His moment of uncharacteristic wisdom sounded like condescension.

"And you aren't?"

"Of course I am, but I don't let it disturb me," Jon responded in a whisper, for the Viscount Loki's servant, Minion, came to sit at the table.

"It doesn't disturb me that much," Patrick lied, also whispering and trying not to make eye contact with the little man who was for some reason methodically touching every utensil and plate near him. "I was just making an observation."

"Well, what is past is past, so..." Jon paused to pass a fork to Minion, whose arms were too short to reach it. "So we must try ever harder to prove ourselves."

"I have been trying." The Irishman smirked, not bothering to whisper anymore. "It doesn't seem to be doing me any good. And I don't see what Gregory did that was so special to be chosen."

"Maybe you need a whole new approach."

Minion was now biting on the fork. "Like what?" Patrick asked.

Jon looked about as if he were about to divulge an important secret, whispering even more quietly, though Minion was already moving on to the next utensil, oblivious to the knights' conversation. "You need to win your way into the confidence of the key players in the keep."

Patrick slapped his hand to his face. Of course Jon would say that. "I have no intention whatsoever of demeaning myself to 'win' anyone's confidence. I want to become an Avangarde by my merits, not by whose arse I sniff."

"Look, Gawain, if you really want it, you have to become creative. A knight's skills do not lie in the sword alone. Sometimes it's necessary to be a diplomat, not a warrior. For example, I hear that the staff is going to try a new chaperoning method to divide the duties among the staff and Avangarde. They are going to let the Guests choose by whom they are chaperoned when they go outside the keep, or are tutored, and so forth."

"So?"

"So if I can convince a certain Guest, a certain older and influential Guest, to request me as a chaperone, then that Guest will certainly have positive things to say about me, and thus word will reach those who make the decisions, and eventually I will be a prime candidate for an Avangarde." Jon paused and looked at Patrick for a reaction.

Patrick stifled a laugh. "And just what Guest did you have in mind?"

Jon tried nonchalantly to jerk his head in Minion's direction, which of course, only made it look more obvious.

The little man was now digging through a burlap sack.

Patrick frowned. "I don't think Minion has much influence in these matters."

Jon rolled his eyes. "No, his master...Loki,"

Patrick shook his head whimsically. "Jon, Jon, Jon. If ever I am master of my own kingdom, I certainly would want you as my advisor, for humor's sake if nothing else."

Jon smiled. "Well, we'll see."

Minion departed then, not having eaten anything, slinging his sack over his shoulder.

"Where's my fork?" Patrick frowned as he searched around his seat.

"Look, there is Viscount Loki now," Jon said excitedly. He straightened out his collar and quickly ran a hand through his thick blond hair. "Wish me luck," he said, and left. Patrick smiled and shook his head.

"Ho, Jon!" Sir Peredur, an Avangarde, intercepted the Reservist in the middle of the dining hall. "Ho, Jon. Where are the scissors I lent to you?"

Patrick saw Loki glance at the two men, and pass out of the room. Jon didn't notice. "I left them in front of your door, as always."

Peredur was angry. "If someone else borrowed them they would have left a note."

Jon crossed his arms over his barrel chest. "Just what are you suggesting?"

Peredur raised his hands defensively. "Look, Jon, I know that they are handy and you have been busy, but those scissors were a gift from the finest smith in my home city. Their handles are gold. Just bring them by later tonight and everything will be fine."

Jon's face turned crimson. "*I left them at your door.*"

"Just bring them back," Peredur said, stalking away.

#

Minion entered the kitchen unobtrusively and went straight to the drawers that held the keep's silverware. Unfortunately, most of it was made of wood and iron.

"Can I help you?"

Minion stopped his rummaging and turned to find Rosa, the kitchen madame. He swallowed hard under her stern gaze, then fumbled in his pocket and produced a piece of paper.

"I'm looking for a bottle of vinegar?" he squeaked after looking over the list.

"Well, you're not going to find it there," Rosa said in her thick Italian accent. She reached up into a cabinet and produced a small earthenware bottle with a red ribbon tied about its neck. This she handed to the little man. "Now you bring that back when you're finished."

"Yes'm," Minion replied, snatching the bottle and running.

He stuffed the bottle in his belt and moved through the corridors towards his destination. On his way he came across Father Hugh walking ahead of him, a glistening string of silver prayer beads dangling from his cassock belt. Minion surreptitiously unhooked them and stored them in his sack. Shortly after, while passing through the dining hall, he grabbed a pitcher of water off a table—leaving a Guest scratching her head after turning to fill her cup.

Thus armed, he arrived at the corner of the keep where a spiraling staircase wound its way up to the second and third floors. Minion made the short but taxing climb, lugging the sack over his shoulder. It was here that Loki had parlayed sumptuous lodgings for himself and his servant—sumptuous by Greensprings standards. The apartments were meant to house distinguished visitors away from the hubbub of the Hall for Guests, and had more than one room, a fireplace, and a view overlooking the main courtyard. Once upon a time, these rooms had been a part of the keep's corner watchtower, hence its circular main room and pointy roof.

"Ah, it's about time," Loki said when his servant entered their apartments. "I was starting to wonder. We have much to do."

Minion approached the central table and deposited the burlap sack there, followed shortly by the pitcher of water and bottle of vinegar. Loki stood up from his chair next to the window where he had been handling what looked like a clay jar. He approached the table, touching on his way the largest object in the room, a pottery wheel. He set the clay jar and a butter knife on the table, wiping his hands on an apron splattered with drying clay. His sleeves were rolled up and his hair unkempt— he had been at work for long hours.

"I hope you have the last of what we need," he said, sifting through the sack's contents. "Any more scavenging forays and people will become curious."

"I'm curious," Minion said.

"Soon, soon," Loki responded, picking through the assorted spoons, forks, and knick-knacks. "But it will be far easier to show you." Loki frowned at the contents. "There isn't much here in the way of precious metals."

Minion squirmed. "I'm sorry master, but there are very few true pieces of silverware about. Perhaps if we waited until a festival or holiday when they bring out the good stuff…"

"Ah-ha, that's more like it!" Loki said energetically, snatching something out of the pile. He held in his hand a pair of scissors with gold handles. Neatly engraved along one of the blades was the name Peredur. "This more than makes up for your ineptitude. Silver would have gotten the job done—not that you brought very much—but gold is much better."

Loki moved to another part of the room where a small anvil stood near the fireplace. On top of it rested an iron mallet. He grasped the scissors by the handles and laid the blades on the anvil such that they mostly hung over the edge. With the mallet he swung down and neatly broke the blades off.

"That should do nicely," Loki said, examining what was left in his hand. He tossed the hunk of metal to Minion. "Heat and soften that in the iron pot, then beat it on the anvil into roughly a cube." Loki retrieved the pitcher of water and moved to a basin where he used the water to wash his hands of the dried clay. "I don't know what was more of a coup, you finding those pair of scissors or the pottery wheel with which to make the jar."

"Thank you master!" Minion said, basking in the rare praise.

Loki went back to the table and brushed aside the pile of material from Minion's latest haul. He hefted the earthenware bottle from the kitchen, unstopped its cork and sniffed the contents.

"Excellent! We are almost there." As Minion removed the hot piece of gold from an iron pot sitting over the fire with a pair of tongs, Loki grabbed the clay jar and butter knife and finished fashioning a hole in the top of the otherwise closed container. The jar was much smaller than the water pitcher Minion had brought, but still large enough to contain a fair amount of liquid. On the pottery wheel, Loki had essentially created a completely closed capsule, then poked a small breathing hole in the top for the firing process. Once hardened in the fireplace, Loki took the butter knife to the hole to widen it out and smooth its edges. Satisfied with his work, he blew the dust off and set it on the table. He then filled the vessel with the kitchen vinegar.

As Minion began beating on the piece of gold, Loki set to making a fresh batch of clay in a bowl. He threw in some powdered raw material and the water from the washbasin, then kneaded the mix into a fist-sized lump of sticky mud. After washing his hands again he took the bowl to the table and drew from his apron an iron spoon beaten flat, wrapped by a sheet of copper that had once been a small mirror.

"There, master, it's finished," Minion said, proudly holding up the pummeled gold with the tongs.

Loki looked down his nose at the object from across the room. "It's not as pretty as me, but it will do. Now bend a copper fork about it as if wrapping a present, leaving the fork handle hanging out like an excess strip of ribbon."

As Minion carried out the task, Loki inserted the rod into the hole of the clay jar, pleased to see when looking down that the vinegar rose to fill the spaces between the spoon and the many folds of copper. Next he packed the fresh clay around the rod so that it stood propped up and snug, leaving only the rod sticking out. Finally, he took from another pile of loot a daisy chain of copper necklaces, bracelets, and even a candle-snuffer pounded together end to end. He handed this to Minion.

"When you're finished, attach the fork handle to the end that isn't the candle-snuffer."

After that, Loki turned to his personal luggage and rummaged through a leather satchel. After finding a gold locket, he pulled a chair up to the table and waited for Minion to finish. Once braiding and pounding the pliable metal together, Minion brought the ball-and-chain contrivance to the table where Loki examined it with a critical eye.

"It will do," he said simply, as Minion stood nearby rubbing his hands.

Loki held up the gold locket. "Recognize this?" he asked.

"Yes my lord, it is yours. A fine piece of jewelry, but you never wear it."

"That is because it is much too precious to risk losing or having stolen," Loki replied, slowly opening the locket on a hinge. Minion reacted, having thought all along the teardrop shaped object carved with unknown symbols was solid through and through. Loki presented the contents, a fine white powder, at a safe distance.

Minion tried bending closer for a better look, but Loki pulled it away.

"This, my little helper, is magic powder." Loki held the locket in the palm of his hand, the lid open. With his other hand he made a waving gesture over it and it began to levitate. Minion gasped. "With great effort, I can make objects move such as this," Loki explained, concentrating on the floating locket. "But with each passing day, it becomes more and more difficult. Once upon a time common people could do this, but few can do it at all any more. The world is changing." He made another gesture with his free hand and the powder rose from the locket, swirling in the air like smoke. The locket then slowly settled in his hand as the powder danced above it. "But with this powder, I can do this all day. I can make whatever it comes in contact with levitate as well…" He made a tossing gesture and the powder engulfed Minion in a cloud. A moment later, Minion gasped and kicked as he rose off the ground. "That is but just a sampling of what this powder is capable of." Loki snapped his fingers and the cloud coalesced and shot back to its resting place in the locket.

Minion fell to the floor with a thud.

"Many uses," Loki said, snapping the locket shut and placing it in his vest pocket, "like making invisible doors open as wide as I want them to."

Minion brushed himself off, though not a trace of the powder was on him. "So why are you waiting to do it?"

Loki sighed heavily. "Alas, this here is the last of what I have. Most of the uses for the powder require that it be consumed. Some was lost in just that small demonstration. But that is what all this is for." He gestured at the gathered paraphernalia on the table.

Minion frowned.

"We are going to make more," Loki explained. "Please, touch the tip of the rod sticking out of the jar."

Minion did as commanded.

A blue spark arced from the rod even before he could touch it, and he leapt back clutching his hand, crying out.

"You see, the powder comes from gold or some other equally precious metal. In order to turn gold into the powder, you need this." Loki stroked the outside of the jar, which did nothing. "Once I've converted that lump of gold into the magic powder, and with the proper celestial bodies in alignment in a few months time, I can float an entire galleon through that portal into the fairy realm at the lake!"

Minion jumped up and down, infected with Loki's energy. "Let's do it master! I want to see the gold change!"

"Yes, yes, let's," Loki said, and caught himself rubbing his hands together like Minion. He wiped his hands on his trousers, regained his composure, and reached for the candle-snuffer end of the chain.

He positioned the snuffer over the tip of the metal rod protruding from the jar, dropped it, and jumped back when a spark sizzled at the contact. His eyes were big with anticipation, his fists raised in the air ready to be jubilant.

Aside from the gold color fading some, however, not much else happened.

And though his fists remained in the air, Loki's expression faded as well.

Minion maintained an idiot's grin, but it was strained as he looked nervously between his master and the lump of gold.

"Touch the gold," Loki said.

"But master..." Minion whined, clutching his still-stinging hand.

"*Touch it.*"

Closing his eyes, Minion reached out and grasped the lump of gold and sighed when he felt nothing but lukewarm metal.

"Dammit!" Loki pounded his fist on the table, causing the jar to bounce and Minion to jump back. For an encore, Loki picked up the whole jar and threw it against the nearest wall, where it exploded into a shower of shards, acrid liquid, and jangling copper parts.

He turned the table over in a cacophony of tumbling metal utensils and moved to the window like a whirlwind of rage. At the window, Loki threw the shudders open and once again shouted, "Dammit!" and beat his fists on the windowsill.

Then just as suddenly as his outburst started, it stopped. He plopped down in the chair before the window, a sullen look on his face. Minion crouched in the corner.

"That size a jar should have sufficed," Loki mused out loud after an interminable amount of time had passed. "Perhaps I would have had to refill it once...maybe twice...with fresh electrolyte, but it should have worked."

He looked up, a spark of hope in his eyes. "Maybe the materials are too crude...or maybe, I need a bigger vessel!" But just soon as he reasoned this to himself, the spark in his eyes went out. "No, no, the gold barely turned *color*! The best material and a jar ten times that size probably wouldn't do either."

At length, he leaned over and put his head in his hands.

"Has the world changed that much?" It was more of a statement than a question. Minion didn't dare make a noise. "This place, Avalon, is the best the world has to offer? So what if the weather is near perfect? So what if the sky is bluer than blue, the grass greener than green, and the air perfumed of apple blossom? What good is all that to me? I hunger for..."

Loki froze. Something in his view caught his attention.

"Perfect weather," he said detachedly. "Rarely a cloud in the sky...but rainbows."

His voice trailed off as he stood and leaned out the window and took a good long look at the countryside beyond the keep walls. At rolling green hills, at lush forests and at the dazzling blue sky.

He sat back down in his chair, a dumbfounded look on his face.

"Could it be?" he whispered.

Chapter Eight

The end of the world began with sand hissing against a tent, a sound like the grains disappearing down the throat of an hourglass. Lokutis sat up clenching his chest, legs hanging over the edge of the mattress, and waited for a long moment until a deep breath rattled out of his lungs, and then he collected himself. He wrapped a crimson robe about his pale shoulders and ducked outside to wait for dawn.

As the tent flap fell shut, the air filled with the sound of fluttering wings. Something large had been resting above the tent door, and was taking flight directly into the sunrise. A solitary sand-colored feather drifted down to him, and he shielded his eyes to get a better look at his visitor. It looked like a large vulture, but the crimson light tangled around its silhouette. Something about the creature struck him as odd, but it was gone, and other problems weighted his thoughts.

Lokutis plodded through the sand, picking his way through obstacles that were at first just rocks, then mason stones, and then broken portions of walls. He looked back one more time, just to check. The tent was of the nomadic design, but enlarged to make a small mountain of shimmering silk, crimson like his robe with gold trim. His simple black banner oscillated serpent-like from the pinnacle. The sky above it was empty.

He stopped at a waist-high circle of mortared stones that contained a spring—the pool spilled continuously over the stone lip and soaked into the sand. He thrust his hands into the cool water and splashed his face. He let the water run down his throat and robe. Then, leaning heavily on one elbow, he cupped more water in his palm and wiped it across the back of his neck. He let the liquid wash away the night's sweat, but it could not wash away the memory of the nightmare.

"Magnificent, isn't it?" said a voice behind Lokutis.

He turned and saw his advisor, awake, silhouetted in the first razor thin line of sunlight. His violet robe and black sash fluttered around his lanky form. His skin was as dark and as smooth as obsidian. His strange almond shaped eyes did not rest on his master, but gazed past his shoulder to the tower.

"Indeed, Akahamet," Lokutis replied.

"Do you intend on finishing it?" Akahamet asked, arching a painted eyebrow. The rising sun glinted off his shaven head. "Is that why you asked that the meeting take place in its shadow?"

Above the valley walls the sun washed the ruins, turning them surreal and red, more alive than at midday when everything became the same dead color. A field of toppling columns sent fingers of shadow across the valley floor, toward the megalithic ruins, ruins so huge that from a distance they easily would have been mistaken in the darkness for another of the valley's craggy peaks.

A tower. A monster.

Well, it should have been. A broad road started at the base, then circumscribed the bottommost tier and appeared on the outside of the next highest, now more narrow. This concourse continued ever higher right up to the point where construction had ended. Even there, if the dimensions stayed relative, the road must have been broad enough to allow four oxcarts to travel abreast of each other, miles above the valley floor.

In the distance a large pair of wings coasted around the tower, hunting. It was probably the thing that had crept up to his tent—probably a vulture that had been enticed by the smells of his camp. It circled the road and disappeared around one side of the tower, the side that was partially collapsed. There, the architecture was exposed, and probably sheltered many rodents in the great halls meant for men.

Each of the tower's tiers was a man-made shell circling the outside of a core of natural rock—the tower was constructed around a landform. Monstrous arches fixed the shell walls to the mountain core, and six of these radiated outward at each tier. Between the arches stretched out secondary arms, from each corner, that reached out to one another. They united in the center, like four hands clasping together, forming a vaulted ceiling for one section of a tier, which in turn would be the floor for another. The network of keystones that kept the megalithic bridgework suspended in air was mind-boggling.

The mountain core was un-hewn at its lower portions, but its peak had been shaped into a perfect cylinder—chiseled down to a smooth circular platform. Not satisfied with the height at this point, the builders had used this platform as a new base for a lattice of arches that supported yet another tier.

It was at this point that construction had come to an abrupt halt. Arching spans hung incomplete. The shell wall was only partially bricked, exposing the frame. The winding road emptied into nothingness. Judging from the width of the last level, there was plenty of room to continue skyward with the tier within tier method of construction before it had to come to an inevitable stop. With one level growing out of another, reaching ever higher, it gave the impression of something organic—like a hollow reed of marsh grass. Or perhaps, with its side crumbled away, revealing a thousand-score arches and chambers, a honeycomb, or the broken shell of a nautilus. Were the builders trying to copy nature? Improve upon its perfection? Or were some designs simply inevitable?

In any case, the tower was a wonder. To see a manmade structure rising from the valley floor, subduing an entire mountain, first inspired shock, followed briefly by disbelief, and then paralyzing awe. It was a city in the sky.

"Were I to finish it," said Lokutis, "Jhove would curse me and thwart my efforts, just as he has done to every generation that has presumed to build on it."

Akahamet nodded. "How long is man's memory? A thousand years? It seems that every millennium some king tries to complete it, believing that he is the one whom Jhove will overlook while they build a monument of self-aggrandizement. But you would know more about that than I."

Lokutis raised an eyebrow. "About what? Self-aggrandizement?"

Akahamet laughed. "That too, but I meant more about the time between attempts. You are the ancient one, the Nephilim, not I."

Lokutis laughed as well. He liked his advisor's sense of humor. "No, I will not be finishing the tower," he said, splashing more water in his face. "Jhove may be an absent god, but the minute you do something to capture his attention—" he gestured at the tower, "—he will make up for all the millennia he was silent. And not by way of a friendly apology. No, I prefer to keep to the shadows and run my little empire from there. As for who will build on it next, I don't know. Perhaps it will be Marduk. Perhaps that is why he asked for this ridiculous transaction."

Lokutis turned to the camp and started back towards the array of tents. They looked like paper lanterns strewn among the sand and rocks. The sight of his own tent door reminded him of his abrupt awakening; he had gone out seeking water, hoping to ease the knot in his stomach brought on by the dreams. He rubbed his temple, rubbing at the images of jeering children, their rocks hurling at him. Their shouts and taunts.

Akahamet trailed behind. "In all seriousness, my lord, your captains are wondering why you chose to hold the meeting here."

"What? Oh. Marduk and his people are a superstitious lot. They will be less likely to commit treachery while in the presence of a testament to what happens to oath breakers." And he added, "It is practical, too. The captains should understand that. We may need the narrow valley mouth and our soldiers today."

"You are worried, then?"

"No, not worried. But it pays to be cautious."

Movement commenced in the camp, slow at first, then picking up pace as tent flaps were flung open and a few of the captains and the camp herald prepared for their duties.

Akahamet said, "You rose early for some reason, my lord. The dreams again?" When Lokutis did not respond right away, he added, "But it is none of my business."

Lokutis grunted, and mused out loud, "The past should stay buried, and not resurface in dreams. The dead should stay buried."

An awkward moment passed. Akahamet turned his attention back to the tower.

"You know what I think?" he said. "It's as you say: Jhove is an invisible and silent god. The people build this tower, over and over again, not to flaunt their accomplishments, not to compete with his creations...but to get his attention. So he will react. It's like a child acting out. A cry for attention. Even bad attention is better than none."

"You are wise, my friend," Lokutis said, smiling. He placed a hand on Akahamet's shoulder as they walked. His advisor knew the story, and his oblique comfort found its mark. He leaned against the well. "Godhood, it's about giving the people what they want. I fulfill their needs and they worship me for it. I fill the void where Jhove is absent."

"You needn't be a god or even a Nephilim to receive my thanks and praise, my lord," Akahamet said, his voice once again deep and sincere. "If it were not for you, I'd still be a slave in Cush."

Lokutis faltered briefly, an image of shackles around his own wrists flashed across his mind. "If you really wish to thank me, you can stop calling me Nephilim. It sounds too much like 'half-breed' to me. 'God' will do just fine."

They both laughed and Lokutis felt the knot in his stomach completely unravel. The sound of jeering children quieted in his head and the image of a dirty boy hiding under a building blurred away. The laughter felt good and he let the morning breeze carry his tension from him.

"Woe!" boomed a strange voice.

They spun in its direction. On top of a weather-worn pillar was a peculiar creature. It was about the size and shape of a leopard, but with plain sandy colored fur. Its feet were chitinous talons, like a hawk's. On its back, extending from between its shoulder blades, were a pair of great motley wings, and if all that were not strange enough, its head was crowned with a mane like a lion's, but peering out from it was a vaguely human face.

"Woe!" it cried again. "Woe to the beasts, the creeping things and the birds of the air! But most of all, woe to man! The sun also rises, but too late for today! The sun also rises, but it is too early for today! Only gopherwood!"

"What by the stars is that?" said Lokutis, brow furrowed at the gibbering creature.

Akahamet grunted, but he wore a look of mild awe. "It's a sphinx, though I've never heard of one this far north. They are not uncommon in the lands south of Egypt."

"Terry, terry, terrestrial!" It continued with its tirade. "Wisteria! Nameless and blameless!"

"What the devil is it ranting about?" Lokutis asked, and blinked when the creature's head rotated a full circle, yet its eyes stayed fixed on him.

"Pay it no attention, my lord; they are full of lies and nonsense. They are known to taunt their victims with riddles, promising not to eat them if they answer truly. However, their riddles are meaningless."

"The flood gates of the sky will open! The wellsprings of the abyss will rise!" "Shoo! Be gone, stupid creature!" Lokutis shouted. He bent over to retrieve some rocks and threw them at the oddity. He missed, but it ruffled its feathers.

"Woe to you, O human! Woe!" Its head rotated again.

"Oh really? Riddle me this," Lokutis said, and snapped his fingers. There was the sound of thunder, and a portion of the pillar just beneath the sphinx burst into a shower of dust and rocks. With laborious flapping, it flew away and disappeared among the craggy peaks of the valley.

"That will teach you!" Lokutis called after it. "Threaten me? I'm a god!"

"We should be going, sire. Marduk and his entourage shall be here soon," Akahamet said.

Lokutis pulled away from the scene and headed back to his tent. He had been more amused by the encounter than anything. Akahamet, however, paused before turning to leave. He looked in the direction of the sphinx, a hint of concern creasing his brow.

#

By early afternoon, Lokutis stood in his tent with his arms outstretched as Akahamet dressed him. Being a god was delicate business, and he wouldn't let just anybody dress him.

His robe was of luxurious lavender silk, tightly belted at the waist with a gold chain. A gold breastplate adorned his chest with at least one of every kind of precious gem. A gold ring encircled each of his fingers. Rings also dangled from his long pointy ears, which seemed to move independently of his head, scanning the room for the faintest of sounds. His dark hair glistened with expensive oils and perfumes, as did his beard, which hung in coiled ringlets from his angular chin. A pointy bronze helmet held the boar's tusks above his brow, each of which was sleeved in bronze.

"Marduk approaches?" Lokutis asked.

"Yes, my lord." Akahamet was almost as richly dressed. His garb was his customary violet robe and black sash, but now he wore a bronze skull-piece that fit the contours of his shaven head. His wrists were covered in bronze braces. A large gold ring hung from his ears and nose, and an ivory-handled short-sword hung from his hip.

"He is accompanied by the agreed-upon number of men?"

"Men, yes," Akahamet said. "But he pulls in train twenty women, most likely as tribute gifts or as incentives for the transaction."

Lokutis scowled, deep in thought. Akahamet now applied kohl to his master's eyes. He had already painted his own eyes and brows with gold dust.

"Speaking of the transaction, does it appear that they bring the gold?"

"It's hard to tell. Their beasts of burden pull heavily laden wagons that leave deep ruts in the earth, but the cargo is shielded by cloth."

Again Lokutis scowled. "And what do the scouts at the valley mouth report?"

"All is well. There are no others in sight. If Marduk brought an army, it is well out of range."

"But none of this is what troubles you, is it Akahamet?"

His advisor paused in applying the kohl, but then continued with his strokes. "It's nothing. Mere foolishness on my part, really."

"Out with it," Lokutis insisted. "You are my closest advisor for a reason. I trust your intuition."

Akahamet drew in a breath. "It's the sphinx, my lord, and all its talk of doom."

"But it was you who said that was just nonsense."

"If that were all of it I'd agree. But that, the strange nature of Marduk's request, the location we've chosen for the transaction, the storm brewing in the east, and now I hear from the scouts that they have come across a crazy man and his family outside the valley who have fashioned a giant boat in the desert. All ill portents."

"A giant boat?" Lokutis said. "Surely you're jesting."

"No my lord. The man is a simple farmer, Noam by name, who claims a flood is coming and has convinced his children and their families to take refuge in the boat."

"There isn't a large body of water for hundreds of leagues from here. Sounds like a crazy, harmless old man whose family is humoring him."

"Perhaps, but it's the sheer size of the boat that concerns me," Akahamet continued. "It's the size of a fortress. Large enough to hold a thousand families. No small amount of time and resources went into its creation. It wasn't made on a whim."

"A fortress you say? Did the scouts thoroughly check it out?"

"Absolutely. They said the insides were just more craziness: doors that opened into nothing, stairs that ended at the ceiling, cubit after cubit of stalls, but no animals. A group of locals that was there jeering him said that he had been working on it for months—longer than when we had first made plans to meet Marduk here."

"Well, there you go," Lokutis pointed out. "It has nothing to do with Marduk, thus nothing to worry about."

"As I said, my lord, just foolishness on my part."

A horn sounded somewhere in the camp.

"Speaking of Marduk," Lokutis said. "Akahamet, my cape."

Akahamet retrieved another swath of dark silk from the full-sized wardrobe Lokutis took with him on his journeys. He hung this on his master's thin frame, propping up the collar and clasping the chain across his throat. Lokutis grabbed its edges and spread his arms like a great bat, revealing more of the lavender lining.

"How do I look?" he asked, turning his head in profile.

Akahamet smiled. "Truly like a god."

"That was the correct response. For your reward I shall let you live another day and not destroy you."

They both laughed and exited the tent.

#

A light haze obscured the sun and on the eastern horizon, dark clouds confirmed Akahamet's report. Fortunately they looked far enough away that the day's business would be concluded by the time they blew in. The morning's breeze had turned into light yet persistent wind that whipped up dust devils.

"All right already," Lokutis snapped at the herald, who announced the arrival of Marduk and his entourage. "I can see them."

The herald tucked his ram's horn under his arm, bowed to Lokutis and stepped down from the stones.

The meeting place was perfect for this transaction. A natural throne rose before a slab of rock that had been a sacrificial altar at one time, complete with blood-gutter that ran to a drain hole. These two objects sat on a field of massive flagstones and behind the throne were remnants of an amphitheater. Evidently sacrifices were popular. Opposite the throne, altar, and seats was an open space surrounded by columns in various stages of collapse. It appeared as if there had been an enclosing wall of mortared stone at one time, but villagers seeking a ready source of quarried stone had scavenged it over the millennia.

Marduk entered the field enclosed by the columns as Lokutis had planned. Here there was enough space for Marduk to feel comfortable, but confined enough to discourage his men spreading from out in a tactical formation.

Lokutis took his seat on the throne and Akahamet stood at his side. Lokutis's one hundred soldiers and scores of servants stood on the amphitheater seats. They wore his black and purple, and the soldiers also wore headscarves that covered their faces in the desert nomad fashion. They carried Lokutis's black pennants, which flapped in the rising wind.

For Marduk, all was red. His approaching entourage looked like an ocean tide rolling in, tinged with red foam. The sort of foam that occasionally washed into coastal towns after a war on an opposite shore, or when the tide carried poison that left gull and seal and fish carcasses strewn along miles of beach. Lokutis did not plan on being a casualty of such a tide today.

The bulk of the entourage was a regiment of crimson clad soldiers each carrying the black-fringed banner of the House of Marduk. Belted at their waists were scimitars. Their uniforms were spacious black pantaloons, and their feet were covered in leather and silk slippers whose toes curled in on themselves, and short, tightly wrapped turbans. Their faces were hidden behind bronze masks fashioned into the appearance of a bearded man, albeit a man with a single slit for an eye. These masks shone like mirrors.

Behind the soldiers next came servants pulling a silver chain that connected a train of twenty women bound at the wrists by silver shackles. They stumbled along, mostly concealed in bright blue burqas. Though only their eyes were exposed, they were certainly women and not soldiers in disguise, as the thinness of wrists and shortness of stature attested.

Next came four wagons pulled by oxen that kicked up a large cloud of dust. Tarps concealed their payloads.

And above all, surrounded by the soldiers in a sea of red

flags, was Marduk's barge. It was a magnificent yet functional work of art: a colossal elephant's head, plated in gold, ears fanning out to either side like two great wings. The tusks were real, taken from some mammoth or mastodon from some far corner of the world. All around the fringe were fist-sized rubies that flared in the sun. At the center of the barge was a flat stage from which the elephant trunk extended and curved back on itself, forming a staircase to the platform. At the back of the stage, recessed between the elephant's eyes—which were made of smoky glass—was a throne.

Upon this seat sat Marduk.

He was a giant of a man, perhaps half again the height of a normal man. His bare chest was broad and muscular, as were his tree-like limbs. His head was shaven; his dark beard was fashioned into three separate jagged points like three black lightning bolts shooting from his jaw. His brow was so prominent and thick that it overhung his eyes and hid their nature.

Each finger was bedecked in a gold ring of some gaudy design. Gold bands, one of which was a serpent creeping elaborately up his forearm, encircled his wrists and upper arms. Both his massive nipples were pierced with rings almost the size of ox leads.

The red tide came within speaking distance of the throne and stone altar. As it did, the soldiers before the barge parted to allow an unobstructed view of Marduk in his splendor. The train of blue robed women took up position to his right and the wagons to his left.

When the soldiers parted, Lokutis saw that the barge hovered above the ground by no apparent means of suspension.

Marduk stood and extended to his full height, crossing his arms over his massive chest. He wore only a white girdle about his waist and sandals whose straps laced up his corded calves to his knees. His skin was deeply bronzed by the sun, in deep contrast to Lokutis's skin which was so pale it was almost transparent. It was, however, just as smooth and blemish free as Marduk's.

Bronze and alabaster squared off as the barge slowly descended to the flagstones.

"Nice transportation," Lokutis said. "You're not trying to compensate for something, are you?"

Marduk ignored the statement and continued to glower from underneath the jutting brow. A man stepped forward, similarly dressed as the flag-bearing soldiers.

He drew himself up and boomed: "My Lord Marduk graces you with his presence! Marduk, God of the Eastern skies! Bringer of Thunder! Vanquisher of Tiamat! Lord of the Wind! Ruler of Nibiru! Architect of Eridu! Slayer of Kingu! Overshadower of Enlil!"

When the herald at last was silent, Lokutis rolled his eyes and bowed at the hip. His entourage followed suit. When this was done, Akahamet stepped forward, made a flamboyant gesture at Lokutis and boomed right back: "Lokutis, God of the Mountain, Lord of the Fires of the Earth, Proprietor of the Forge of Power, Maker of the Food of Kings and Gods, Guide to the Netherworld, Provider of Dreams, Bringer of Pleasure and Might...is well pleased to tolerate your divine presence." Akahamet bowed deeply and stepped back.

Marduk sneered and his balled fists quivered, but after a long pause he bowed at the hip and his people followed suit.

"Well, now that we have that nonsense out of the way," Lokutis said, sitting back in the throne and crossing his legs, "let's get down to business shall we?"

Marduk remained standing, arms still folded. "Yes, let's." His voice was booming and unnaturally deep, a sure sign of his own Nephilim nature. "You have the Mizkift?"

"Yes," Lokutis responded.

Marduk looked around, being slow and obvious about the

gesture. "I don't see it. Nine pillars' worth of Mizkift should be fairly obvious. Where is it?"

Lokutis stood up from the throne and stabbed a finger at the five wagons. In particular at one whose concealed load was smaller than the rest.

"And where is the five pillars' worth of gold as compensation? I see, at best, four and a half. No trickery in this exchange will be tolerated!"

Marduk sneered again and gestured with his chin to his men near the wagons. "I knew you would go into a passion over that. Allow me to enlighten you."

The wagons were uncovered to reveal brick upon brick of lustrous gold neatly stacked into trapezoids. The smaller load was silvery in the sunlight.

Lokutis' back went rigid and color entered his fair face. "*This*, for my services and my product? Even if your mines were empty of gold, there should be four pillars' of silver to compensate, not half of one!"

"Lokutis! Be still!" Marduk's otherworldly voice stirred the black and purple flags. "It is not silver." Marduk gestured, and one of the wagoneers laboriously removed an ingot of the material and walked it towards the throne and altar.

"You may be the master of converting gold into the highward firestone, what you call Mizkift, but I am the master of smelting gold from ore." Marduk's voice was calm, and bore a touch of pride. "Only those accustomed to mining and smelting as much gold as I in my empire are aware of this material."

The ingot was half the length of the servant's forearm and twice as thick as his wrist. He approached the altar, and Akahamet intercepted him and took the object. In doing so, a surprised look crossed his face. He hefted it and carried it to Lokutis.

"At first we deemed it a troublesome impurity that was difficult to separate from gold in the smelting process..."

Akahamet handed the brick to Lokutis, murmuring, "It's true my lord, it is not silver. It is much heavier."

"...but then we performed experiments on it. It is its own noble metal. More lustrous than silver and more dense. It does not tarnish nor corrupt. It is harder and stronger than both silver and gold. And most of all..." Marduk paused for emphasis. His smooth voice would have belied his brutish appearance, but when he smiled, he revealed many sharp teeth. "It produces almost twice the amount of Mizkift as gold when fired."

Lokutis examined the metallic brick in his hands with raised eyebrows. After a moment he handed it back to Akahamet.

"Platinum," he said simply. "I am not ignorant of its existence."

Marduk motioned to his herald, who approached the altar with a clay tablet. Again Akahamet intercepted and took the item.

"The calculations for formulation are noted on this tablet, and the resulting yield," Marduk said.

Akahamet handed the tablet with a multitude of cuneiform chicken scratches to Lokutis, who merely glanced at it and handed it back to his advisor.

"Being the Lord of the Forge, whose prowess for creating the purest of Mizkift is legendary, you should be able to coax more than three quarters of potential yield from the platinum. Right?" Marduk flashed his sea-monster teeth in the most condescending of smiles.

"You assume a lot." Lokutis sounded none too pleased. "None of this was agreed upon. Despite your calculations, I could stand to be at a disadvantage. You could walk away with more Mizkift than I with noble metals, and that's even taking into consideration the ten percent extra you are to have brought in consideration of my stores. Do you have any idea how far you've depleted them, ordering your ridiculous amount of Mizkift?"

"I understand." Marduk sounded uncharacteristically contrite. "It is unexpected, and some measure of risk comes with accepting new terms. That is why I am prepared to offer you these to offset any potential shortfall on your part." Marduk swung a hand in the direction of the chained women. His herald moved towards them. "Personally, I think you are getting the better end of the deal. But this transaction is important enough to me that I'm willing to pay a premium."

His herald tugged the foremost woman's veil; it hung from her bound wrists. She certainly was an exquisite creature. Narrow of waist and broad of hip, she stood gracefully in gauzy pantaloons. Two strips of the same transparent material crisscrossed her torso, covering but not concealing her breasts. Her abdomen rippled with muscles, as did her arms. A dancer's physique. Her skin was the color of coffee, her lips full, and her hair was a dark silky mane hanging down her back, braided in gold strands. Her eyes were almond shaped, and despite looking down demurely, Lokutis could see that they were a strikingly rare emerald color.

Lokutis took in the sight, and Marduk let him, remaining silent. Lokutis cleared his throat and mentally slapped his own face to recompose himself. Marduk certainly knew his weaknesses.

"You are very fortunate that I have knowledge of platinum, otherwise I'd put an end to these proceedings," Lokutis sniffed. "As it is, I accept your gift and we can proceed."

"I thought you might," Marduk said, not-so-contritely. "But that does bring us back to my original question: Where are the nine pillars of Mizkift?"

"Why, they are right here." Lokutis gestured to Akahamet who moved around the amphitheater seats and gestured to yet another helper. He stepped out from behind the seating and approached a clay amphora situated among the rubble. He was dressed all in white, in a material that looked more like finely woven metal than cloth. He wore gauntlets and a hood of the same material, and the hood was fitted with two glass disks over the eyes. A breastplate on his chest bore several stones that glowed with an inner light as he drew near the amphora. He reached up to its lip, which was a little higher than his head, and removed a loop of densely woven copper wires from a metal pole in the lid. The copper loop was the terminus of a copper cable leading away from the amphora, partially buried in the sand. The cable split in many directions, and drawing a subdued collective gasp from Marduk's entourage, their terminals revealed themselves.

A multiple sunburst of white light strobed the area. Nine objects slowly materialized in the air. Each object was a trapezoidal stack of white ingots similar in size and shape to the gold and platinum bars. A line of the copper cable ran to each stack and was sandwiched between the bricks. And just as Marduk's mobile throne had been levitating above the earth, so too were the piles of white material. But the moment the copper loop was lifted from the jar, they slowly descended to the ground.

Marduk raised an eyebrow, and then said somewhat grudgingly, "Truly you are a magician of the highest sort, and with a flair for the dramatic."

"Why thank you." Lokutis bowed to the rare admission. "Please have one of your people choose a sample at random."

Without having to be told, Marduk's herald scurried forward and gingerly removed a brick from the nearest pile.

"That is clever to hide the Mizkift within the Plane of Light right before us," Marduk said, then gestured at the amphora. "Though I can't imagine what your plans would have been had the negotiations gone sour and had the charge of electrikus in the capacitor had been depleted."

Lokutis shrugged. "I knew you were good for payment."

Marduk smirked.

The herald placed the white substance on the altar and another red-clad servant came forward with a tray holding cups and a flagon. Akahamet positioned himself before the altar. The herald placed a cup before himself and Akahamet. He then raised the flagon with one hand by an ornate handle on its side and steadied it with the other hand at its base. He presented it to both camps. "This is Nektar, drink of the gods. This I attest to." He placed it back on the tray.

Akahamet reached over and took the brick of Mizkift and raised it above the flagon. "This is God-Cake," he announced loudly, and broke off a chunk of the substance in his hand, crushing it into a powder that dropped into the flagon. "Purest of Mizkift, the highward firestone. This I attest to." It was Akahamet's turn to grasp the container. He moved it in a circular motion, mixing the contents inside. He then re-presented the flagon, stating, "Nektar and Mizkift create Ambrosia, food of the gods." He then set it back on the altar.

The herald picked it up and delicately poured into each cup. A pale rose-colored liquid filled each one. When this was complete, each servant dutifully carried his chalice to his respective master. Marduk and Lokutis saluted each other with their cups and took a long drink.

Though he had drunk the Ambrosia elixir many times before, it always felt like his first. By itself, Nektar was heavy and sweet and imparted a deep-seated euphoria. With Mizkift added, the sweetness was tempered by the metallic bitterness of the powder, which transformed the Nektar euphoria into an acute awareness of the universe.

Lokutis was vaguely aware of handing the cup to Akahamet as his eyes rolled into the back of his head, which lolled towards the sky. The taste assaulted the back of his tongue, first smothering it with an overwhelming berry-honey taste, and then followed it by a metallic tartness that drilled ruthlessly into his taste buds. As the euphoria settled in his chest and loins, the tartness shot through nerves like lightning to his brain. A simultaneous burst of light exploded at the center of his mind and across his vision, leaving an afterimage even as the initial explosion turned to sputtering shooting stars. As the initial sensation receded, Lokutis opened his eyes and looked around.

The world around him was transformed. Everything was sharp and crisp. Colors were more vivid. Lokutis could count the pores on Marduk's skin, which had previously seemed as solid as polished bronze. He could hear the heartbeats of all living creatures around him and the hum of the giant jar-capacitor. He heard the frenzied work of fire ants under the ruins—it was scrabbling, hurried, frantic work, exceptional even for their hardworking kind.

The swirling dust and sand and the flapping banners had meaning. Their movements were not the least bit random. The rocks themselves had a story to tell by their very resting positions and Lokutis could hear them whispering their deepest desires, where they wanted to move to next...and when. Their desires were urgent and immediate; the stones were impatient to go. If he had the time and elixir to spare, Lokutis was certain he could study the air and discern the equation Jhove used to create it. Maybe even improve upon it. Lokutis became more and more aware of his people and those of Marduk. Their heartbeats became a deafening drum and their breaths a howling wind. The blood flowing in their veins was a rushing river and their minds were screaming in awe at being in the presence of gods. Their adoration and their love were suffocating.

Lokutis squeezed his eyes shut, overwhelmed by it all. He rubbed his temples and took deep breaths until eventually, inevitably, the sensation passed and he was left with a more manageable feeling.

When he opened his eyes, he was gratified to see that Marduk was still under the effects of the elixir. The big man was laid back in his throne, massaging the bridge of his nose with thumb and forefinger.

Lokutis was also pleased to see that Marduk's head servant, the herald who had introduced the Ambrosia, was swaying himself from having partaken of the ceremonial drink—unlike wise Akahamet, who still held the cup, alert and ready for action should it prove necessary during his master's brief moment of vulnerability.

It wasn't much longer and Marduk stood.

"The quality of the product is satisfactory," he sniffed.

"Your Nektar isn't half bad either," Lokutis smirked, knowing full well the Mizkift was more than just satisfactory. "Someday you must tell me who your supplier is among the Olympians."

Marduk ignored the comment.

Several crimson-clad individuals moved among the stacks of Mizkift with clay tablets and styli, tallying the product for their accounts.

Likewise, black and purple clad men moved among the women, removing their robes to ensure the quality was consistent. Lokutis wouldn't put it past Marduk to hold up one beautiful flower as an example among many concealed weeds. So far, Lokutis liked what he saw.

Marduk sat and glowered while his people counted the Mizkift. Lokutis sat as well, throwing a leg over an arm of the stone chair.

"So Marduk, what on earth do you need so much Mizkift for? Such a quantity is unprecedented." The big man did not react immediately to the question. He merely drummed his fingers on the arm of his throne. "Do you need a lifetime supply of repelling force for your floating chair? Hmm?"

"It is none of your concern," Marduk said at last, glancing at the accountants anxiously. "You have been paid in full. What I intend to do with it is my business."

"You see, that is where I disagree," Lokutis said. He swung his feet to the ground and stood, and his tone was still deceptively light. "This is a huge amount of Mizkift to be loosed upon the world all at once. Surely something unusual is afoot, and I don't like the sound of it."

Lokutis made a waving gesture with his hand in the direction of the Mizkift. The stacks levitated and disappeared in a sunburst of white light, leaving Marduk's accountants stumbling back with open mouths.

Marduk was on his feet, looking in disbelief at the empty space. Lokutis had accomplished the feat without having the capacitor jar reconnected to the Mizkift. "What is the meaning of this?" He turned to Lokutis. "Do you dare forfeit on the agreement?"

"I am not forfeiting! You will get your God-Cake, just as soon as you tell me what you are going to do with it! However, be quick about it. The longer it rests in the Plane of Light, the greater the risk of it being lost there."

Marduk's entire head turned scarlet and the cords in his neck stood out. Men in both camps put hand to sword hilt, but stopped short of drawing them. Despite the escalation of tensions, Lokutis suppressed an urge to chuckle at Marduk's comical appearance. That alone was worth the trouble to meet.

"Disclosure was not a part of the original agreement, Lokutis. Why do you care?"

"Because I care not for letting you manipulate me into slitting my own throat."

Marduk raised an eyebrow. "Oh, and just how do you come to that conclusion?"

"This amount of highward firestone is only meant for one of two things." Lokutis's voice was becoming shrill and his movements agitated. Eclipsed by his legendary temper, what little mirth he felt withered. "Either you plan on weaponizing it and using it against me," he continued, "or you plan on disseminating and selling it yourself at a considerably lower price just to drive me out of business and out of the region."

Marduk bared his teeth, shook his head and laughed. "You are truly paranoid, even to the point of destroying a perfectly good business transaction."

"You deny it?"

"I don't need to convert Mizkift to light energy or even to bankrupt you so elaborately. I can crush you anytime. Take my gold, my platinum, my women and leave. You needn't concern yourself with me any longer. Now bring it back!"

Lokutis's face felt hot. "How can I possibly leave you with this much power and turn my back on you?" Spittle was flying from his mouth. He was losing control of himself, letting fear get the better of him, and yet he couldn't keep his mouth shut. "You had to have emptied your entire treasury to come up with this much gold! You must be preparing for some sort of final attack to consolidate your power!"

Marduk paced back and forth in a rage. He glanced between the empty spot, his soldiers and those of Lokutis, weighing his options.

"Very well!" Marduk boomed. His voice echoed up and down the valley, shaking the rocks. "If it will get me out of here sooner, I will tell you." There was a moment of silence. He paced closer. "I intend to permanently enter the Plane of Shar-On, the Plane of Light."

Another moment of silence as the gods faced off.

Lokutis blinked and shook his head as if to clear it. "Come again?"

"You heard me. I intend to use the Mizkift to open a portal into the Plane of Shar-On and enter."

Lokutis once again shook his head in disbelief, but on a grander scale. "What? Are you mocking me?"

Marduk stood with arms crossed, unresponsive.

"Nobody *enters* the Plane of Light! It is a dimension of

energy where Mizkift goes when sufficiently energized. That is all." Lokutis scoffed. "The only ones who believe otherwise are the pharaohs who have some notion that, after a lifetime of ingesting the cake and saturating their flesh with it, they will wake up there after death. And I know what you think of the pharaohs."

"You don't exactly dissuade them from that belief, Lokutis, do you?"

Lokutis feigned shock. "Of course not. Who am I to trample all over somebody else's dogma? It would be bad for business."

"Bad for business indeed," Marduk sneered. "Which is why I don't understand why you're willing to make an exception in my case."

"The Egyptians do not demand this much all at once! It is suspicious!"

"This much Mizkift is necessary to force a doorway open. And as I pointed out, if I am successful, you'll never see me again. There's as good a reason as any to bring it back now."

"Even if you were to force your way into the dimension, assuming you didn't blast yourself out of existence in the process, what do you expect to find there?"

"A new beginning," Marduk said solemnly. "An escape."

Lokutis stared. "From what? Reality? All you have to do is mix a little Mizkift with Nektar to make Ambrosia to do that. You don't need nine pillars of it."

"I do not intend to hide in a drunken stupor, but to literally escape this world." Marduk took to pacing again like a caged animal.

"Another world?" Lokutis scoffed. "You wish to conquer another world? Then invade one of the sanctuaries of the Elohim. Again, a feat that does not require a mountain of highward firestone."

Marduk stopped his pacing. He did not respond. Rather, he looked sidelong at Akahamet and to his own herald. Something about Marduk's manner struck Lokutis as strange. Over the ages he had come to expect certain behavior in his dealings with Marduk as normal: pomposity, arrogance, bravado, megalomania. The sort of fare that afflicted all the gods. The sort of conduct from which Lokutis himself was not immune.

But now, there was sincerity in his voice, as well as something else. That same something that was in Akahamet's voice when his advisor had spoken of the approaching storm, his misgivings of the meeting place, the appearance of the sphinx, and the mention of the madman, Noam, building his ark on dry land. It wasn't just concern—it was fear. But this was coming from a god.

Lokutis narrowed his eyes and chewed on his lower lip. The horizon behind Marduk's head had become deep purple, with occasional streaks of lightning. His crimson host shifted uneasily, glancing nervously at their god, and Lokutis could sense his people were doing the same.

He turned to his trusted advisor. "Give us a moment, will you Akahamet?"

Akahamet blinked in surprise at the request, but dutifully bowed at the waist and withdrew a respectful distance. Marduk likewise made a sharp gesture to his herald, who seemed pleased to put distance between himself and the feuding gods.

"A sanctuary?" Marduk said at last, bitterly. "One of the hidden realms created for those Nephilim beloved of Jhove? That is precisely the last place I should go. Jhove perceives you and me as monsters. Freaks! Mistakes!" He allowed a moment for the words to bite, and they did. Then he said, "But the Elohim, the Shining Ones, Jhove had pity on them even though they had the same Grigori fathers and mortal mothers as we. And why? Because they were beautiful? Bha! Should I force my way into one of their kingdoms hidden behind walls of air, Jhove would strike me down in a heartbeat. No Lokutis, I intend to hide this face in a realm even Jhove cannot reach."

At Marduk's words, Lokutis remembered the dreams from earlier that morning, followed by the memory of an angry man beating him with a switch. *Fatherless bastard.* So many accusations. Then a woman, throwing herself across his bleeding body, taking the lashings and pleading for the man to stop. Yes, the Nephilim, the Elohim, they were mistakes. Never meant to exist. Incomprehensible creatures, born different, children of the Grigori, the Watchers. These were servants of Jhove who were sent to teach mankind, but instead ended up falling from grace and being banished for lying with mortal women.

Lokutis closed his eyes and rubbed his temple. The image of the woman being strangled by the angry man wouldn't leave his thoughts. He rubbed harder when the memory turned to the woman's eyes going lifeless, her head lolling to one side. He opened his eyes and stopped the rubbing. It wouldn't pay to show signs of weakness before his fellow god. Even as he told himself this, though, he thought of the angry man brushing a spider into a jar, and tossing it away. Somehow that image, the hairy creature in its glass vessel, was worse than the memory of his mother dead at her own father's hands.

What Marduk desired was not unfounded, so Lokutis was stern but not unsympathetic when he said, "The Plane of Shar-On is not a place one can go to. If you truly are looking for a change of habitat, then you should invade a sanctuary. If for no other reason than because it is our birthright. We belong there just as much as the Shining Ones."

Marduk ground his teeth. "I have reason to believe Jhove will lay waste to this world he created, to wipe it clean of all the mistakes that populate it. Just as he did to this accursed place eons ago." He thrust his finger at the giant tower that loomed in the background. Its uppermost portions had become veiled by heavy grey clouds. "But it won't be a localized event this time. It will be the entire world. And I intend to be gone from here, and not in an Elohim fishbowl, either, where it will be easier for Jhove to see that he missed one of his mistakes."

"Who is paranoid now? Wherever did you come by such prophecy?"

"The signs are all around you, Lokutis, if only you would look. Mostly it says so in the stars. You would know that if you spent some time outside that cave of yours. Even the fool villager crafting that giant ark outside this valley knows it."

It was Lokutis' turn to pace.

"Really Lokutis," Marduk growled, no longer staring at the empty space where the pillars of Mizkift had stood. His voice was now full of soothing and rationale, at odds with the sweat that started to bead on his pate. "If I am wrong, then I will destroy myself in a blaze of white Mizkift-light. If I am successful, then I will enter either an airless field of energy and perish, or enter a new world and you will never see me again. In any case it will be a boon to you. My empire will need a god."

A bead of sweat fell from his temple. His smile was strained.

Lokutis' eyes narrowed as he returned the big man's gaze, weighing all the information and possibilities. The sky was now dark and distant thunder rumbled. The gentle desert breeze was now a full-grown gale.

"Liar!" Lokutis at long last cried, stabbing an accusing finger at Marduk. "Surely you must take me for some kind of fool with this preposterous excuse! I still say you are up to no good...and in this world, not the Plane of Shar-On!"

Marduk dropped all pretenses of calm and civility. "You miserable wretch! You had this planned all along, didn't you? You never had any intention of handing over the Mizkift! You mean to take my gold by force, don't you?"

"Don't change the subject!" Lokutis shouted. "This is about you taking my God-Cake and using it against me!"

A shouting match ensued and they gestured furiously at one another. Their respective camps held hands firmly to sword hilts and their eyes flicked from one enraged god to the other.

Inevitably, somebody drew a sword, setting into motion a scraping chorus of metal drawn from sheaths on all sides.

"Lokutis, this is your last chance. Relinquish the God-Cake or I will squeeze from you the knowledge of how to retrieve it myself."

"I'd like to see you try!" Lokutis shot back.

Marduk raised his wrists and banged together the metal jewelry.

At the sound, the women slaves tugged apart their shackles, made space between themselves, and commenced to whirl the chains above their heads. The once demure eyes were now intense and focused.

Lokutis bared his teeth at these women, who, as it turned out, did not have the hard bodies of dancers, but the hard bodies of warriors.

Marduk's force now stood one hundred twenty to Lokutis' one hundred.

"I thought you might try something," Lokutis sneered. He snapped his fingers as he had done earlier to drive the sphinx away.

The earth rumbled and shook, and outside the ring of columns, forms rose from the ground. They spilled sand and dirt from their bodies. They were pale and dirty giants, bipedal like a man, and stood another man's height above Marduk. Their limbs were long and deformed with gnarled muscles. Many were bow-legged or hunched, others better formed, but all bearing the heavily muscled bodies of labor and the scars of battle. Naked, hairless, their heads were oblong. Their mouths hung open and trailed strands of drool. These creatures numbered ten and circled the meeting place, encompassing Marduk's forces—including his warrior women.

After a dramatic pause, Marduk spoke. "You can call upon all the help you want, but you and your menagerie of freaks will not keep me from what is rightfully mine."

Lokutis tsked. "Come now, is that any way to talk about your Nephilim brothers?"

"I no more claim these creatures as brother than the Elohim claim you and me. And I tell you, Jhove is coming soon to cleanse this world of such as these," Marduk responded.

"Enough of that ridiculous story! It is obvious you have treachery in mind!" Lokutis gestured toward the warrior women.

Marduk clenched his fists, drew a deep breath and with his unnatural voice rising as he spoke, shouted, "Give me the firestone you insolent little *bastard*!"

Lokutis froze at the word. His face contorted into a caricature of itself—fangs grew from his upper jaw and his eyebrows turned into bat wings above slitted animal eyes blazing lavender. A shimmering aura surrounded his body that seemed to melt his clothes away and his stature tripled in size, becoming a muscled giant. Great bull horns sprouted from his head, toppling his ornate helm, which fell to the sand. He held out fists engulfed in balls of purple flame.

"How dare you talk to me like that!" he growled in an otherworldly voice.

No sooner had Lokutis started his transformation than Marduk commenced one of his own. He too grew in stature, but not as much as Lokutis. His fangs lengthened, and his eyes melded into one great cyclopean fireball. He snatched the serpent shaped bracelet from his wrist and made a flinging gesture. It elongated in his hand and turned into a fiery whip.

"Your true form does not frighten me! Jhove will not have to wipe you from the face of the earth, for I will!"

"Woe!" cried a new voice. "For the hour is at hand!"

The opposing forces turned in the direction of the voice.

There, sitting on top of a column, was the sphinx. Its head rotated oddly.

"Woe to the beasts, the creeping things, and the birds of the air!"

"I told you, Lokutis, your monsters will not stop me!" Marduk exclaimed, shaking the whip at his adversary. It writhed like a living thing, throwing off sparks.

Lokutis scowled. "Deception does not become you. That is one of your agents, sent from the start to distract me."

"Son of Ea," the winged creature said to Marduk, who started at being addressed as such. "Your time has come! Hewn down by the messenger you shall be! There is not even hope of resting among the stars!"

Marduk turned to Lokutis. "What trickery is this? First you make Mizkift disappear without the aid of a capacitor, now you know the true name of my father?"

"Long wanderings!" The beast now turned to Lokutis. "Slow fade! Power drained from your heel! The green man will cut you down and send you to the venomous cave. Only in the last days will you be set free again, just long enough to be destroyed by the bridge-god on the rock of Ragnor! Woe!" The sphinx took flight and flew away from the column in swooping arcs, down the valley, to the scene unfolding there.

The mouth of the valley had become a swirling mass of thunderheads, a vortex crisscrossed with lightning. Something that looked like an ocean of water and light was gurgling forth from this tunnel as from an overturned urn, splashing and foaming its way down the valley, breaking against the rocks and hurling loose boulders in front of it.

Wading through this miasma was a titanic figure around whose ankles the water broke. Humanoid in form, it stood almost as tall as the nearest cliffs and light radiated from its body. It wore richly decorated armor, and girded about its waist was a broad belt with a sword in its scabbard. The light-being grasped in both hands a scythe, which it rested on one shoulder as it strode forward. Spreading from its back were great wings opening and closing like respirating lungs. These looked for a moment like clouds, but soon coalesced into solid pinions.

The first impression was of sheer size, a column of light, radiating mist. But the being's head was what riveted one's attention, and inspired terror.

Whereas its body glowed, its head was absolutely ablaze with fierce lightning. It had not one but four faces, rotating above its shoulders like the sphinx's. The first face was nominally human, with eyes, nose and mouth. The next was a bird of prey, with piercing eyes and a raptor's hooked beak. Another rotation revealed a snorting bull, and the final, a roaring lion.

All who beheld the creature were stricken immobile. It wasn't until a great horn sounded that Lokutis and the others awakened and turned to see where the sound was coming from. A similar creature had perched on the mountaintop and bellowed through a long trumpet. Extended sonorous blasts shook the foundation, causing rocks to slide from the cliffs and the ground to shake.

With the first trumpet blast, large raindrops pelted the dirt, the wind picked up, and thunder and lightning rent the sky. A gushing noise drew Lokutis' attention to the spring where he had splashed his face that morning. It hissed and frothed as if a subterranean sea was rising to the surface.

Servants and soldiers broke and ran in every direction. They collided and scrambled over the top of one another, forgetting in their panic that only moments before they were prepared to put their swords through one another. Marduk whipped his people, cursing them to stay put.

Akahamet stood firm at Lokutis' side. "What are they?" he asked, a mixture of fear and awe in his voice.

Lokutis looked on with disbelief. His form shrank from the bull-horned monstrosity back to that of a slight man. His frame shimmered and his rich clothing reappeared.

He said simply: "Archangels."

"I am with you, my Lord," Akahamet said, reaching out and touching his master's forearm. Lokutis barely took notice. The storm angel drew back its scythe and cut down Lokutis's deformed giants. It hooked their bodies and flung their severed torsos into the air. Another swipe sent crimson-and-black-clad corpses scattering.

The trumpet blared without cease now, the rain plastered Lokutis's hair and clothing against his skin, and the scythe-wielding archangel was almost upon them, reaping its grisly harvest.

To his credit, Marduk stood his ground and lashed out with his whip, sending bolts of red energy at the thing. But it was to no avail, for the bolts passed through it as if it were made of mist. Marduk cast aside his whip and the sparking, sputtering weapon turned back into a coiled piece of metal. Even as the scythe bore down on him, he raised his fist and raged.

The weapon passed through him swiftly, yet did not cleave him in half. He went rigid, and a ghostly image of himself was ripped from his body in two pieces. The top half was Marduk's face, contorted in torment, and the image faded into the wind. His body collapsed. On the ground his head lolled to one side and Lokutis could see that his eyes were glazed with cataracts as if he'd been dead for hours.

"My lord, look out!" Akahamet cried and pushed Lokutis aside.

The scythe plunged. Lokutis crashed to the ground and saw Akahamet take the blow. As the man's body fell on top of him, Lokutis saw Akahamet's forlorn specter float away. He struggled out from under the body, but froze momentarily when he made contact with Akahamet's white lifeless eyes.

He snapped out of his horror. The archangel stood above him, raising the scythe.

A wall of water engulfed him first, obscured his assailant,

and lifted him off the ground and swept him away.

He flailed in a turbulent current, reaching and grasping for some sort of hold, hoping he wouldn't be pounded against one of the stone columns. His lungs started to burn, and he struggled out of his breastplate and cape. When he was free of the metal, the current popped him to the surface.

The landscape, or lack of thereof, was now completely different.

Gone was the threatening archangel. Gone was his tent. Gone were Marduk's corpse and the gilded elephant. Even the meeting place, with its altar, throne, and amphitheater were gone, replaced with a foaming, swirling, disorienting sea. Though much of the tower was still visible, the tips of the valley's mountains protruded from the water, and those were quickly being swallowed.

Lokutis flailed around to find some haven of safety. He had no immediate foothold on anything, and he considered swimming for the tower, even though it was leagues away. And should he make it, then what? Hide in its honeycomb vaults in the sky, snacking on rats?

He squinted into the driving wind; the rain beat his face and he couldn't see. He paused in his treading water long enough to shield his eyes with one hand.

The sea-foam was lifting off the surface of the water and gathering in the air like a flock of birds, and then migrating towards a light in the sky that was brighter than any sun. It lit the foam around him, and made it glow like the luminous plankton of the oceans.

Except it wasn't plankton.

Roughly the size of his fist and alternately round or spherical, depending on how you looked at them, they were little creatures covered in eyes. Human eyes.

They turned like fiery little wheels and bobbed like bubbles in the water. They behaved just like sea-foam, but then rose like smoke or mist, pausing just long enough to stare curiously with that multitude of eyes at Lokutis as they passed by.

"Thrones," he said, calling the angels by their name in the hierarchy of the Heavenly Host. Never had he heard of the beings coming anywhere near Jhove's earthly creation. Not since it was first made many, many millennia ago. Lokutis now understood what he had seen earlier, pouring out of the maelstrom in the sky like water out of a gourd. It had been the Heavenly Host coming forth to purge the earth of its wickedness and its monsters. Monsters like him.

Marduk had been right.

The last of the shining beings floated away from him and then suddenly something obscured the light in the sky and cast him in shadow. When his eyes had adjusted, he got a good look at what had blocked his vision: It was a giant boat, simple but sturdy. Essentially a cube with another cube on top, a sort of cabin surrounded by a deck.

And just when he thought things couldn't get any more surreal, Lokutis saw all manner of animals gathered on the deck, in particular a pair of giraffes staring down at him as if *he* were the oddity.

A violent undulation of the water took the vision from his sight and he was cast among the flotsam. Tree branches, uprooted shrubs, the carcasses of dead birds and domesticated animals, and even the corpses of his own servants. Another heave of water shifted his view again, this time setting him before the great tower, still far away.

The light in the sky burned above the tower like an eye, lighting up the carved cylinder of the mountain. He was amazed to see that a significant portion of it still rose above the waters, but the dark currents clawed at its stones like demons. An arch collapsed and sent a portion of the shell wall into the water, sending up a wall of spray. Though this caused more of the innards on the upper tiers to be exposed, the lower ramparts survived the assault.

The last of the Thrones disappeared into the light, and the light began to dim. The tower darkened with shadows, starting at the base then working their way up to the top. As the shadows grew, a chill that had nothing to do with the water crept up his spine and he watched helplessly as the light slowly collapsed in on itself. The light winked out. The world became bereft of light and warmth, as if a door had closed. Only the cold rain, the turning waters, and the tower, somewhere in darkness, remained to watch Lokutis's slow death.

As he struggled to stay afloat, a revelation came to him. The entire world was destroyed, wiped clean this day. Yet the simple villager, Noam, and his family most likely survived in the ark. This wasn't the end of all things.

Jhove meant to start anew, and he had left the future generations something: The tower.

When the waters had subsided and Noam's descendants repopulated the lands, they would eventually come across the tower again.

And it would call to them.

Tempt them.

Just as in the ancient stories, where Adam and his wife were set in a beautiful garden with a forbidden tree in it. That is why Jhove left the tower standing and intact, yet incomplete. Future generations would have to decide for themselves whether to leave it alone, or try to finish it.

Lokutis didn't have much time to ponder what the chances of either happening would be, for another great wave overcame him and this time all went dark.

#

The sound of the surf told Lokutis he was still alive. Salty air washed over his skin, and all around, seagulls made their excited cries. He could not move, and to open his eyes was to drag shards of glass underneath his lids, and to swallow was to gag. But there were voices and movement around him, so he forced himself to open his eyes.

The light hurt. He wanted to be blind. But then the brightness coalesced into forms and colors, and he was staring into a blue sky, at wispy clouds, at gulls coasting on arched wings.

"Ah, our guest is awake," a deep voice announced.

There was more movement about him and a face swam into view. This person reached down and helped Lokutis sit up.

"I imagine you have an incredible tale to tell," the voice said, and eased something soft behind Lokutis' back to prop him up, "but by the looks of yea, the tale will have to wait a spell. No matter, you are in good hands now."

Lokutis took a good look at the owner of the voice, who now crouched before him. He was a large man, with full beard and head of hair so dark that it had a blue sheen to it, and was streaked with silver. His skin was very pale, as pale as Lokutis himself. His eyes were piercingly blue, set deeply and fringed with crow's feet. His teeth were big and straight on an expansive face; Lokutis assumed he was a nobleman in some faraway land.

"Can you at least tell us your name?"

Lokutis swallowed the rocks in his throat and licked swollen flaking lips. Even his tongue was dry, but he managed to say, "Lokutis."

The large man frowned, yet maintained his fatherly smile. "My, that's a mouthful. How about we shorten that to something more manageable, shall we? Loki."

Loki moved his eyes around his surroundings. He was on a rocky beach at the foot of a slope. Snow and scree rose up to a high mountain peak. The air was cool and the rough, grayish foliage was alien. The only things that looked remotely familiar were the trees, some relative of his native cedar. His host wore coarse clothing of wool, leather, and animal skins.

Loki lay on wool blankets, under a pile of skins. The pleasant smell of roasting meat drew his attention to a campfire nearby on the beach. What looked like a boar was turning on a spit above the flames. A kettle boiled in the flames. Many people, dressed as roughly as his host, were gathered there and drinking from horns.

"Frigga, bring our guest some broth, he must be famished...and something to drink."

A stout woman acknowledged the request and bent over her kettle.

The man turned back to Loki. "Frigga, my wife, she will fix you up nicely."

Loki gestured weakly. "W-where am I? Who, you?"

"I am Woden, son of Bor, and you are in the highest reaches of Midgard, where we retreated from the Deluge. We have been here well over a moon now, waiting for the waters to recede. I sent out my birds to see if the waters had started to do so. They came across you, clinging to a log." Woden gestured to two large ravens sitting nearby on a tree branch. "You have Hugin and Munin to thank for being rescued; otherwise you would have floated right by us."

The ravens bobbed their heads. "Drowned rat! Drowned rat!" they croaked.

The woman Frigga brought a steaming bowl and a large wooden spoon. She was large of girth, but had a friendly round face that was not at all unattractive. Her blond hair was braided into a rope as thick as Loki's arm. Woden took the bowl, spooned some broth and put it to Loki's lips. With his aid, Loki managed to swallow some. Considering the circumstances, it was the most delicious thing he had ever tasted.

After a few spoonfuls of the broth Woden reached for the drinking horn. "I imagine everything and everybody you knew previously are gone now. But as I said, you are in good hands. You are one of us now."

"There you go again, taking in strays," somebody nearby scoffed. "Someday it will be your undoing."

Loki looked in that direction. Sitting apart from the fire was a giant of a man with a flaming red beard and wild head of hair. He scowled as he wrapped a leather strap about the shaft of a great war hammer. The weapon was so huge that no normal person could wield it. But the redheaded stranger had arms as big around as Loki's torso. All in all, he made Marduk look like a child.

Woden ignored the comment, but lifted the drinking horn to Loki's lips. "My son Thor, he is a dour and taciturn sort who is slow to trust and even slower to befriend. But you needn't worry; he will love you as a brother soon enough and there is no greater ally."

Loki sipped at the dark liquid in the horn, and almost immediately gagged. His reaction drew much laughter from those gathered around the fire.

"Mead is an acquired taste," Woden admitted.

"Father, look!" A new voice cried.

All in the camp turned towards a figure standing on the rocks at the ocean's edge. He was another large man, and an elaborately carved horn hung from a strap around his neck. He pointed out into the sky. A hushed gasp rippled through the crowd. Arching across the heavens was an iridescent arc of many colors, which was simultaneously solid and ephemeral. Light emanated from it powerfully, so much that Loki could not look at it for very long.

"Isn't it beautiful?" the man on the rocks said.

"What is it?" Frigga asked, mouth agape.

"It has something to do with the Deluge, I'm certain," Woden said.

"Hemdal," called Thor. "What do you make of it? Nobody knows the powers of the earth and sky as you do."

Rapt with the bow in the sky, Hemdal turned to address the

camp. "It has much power, I am sure. As if the song of the world itself was harnessed and made manifest. I can only imagine that it comes from the Creator himself. Why he would leave such a powerful thing unguarded, I do not know." Hemdal seemed entranced, and his gaze turned inward. "What one could do if they could make it their own!"

Loki groaned.

Though he had floated to the ends of the earth, as far away from the tower as possible, he still bore witness to the sort of folly that lead to the Deluge. He did not know the true meaning of the prismatic bow, but he was sure Jhove had not put it there to be coveted.

As the camp stared in wonder at the beautiful arch, Loki reached for the spoon and bowl and sipped the broth gently.

#

At long last Loki stirred from his reverie.

He was silent for so long that Minion thought that perhaps he had fallen asleep, though that didn't stir him from his corner to go check on his master.

"Minion, go to the instrument case and bring me the item that looks like a glass bulb with bits of metal in it," Loki said without taking his eyes off of the sunny day outside their window.

"Y-yes, master," Minion complied.

The little man crept out of the corner to the area where their luggage was stored. Against the wall were all sizes and shapes of valises, satchels, and trunks. He dug out a medium sized leather bound box and opened it on its hinge. Inside were many odd pieces of equipment. The object Loki requested was shaped like the bulb from a tulip, but made of clear glass. Inverted with round end facing up, it rested on a wood pedestal. Inside the glass, rising out of the foundation, was a thin wire that stood up straight and was capped by what looked like a tiny helmet of the sort the knights about the keep wore when on duty. Sprouting from this helmet were four more wires that pointed in opposite directions like the arms on a windmill, but horizontal. At the end of each arm was a bit of tin beat so thin that wind would have easily blown it away were it not housed inside protective glass and attached to the wires. These kite shaped pieces of metal stood perpendicular to the arms like a man holding out signaling flags. Each bit was colored: dark on one side, light on the other.

Since the curious assortment of wires and foils jiggled with the slightest of movements, not to mention the delicacy of the glass housing, Minion brought the device with great care to Loki. Loki set it on the windowsill and opened the shutters wider.

"What is the most defining feature of the island?" he asked with a bit of excitement in his voice. Before Minion could even debate venturing a response, Loki answered his own query. "The weather! That and the fact the island lies hidden behind a wall of mist, yet another phenomenon of weather. And—" this time he turned and addressed Minion directly—"how many times have you seen rainbows about?"

Minion shrugged. "Many...?"

"Precisely! Now, how many times have you seen rainbows about...though it hadn't rained recently?"

Minion's eyes widened. But before he could respond, Loki pointed down to the glass device with a child's delight. To Minion's surprise, the arms were rotating about the helmet like the spokes on a wheel. The little metal flags were almost a blur, moving like the horses on a child's carousel.

"Now, let's see what we really have," Loki said, moving his hands over the bulb like a witch scrying into a crystal ball.

The spokes moved even faster and now the little flags really were but a blur. Loki's gestures became more elaborate, as if working a marionette on strings, and when doing so the black and white blur started to change colors, turning to reds, blues, yellows, and every shade in between.

Soon afterward, Minion's jaw dropped and he stepped back from the window. The whole room became filled with prismatic colors as a rainbow alighted right into the window, arcing from the sky and spanning some distance over the entire keep. It mainly came to rest on the device in the window, but much of it spilled into the room, painting everything with rich and splendid colors.

"Isn't it incredible?" Loki called, silhouetted in a mauve aura.

"Yes master!" Minion hadn't realized it, but there was a rushing noise as well, like a wind whipping about the chamber.

Loki made a chopping gesture that ended with his hand in a fist over his chest. The color and wind were snuffed out. The miniature carousel turned lazily in the glass bulb.

Loki sighed heavily and fell to his knees beside Minion, ecstasy on his face, and he embraced Minion with a single arm while gazing wide-eyed out the window in a very un-Loki moment.

"This is better than my wildest dreams."

Minion had no idea what he meant, but rubbed his hands together excitedly just the same.

#

"Oi! Watch it Patrick!" Corbin complained as he ran into the Irishman's backside.

Patrick had stopped mid-stride in the courtyard. "Did you see that?" he asked, shielding his eyes in the sun and looking up at the old watchtower—the Viscount Loki's apartments.

"See what?" Corbin asked, shielding his eyes in the same direction.

"A rainbow just appeared out of thin air and landed on the roof of the watchtower there."

Corbin's face scrunched up with disbelief. "Are you daft man? Rainbows don't come and go like that."

"I'm telling you, right..."

Corbin waved him off, mumbling. He left Patrick standing in the courtyard scratching his head.

Chapter Nine

Patrick Gawain lifted his head from his pillow. There was an alien sound coming from his door. After the sound had repeated itself several more times, he finally recognized it: someone was knocking.

He dropped his head back to the pillow and groaned. It could only be one person. He felt no desire to rise, so he called out, "Enter."

Sure enough, through his blurry eyes Patrick saw Aimeé's blonde head poke inside the room. Every now and again she brought him breakfast in bed, mended and washed his clothes, and he suspected her of feeding Siegfried extra, which was causing the horse to become fat.

Patrick, like everyone, was aware of her infatuation. He had tried ignoring her, but to no avail, and the one time he had tried telling her that her efforts were best applied to her regular duties, she looked completely shattered. So Patrick let her do him favors, at the cost of some ridicule from the other knights and his own respect for the girl. She was either incredibly thick-skinned or incredibly naive.

He ducked underneath his covers. He could hear her pull up a chair next to his bed, which surprised him. Usually Aimeé laid down a tray of food, tried talking for a while, then left.

"Are you going to hide underneath there all morning like schoolboy?" The voice was deeper, and harshly accented.

Patrick looked up. The girl laughed. It was not Aimeé, but Lady Katherina.

"What is wrong?" she asked.

Patrick rubbed his eyes. "I thought you were someone else." He suddenly felt awkward. A servant being in his room while he was in bed in a nightgown was one thing, but a Lady Guest was quite another.

"Someone else?" Katherina said, her mouth turning into a mischievous smile. "So you have many Lady coming into your room. I have heard this."

"Not exactly," Patrick replied. He noted her strange accent that he couldn't place. He pulled the covers up to his neck and studied the young Guest. He now couldn't understand how he could have mistaken the platinum hair of the Lady for Aimeé's earthy blonde. Katherina seemed at ease before an undressed knight, unescorted in the Hall for Boys. The look in her hauntingly clear eyes told him that she'd come to talk about something important.

Did she come to discuss the death of Jason McFowler? Patrick was uncomfortable. She had made him uncomfortable ever since the funeral.

"What can I do for you, my Lady?"

She studied him for a moment, then said, "We are told that we may choose chaperone. I wish to go outside wall today and fly kite. I choose you as chaperone."

Patrick frowned. "Why me?"

"Why not?"

"I have my regular guard dut..."

"Sir Corbin says it is...is..." She struggled with the word. "Acceptable. In fact, he was pleased."

Patrick smirked. *I'll wager he was.*

Katherina stood. "Very well then, after midday meal, at the

main gate." She turned and left the room.

Patrick put his hands behind his head as he lay in bed, groaning for the third time. He wished it had been Aimeé after all.

#

In the dining hall at breakfast, Patrick came across Sir Corbin, who was all smiles.

"Thanks," he said.

Corbin laughed. "Of course, what are friends for?"

Many of the knights and staff ribbed him over the matter. Evidently he was the first knight to be selected by a Guest as a chaperone.

"She zeroed in on you like an arrow to a bull's-eye." Corbin winked at him. "We told you the Ladies have an eye for you."

Patrick suppressed a shudder. "I'm not so sure it's like that."

Corbin frowned. "Why not?"

Patrick waved the matter aside. He couldn't exactly explain how she had looked at him during the funeral, as if he had been responsible for Jason. If not that, then he felt guilty for having the affections of Jason's old flame. And yet still, he didn't want the repeat the episode with Lady Christianne Morneau. He was determined not to let another thief into the confines of his heart to steal another portion of his pride, what precious little of it remained.

#

Patrick met the Lady Katherina at the main gate. She carried a delicate and colorful kite. Without a word, she handed the thing to him and strode over the drawbridge. He was obviously meant to follow.

A small band of Avangarde in the courtyard saw this transaction, and several of them went down on one knee and swooned. Patrick made eyes at them to tell them to keep quiet, but this only caused them to laugh all the more.

Patrick followed the Lady Guest up a gentle slope. At the top, she took the spool from him and told him to stay put while she unraveled it and pulled it some distance away.

She talked nonstop. She spoke of keep affairs, the previous night's play, and what committees she aspired to join. She seemed to talk for the sake of talking, rather than with (or even at) the Irishman. Her accent and grammar grated on him; she constantly forgot to use articles, or indicate the appropriate number of subjects in a sentence. Patrick was no master linguist, and even he admittedly had problems speaking French or the Anglo language, but there was something arrogant about her butchery. She obviously had a command of vocabulary, but refused to string it together correctly.

"Sir Gawain, you are listening to me?"

"Yes, my Lady."

She went into another monologue. Patrick shifted his weight to the other foot. He felt stupid standing there holding a kite, trying to figure out what the girl was up to.

She told him to throw the kite into the air. He did, but couldn't manage to get it aloft.

"Oh stop it, let me do it before you break it." She came forward and took the kite, thrust the string into his hand and expertly sent the contraption into the air where it pulled the string taut. He tried handing it back to her.

"No, you keep. You obviously have need of learning how."

Patrick's brow furrowed. "My Lady, I don't think that it is a good idea for your chaperone and guardian to be preoccupied with a toy."

"Why not?"

"The idea is to protect you, which I cannot do if I am..." He trailed off, struggling with the airborne kite that fought in his hand like a living thing.

"There are many knights about now," Katherina replied, and

indeed many Guests were on the grounds outside Greensprings since she and Patrick had arrived. They all had their Avangarde escorts, and there were more patrolling on horseback at the edge of the woods. The place was quite busy, actually. "Besides, you are knight. You are supposed to do my bidding. Now, fly kite."

She turned her back on Patrick to watch the kite's antics, which perturbed him all the more. She commenced talking again. "You know, Irish-man, I would like to go on picnic someday. I tire of looking at Greensprings with all the silly girls here. I want to go somewhere different for a little while..."

He was not a servant, not a playmate; and she was a headstrong arrogant little noblesse. He no longer wanted to play polite games. He wrestled with the string and noted the end had been rubbed with wax and formed into a hook. He imagined this was to keep it secure when all the string was wound. This gave him an idea. He didn't care if it resulted in him being reprimanded. He would blame it on Corbin for mismatching Guests and chaperones.

"...think I would like to see ocean. Yes, ocean, that would be nice. Birds, breeze, make sand castle. Can you make sand castle, Sir Gawain? Sir Gawain?"

She turned and the Irishman was gone. She looked angrily to the gate and could see him walking away. "Sir Gawain! Come back here this instant!" She stepped forward to pursue him, but something caught on the hemline of her gown. She looked down and saw the kite string attached to the hem of her dress. It was currently slack, but then the wind gusted and it was suddenly pulled taut. The kite yanked on the string so that it pulled the dress up over Katherina's head.

#

The Lady Katherina walked briskly down the corridor carrying her kite and tangled string with her. Her hair was in disarray, and her jaw firmly set. She approached the door of Reservist Patrick Gawain and pounded on it. A moment passed and the door opened. Patrick's stomach flip-flopped when he saw the disheveled Lady. He hadn't expected her to hunt him down to his quarters.

She shoved the kite into his hands. "String is tangled!" she growled. "Fix!" She then marched away. After a few strides, she halted and turned. "Tomorrow we go on picnic. Be ready." Then she left for good.

He stood there in shock, holding the kite. Sir Jon and William of Monmouth had stepped into the corridor to see what all the commotion was about. They were smiling.

"What are you looking at?" he growled, and went into his room and slammed the door.

#

Patrick had planned on not catering any longer to the Lady Guest, but Sir Corbin gave him a stern warning.

"It is not like an Avangarde to shirk his duties. Just because you find your charge unpleasant does not give you leave to neglect your responsibility." Corbin was right; Patrick just didn't want to admit it. He shook his head sadly. Corbin quoting the Creed?

First Mark, now Corbin. The burden of responsibility must indeed be heavy if it caused normally fun-loving knights to behave so stiffly.

So Patrick accompanied the Lady Katherina on horseback to a locale of her choosing, which turned out to be a pleasant spot past the orchards along a brook.

"I am not sure we should be this far from the keep," he complained.

Katherina flashed her eerie eyes. "Why?"

"Since the attack, the land may not be safe."

"Everyone who is anyone at Greensprings says this attack

was once-in-a-lifetime occurrence. And where is your sense of adventure?" She clucked her tongue.

Patrick hated her.

She dismounted and tethered her horse without aid. She also set out a blanket and the midday meal. She was a very capable person, unlike most of the Lady Guests who needed to be hand-held and pampered.

They sat and ate silently for a while.

"Why did you want to come out here for a picnic?" Patrick asked.

"I told you, I wanted to get away," she replied.

"All right then, why me? You could've asked anyone to be your chaperone."

"Because, I wanted to come with someone I would feel comfortable with. You were Jason's friend. If you were his friend, then I imagine that I could feel at ease with you."

"Jason was friends with everyone, and I, arguably, the least of them." Patrick felt uneasy. He knew this would happen.

"You didn't approve of him then?" She seemed to be prying him open with her eyes.

"On the contrary, I loved him like everyone. It's just that I don't think he felt anything special for me. I was just another colleague, and to his credit, he treated us all equally. McFowler did have his true friends, but I dare not say I was one of them."

Katherina poured more wine into her cup, but only looked at it. Finally she said, "I believe this is correct. I was not close to him, either. But I felt comfortable with him."

Patrick realized he had been holding his breath. Then there was no special relationship between the two as first he thought. McFowler really just wanted her to sing his music.

"And," she continued, "you intrigue me. You are not like other knight. You are not like other noble. You are different. Don't talk much. Other knight try make conversation, involve Guests. You hide."

He shrugged. He had no idea it was that obvious. He had hoped that his personal shortcomings had faded more by now. He didn't feel like discussing them either.

"Other knight are predictable, you are not. I don't like conventional."

"So I've noticed," Patrick said. So she had singled him out because he was different. He didn't know whether to be flattered or offended, considering the source.

She stood and tugged none too gently on his surcoat. "Let's go exploring." He hesitated to leave the open blanket, plates and cups, but she was already working her way down the bank to the water. She pulled up her gown and kicked off her slippers, then waded ankle-deep into the water.

The forest lay on the opposite shore. It was fairly clear, not densely wooded, and it made poor cover for attackers (well, earthly ones in any case; otherworldly and shadowy ones were a different matter). At least it was broad daylight. The goblins that had attacked had come at night—perhaps that was all they could do. Maybe Katherina was right, maybe that had been a once-in-a-lifetime occurrence. Still, he kept one hand on the hilt of his sword. He was not enjoying escorting the Lady Katherina.

"Maybe we should be going now," he suggested. He was met by a cold stare, and she started to meander upstream. Patrick paralleled her on the bank.

"Tell me something about yourself," she said.

Patrick sighed. "I'm Irish, I'm a knight, I carry a big sword."

She gave him a sarcastic look. "I mean it. Tell me something personal about yourself. You were Crusader, right? Tell me about this."

Patrick paused. Though his face had become devoid of expression, his hand seemed to move of its own accord to his head. He began to rub his temple with his fingers as he squeezed his eyes shut. For a brief moment, he heard the distant din of battle; metal on metal, cries of men.

"Sir Gawain?"

Patrick realized that the princess was staring at him.

He did his best to make his temple-rubbing gesture look natural by running his hand through his hair. He smiled wanly. "It was terrible. The worst thing anyone could do."

Katherina frowned. "But it was for good cause, to take the Holy Land back from heathen." She fingered the crucifix about her neck. It was an oddly shaped one. Its cross was angled rather than straight, with rope cords wrapped around either end.

Patrick swallowed hard. "It...was not...the purest of missions. Believe me. It was hard; physically, emotionally and...spiritually."

Katherina was now wading into knee deep water. She hiked up her gown even farther. In doing so, she exposed more leg and thigh than Patrick was used to seeing on most men. His heart beat faster.

"Then why did you do it?"

He flashed a brief smile. "It seemed like a good idea at the time."

"I wasn't aware that Irish-men went to Crusade," she said.

"They don't, normally. I knew of few others who did."

"Then why did you leave..." she struggled with her memory. "...Eire? Were you running from something?"

Patrick must not have guarded his look well enough, because she looked immediately contrite. "I really don't want to talk about it," he said. "Why don't we talk about you for a while, shall we?"

She pulled up her gown a bit more. Patrick couldn't help but glance at the long white legs. "Very well," she said. "What do you want to know?"

"Where are you from?"

"*Uhkraani*," she said. The sound of the word almost hurt Patrick's ears. She smiled apologetically. "I'm sorry, I don't know word for it in Latin or French...or Gaelic for that matter."

"Where on earth is it?"

She shrugged. "Far away. It is beautiful land. It has golden fields in the good season. Eternal snow in the bad. It is much different than here. Our language, our clothes and customs, even our buildings are shaped different."

He was puzzled. "Just how are your buildings shaped?"

"They are like, um, onion." She struggled again with the explanation. Patrick nodded. He had seen the roofs of the palaces and mosques in the Eastern lands with their spiraling and bulbous shapes.

"We have contact with Europe, though. We know of warring brothers in England and Normandy, of scheming French Phillipe, of Crusade, of Pope Urban, of Antipope Clement. We are not barbarians like..." She shrugged one shoulder.

"Me?" Patrick leaned forward on one knee. Katherina blushed. She continued to stroll through the water. They came to a tiny stone chapel along the brook. He reached down to help her up the bank.

"You are much stronger than you look," she commented when placed back down to earth.

"Thanks, I think."

She plucked a flower from the edge of the brook and offered it to him. "For your efforts today."

Patrick reached for its stem, but then cried out and withdrew his hand. He held his fist gingerly and looked at the flower as if it were evil.

"What happened?" Katherina laughed.

"A thorn or something," Patrick said angrily.

"That should be lesson to you—you shouldn't reach for beautiful thing so quickly. Do you care to try again?" She continued to laugh, holding the flower forward.

Patrick shook his head. "I never did like flowers that much anyway."

"Would you not give flower to woman?"

"No."

She tossed the flower aside. "That is too bad."

The chapel was crumbling and obviously hadn't been used in years. There were intricate carvings on the walls on the inside. No villager made these; they were of too high a workmanship. Patrick wondered who had made this place. It seemed older than the village or the keep. Was there a race of people who had been here before the original knights of Greensprings? Were they the same people who had set the numerous standing stones on the isle?

"Why did you come to Greensprings?" he asked. It was impolite, but she had made him uncomfortable by asking personal questions.

She did not readily answer. When she did, she put on an exaggerated smile. "Would you believe that my mother sent me away so that I would not be captured by the powerful sorceress Baba Yaga, who flies over the land in her cauldron in search of children to eat?"

Patrick smiled. "No."

She put her head down and toyed with her crucifix. She sighed. "My mother, actually, did send me away for my protection. Though it wasn't because of an evil sorceress..." Her voice sounded thin.

Patrick felt a pang of guilt. "You don't have to talk about it if you don't like."

She waved him off. "No, I want to." She tucked the crucifix back beneath her collar. "My uncle wants to take throne away from my family now that my father has passed away. My little brother, who is rightful heir, is still too young to rule. My uncle wants to seize power now. So, to secure his position, he wants to...marry me."

Patrick's stomach turned. Katherina hugged herself and rubbed her arms, but shrugged to cover the gesture.

"That wouldn't be completely out of ordinary; royalty do this sort of thing for the sake of politics. And ironically, I am normally attracted to such man as my uncle: older, commanding, confident. But he made me feel like object. Like one of his horses or worse, like one of his other women." Her eyes were wet, and she quickly turned so that Patrick would not see, but he did. "He try several time, married or no. He has no scruple. And when I resist, he hit me often. So, my mother send me to associate in Rome. Then I come here. That is why I am here." Katherina sighed and her shoulders sagged.

"I'm sorry, I shouldn't have asked."

She smiled. "Why not? It is truth. It is life. No point hiding it. Besides, it is good to talk about it. If you keep bad things inside you, they will eat you up." She looked at him as if she knew something. "You should try it sometime. Talk. Get it out. Before it eats you."

Patrick averted his gaze. "What's mine is mine."

She shook her head, and her eyes glistened as if still wet with tears. "No man is island."

"What of the island who is a man?" Patrick countered.

She didn't seem sure how to respond to that. "You are poet."

The Irishman shrugged. There was a moment of silence while they surveyed the walls of the chapel, admiring the rich engravings. Katherina placed a finger on a particular image, which was part of a story line. She had a mischievous air about her.

"Sir Gawain, what do you make of this?"

He came forward and scrutinized the picture. It was of a knight, bearing arms and armor, leaving a battle. A woman was running to meet him. She was weeping. Patrick explained this much to Katherina.

"Yes," she said, "but what does it mean? Why does woman cry?"

He shrugged. "I don't know. The meaning is lost long ago to

the original patrons of this place. Perhaps there are some villagers today who can..."

Katherina smiled while shaking her head. "No, Sir Gawain. *You* tell me what it means. Tell me story. You are poet. You can do this for me. Tell me what it means."

Patrick's brow lifted; such a request had never been made of him before. He pulled back from the wall and examined it from a distance. "The woman," he began, "is the lady of the knight. He is returning from battle."

"What was the battle about?" Katherina asked, standing closer.

"It...was about her. You see, another knight in the land wants her, but she will not go to that knight, for she loves her man very much. So, the other knight, in jealousy, tells everyone in the land that the woman was once a harlot and unworthy of any man. This angers the husband of the woman—that man there—and he must defend her honor, so he goes to meet the man in personal combat. But when he arrives, he is ambushed by the evil knight and his henchmen, for they have no honor."

"Obviously he survives, for there he is arising victorious," Katherina said, gently touching Patrick's forearm. "But how, if he is only one man?"

"You are getting ahead of the story, my Lady—you see, the good knight is just and right. No man who is just and right can be defeated. Yes, he is ambushed by three times his number, but because of his cause he suddenly has five times their strength, and can defeat them all. He fights long and hard, and is victorious, and saves the honor of his lady. He returns home to his wife, who cries with tears of joy to see him still living. That is what it means."

Katherina's clear blue eyes were glowing in the dim light of the chapel. She still held on to his forearm. "You are not just poet, Patrick, you are romantic. Even if you would not give flower to girl."

Her touch made him uneasy and he pulled away. "Well, one man's romance is another's foolishness. It was just a story. I meant nothing romantic about it."

Lady Katherina pulled her hands behind her back and strode to the entrance. She looked over her shoulder at Patrick and said, "You're right. It wasn't romantic. You're not romantic. As a matter of fact, it wasn't even very good." She slipped out the door.

"What," Patrick said angrily. He followed her out the door. "Just a moment ago you said it was romantic."

Her back was to him. "Ha, you call that romantic. I can hear better from boy half your age."

"Is that a fact?" Patrick growled. He really didn't understand this girl, and wasn't sure if he wanted to. He was already starting to see the writing on the wall. Which was fine, because he didn't need another Christianne.

"That is fact, Irish-man. A man coming to my window at night, and then reciting poetry to me, is romantic." She returned to the picnic site and began to pack the blanket into her horse's saddlebag.

"That would be a neat trick, considering that any boy trying to go to a window in the Hall for Lady Guests would be caught and punished."

"A resourceful man wouldn't. A *romantic* man wouldn't," returned Katherina, while mounting her horse. "That is what would make it romantic: the danger. Besides, what do you care? You don't have romantic bone in your body. Let us go back, I am tired."

He stood for a moment, fuming. His fingers drummed on his sword belt. Finally, he mounted Siegfried and didn't say a word all the way back to Greensprings.

#

"You want me to do *what*?" Sir Jeremiah exclaimed.

Patrick gestured wildly with his arms to hush the exclamation. "I want you to keep your back to the Hall for Lady Guests for about a half an hour. Trust me, nothing is going to happen." Patrick wished it was Waylan guarding the wall instead. It would make things so much easier. At least he had the good fortune of it being another Reservist.

Jeremiah wrapped his cloak about him tighter in the chilly night air. "Pat, do you have any idea what kind of trouble I could get into if someone finds out you were fooling around the Hall for Lady Guests?"

"Well, if your back is turned then you personally won't be seeing me in there, and won't be in any trouble yourself."

Jeremiah shook his head sardonically. "All right, it's your funeral."

Patrick smiled. "Thanks, I owe you one."

"Damn right you do."

#

Patrick waited for the Avangarde patrol to pass the Hall gate, then he left his cover in the bushes and slipped into the courtyard. He stepped into the shadows and calculated his next move. The main doorway was across from him, but he knew that a nun sat inside all hours of the day. He moved to the side of the building and searched for the window he needed, using information gleaned from Sir Jon the Informant (what they were calling him now).

Patrick found the correct window, and to his delight, plenty of ivy grew thick and high on the wall.

"Call me unromantic...no romantic bone in my body..." he mumbled as he climbed. He reached the window and grabbed onto the sill and pulled himself up. A momentary doubt surfaced—he hoped this was the correct room, or else he was going to have a hard time explaining himself. He landed gently on the floor and concealed himself behind the curtain, and waited.

#

He didn't have to wait long. The Lady Katherina entered the room, went to her bureau and stood before her mirror. She removed a pin from her almost-white hair and started to unravel the plaits.

Patrick moved out from the curtain and stood silently, grinning. A few moments passed before she noticed the knight in the mirror, leaning against her windowsill. Her hands froze for a beat, then continued undoing their plait.

"You are just in time," she said with an almost undistinguishable smile.

"Oh? For what?"

"Come here," she said.

Patrick came up behind her. "Yes?"

"Help me unravel hair. I must brush before I go to bed."

Patrick did as ordered, slipping his fingers through her cold, smooth braids.

"You've done this before?" She sounded surprised.

"I have mother and sister," he replied, mimicking her accent.

"You have poem?"

"Not a very long one, a little one," he replied.

Katherina gestured impatiently for him to commence. He cleared his throat and said:

There was a king of incredible self
who had gold and gems.
Beyond imagination was his wealth.

His kingdom rich,
his land expansive,
and he had powers with which

he could cause the winds to sing him praise,
float the moon across the sky,
or cause the stars to shine in the days.

And with a mere thought

he could cause the sun to rise at his command,
but it was all for naught,
for he had no subjects in his land.

And his brother's daughter he wishes to marry,
in this sometimes land of snow,
but her mother is wary

and the snow princess must go.

She lands in Greensprings,
where she is safe,
and there she sings.

Katherina was silent for a moment, then grabbed a hairbrush and moved to the other side of the bed.

"No, no, no," she said. "Typical, typical." She pulled the brush hurriedly through her hair.

Patrick crossed his arms and frowned. "Just what do you expect? What do you want?"

She shrugged. "Spontaneous. Something not fabricated."

Patrick nodded. He came forward and leaned on the bed post before her. "I see, you want of the moment. Like your eyes."

"My eyes?"

"Yes. How they are like the color of a magical lake where the fairy princesses dwell. Where they wait for the handsome mortals to come and drink so that they may seduce them to the bottom of the cold waters. But only to find that it is they who are seduced by the handsome men, and must choose between their fairy world or the mortality they must have in order to love their would-be victims."

Katherina's lips parted and she was speechless. Patrick stepped up next to her and stroked her cheek.

"Or your skin," he continued.

"My skin?"

"Yes. How it is like moonbeam. How it enchants all who gaze upon it and ever afterward cannot step outdoors and lay eyes on that celestial body in the sky, and not be reminded of you and not be rid of the memory until it wanes away like love dying."

Katherina stood with her head to one side, gazing upon Patrick as if seeing him for the first time—truly seeing him.

"Your smile is poetry as well," he continued. "It lights up a room like sunshine after a cold night."

Some of the glamour left her eyes. "You lie," she said. "It is a big hideous thing anchored on either side by holes."

Patrick shook his head, admiring the corners of her mouth as if they were the most fascinating of gems. "Dimples are nothing to be ashamed of. It merely means you were kissed by angels as a baby."

She abruptly turned to hide the color rising in her face, and resumed combing her hair.

Patrick came closer and whispered near her ear, gently touching the curve of her hips. "They say the universe is shaped like this, like a woman's hips, from whence life comes."

Katherina swallowed hard. She was swaying where she stood. Patrick moved to her hair and caressed it. Undone it was much, much longer and thicker than he had imagined. He started to say something, but then there were footsteps in the corridor.

#

Mother Superior entered the room. She looked from side to side as if expecting to catch a prowler in the act. She saw only the Lady Katherina lying in the bed, which was piled high with blankets and pillows. She leaned against the pillows as she read from a small Bible by candlelight.

"Mother Superior! Can I help you?" Katherina asked.

Mother Superior came forward, a forced smile on her face. She may have been comely to look upon once, but now she was the epitome of sternness. "No child, I just thought that I heard voices coming from your room. Possibly a masculine voice involved, and as you know, that is explicitly against policy."

Katherina feigned shock. "Mother, you offend me. Do I seem the rule breaking sort?"

Mother Superior opened her hands. "You are the headstrong sort, and I am entrusted to enforce the policies in this Hall." She prowled the chamber, closing the window shutters, looking behind the curtains. "Nothing personal, child, I must suspect everyone and everything." She opened the closet to find only clothes and slippers.

"Well, I assure you there is no man, unless you count God."

Mother Superior smiled and stood by the bed. "I suppose you are right. I shall be going now." She turned to leave, then suddenly bent over and looked underneath the bed—and found nothing. Katherina giggled.

"Good night, child."

"Good night, Mother Superior."

The old woman left. Moments later Patrick's head rose from the covers next to Katherina's body.

"That woman definitely takes her duties much too seriously," he said.

Katherina slapped Patrick's head gently. "You were breathing much too heavily on my thigh...and you need to shave."

"Sorry," he said. He rolled over next to her and put his hands behind his head. Had someone told him six months ago that he would be in a young Lady Guest's bed like this he wouldn't have believed it. Her bed smelled like her perfume.

Katherina asked, "Why are you here?"

Patrick shrugged. "Why didn't you give me away?"

It was her turn to shrug. An awkward moment of silence passed. She sighed. "What are we doing?"

"I don't know."

"Well, we better know, before something goes wrong."

Patrick frowned. "Like what?"

"Like hurt feeling, because we did not talk." Patrick drew in a deep breath. What indeed was he doing? Katherina had drawn a line in the sand before him—daring him to do this—and he crossed it. He didn't stop to think why, just wanted to prove himself and massage his pride. She had angered him. He fully intended on not letting what had happened so many times in the past with so many people happen again.

"I don't even know how long I will be here. As soon as I know it is safe to go home, I will. As soon as uncle is disposed," Katherina said.

"When will that be?" Patrick inquired.

"Soon," she replied, though not very convincingly.

Patrick mulled it over more. If he could prepare himself for what he felt was the inevitable, then he knew it wouldn't hurt as much as it did with David of York, Christianne Morneau, Jason...so many. He had the advantage in this situation because this time he could see it all coming. Patrick smiled confidently.

"There will be no hurt feelings," he said, moving to the edge of the bed.

"Oh, and why not?"

"Because there is nothing particularly special going to happen between us. We are only going to be friends. If we can do this, than nothing bad will happen, right?"

She moved to his side on the edge of the bed. Her face was now close to his. Patrick could feel her breath on his lips, and feel the warmth of her leg pressed against his.

"Right," she replied. She seemed surprised to have a man this close to her. "Only friend, what could go bad? It is better this way."

Patrick toyed with the leather-bound Bible on the bed. The fact that she had such a fine treasure showed that she indeed was royalty from somewhere. "We still can be special friends, though," he pointed out. "There is no reason why we can't share secrets and whatnot."

"You mean like telling me about servant girl?" she asked coyly.

Patrick frowned. "What do you mean?"

"You know what I mean, the French servant girl... Ay-me," Katherina taunted.

"That is nothing. Nothing has, or will ever happen with her."

Katherina didn't seem to believe him, but he decided not to pursue the matter. He jumped from the bed and moved toward the window. He felt that he was pushing his luck by spending so much time here. "I should be going, and we really shouldn't make a habit out of meeting like this," he said.

Katherina nodded. "Shall we have breakfast together in dining hall?"

Patrick stuck his legs out the window. "Yes, I'd like that." He started to lower himself.

"Tomorrow then," she said, walking toward the window to see him out.

Before dropping out of sight, he asked, "Friends?"

Katherina leaned forward, quickly kissing him on the forehead. "Special friend."

When he landed on the ground and sneaked off the grounds, he couldn't help but to feel happy. Happy that he had been in command of the situation, averted another possible tragedy, and still managed to make a friend in the process.

\#

For days afterwards he avoided Katherina. He didn't know exactly why. Perhaps he didn't want to ruin the memory of the other evening by finding that she had thought nothing of it. Maybe he was afraid he would start enjoying her company too much. Whatever the case, she didn't fail to notice it. She tried several times to recruit him to chaperone appointments, but he politely declined, citing that he had other duties.

One evening in the dining hall, the Irishman hurried to take a seat among the Avangarde before Katherina could enter the room and ask him to dine with her.

"Patrick!" Sir Waylan greeted him. "You dance with Jon, you wrestle with Willy in his bed, now you are avoiding beautiful woman. We're starting to worry about you."

Patrick shrugged it off. "She is hardly a woman. Really no more than a girl. I'm only doing the right thing."

Waylan gave him a sarcastic salute.

Katherina entered the hall alone. She had no lady-in-waiting, and rarely did she dine with other Lady Guests. Patrick never noticed who she had dined with before. He was only now realizing what a loner she was. It wasn't surprising; she was more headstrong and mature than the rest of the girls. In her own right, she didn't quite fit in either.

Sir Geoffrey materialized at her side. Patrick could not hear the conversation from across the room, but imagined the crimson-caped Geoffrey inviting her to dine with him. Her physical language at first said no, but then she laid eyes on the Irishman. Suddenly, she smiled to Geoffrey and followed him to his seat. She stuck her tongue out at Patrick. He smiled and crossed his eyes at her.

If she enjoys the company of the likes of Geoffrey, then I certainly am doing the right thing, he thought.

The servants brought the food, and the hall was abuzz with the sound of conversation and dining, and Patrick had to fight hard to keep his gaze from wandering towards Katherina's table. She seemed to be having a similar difficulty—yet she went out of her way to lean closer to Geoffrey and laughed so loudly at his jokes that the entire hall could hear her.

Patrick drummed his fingers on the table. He noticed that Aimeé was near serving. He gestured for her to come near.

"Yes?" she asked, green eyes glowing.

"What is...that?" He pointed to a round, steaming, crusty shape on a platter.

"That is like a strudel, but it is full of warmed meat and vegetables. I think it comes from Flanders," she said.

Patrick pretended great interest in the food, then gently grabbed her elbow and pulled her in closer. "And this?" he said, pointing to another plate. She leaned even closer and Patrick placed his hand in the small of her back as she described the various dishes. Her duties must have brought her close to the kitchen hearth, for in her clothes were the smells of thyme, hot butter, and rising bread. A sheen of sweat stood out on her brow and her blouse clung to her waist and shoulders.

The sound of pottery breaking rose over the din. All turned to see the Lady Katherina with hands to her mouth in a gesture of surprise. A bowl of food lay broken at her feet, and Sir Geoffrey was making a fuss: "Are you all right? That bowl shouldn't have been that close to the edge...servant girl, come here..."

Aimeé was gone, rushing over with a towel for the mess.

Patrick rolled his eyes.

The evening wore on, and before long Mark stood to make an announcement. "For our entertainment, we will have a display of dancing. Please welcome William of Monmouth, Trent of Jersey and company."

The keep musicians carried out their instruments, followed

by William, Trent and some other Guests who were dressed in bright costumes. There was applause, and the performers bowed. The musicians began to play, and the Guests moved airily about the room. Patrick had no idea that William was also a dancer. He wondered what his merchant father would think of all this.

After a while, once the rehearsed portion of the performance was finished, the dancers went into the audience and extracted more people. Before long most everyone in the hall had been conscripted into the dance. Patrick now understood why Wolfgang had gone to great lengths to train the Avangarde to dance; he didn't want his elite troops looking like oafs at a social occasion.

Katherina was indifferent to the dance. She sat with one leg crossed over the other, bobbing her foot out of time with the music. She grabbed a grape and chewed on it irritably.

Geoffrey leaned over to her and motioned to the floor where increasing numbers of people were joining the dance. Patrick drifted nearer.

Katherina looked at the knight languidly. "Geoffrey, you have something between your teeth." She sat up and moved towards the exit while Geoffrey tried inconspicuously to see his reflection in a silver plate. She looked over her shoulder at Patrick before slipping out. He slipped out of the hall also.

He could see Katherina in the dark corridor, and when she saw him too, she picked up her dress and dashed for the stairwell. Patrick raced after her up the steps.

He ascended the dark stairway and found her up against the wall on the dim balcony above the dining hall. He went to her and tried to grab hold of her, but she pushed him away. She dashed across the balcony window that momentarily illuminated her bright green dress, but then pressed herself against the next wall.

The residents of Greensprings were laughing. They twirled

and swooped in a colorful mass that rose and fell like the swells of an ocean. To them, the dance occupied their senses and they may as well have been the ocean, for they flowed and pulsated as a single entity. They exchanged partners and danced with each other as water is one in a fluid body: having mass, but no true form. It was a colorful and vibrant sight.

Patrick again went to Katherina, and again she pushed on him, but this time he did not let her go. He held fast to her arms, then slipped his hands up to her wrists and pinned them against the wall above her head. He leaned his face into hers. He could feel her breath on his face, then she turned her cheek to him.

Patrick released her wrists and took a step back. She immediately reached forward and clasped her pale hands around his neck and drew him closer. He took her waist in his big hands just above the curvature of her hips, and lifted her. She wrapped her legs about his waist, and he pressed her against the wall. Their lips met fiercely.

Patrick felt as if his heart would burst. He had envisioned this moment a hundred times, but never thought that this warm moistness he now experienced would be so stirring. He felt as if he could lose himself in the sensation as he moved his hands from her waist to her legs and pressed harder into the wall. He was inadvertently bunching up her dress and he could feel the bare flesh of her legs. He thought he was going to explode.

Suddenly, Katherina grabbed either side of Patrick's face and pushed back to dislodge their embrace. She took in a breath and her mouth was wet.

"Only friend, right?" she gasped.

Patrick kissed her fiercely several more times. "Yes, only friends," he replied between them.

She grabbed his face and pulled it harder against hers.

#

There was a marked change in Sir Gawain's behavior. He

had a certain bounce to his step that had not been there before; he more often acknowledged others while passing them in the keep corridors; he was more apt to smile and make conversation; and there was a definite sense of confidence in his attitude. Not only his behavior had changed, but he was now more prone to comb his hair, which was trimmed. His clothes were pressed, his boots dusted. He seemed to enjoy the attention these changes attracted, but he did not explain the sudden difference. When others offered their theories (which were often too close to the truth), he did not go out of his way to confirm them.

It was no secret, however, that he was spending much time with the Lady Katherina, just as it was no secret that King Mark was being flowered with the affections of the Lady Christianne Morneau. Yet no one mentioned it publicly. It was not truly forbidden by the establishment for staff and Guests to consort, but it seemed to be discouraged for obvious reasons. Sir Geoffrey did not win any support for Greensprings by wronging his former fiancée, the Lady Amy du Lac. Yet, oddly enough, no one talked about that, either.

Patrick was still learning the nuances of Greensprings etiquette. He didn't know where it was all going, or how long it would last, but he knew that he would be prepared when the time did come. In the meantime, he was going to enjoy it.

#

He took long walks with Katherina in the orchards, sat and talked in the gardens, dined with her, and went for afternoon picnics—as was the case today. He sat across from her and studied her closely. She chewed unceremoniously on a honey-spread biscuit, and honey smeared one corner of her mouth. Patrick frowned in puzzlement. How could such a noble lady have such unladylike eating habits?

She wasn't always this way. Obviously, she could be very

feminine when she wanted to be, and often used it to her advantage. But sometimes, when she was at ease, she seemed to let down a certain guard and her boyishness shone through. Patrick assumed it was this lack of refinement, this irreverent boldness that he found charming.

"Patrick, what are you staring at?" she asked. "Patrick? Patrick?" She leaned over and shook his shoulder.

He snapped back to attention. "Sorry," he muttered.

"Where do you go when you do that?" she asked.

"Pardon?"

"It seems at times that you are, at best, half-there," she replied. "It looks as if you are in other world. So, where you go?"

Patrick shrugged. "I'm just thinking, I guess." He picked up a cloth napkin from the picnic basket and wiped the spot of honey from her lip.

She pulled away like a child being cleaned at the dinner table. "What do you think about?"

Patrick shrugged again. "Stuff."

"Like?"

"Stuff. Things that happened. Things that could happen. Things that could have happened differently if I had done differently. You know, stuff."

Katherina leaned forward and cradled his face in her hands, her eyes looking into his. Patrick, in his reverie, saw his mother cradling his face in a similar fashion. She was standing before him next to his horse that was saddled and loaded. She seemed so tiny and frail in his arms. Who would have guessed that the woman was so strong? *She won't take you back, Patrick, even if you return wealthy and famous,* she said, speaking of Kellie. He had sighed then, as if the last bit of his soul had rattled out of his ribcage.

"Sir Gawain? Patrick? You're doing it again." Katherina looked concerned. She was stroking his raven-dark hair.

Patrick shook as he snapped out of his daze. He grabbed at

Katherina's wrists to keep her from fussing with his hair and held them gently. "I'm sorry," he said. He started to realize that he was saying, "sorry" often. "I don't mean to be a bad companion."

"You are not. I just don't understand. Every now and again you have this faraway look in your eyes, and the play of emotions across your face is more...more..." Katherina struggled with the vocabulary, "...vivid. Why?"

Patrick put her wrists down and attempted to stand, but she maneuvered herself onto his knees and pinned them down so that he couldn't. She locked her wrists across the back of his neck. She was delicately built, but she had the ability to manifest her strong will into her limbs and grip.

"You are not going to pace like animal again. I won't let you run away this time. I hate it when you do that."

Patrick sighed. "Why do you want to know?"

"Because I care. Is that so bad?"

"Sometimes, yes."

"What happened in Eire that was so bad that caused you to leave?"

Patrick swallowed hard. He gathered the little Uhkraani princess in his arms and placed his head against her breast. She unraveled her legs and surrounded Patrick's torso with them while stroking the back of his head. He was a long time in saying anything.

"It was a girl, it was failure, it was hopelessness. It was many things."

"Tell," Katherina encouraged.

"I come from a modest house. My father was a knight, and lord of a small estate handed down generation to generation. I have three brothers, all older, all to receive the inheritance before me. I had only the name Gawain as my legacy. I could have stayed at home, working for my eldest brother on the estate, but not as much more than a servant. You see, I had no future in that way. I opted to do what my uncle had done when faced with the same situation when my father took over after my grandfather passed away. I trained underneath him, as did my other brothers, to become knighted. I had dreams of finding my own lands and wealth, as my uncle had done.

"If I had stayed with my family, I'm sure that I would have been treated well, but the idea of never having anything my own irked me. Despite that feeling, I almost fell into that trap. I met a girl. Well, rather, I fell in love with a girl whom I had always known in the village. She was Kellie O'connor. She had eyes bluer than a summer sky, hair darker than midnight, and the face of a Madonna."

Patrick had withdrawn his face from Katherina's warm bosom to look her in the eyes as he told his tale. He paused momentarily to swallow again. His eyes burned, but no tears spilled.

"I spent two wonderful years with her. She was my first love, my only love. I treated her like a princess, and she almost was in comparison to myself and my family. I thought I did all the right things, said all the right things. She said she loved me, even up to the end."

"What happened?"

"She found God. She started to spend more time in church than out of it. She took to praying constantly. Even though we were betrothed to be married, she changed her mind. She said that she wanted to join the convent. She said that was where her destiny lay, in marriage to Christ, not to me.

"It was hard at first, but she spoke with such passion about it that I began to see that she indeed wanted this. And it did seem to me that something was missing in her life that I just couldn't fulfill. I thought perhaps that was what she needed. I wanted her to be happy. I didn't want my selfish needs to stand in the way of hers. So I gave her my blessing, and she went to the convent to ready to become a bride of Christ." His grip on

Katherina tightened and his voice was rough in his throat. "But then I learned that she changed her mind again. She met another man, and decided to marry him, and she did.

"I went to her and talked. Asked her why, how this could happen. She told me that we just weren't met to be. She said that she was sorry, that she still loved me, but not as before. She had the audacity to lecture me on the fickle nature of fate as if this all was no consequence whatsoever."

He fell silent for a while. Katherina watched as the wheels of thought turned in his mind, animating the experience again and again.

"So you left then, for Crusade. To find fortune for yourself, and to be away from Kellie," she said.

Patrick silently nodded, his eyes still burning. "Yes. I couldn't stand to see her every other day in the village, walking hand in hand with another man, knowing that I couldn't have offered her anything to have prevented it. As I said, I did all that I humanly could have. I knew that it was a matter of time before I saw her with child...his child. I knew that soon that Sean, my eldest brother, would be taking over and ordering me around. I had to leave.

"So, it was an easy decision. Pope Urban had addressed all the Christians to go on the Crusade the previous winter. I left immediately for Flanders, where I heard many of the Frankish princes were gathering to do just that. Adventurers, merchants, common men, nobility, everyone, was going. So I decided to do so, as well. It was hard on my mother in particular. But she knew as well as I that there was no better alternative.

"My reasons weren't entirely material. I thought that perhaps I could become closer to God by taking up this Crusade. I thought I could become a better person. I thought I could find it in myself to truly forgive Kellie like I should, like a good Christian. As it was, hatred and sorrow were consuming me. I needed the journey, so I went to Flanders across the sea from my Green Isle."

"Did you? Become better Christian? Do you forgive Kellie now?" Katherina persisted.

He was silent for a moment. His mind still turning. "Yes, and no," he said at last. "I am a better person, even a better Christian, but for completely different reasons than I had expected. As for Kellie O'Connor, I forgive her. I always did. I cannot be so arrogant as to expect life to bend to my will and do as I please. She took the path she had to. But, that knowledge does not lesson the pain any. It still hurts to this day, and always will. I will always love her... and hate her in equal measure. I would like to think that I will always remember the better times rather than the bad. But sometimes I wonder."

"You said you became better, but not in way you expected." Katherina let Patrick up. His fidgeting and agitating had finally forced her to relinquish her hold. He now paced on the soft grass.

"Yes, the Crusade changed me...ultimately for the better. But not because it was a Holy Crusade, but because it was a series of events that life threw at me. One can't help but learn from them. Even the bad decisions I made taught me not to make them again."

"Then why do you dwell on it as if you failed miserably all around?" she asked.

"Because, it wasn't easy. It hurt. It was over three years of pain, discomfort and disenchantment. Like I said with Kellie: knowing doesn't make it hurt any less. It still happened.

"I grew up believing in the Church, in God, in a certain way, and the Crusade shattered all those ideas over time. When I arrived in Flanders, I found a massive rogues' gallery of misfits looking for a fight. They were uncouth, unclean men looking for any easy out from any crime they had committed in the past against man or God, because that is what Pope Urban promised.

"Certainly there were the true knights of the households of

the Princes Bohemund, Godfrey, Tancred, Baldwin, Robert and so forth, but they were in the minority compared to the rabble that followed them in God's name. Raped and pillaged all the way to Jerusalem in that same God's name. In the beginning I didn't know any better. I fell into bad company. The only company that would accept me at first. I was a foreigner, I didn't even speak that much French. They took me under their wing. I stayed with them for the better part of a year. They weren't much better than bandits.

"After Constantinople, we faced the real supposed heathens—the Moslems at the battle of Nicaea, which wasn't much of a battle for me. The Moslems were so overwhelmed by our numbers that they surrendered. Then came the battle of Dorylaeum. *That* was a battle. I thought more than once that I was going to die. I was covered head to foot in blood and gore. If the Crusade hadn't seemed all that Holy to me at first, it certainly didn't now. It was my first real battle, and I saw my companions commit acts unholy upon those people, even after they had admitted defeat."

Patrick paused as he paced. Then he knelt and looked into her pale eyes. "Do you know that in our march to Jerusalem, once in the Eastern lands, our foods and supplies came from Moslem merchants? We could kill their soldiers, take their land, rape their women, but it was perfectly all right as well to buy their goods in the marketplaces. They treated us like kings. They were a pleasant people...helpful, friendly...and they bathed and smelled of perfume. They did not smell of dirt and shit like the men I walked among. Their cloth, their armor and weapons, were superior. We bought them as treasures. I wear mine to this day. These were the heathens we were sent to destroy? I was starting to wonder who the barbarians were: us or them."

Patrick stood and took to pacing again. "It was then that I took note that even our shining leaders, the princes whose offices were supposedly divine, weren't much better than the thugs I traveled with. They took side expeditions to conquer Moslem establishments that had nothing to do with Jerusalem. They just wanted to fill their coffers. While they were doing that, we common soldiers were crossing the desert in high summer. We ran out of water and food because we were once again ill prepared. I thought I was in hell for the longest time, staggering along with parched and cracked lips.

"But then we came upon the city of Antioch, an ancient place that stood between us and Jerusalem. Here I could understand besieging. Here there was food and water. Here was an obstacle to our goal: the Holy Lands. Here were hostile Moslems. I thanked this opportunity for once."

Patrick ran his hands over his face and through his hair. "I thought too soon. We did not easily win access to the city like we thought we would. It took eight months. Eight months of then wintry weather that killed more of us than the Moslems did. We hid in wet holes in the earth covered by moldy blankets. We subsisted on marsh reeds.

"I asked myself many, many times—why did I stay? To this day I'm not sure. I often wonder what my life would be like if I had left. So many were turning back and returning to Europe.

"I think I stayed because my fear of returning home empty-handed and beaten was more severe than the torment I was then experiencing. I was nothing more than a nobody in Eire, but I still had my pride and I wasn't about to give up. Especially not in the eyes of God. For all the ungodly things that I had seen, I still actually at that point believed that this was all for God. Even if the means were somewhat convoluted."

He was pacing more furiously and gesturing more wildly with his hands. "Merchants set up camp outside ours. They brought their opium and harlots. Many a Christian fell into temptation there, and they were not ashamed to admit it. These were the chosen, who were to take back the Holy Land? I had long since lost my innocence and naivety, but still held on to certain beliefs. Perhaps I shouldn't have, because it would have made things easier on me spiritually. I could have been numb to the horrors that followed. I could have been jaded.

"Eventually Antioch fell. Just in time for us to be the besieged—an army of Moslems came from Mosul to besiege us inside those very same walls. Many more Crusaders left then to Europe. And still I did not go. I think then that is when I started to slip into insanity. I think perhaps I searched for death as a form of liberation from evil and that the Moslems were bringing it. So I stayed.

"But lo and behold, from the hills came a vision of a saint carrying a holy spear that inspired us to sally forth and defeat our captors. I was then truly insane. Gibbering and talking to a God that did not respond. I fought with valor in that battle, and for that valor I was welcomed into the camp of Godfrey de Bouillon, a Duke of Flanders. He was a good man. It was widely known that he actually came to the East to vanquish the infidels and not for gold alone. It was the happiest moment of my life at the time.

"Even though I never really met Godfrey and was just another knight lost in the ranks, I wore the white surcoat with the red Cross, and I could leave behind the rogues I had traveled with, even though I had become well acquainted with many of them. They were unwholesome, but they had accepted me and stood by my side.

"Even after I had started to hear the rumors that the vision of the saint and the holy spear were a fraud, a theatric to convince the men to fight, I maintained the belief that it was all for God. That I would find an inner voice that would tell me all was well. So I marched with my chin up.

"When we came to Jerusalem at last, we found the Holy City locked up, waiting for us. Our arrival was no secret. They offered us peace and guaranteed safety to all Christian pilgrims and worshippers in the future if we would just leave them alone.

But the Franks wanted only unconditional surrender and the Holy City delivered into their hands. So we laid siege to her.

"Forty days we assaulted the walls, and they turned us back. But eventually, during that hot and dusty month, we won entrance. Some of us by deceit through the front gate, and some of us victoriously over the walls with Godfrey and Tancred. I was with that group. I was wild eyed, half starved, smudged with blood, soil and soot, and full of what I thought was God. As it turns out, I was just insane."

Patrick grew silent. He had been recounting his tale to Katherina with full eye contact. But now he once again had slipped off into a faraway stare. His shoulders slumped, he swallowed hard.

"They say when one is insane, that all becomes crystal clear within a certain frame...well, I certainly saw with clarity. A vision that was so clear it was painful, yet unreal, like a vivid nightmare. Nightmares have the grace of being just that, nightmares—dreams that are unpleasant, yet not real. I had, however, no such grace.

"After the initial assault into the city I fought hard side by side with my comrades. It was bloody, but it was also glorious as battle can be when you are filled with the lust for it. It is the lust that drives a man to become a career soldier. But once the Moslem soldiers were defeated, I thought we had won and the civilians that ran before us would eventually calm down and accept their new conquerors. But that was not the case. They fled screaming, and with good reason.

"I watched helplessly as my fellow Crusaders butchered civilians only for the sake of butchering them. Because they were there. They chased them down for sport, stabbed women and children, ripped babes from mothers and dashed them against stone walls, forced innocents to jump from windows and walls..." Patrick was swaying back and forth, but he didn't seem to notice. There was once again a long moment of silence.

Katherina tried to hide a grimace. "I didn't understand. I stood dumbfounded. I had witnessed such behavior from the common rabble, and at first I thought they were the foot soldiers of God doing His unpleasant work to the non-Christians, but that attitude soon passed. The more time I spent in the Eastern lands, the more I came to understand that the Moslems were people like you or I—misguided perhaps in believing in what they believed—but certainly not deserving of this sort of torment. And these were knights and nobles committing these acts. I had been filled with the passion of battle, but not like that.

"Everywhere I went there was blood running like water in the streets and gutters. Heads and limbs were in piles...little child hands...bodies so full of arrows you couldn't tell if they were man or woman, or sometimes even man or beast. This brand of Christian justice went on for a week. Beheadings and tortures followed by death by flame. Even the surviving Jews in the city were herded into the synagogue and the place burned to the ground. I couldn't believe that I had been a part of it.

"By the end of the day, and still even the end of the week, I wandered the streets of Jerusalem. I was caked with dirt and blood. I was a ghost. My head ached constantly, I couldn't think, and I felt hardly human. Who I was had long ago disappeared, I couldn't even remember the old Patrick.

"I had left Eire to escape hopelessness and pain. To find myself, to find God. I felt cheated. I felt empty. I had gambled and lost by choosing this path in life, and nothing was going to change that—ever."

Patrick was quiet for so long that Katherina wondered if he would talk again. She asked, "But you survived it and left. And you say that you are a better person for it."

Patrick nodded. "A man found me wandering. He was an Englishman who had joined Godfrey at Antwerp. He too had heard the Pope's call to liberate the Holy Lands, and he too had sought to make himself a name. Ultimately, he too felt as I, but he was not as devastated. He took me aside and cared for me. He brought me food and talked me back to my senses and made me human again. His name was David of York. He too was under Godfrey's banner. We became fast friends and I joined his regiment in Godfrey's knights. We stayed for the better part of a year, watching our own leader, Godfrey de Bouillon, being named the Protector of Jerusalem, and reaping the rewards from the status we received because of it.

"But we, and several others, were disenchanted by what had happened, and when we heard that the Moslems of Egypt were coming to fight us, we opted to leave, lest all this happen again. We had accumulated a modest amount of wealth and we left with it.

"On the journey back to Europe, I eventually did find something akin to that little voice inside my head that said all was well. But I can't say that it is God. All I can figure is that such horror, such carnage can only be explained in the afterlife by God. I believe that he remains silent and watches us find our way blindly in the dark to Him and Salvation, and that is what the Crusade was about: the darkness we must cross on our way to Him.

"In the meantime, I must suffer the world and its heartaches. But as I have previously pointed out, knowing doesn't always make the pain any less."

Patrick truly was done speaking now. He toyed with a leftover bread crust while Katherina sat, thinking. Patrick turned his attention from the food to some standing stones nearby. He could tell that she still had more questions in her, and though the conversation had been liberating, it was also exhausting, and wasn't sure if he wanted to continue.

She suddenly came forward and once again wrapped her legs about his torso and cradled his face. "I cannot say that I completely agree with your philosophy, but I understand you a great deal more now. But I still don't understand why you distance yourself so from everyone. Why are you Sir Silence?"

Patrick reached up and stroked her hair as she had been doing to his. "I think perhaps it is because I know that everyone I meet will eventually abandon me."

Katherina frowned. "What do you mean?"

"Just that: everyone who comes into my life enters only briefly, then departs. They win my confidence, my friendship, even my love, then they abruptly leave. I believe it is a curse that afflicts me like so many tragedies that commonly afflict others in this world. But this particular tragedy is my own personal curse, and I must bear it always. It is my test in life."

Katherina's frown turned to a whimsical smile. "You are so serious, it is amusing. I think only curse is your overactive imagination. I will never abandon you, even if I must go back home. Always be special friend to you, even if it must be through correspondence."

"So you say," Patrick said quickly, "but even if you have the best of intentions you are still only the tool of fate and will be used by it to visit this curse on me."

Katherina gently slapped his head. "No, Irish-man, and I will prove to you by not doing that."

Patrick shrugged. "I have heard that before, even from David of York."

"No, no, no." She stuck her tongue out at Patrick.

Patrick shrugged again, but now he was smiling. "Promise?"

"Yes, yes, yes."

The Irishman tickled her ribs and she giggled and squirmed.

"You know Sir Patrick, you are not Sir Silence at all, and you are certainly not shy," she giggled uncontrollably as he ran his hands over her ribcage and body. "Once one comes to know you. Another thing, you still do not cry. I have heard perhaps the saddest of tales from you and not a single tear has fallen from your eye. I see they struggle to come out, but you don't let them. This is no good."

"Don't you think I have tried? Tears are not at my beck and call," Patrick said.

She took his hand from her waist and just held it. "When was the last time you wept?" she asked.

Patrick thought, calculating. "Before Kellie left me. A long time ago. I do not know why I no longer have any tears. I fear if the day does come again that I weep, it will be an absolute deluge."

Katherina looked shocked. "That long? Even after all these tragedies? That is not right, Patrick."

"You know what my theory is?" Patrick pointed out, still smiling. "Everyone else has the problem, not I."

"Once again I can't necessarily agree, but that sounded like the most positive thing I have heard you say ever, Irish-man." Katherina escaped Patrick's grasp and started to pick up the picnic site. "Come, let us go back to Greensprings, I have to be at loom soon."

Patrick bent to assist her, but then suddenly stood up and looked off to one direction.

"What is wrong?" she asked.

"Those standing stones, I could have sworn they were over there, and not there, a minute ago."

Katherina's brow furrowed. "You certainly do have active imagination. Do you always see things Patrick?" She grabbed his hands and put her face close to his, and in their kiss, they forgot all about the stones.

#

"How do I look?" Patrick asked Sir Jon.

Jon surveyed him. "Your usual dapper self. It's only a concert, not a state dinner, you know."

Patrick wiped his sleeve over the polished bronze shield that hung on the wall near the Practice Field, just inside the keep. His efforts did not improve the blurry image.

"Jon, I'm amazed at you. Were you not the one who insisted that a presentable image was necessary if one wanted to improve one's station?" Patrick straightened Jon's cape and patted him on the chest. "How goes your attempt of winning the Lord Loki's endorsement as an Avangarde candidate?" Patrick's eyes scanned the yard from the colonnade; the evenings no longer were chilly, and the grounds around Greensprings were alive.

Jon pouted. "He said my efforts were best applied elsewhere."

Patrick grimaced. "That wasn't a very nice thing to say. I'm sure he phrased it more gently than that, right?"

Jon shook his head dourly.

"I'm sorry to hear that Jon. I don't know what to say." Patrick placed a friendly hand on his shoulder. "You're a good man, and you deserve something for your efforts."

"Well, you give me hope," Jon confided as they moved towards the exit of the keep, and the practice field beyond.

Patrick was genuinely surprised. "How so?"

"Despite your best efforts at being anti-social, you've still managed to win the attention of a noticeable Guest, the Lady Katherina. I am sure she will gladly recommend you become an Avangarde once the next position opens. So, you see, you've accomplished what I've been trying to do without even trying."

Patrick waved him off. "I've done no such thing."

Jon smiled. "You're probably right. It probably has more to do with the fact that she is a bit of a misfit herself. Birds of a feather and all."

"Katherina? A misfit?"

"Yes, she is much like you. Dines alone, doesn't spend much time with the other lady Guests, doesn't participate in..."

"OK, OK, I get it," Patrick frowned, more than just his feathers ruffled. "She's been through a lot. She is far from home and she barely speaks any of the common languages here. That alone will isolate you. It wasn't until a year into the Crusade that I finally began to fit in, after I started to get a sense of French. Loneliness will drive you to do odd things..." Patrick trailed off, feeling pulled toward dark thoughts.

"Still, you will win recognition—Avangarde sort of recognition—for counseling her during her difficult time. All I have to show so far is that I annoyed the Viscount Loki."

Patrick was about to comment when the sound of hurried footfalls came up behind them in the form of Trent and Willy, on their way to the concert. Willy caught sight of Patrick and wagged his finger.

"Ho, Sir Patrick, I say you've gone too far this time."

Patrick frowned. "What's that?"

"You know very well. You slipped into my room and absconded with my pottery wheel."

"It is missing?"

"As if you didn't know," Willy stopped, hands on hips and a serious attempt of a disapproving scowl on his face.

"What makes you think I took it?"

"Because you, Sir, are a hater of art. You always protest my craft."

Patrick smirked. "I like art just fine, William. It's your crafts that make disagreeable noises I do not like. Your pottery-making doesn't disturb my sleep, therefore I have no motive for absconding with your pottery wheel."

This seemed to stump Willy. "Very well, you are off the hook." He thrust a finger dramatically into the air. "But I demand a formal inquest into the matter!"

Patrick smiled. "I will look into it first thing in the morning."

Satisfied, Willy and Trent continued on their way to the concert, but before doing so, Trent called back, "Oh, I almost forgot, King Mark needs help carrying something out of the keep."

"What about you?" Patrick called after Trent, but to no avail. The gangly boy had already strode out of earshot.

"I'll go, Jon. Cheer up. You are a good man, forget what Loki said. He's wrong." Patrick patted Jon on the shoulder again, and they parted ways outside the keep.

#

Sir Patrick strode down the corridor with a bounce in his stride and he whistled softly to himself. He had not been in this part of the keep since the inquest, and it still seemed gloomy, as if haunted by the old men and their questions. He wondered what Mark was carrying to the concert.

An icy breeze caused the tapestries to flutter. Patrick stopped his saunter. The keep was drafty, but nothing like this, and a shiver ran up his spine. He didn't like the feel of it.

Then at the far end of the corridor was the shape of a robed and hooded figure. It walked slowly with head down and arms tucked in either sleeve. Patrick's heart pounded. "F-Father Constant?" he called, but he knew better. He knew that it wasn't Hugh, or any of the other clergy. It was his own personal tormentor, returning from its absence. As it approached, the Apparition raised its hooded head, and only blackness filled the gap. It thrust forth its accusing finger.

Patrick stood stiffly, jaw clenched. "Who are you?" he said between his teeth. "What are you, and what do you want with me?"

The thing stopped before the Irishman and kept pointing. Patrick flinched, but did not run. He stood with his back straight.

"I will not let you do this to me any longer. Take what you come for, and get it over with. Otherwise do not waste my time, wraith!" Despite his bold words, Patrick shook like a scared child.

The Apparition backed up a step, turned, and walked away. It took a few steps, looked over its shoulder, then continued on its way, fading into nothingness as it did. It was gone.

Patrick let out a long breath that he didn't realize he had been holding. He shook terribly and his brow was wet.

"Sir Patrick? Is that you?" The human voice in the corridor brought him back to reality. He looked up to see the Lady Christianne Morneau approaching from the other direction. When she was in sight of the knight, she gasped. "Are you well? You look as if you have seen a ghost."

Patrick laughed nervously. "I think I am coming down with something, but I believe it will pass soon."

Melwyn was with her, trailing in her shadow. She peeked over Christianne's shoulder and gave her characteristic vacuous giggle.

Patrick smiled and bowed deeply. "Good day to you, Mademoiselle Melwyn."

The servant laughed again and her face disappeared behind Christianne's back. She long ago had lost her fixation for William, and knew that Patrick was no lover of young men, but she still made a game of it.

"You certainly have a way with the Ladies," Christianne said. "Melwyn, why don't you run ahead to the concert? I'll meet with you there."

Melwyn conceded and made a wide berth around Patrick as she departed, laughing. He watched her leave and shook his head.

"I mean it Patrick, you certainly have a way with the Ladies," Christianne said once Melwyn was gone. Patrick didn't know what she meant, and frowned at her. "I was surprised to see you with the Lady Katherina."

The knight understood her train of thought. "We really are just friends."

Christianne wrung her hands. "No, you're not. Anyone can see that."

Patrick shrugged. He didn't make any confession, or made any more effort to deny it.

The Lady Morneau looked away, struggling to say more. "I just wanted you to know that, well, I never meant to..."

Patrick put up a hand. "You don't have to explain. I don't have any ill feelings for you. Were you still passing your time with Geoffrey, maybe then I would, but you're not. I like Mark very much. I am happy with the way things are now. Does that make sense?"

Christianne came forward and embraced him. "Yes, very much. Thank you."

He hugged her back. This, for some reason, was more of a relief than seeing the Apparition turn away.

#

Patrick found Mark in his apartment. Crates of yellow and red and blue pennants blocked the window and stopped the door from swinging all the way open. They'd been in storage awhile and some of the crates were moldering and unstable, but Mark wanted to hand them out at the concert, and needed help transporting the load of them to the field.

"Why for a concert?" Patrick asked.

King Mark shrugged. "They have been lying around here for a long time now, and I have been wanting to pass them out for some occasion. I just can't find one that suits well enough. I figured the concert was just as good as any. They're taking up space in my quarters."

"I have an idea," Patrick suggested.

"Oh?"

"I've been thinking about organizing something in the way of a jousting tournament, or perhaps a mock melee with us knights choosing teams and fighting it out. We could hold it on the Practice Field, put up balconies for the Guests as spectators. That would be a more suitable occasion to pass out pennants to wave than at a music concert."

Mark blinked. "Why, yes. That sounds absolutely grand. I'll make sure everyone helps out. That is a terrific idea." He looked at Patrick with a new appreciation. "Why the desire to be so involved all of a sudden?"

Patrick rubbed the back of his head, and turned halfway away. "Let's just say it's been pointed out to me that I tend to avoid things and should be more involved."

Mark nodded with a smile, but his expression turned inward as he reevaluated the piles of crates. "Unfortunately, that means I must put up with these damned things in my bedroom for a while longer." Mark dropped the crate he was holding and brushed his hands. "But it also saves us from carrying them out there now. Let's go to the concert."

It was a quick trip out of the keep to the practice field, where wooden scaffolding was set up for the spectators. These were mostly occupied by the older Guests and keep staff, while the younger Guests and junior staff were content to sit in the grass before the stage, where members of the troupe were warming up their angelic voices.

The Lady Katherina intercepted him, and guided him to the front of the crowd before the stage. There, they found William, Trent, and Jon. "Gentlemen," he said, "may I present to you the Lady Katherina." The trio rose to their feet and bowed at the hip and Katherina returned the gesture with a curtsy.

"Pleased to meet anyone who can extract that stick from Sir Patrick's arse," Willy said.

With just a hint of color to her cheeks, the Lady Katherina covered a dainty smile with a hand and said nothing.

"Can we sit down, please," Patrick said, mortified enough for the both of them.

"Don't worry," she said. "It mean they comfortable with you. You should be happy."

"I'm ecstatic,"

"What is wrong with the big one?"

Patrick noticed that she was looking at Jon, who was still gloomy.

"He's not having such a good day. It's a long story."

Katherina pouted. "He need cheering up. Or maybe girlfriend."

Patrick shrugged.

#

"Ah, there is our illustrious leader. Maybe now we can get on with this ridiculous sing-fest," the Viscount Loki growled, as Mark took his seat.

"Music is not your fancy then, Viscount?" asked Sir Geoffrey, who sat next to the older Guest. Both were impeccably dressed and had spent time on their hair. A few of the other young men had begun to imitate them.

Loki sniffed. "Not such an amateur showing as this, of course not."

"Surely give the youngsters some credit, they're working hard to amuse us. Though I wouldn't mind some of them doing something else for my amusement," Geoffrey said. His eyes wandered over some of the older Lady Guests in the choir.

Loki raised an eyebrow. "And what has prevented you from asking?"

Geoffrey waved a hand. "I haven't had much luck lately."

"That doesn't seem to be the case with Sir Mark or Sir Patrick," Loki pointed out, nodding in the direction of King Mark. Mark motioned to the conductor to start the music, and Loki's chuckle was lost in the first notes.

Sir Geoffrey sneered and murmured, "The Lady Morneau is hardly worth the effort. She is all talk. The Lady Katherina, on the other hand, now that is a tragedy."

"Because she is with the Irishman?"

"Precisely," Geoffrey replied. The choir made its first harmony, a sweet, heavenly sound. The two men listened for a few moments, but did not lean back from their heads-together posture.

"You don't like Sir Patrick?" asked Loki.

"It's not that," Geoffrey said, and shrugged. "He is a good enough fellow and a fine soldier. I just don't think he deserves a catch like the Lady Katherina."

Loki smiled. "And you think you do?"

"Well, yes. She needs a real man, someone to show her a good time."

The Viscount's smile broadened. "What's stopping you from showing her that good time?"

Geoffrey shrugged. "She is with Patrick."

Loki clicked his tongue. This seemed to annoy the Avangarde.

"Are you mocking me?" he demanded.

Loki feigned innocence. "Me? No, not at all. It just seems to me that you easily gave up on the notion of stealing the girl away from Patrick. You, who I hear is legendary for making the Ladies swoon with a single word, are letting an undeserving man walk around with your prize. And a *Reservist* at that."

Sir Geoffrey's brow furrowed at Loki's comments, but his gaze turned towards the Reservist and the Lady Katherina, who sat side by side in the grass before the choir. They were accompanied by two boy Guests, and were giving Sir Jon a good-natured ribbing, who was stoically allowing the Lady Katherina to crown him with a chain of daisies.

"You want her, don't you?" Loki whispered in the knight's ear. "People are laughing at you because you have been bested on the battlefield of romance by an unremarkable, fashion-senseless Reservist from an obscure island. Are you going to let that happen?"

Geoffrey shook himself and blinked. "I've already stolen a girl away from him once. He would make things difficult this time."

Loki scoffed. "You need to be subtle. You need her to come to you."

"And how," Geoffrey asked, "do you propose I do that?"

"You're a smart man," Loki said. "You can figure it out. For instance, you might choose a route that would be so subtle that no one would suspect you were the one behind Katherina's leaving Patrick for you."

"How's that?"

"I'd wager you would first go to the servant Aimeé."

"The servant girl?" Geoffrey looked puzzled. "Why?"

"Because, you know that Patrick is also seeing her on the side, as the rumors say..."

Geoffrey's face lit up in acknowledgement.

"...and you would show *her* a good time..."

The Avangarde looked puzzled again. "Why?"

"...because, you, being the man you are, would ruin her for Patrick. She would want nothing to do with him after you got through with her. I'm correct in assuming that would be the case...right, Sir Geoffrey?"

Geoffrey hesitated in answering, and then nodded with a pained look. "Of course." He sniffed and straightened out his surcoat.

"Well then, once Patrick learns that his dessert is rejecting him, he will also learn that his main course is as well."

"Why is that?" Geoffrey leaned closer to Loki to hear better over the choir.

"Because girls talk amongst themselves about that sort of thing. Aimeé will tell Katherina that Patrick is hardly a man, nothing like you. Once Katherina hears of that, and learns that Patrick is seeing another woman, she will naturally come sniffing around your door. You see, you took this path at winning the Lady because it was devious, and the only possible harm done, if any, would be to a mere servant." Loki winked at the Avangarde, who had a thoughtful gaze in his eyes.

"You really think so, Loki?"

"Of course. Such a plan wouldn't work for a lesser man, but for you, with your prowess, it's almost guaranteed."

Geoffrey leered first at the Irishman and Katherina, then at the buxom servant girl who sat among the keep staff.

He was a genius.

#

Aimeé placed the last of the carrots into her skirt, the ones Rosa Maria had rejected because they were too tough and knobby for human consumption, and left the kitchen. It was a short trip to the stables, and on the way she passed Sir Geoffrey.

"Forgive me, m'lord, but I can't manage to bow with this load in my skirt," she said.

Geoffrey smiled charmingly. He liberated a carrot from her skirt and took a bite. "That's quite all right, I'll take this as compensation."

The Avangardesman leaned against the entrance, chewing on the carrot. Aimeé smiled at him, at his choice of food, and entered the gabled building for Siegfried's stall. "Hello big boy, how are you?" she cooed. The big horse came forward and nuzzled her. She commenced to feed him the carrots and smooth his forelock. "My, you're looking handsome today."

A shadow fell across her. It was Geoffrey again. "May I help you?" he asked.

Aimeé blinked, then shrugged. "Suit yourself, m'lord."

Geoffrey stood beside her and reached for the carrots in her skirt; he rooted around in the pile too long and too deeply. She gasped and moved away.

"Oh, forgive me," he said. He fed the carrot to Siegfried. Aimeé withdrew another and handed it to Geoffrey. "Hungry fellow isn't he? I don't doubt he would eat you if he had the chance." Geoffrey chuckled.

Aimeé smirked. "He would have a hard time chewing on me, I'm so tough."

Geoffrey stroked her cheek. "You certainly are tough, but I imagine you would taste sweet."

Aimeé's eyes lost some of their meekness, and she stepped back. "Sir Geoffrey, why, not long ago you were yelling at me for spilling drinks."

Geoffrey shrugged. He continued to touch her face and rub her shoulders. "It's my job, you know, to be a pompous noble. But you might say that I'm not on duty right now." Aimeé wasn't smiling now as the knight's hands moved all over her. "I've been watching you, and I can tell what you like. I like the same thing. So why go through the silly rituals that men and women play to achieve it?"

Aimeé wrung her skirt into knots where she held it to support the carrots. She was looking down and breathing hard.

"Here, let's be rid of this." Geoffrey dumped the remainder of the carrots into Siegfried's stall. "The horse will undoubtedly like us all the more for it."

Aimeé backed up. "M'lord, I think you m-mistake me."

The Avangarde swaggered after her. "No, I don't. It's obvious what kind of girl you are. It's obvious to everyone. Don't be ashamed, it's not as if you were a Lady or anything. It's all right for you." Geoffrey undid his sword belt and he let the weapon rest against a post.

"Please, m'lord. If you'll excuse me."

"Come now, is this how you like it?" the knight said between gritted teeth as he stepped forward and gripped her wrists hard. He struggled with her flailing arms and somehow managed to loosen her corset strings. She slapped a hand across Geoffrey's face, then looked at the hand that did the deed with shock. She hadn't meant to do it. It was a reflex.

Geoffrey's face turned to a mask of rage. He back handed her so fiercely she fell into the straw of an open stall. She lay there, stunned, a trickle of blood seeping from her open mouth. Geoffrey knelt down over her.

"Now give me what you've been giving Patrick!" he hissed and pushed up her skirts. Aimeé gave a scream that was cut short by Geoffrey's hand covering her mouth.

#

Patrick approached Siegfried's stall and called to the dark horse. Siegfried did not come right away, but finally lumbered over.

"What's wrong, old boy?" the Irishman asked, concerned. The animal was bloated and sick with gas. On the ground, dozens of half-eaten carrots and carrot stems lay in the straw. Siegfried usually ate the entire vegetable, and if these were how many were left, Patrick hated to think how many had been there to begin with.

"Dammit, Aimeé, how many times do I have to..."

A sound caught his attention. A whimpering in another stall, and he followed it to its source.

He found the battered servant girl.

"Oh my God, Aimeé, what happened?" He rushed forward, but when he attempted to be near her, she cried out as if in pain and scurried to the other side of the stall, into the shadows. Patrick hung back.

"Don't look at me," she pleaded.

It became evident to him what had befallen the servant. He had seen the same disarray and fear in a woman many times during his journeys in the Crusade. He came forward and sat near her.

"I mean it, don't touch me... I'm dirty," she said. "I don't want you to see me like this."

"I want to help, tell me who did this. I will make sure he pays."

There was a long moment of silence. Then she coughed out what might have been a sarcastic laugh of sorts. "You can't," she said.

"Why not?"

"Because," she almost shouted, "he was like you. A noble. A man. Who can do as he pleases." Her body became wracked with a fresh wave of weeping. "A man who can do...do...this! Or do the exact opposite: treat me like I'm not there at all, not even worth looking at, let alone touching! Often I wonder which is worse."

Patrick hung his head. He knew what she was saying. He suddenly felt like he didn't even have the right to comfort her. Aimeé struggled to her feet. When Patrick offered assistance, she waved him off. She managed by herself.

Now that she stood in the light, Patrick had a better look at her. Her linens were ripped in various places, and it was a struggle for her to hold herself up against the railings, and to hold herself in where her clothing supports had been. The left side of her face was swollen and her lip was split on one side. She was going to have a hell of a black eye.

She limped severely as she made for the door.

"Please, let me help you. Tell me who did this," he pleaded.

Aimeé scoffed. "Why? What would you do? From what I understand there is no glory in defending the honor of a maidservant. If you fought the man who did this, you would only be laughed at. Or, at best, they would think you were defending your territory or property. I do not care to be thought of in that way. I may be only a servant, but I have some dignity."

Patrick cupped his hands underneath his nose almost as if he were praying. Again tears brimmed in his reddening eyes, but none fell.

"You want to hear something funny?" she asked, turning to the knight. "He thought I was doing this with you. He felt he was also entitled."

Patrick bit the end of his thumbs and shut his eyes. "No, Aimeé, I..."

"Maybe it is my fault. The other maidservants warned me of this sort of thing. They said I was too bold, they said I threw myself at the sirs, they said it would all come back on me. I guess they were right." She paused at the doorway. "The funny thing is, I threw myself only at you, and you were the only one who didn't bother to even look."

Patrick held out his hands in frustration. "Aimeé, if there is..."

Aimeé again waved him off. "No. It's not so bad. It's not the end of the world. It's not even the first time." She left him there and disappeared into the keep.

#

Loki held the strange-looking bronze instrument skyward. He then positioned himself better in the window and squinted at the stars through the metal apparatus. He brought it down, looked at it, made some adjustments to its movable parts, then peered at the stars once again with the thing.

"Ah, that's better," he murmured. He held this pose for a moment, and then tucked the device inside his cape. He sighed with a smile. "Only a short while now."

He turned and walked briskly down the keep corridor. It was dark, but brilliant moonlight cast eerie shadows on the walls. Something caught his attention. He moved silently to a tapestry that was gently moving in an air current, and delicately pushed it aside. Inside was a room that he hadn't realized was there. It was open to the gardens and a cool breeze was blowing through. Slumped in a chair in the moonlight was King Mark, asleep. Loki slipped in, smiling.

"Well, well, well. What do we have here?" Loki said as he swooped around Mark like a great bat. His shadow fell across Mark like a cloud blotting out the sun, and the prone knight twitched in his sleep. "Are we tired? Heavy is the head that wears the crown, is that it?" Loki clicked his tongue.

He circled the golden-haired man, studying him and stroking his goatee. "You know, Sir Mark, my dear Steward," he said. "You're not quite as healthy looking as you used to be. You're tired and haggard looking. You look as if you have been through mortal combat, but you haven't been, have you? You've only been reading paperwork and signing this or approving that and deciding who is to be chaperoned by who and who has been skipping church services and should you tell Father Hugh about it and...well... I think you get the picture, don't you?"

Mark jerked more violently in his sleep. His eyes squeezed shut harder and he moaned audibly.

"In fact, leadership isn't quite what you expected, is it? Why, I'd even say that you're not fit for it! And you, of all, know this. But you are proud, and waited a long time for this opportunity to lead Greensprings, haven't you? It's a pity now that you are the leader, you realize you're not cut out for it. That must certainly sting the pride: knowing you're no good at your appointment, but too proud to admit it, let alone relinquish it into another's hands." Loki lunged forward and positioned his face next to Mark's temple. "My, the guilt and sense of failure must be unbearable!"

Mark cried out and he sat upright. He was breathing hard and a cold sweat had broken out on his brow. He looked wildly around him at the room. It was empty. He could have sworn someone had been there.

He leaned forward and placed his face in his hands.

#

When Patrick entered the dining hall, Katherina gasped; the man looked sick to death. "What's wrong?" she asked. He joined her at the table and flicked his hand in the air.

"Nothing." He fumbled with the dinnerware and reached for the food without saying more.

Katherina's eyebrows were still knitted. "Something is terribly wrong. What is it?"

"I said 'nothing,'" he snapped. "It's not important."

Katherina's eyes turned icy and angry. She hadn't looked at him like that for some time. "How can you say that? You are completely...d...distressé? Distressed."

"I just have a lot on my mind. The tournament I said I'd put together for Mark."

Katherina didn't believe him; her eyes got colder.

Patrick glared back. "Look, it's personal."

"What is so personal you can't tell me?" She balled her fists into the napkin on her lap and leaned closer. "We are intimate. We tell secrets. I tell you mine, you tell me yours, right?"

Patrick leaned back in his seat and stared at the ceiling. "I don't have to tell you all my secrets, right? We are not married. We agree that we wouldn't become this committed. I can just as easily tell my secrets to others, right?"

Katherina was quiet. The anger was gone from her eyes, but the iciness still lingered. "Yes, Patrick, that is correct. And I am free to tell my secrets to others as I please."

Patrick bobbed his head in acknowledgement, but the essence of what she had said seemed to escape him as he dug into his meal. They ate without speaking.

#

Patrick approached Siegfried's stall and called to him. Siegfried came to the knight and nuzzled him. He was looking and smelling much better this morning. Patrick applied a metal brush to the horse's mane. "There you go, boy, we'll get those knots out yet," he said, gently but sternly brushing on the animal's glossy hair. Patrick had a thousand things going through his mind. He was finding that organizing an event for Greensprings was much more difficult than it appeared. He was actually going to have to break down and ask Willy or Trent for advice on how to juggle his duties and organize as they had juggled their studies and organized.

On top of that, now there was Aimeé. He felt obliged to do something. Furthermore, he had been cross with Katherina for days. He should do something special for her as well.

He looked up at the sounds of footfalls and saw Sir Geoffrey walking in with a grain bag for his mount, crimson cape glowing in the sunlight. Geoffrey startled when he saw the Irishman, but quickly smiled.

"Good day, Sir Patrick," he said.

Patrick nodded. "Good day, Geoff."

Geoffrey hooked the grain bag in his horse's stall and leaned on the door. "So, how fare you?"

Patrick shrugged. "I seem to be singing the same tune."

"I can understand that."

There was a long awkward moment of silence. An idea occurred to Patrick and he voiced it. As with Christianne, he had long ago lost any hard feelings he felt for the nobleman. "Geoffrey, I am putting together a jousting tournament, or perhaps a melée for the benefit of the Guests. Do you have any suggestions for it?"

Geoffrey crossed his arms, frowned and nodded. "We could have awards for the best competitor, naturally...and we could involve the Guests by having them play roles in the competition, like squires, and mock kings and queens for the teams and what not."

Patrick brightened. "Excellent idea. We could actually make a big scene out of it, like a ballad of sorts, but with live people acting it out."

"There you go," Geoffrey encouraged.

Again a moment of silence. It was Geoffrey's turn to break it. "So, who would you choose as your Lady to champion?"

Patrick laughed, and then shrugged. "The Lady Katherina, I suppose. And you?"

Geoffrey was a while in answering. He had his back to the Irishman. "I thought maybe since we would all be acting and pretending that I would try something radical, not to mention congenial to the servants. I thought I would ask Aimeé."

Patrick's fussing with Siegfried came to a sudden halt.

Geoffrey's face turned just a little, as if watching Patrick from the corner of his eye. "What do you think of that, Patrick? Wouldn't that just surprise everyone, and cause the kitchen staff to herald me as a hero? Why, I would be praised for my originality."

Patrick just stood, watching without moving.

"I'm sure Aimeé would certainly find the idea appealing," Geoffrey continued. "She is a good sport after all. Of course, you already knew that, didn't you?"

"What do you mean?" Patrick asked, puzzled.

"Come now, Patrick, you don't have to play dumb with me. I know about you and the girl. She enjoys your company in a, well, shall we say, primal sort of way. She likes it rough. I know, I've had some of it myself." Geoffrey turned his attention back to his horse.

Patrick came forward and grabbed the Avangarde's arm.

Geoffrey pulled away. "Yes, so what of it?"

"You hurt her and you hardly had her permission."

Geoffrey brushed off his arm and turned his back to the Irishman. "What's wrong, Gawain, don't feel like sharing? The Lady Katherina isn't enough for you? Or is it that Aimeé has no need for you now, after me?" Geoffrey now straightened out his collar and turned again to Patrick. "Besides, Gawain, what are you getting all excited about? She is basically nothing more than a common wh..."

Geoffrey did not have the opportunity to finish the sentence, for when he looked up, his entire vision was suddenly encompassed by Patrick Gawain's gloved fist.

The knight was launched out the doors of the stables in a rolling mass of crimson cape. He rolled to his feet, half-stunned, and Patrick knocked him back to the cobblestones. They rolled together in a mass of surcoats, cape and cloak. Geoffrey managed to come to his senses and pushed the Irishman off him. They confronted each other standing and reached instinctively for swords that weren't there.

When his hand met the empty air at his hip, Geoffrey lunged forward and struck Patrick square in the face. The Irishman fell back and blood poured from his nose.

"You should have better manners around your superiors," Geoffrey shouted, and kicked Patrick in the gut. Patrick grunted, and then again and again as Geoffrey planted his foot repeatedly in his ribs. By the third assay, Patrick mustered enough of his faculties in his painful daze to seize Geoffrey's foot and jerk it out from underneath him.

The Avangarde fell and the Irish knight was upon him. They rolled like children pulling on one another's hair in the barnyard until they were battling next to the fountain near the front gates. Patrick finally got better leverage, and in his rage straddled the poppin-jay knight and bludgeoned his face mercilessly. He could see blood flying and was vaguely aware of a large crowd gathering.

Then, a strong hand gripped the back of his clothing and lifted him into the air. Now released, Geoffrey attempted to let fly with another volley of strikes, but he too was snared by the strong grip.

In the flailing, Patrick realized it was King Mark who held them. He was methodically dragging the two feuding knights into the fountain, where he unceremoniously dunked them. Patrick and Geoffrey were both big men, but Mark was bigger. They were repeatedly submerged until they stopped struggling. Mark then threw them to the cobblestones where they lay like wet rats.

"You two have a lot of explaining to do," Mark said gravely. "Now, to my apartment."

He kicked at them until they struggled to their feet, and then they staggered, heads low, into the keep.

#

"I thought you said there was nothing happening between you and the servant girl?" Katherina said, almost shouting. The close stone walls bounced her voice around and made Patrick's bruised head pound. He was tearing his room apart looking for his other surcoat that wasn't wet and soiled.

"There isn't," he snapped back.

"Then why did you fight Geoffrey? Everyone is saying you fought over the girl." Katherina's clear eyes were blazing and her arms were crossed tightly across her chest.

Patrick bend down and thrust his hand under the bed, and smacked his face on the frame. He stifled a cry and clutched at his swollen cheek.

"Dammit!" he shouted, and punched the bed. Once he had regained his composure he sat back on his heels and looked to the Lady Katherina. "Look, we are acquainted, her and I, but I swear to you nothing happened between us. And if it had, what concern is it of yours? We agreed—"

"I know what we agreed!" Katherina shouted. She threw up her arms and sat on the edge of the bed. She no longer looked angry, but sad. Her lip trembled.

Patrick found his surcoat folded in the chest, where it should have been anyway, and hastily put it on. He went to Katherina and sat beside her, put an arm around her, and started to stroke her hair.

"I'm sorry, I never meant to yell at you. You're the best thing to happen to me in a long time. I don't want to ruin that."

Katherina wiped her nose. "I know how we're supposed to feel about one another, but how can I allow you to run around and consort with anyone you please and have everyone know about it?"

Patrick laughed. "I'm not consorting with anyone...well, except you. Aimeé has been soft on me since I arrived. I've been nothing but a gentleman to her. Geoffrey took advantage of her good nature—in a terrible way—and when I found out it was he who did it, well, then that is when we fought."

Katherina's eyes were red. "Is this truth?" Patrick nodded and crossed himself. "What did King Mark say to you in private?"

Patrick sighed. His smile dissolved. "He was angry. He was more concerned with us fighting in front of Guests and blemishing the image of Greensprings and the Avangarde, than with what happened to Aimeé. He didn't approve of Geoffrey's behavior, but he approved of mine even less for allowing myself to lose control like that. As everyone will see it, Geoffrey broke no law or rule; he only showed bad judgement. As for me, I only showed myself to be a man incapable of solving my problems peacefully. It will be a long time before I will be an Avangarde."

"You care for her don't you?" Katherina said. She hugged Patrick and rested her face against his chest.

"She is sweet, and sad and lonely. I think she dreams of being taken away by a charming prince someday. She was nice to me when no one else was, and I treated her like a servant, not a person. It is the least I can do for her to pummel Geoffrey's pretty face. I rather enjoyed it, actually. For my own sake if nothing else. But I feel nothing special for her. Katherina, please believe me when I say if anything is to happen with her, I would tell you. But I do not see it happening."

Katherina nodded against his chest and said something in assent, but it was muffled.

Patrick felt a warm moistness where Katherina's face was. Patrick continued to stroke her beautiful platinum plaits. He had no idea that she hid such feelings for him. Or is it that he had known it, but did not want to acknowledge it?

Would it be so bad to care for her more? he thought. *Could I break the curse with her, or would it be another tragedy? Perhaps she's worth it...* But the steel doors of logic shut on his feelings. That same logic told his mind that the probability of happiness was unlikely, and letting his guard down would only invite pain and loneliness. Patrick stood and grabbed his sword from the stand.

"I must be going soon. I have guard duty. It appears now that I will be doing the night watch until kingdom come." He buckled his belt and threw on his great-cloak.

"Patrick, I'm sorry for being silly girl," Katherina said, wiping her eyes and trying to smile.

"I'm sorry for being a brute. Are we still friends?"

She nodded.

Patrick dashed for the door, then paused. "Oh, by the way, I think it would be better if we didn't see each other inside our chambers. You saw what kind of rumors circulated about Aimeé and me, and what happened because of it." He ducked out the door, but quickly returned. "And another thing, I won't be able to go for our afternoon walk tomorrow. I will be busy making preparations for the tournament I'm putting together. I'm sorry. Goodbye, I really have to go now." He was gone.

Katherina sat on his bed for a while. "Goodbye, Patrick."

#

When the Lady Katherina entered the garden, the sun was long set. She was in a daze, so it should not have been a surprise to her that she stumbled over her own dragging feet in the dark. Just the same, she cursed in her native language.

"My goodness, such words from a Lady," a silky, accented voice said from behind.

Katherina turned to see the Viscount Loki perched on a wall, cape wrapped about him. From what she could tell in the dim moon and starlight he was cutting an apple into slices with a pocket-knife. "I seriously doubt you understood what I said," she said, and planted her hands on her hips.

Loki smiled. The young lady with her wild bangs hanging in her eyes and the fierce expression on her face reminded him of those little dogs bred by royalty for their cuteness and viciousness. "No, actually, but I once knew a similar language in my days on the shores of the Black Sea," he said. "And I dare say what you said sounded quite harsh, even in a sailor's mouth."

"You've been to the Black Sea?" she asked.

Loki slid off the wall and alighted on the ground next to the girl. He neatly folded the pocketknife with one hand and slipped it into his vest. In his other hand, what she had thought was an apple, was a piece of wood. She got a little glimpse of it—some sort of miniature diorama with tombstones, before he slipped it into another pocket.

"Yes, but a very, very long time ago," he responded.

"I don't believe you," Katherina challenged, but there was a hint of a grin at the corner of her mouth.

Loki drew himself up and made a flamboyant gesture with one hand, followed by a spoken verse in some guttural language.

Katherina's eyes widened and she clapped her hands. "Very good. The old ones in the villages still say this nursery rhyme to children. I have not heard it in long time."

Loki turned in profile and waved a hand over himself. "I am a rather oldster myself, and in my time, it was a drinking song."

"You are Russo?" Katherina asked, intrigued by this new knowledge of a fellow Guest she had previously only known by reputation.

"Not at all. I was an emissary from my people to Holmgard once upon a time."

Katherina frowned. "Holmgard?"

"Well, I suppose people now days call it Novgorad. Peoples change, as do their cities and tongues."

Katherina's frown deepened. "When was this?"

"As I said, a very long time ago, and... Say, isn't it rather late for a Lady to be out and about?" Loki put on a mock scowl and wagged a finger at the girl. "Just where were you going, young lady? Do you not know the hour?"

"I skipped dinner," she admitted, smiling wanly at Loki's attempt at humor, "and go to kitchen to find something to eat."

"But still, rules are rules. You should be indoors, no?"

Katherina threw up her hands in exasperation. "This place has more rules than anything! I imagine they have a rule that say they must make more rule!"

Loki laughed. "I agree wholeheartedly, so your transgressions are safe with me. But skip dinner? I thought people around here lived for the social occasion of dining."

"I wasn't feeling very hungry."

Loki leaned in closer to get a better look at her face in the shadows. "Is there something troubling you?" he asked.

"N-no, why do you say that?" Katherina asked.

Loki raised a pointy eyebrow. "Well, usually someone as lovely as you doesn't have red eyes and streaks running down their cheeks. It is usually the boys who chase them that look so heart broken."

Katherina blushed, hoping Loki would not be able to see the color in the dark. "I'm not heart broken, I'm just..."

"Confused?" Loki offered.

Katherina shrugged, and then nodded in assent.

"Why, you don't strike me as the type to be confused," Loki said. "You strike me as a princess who is used to commanding and having your way. Someone who knows exactly what they want, and then takes it!"

Katherina crossed her arms. "Usually, I am. But I am not used to feeling this way about someone."

Loki stroked his goatee. "Madame, if you don't mind me saying so, anyone who causes such pain in beauty such as yours, is not deserving of it."

Katherina was silent for a moment. "No, I don't mind you saying so. But I assure you that ultimately what I decide to do about it will be my decision."

Loki clapped his hands. "That's the princess I see in there! I wouldn't want it any other way."

Katherina smiled. The Viscount's antics lighted her spirits, which had been heavy with thoughts of Patrick.

"Now, if I were that heartbreaking boy, I would be on the look out," Loki drew up his cape and masked all but his eyes that peered over his arm and darted back and forth. "For your wrath would be upon me," he stalked about in an exaggerated manner, looking side to side as if being hunted.

Katherina's smile broke into a laugh. "Are you always so dramatic?"

Loki straightened up and smoothed out his cape. His face was cool and calm again, and he said dryly, "Usually not, but when confronted with otherworldly charm such as yours, I seem to lose complete control." His serious face cracked into a smile.

Katherina laughed and shook her head.

"If you continue to cry, may I offer you my shoulder to lean on? I'd be incredibly flattered if you let me," Loki asked.

Katherina tilted her head to one side in thought, and then asked, "Why?"

"Because, like you, I am far from home and find myself surrounded by unfamiliar Franks, Anglos, and other ragamuffins who do not understand me. I need a friend, too. Someone I can tell *my* secrets to. Someone with whom I can, perhaps, shake the rust off of an old Slavic poem or two I used to know."

Katherina gingerly touched her lips and swayed side to side. "Very well, you may be official leaning shoulder."

"Yes!" Loki shouted triumphantly and shot his arm into the air as if at a competition.

Katherina giggled. "You are silly man."

Loki bowed.

Katherina calmed her giggling. She was starting to sound like a girl half her age, and was not at all happy with herself for letting down her guard. "I must be going," she said, putting on the air of protocol. "But if you like, we can test out these poems, shoulder-leanings, and secret-tellings at another time."

"That would be most gracious of you." Loki's bow deepened.

"Good evening, Lord Loki. It is pleasure to finally meet someone who recognize my language and home." Katherina curtsied her goodbye and turned to leave. She didn't get very far, however, when she realized that they had been walking and talking this whole time and she was now in an unfamiliar part of the keep grounds.

"I think you might find the kitchens in that direction," Loki pointed out, "and if I might make a suggestion, use the servants' entrance: Better to avoid those rule-loving Greensprings folk."

Katherina nodded her appreciation and slipped away, a silvery silhouette in the moonlit darkness.

Loki watched her go, admiring her form.

About then, Minion came along and stood beside the Viscount.

"You're late," Loki said. "But no matter, you caught me in a good mood."

"Who was that, Master?" Minion asked.

The Viscount stroked his goatee. "A very lovely Lady. Nice childbearing hips, wouldn't you say?"

#

Patrick entered the dark kitchen apprehensively, first poking his head through the doorway and looking side to side, then dashing across the main work area to the cupboards. He felt awkward being there after hours, let alone at all. Rosa Maria was notorious for browbeating and wielding a broom at anyone who didn't belong. And even King Mark was known to have his hand slapped for trying to steal some marzipan.

Patrick's growling stomach finally overcame his tentativeness and he moved to the larder. After he had begun to rummage around beneath some spice tins, however, he became aware of someone in the room.

"Ah hell," he muttered.

A portly figure in linen clothing came out of the shadows. "Excuse me, but Rosa Maria does not... Oh! M'lord forgive me." She curtsied when she recognized him as a knight. "I did not know you were a sir. Still, Rosa Maria would be angry if she knew that I at least did not try to deter you from raiding tomorrow's food."

"I'm sorry," Patrick stammered. "I was assigned late guard duty, and I missed dinner. I was just looking for something small to eat."

Another voice came from the shadows and another portly figure came forward. Patrick recognized them as the duo Anna and Claire, who often worked together. "Leave the poor lad alone. He's tired and beat-up looking. He could use a meal."

The first maidservant, Anna, was still nervous. "But..."

Claire elbowed her. "That's the Irishman, silly."

"So?" A knowing look from Claire caused her to brighten and she exclaimed. "Oh! *That* Irishman. Well, Sir Sile-er-Patrick, please help yourself."

The two maidservants rushed out of the kitchen, tittering in their Anglo slang. Patrick watched them leave, then shrugged to himself and opened the pantries. He found some cheese, a not-too-rubbery chunk of bread, cured ham, and even a flagon of wine, and sat down with his meal at the table by the door, where the scullery maids sat to cool off whenever they had a moment.

He was halfway through the bread when a sleepy-eyed Aimeé appeared in the doorway. A hand pushed her from behind and she was forced farther into the dying firelight near the hearth. She turned behind her and then turned to Patrick, then again to the doorway she had just come. Her expression was just as confused as Patrick's.

The Irishman stood. "Good evening, Mademoiselle de la Chasse."

Aimeé pulled the blanket she still wore about her. "You remembered my full name."

Patrick nodded.

There was a moment of silence. Aimeé looked about the room to pass the time. She looked everywhere but at Patrick.

"Please, won't you have a seat? Join me for some food," he said finally.

The maidservant shook her head. "I'm not hungry, but I will sit with you, if you like."

"I'd like that very much." Patrick offered her a seat next to him at the kitchen prep table. "You look in much better shape than I," he said when she sat. "Your face, I mean."

Aimeé smiled. "I'd agree. You look as if a hundred wild horses trampled you." She looked away. "I heard what happened between you and Geoffrey... I guess you fought over bragging rights, eh?"

Patrick's brow furrowed in anger. "No, mademoiselle. It wasn't like that at all. And if you knew me any better, you would know that."

"But that is it, isn't it? I don't know you at all," she quipped, losing some of her fear. Under the deference, she wasn't so unlike Katherina.

"I'm sorry for that. I behave the way I do towards you not because you are a servant, but because I feared liking you...and lately in my life, I have feared liking anyone."

The hard line of Aimeé's mouth softened a bit. "That doesn't seem to be the case with the Lady Katherina."

Patrick picked at his ham. "Well, the only reason she reached me to any extent to begin with is because I was obligated by duty to spend time with her. She was in a position to work her way into my life."

"You sound as if you almost regret that."

Patrick was quiet for a moment. Aimeé didn't rush his answer, but found a whetting stone and produced a small knife, the kind all the servants carried, and worked on the blade. It was short and narrow, and her hands moved as if this was a task she'd done so many times that she no longer needed to pay attention to her work.

"Maybe I do regret that." Patrick shrugged. "As I said, I've been afraid to let any one near me. They have a tendency to leave me in one way or another."

"That sounds like a classic man perception," Aimeé laughed. "Does Katherina know this? Or are you doing another classic man-thing and letting it all happen without her knowing your intention." She turned the blade and whetted the other side.

"We have talked about it much. She knows how I feel, and I know how she feels. We have a common understanding. We are only the best of friends. As for my intentions, I have no idea what will happen."

"Most men don't." She rolled the knife back into the waistband of her skirt.

Patrick was glad to see the maidservant in good humor for once. He finished the last of his meal, stretched, and shivered a little. "It may be spring, but this Avalon evening was cold. I think it will be a while before I recoup my warmth."

Aimeé opened up her blanket. "We can share, if you like."

Patrick hesitated.

"You're cold," she said, "so here's a blanket. I'm cold, so I want some too. Be practical." She extended the blanket and he wrapped the opposite side about him. He now sat next to her body, trying to preserve an inch of propriety between them. They sat silently for a while, watching the dying embers of the fire. The light was a brilliant orange and the heat felt good.

"Sir Patrick?" Aimeé said.

He grunted.

"Can I be your friend?"

"Yes, of course."

Another silent moment passed and Aimeé ventured another question. "Would...would you put your arm around me? It's not the same from another woman."

Patrick hesitated again, then relaxed a little and lifted his arm. "Yes, I can't see why not." She slipped under his arm and held on tightly. After a moment, he held her back just as strongly. Now that he actually touched her, he was surprised by how firm her body was. Her skin was smooth and the color of buttermilk. Except for her hands; they were calloused from years of work and perpetually off color. He expected her to smell of wash water and sweat, but she did not at all. She smelled of apples and heather.

The servant girl's body started to shudder almost imperceptibly, and the shudders grew into little convulsions. Sobbing noises came from her chest.

Patrick stroked her thick wild hair and rocked her gently.

#

In the darkness of the corridor outside the entrance, the Lady Katherina stood watching. Her wintery eyes iced over and her jaw set firm. She turned and briskly walked away.

#

Sir Corbin jogged down the path, holding onto his sword so he would not trip over it. He called to the Irishman. "Patrick, hold up." He didn't have a hard time catching Patrick; the poor fellow looked exhausted.

"Corbin, what can I do for you?" Patrick asked, and then smiled. "Actually, what can I *not* do for you?"

Corbin slapped a hand to Patrick's back, then looked over their shoulders and steered him in another direction. "I have a request for you."

Patrick nodded. "Easy enough, what is it?"

"I'd like you to be the one to go to Aesclinn and tally up what we owe the pig farmers for this week's account."

Patrick stopped in his tracks. "The pig account? Why me? That is such a tedious and menial thing to do. Besides, it's Waylan's turn this week, isn't it?"

Corbin made a face and rubbed his pot belly where it hung over his belt. "The truth of the matter is, you are scheduled for valley patrol today and so is Geoffrey. We thought it would be best if we kept you two boys apart for a while. Otherwise you will kill each other. Then where will I be? A dead Avangarde, a dead Reservist, funeral arrangements, explaining to do..."

"So send Geoffrey on pig patrol. He'd be right at home with the swine."

Corbin laughed. "Maybe, but there is that pesky seniority thing."

Patrick nodded. "All right, all right. I'll do it if it helps."

Corbin winked at the Irishman. "There's a good man."

#

Before he left the keep for the day, Patrick went looking for Katherina to tell her that he would be late for their afternoon walk.

"That is fine, Patrick, I already made plan," she said.

Patrick blinked. "What? Why?"

Katherina returned her attention to a complicated piece of embroidery. "You have been very busy lately, I thought you would have to skip on walk again. So when someone invite me on carriage ride, I accept. Is there problem?"

"I, uhm, well no. I don't mind."

"Mind? I hope not. After all, we agreed..."

"Yes, yes. Serves me right for even starting to be selfish. I hope you have fun."

"Oh, I will."

Patrick hesitated in the doorway. The options were to either leave and torture himself, or ask and look like a fool. His hand lightly traveled the grain of the door, and he frowned. "Just out of curiosity, who is it that invited you?"

Katherina crossed her arms. "Viscount Loki."

Patrick winced. But on the bright side, he thought, once one came to know the Viscount, his abrasive nature was obvious enough. Katherina would not tolerate such a man for long. "Well, I must be going. Have fun."

"Duty calls, I know, Sir Patrick. I will enjoy myself."

#

Patrick was irritable throughout the bargaining session with the farmers. It wasn't really much of a bargaining session: the farmers quoted what they felt they should receive and Greensprings offered the money, and not much negotiation went into it. Any staff member from Greensprings could have done it, but the duty was left to the Avangarde. It was a continuation of Wolfgang von Fiescher's vision of a humble order of knights. When the money had changed hands, he left Aesclinn in a hurry.

His last words with Katherina troubled him. She had seemed cold and distant and annoyed that his duties interfered. She had so often encouraged him to become more active with the knights, and now that he was, she was jealous of his time. He still didn't understand the girl, but he was eager to see her and try to patch things up.

While putting up Siegfried, he noticed that Loki's horses were still in their stables. Pig duty had taken several hours, but that was not long enough to go out for a proper ride and come back.

He searched for her then in the keep, and came up empty.

Jon the Informant, of all people, would know where she was. Patrick came across Sir Jon and Sir Jeremiah at the edge of the garden.

"Did they not go on a carriage ride?" he asked.

Jon looked puzzled. "As far as I know they never intended on it. That would require an escort, and they never ever requested one."

Patrick pursed his lips. "Are they together at all?"

Jon looked defensive and a little uncomfortable. "Yes."

"Then where are they?"

Jon tilted his head in the direction of the path to the garden. Patrick's heart stopped. The garden was the place people went for privacy. That would explain why they did not go on a carriage ride, because that would require going outside the walls of the keep and an Avangarde escort...which would negate privacy. But why would Katherina lie about it?

The secrecy, Jon's hesitant behavior, Katherina's distancing. His heart not only stopped, it fell from his breast onto the dusty ground. He approached a stone pillar and leaned on it heavily. Sir Jon and Sir Jeremiah rose and touched his shoulder, and headed back toward the keep, sensing that he wanted to be alone.

It became incredibly apparent what had happened. What he had allowed to happen. How could he be so stupid? Why did he let this happen? He wasn't quite sure what he was more angry at: that he had let Katherina down by not paying her enough attention, or by letting himself down by allowing himself to fall for her when he was trying so hard not to.

He sighed, sat on the bench, and hung his head. He rested like that for some time, damning his luck and pondering what to do next. He had just started to laugh again with her. To be carefree and liberated of worldly matters. She had made him feel good and gave him attention and affection. Even the annoying arguments she caused, he enjoyed. However annoying they had been, they had made him reflect and question his beliefs—and consequently he had taken steps to better himself which looked good in the eyes of the Avangarde. And he had fallen into the trap of taking it all for granted. He was under the blatantly idiotic impression that she would always be there. And he had been absent, inconsiderate, and less-than-honest on such matters as Aimeé.

He felt stupid and sick.

Yet this was exactly the behavior Katherina would condemn. She did not tolerate defeat. He stood and strode quickly into the garden. He would find her, apologize for his insensitivity, and to hell with this "agreement" they had forged. He would let his true feelings be known and show her he had changed. He would not be Sir Silence.

Along the garden path, he stopped at a rosebush and plucked a flower, careful not to prick himself on the thorns.

#

"So, Lady Katherina, your face isn't quite as long as it once was. Does this mean you have taken command of the former situation that caused you to have difficulties walking earlier?" Viscount Loki asked. He walked slowly with his hands grasped behind his back. The sun beat down hot and bright on the flagstone path and white rose blossoms.

"Let's just say I take command of my heart." She too walked with hands behind her back. "Lord Loki, why did you cancel our carriage trip for this?"

He shrugged. "I thought it would be more comfortable to speak in private. I doubt you wanted a knight riding beside us, bending his ear to our every word. Rumors find their beginnings in such a manner, and can have unpleasant repercussions."

"Some more evident than others."

"What was that, my Lady?" Loki inquired.

Katherina politely waved him off. "Nothing."

The came to a central fountain, and Loki sat at the water's edge and traced his fingers across its surface. The fountain was a masterful piece of work, almost magical in its elegance. It caught the sun and glowed whiter than the roses. Loki motioned for Katherina to join him. "Tell me, are you in need of a shoulder to lean on yet?" he asked. "The offer still stands."

Katherina smiled. "Do you speak in symbol, or want me actually to lay head on you?"

Loki shrugged. "I must admit, I would rather it be literal. It would make me feel good to be of service to someone—but whatever makes you happy... I would be pleased either way. I am fortunate just to breathe the air around you, and I hope never to cause you to be so distracted that you would trip over your own feet in the darkness, as I witnessed some nights ago."

Katherina's eyes flicked up in a faint roll. "Don't say things you don't mean. I have had too much of that recently."

Loki gently grabbed her chin and looked at her with intense eyes; they swirled like a lightning-filled storm cloud. "I do not make promises I cannot keep," for a split second, his demeanor became fierce, almost wicked, "and I do not tolerate those who do not keep theirs."

Katherina stiffened at his sudden touch. He was leaning into her personal space, pressing his body against hers. Her jaw firmed and she nodded slowly, refusing to shy away from his gaze.

"I see," she said, leaning away and breaking their contact. "You are sort who not suffer fools lightly. You take charge of situation. You set the rules. Am I correct?"

Loki shrugged, smug in his silent assent.

"You remind me of my uncle," she said after a moment of staring off into space.

Loki's teeth flashed. "Why, thank you."

Katherina turned to him with a cold stare. "Not a compliment."

Loki's expression fell. "Oh, well, my apologies for being me." He stood and wrung his hands nervously. "I sense there is a story with this uncle-fellow, but I won't pry. I can assure you I'd never use my ego, considerable as it is, to hurt you."

"Then I hope what you said earlier is true, that you keep promises."

Loki kneeled at her feet, gesturing over his chest. "Cross my heart, hope to die, may you stick daggers in my eyes."

Katherina's eyes flared and a hint of a smile creased her lips. She leaned forward and cradled the Viscount's craggy face in her hands. "Careful what you wish for."

Loki reached up and pressed her hands into his face, his smile deepening. "As long as it is these hands pushing those blades."

Katherina once again broke contact and pulled away. "Being confident is not bad thing—in fact, it very attractive. But when it becomes arrogance, it no good."

"I concur," Loki said, standing. "I take it this uncle was insufferable. If you would be so kind as to tell me what it was in particular about him that put you off, I shall find it easier to avoid making his mistakes."

Katherina went icy. "I would rather not talk about him, or why I am in Avalon."

"I beg your forgiveness," Loki said, bowing at the hip. "Despite my earlier statement, I find myself prying. I mean only to win your trust."

"Then just be friend."

After a moment of silence Loki said, "Certainly, but I have a suggestion as well. I want to tell you something about myself. Something I haven't told anybody here. I have no one to share such things. I'd be honored if you would listen to me, and at the same time hope you will better understand and trust me."

Katherina's lips parted slightly but she did not speak. The awkward silence hung in the air. "I—I suppose that is acceptable."

Loki took a deep breath. "Splendid."

He stood then and paced, not saying anything for a while, keeping his back turned to her. At last he said, "I know it is not proper to divulge one's reasons for being here. It is a sanctuary, a safe haven from the outside world and one's problems there. Well, I do not mind telling you that I am in exile. I was forced away from my people due to a misunderstanding." He turned his head over his shoulder to look at her as he spoke. "I say 'my' people, but they actually adopted me into their clan after tragedy had struck my homeland before that. They took me in when I had nothing. Their leader made a blood-brother out of me. It wasn't long before they truly treated me like one of their own." Loki started pacing, staring off into a different time.

"They were a big-hearted and magnanimous folk, especially their leader and his wife. I called them 'Father' and 'Mother.' We really were one big happy family.

"But for all their kindness and generosity with me, they were a simple and barbaric people who acted from their hearts more often than their minds. They were unsophisticated, even naive. They made enemies just as fast as they made allies. I am from a more diplomatic people. I used my skills on behalf of my new family and many times saved us all from tragedy. It wasn't long before we were a secure tribe, and powerful. Father thanked me and was gracious, even when my personality and nature began to chafe the others. Father stood up for me when others grumbled, which became often. I found myself more and more at odds with my siblings. I tried to change them, modernize them too quickly."

Loki kneeled before Katherina, staring into her eyes. "I meant well, I really did. But in my youth and arrogance, I made the mistake of talking down to them, treating them as lesser. They started to contradict me at every turn, fight me at every chance, even when they knew I was right."

Jittery with angst, Loki stood again and paced. "Then came the day of my greatest mistake. Again, born out of a desire to help, to be of use and to show gratitude to the people who took me in..." He paused. "Balder: Father's youngest son, the golden child and beloved of all, wanted to be a hero, wanted to make a name for himself. I must admit he idolized me, looked upon my abilities with wonder—I could calm entire armies and send them packing without raising a single sword. He must have thought I was magic. He was like my shadow, constantly asking questions of my craft, trying to be like me, using the art of the silver tongue to accomplish what his bigger, older brothers couldn't with the sword and the hammer. You see, among this family, to be a powerful warrior was the be-all, end-all. But Balder was smallish in size, and though a prize with the ladies, he could never seem to win the respect that he craved from his brothers.

"So the day came when enemies came and laid siege to the city. Balder was acquainted with the commander of the opposing army, and thought to convince him through statecraft to leave. Somehow turn the enemy away, while at the same time making a business deal that would profit both sides down the road. Such was my way. But Balder did not consult me in his plan. He wanted to do it all alone, to receive full credit and be a hero. I did not begrudge him for wanting that. What I couldn't allow, what nobody could allow, was how he wanted to go about it."

Loki turned to the Lady Katherina with hands behind his back, the straight face of the narrator. "He thought to win the trust of the commander by presenting the keys to the city. He had learned from me, in order to win something in negotiations, you must first give something of equal value." Loki squeezed his eyes shut and rubbed his temple. "What made him think that giving the *keys* to the city was a good idea is beyond me. I heard of his plan and tried to stop him. But it only resulted in a bitter argument that made him even more determined to carry out the plan on his own. I was helpless to do anything to stop him. You see, my behavior had alienated me from the others and I knew no one, not even Father, would listen to me. Especially if it involved disparaging Balder, his favorite son.

"So I went to Balder's brother, Hoder, who would at least listen to me with an impartial ear. Because Hoder was blind from birth, he was not a hotheaded warrior like the other brothers, and I thought Balder might listen to the soft-spoken Hoder. I trusted Hoder to stop his brother by any means possible. Unbeknownst to me, Hoder took the 'by any means possible' portion of my request a little too seriously. Hoder, though blind, had many talents, one of which was concocting potions from herbs." Loki smiled sweetly, his voice trailing off a little. "He made many a love potion for people in Father's court."

Loki shook his head and resumed the original pace of his story, but with a sadder voice. "I do not know if Hoder intentionally poisoned his brother, or if it was an accident, but he added too much mistletoe to the brew, and tricked his brother into drinking it the night before he was to hand over the keys. Balder, the golden child who only wished to save the kingdom, died a horrible, painful death. In the end, the enemy was driven away by force."

Loki sat down on the fountain's edge, the day's heat starting to create damp spots at his armpits and chest. He gathered a handful of water and rubbed it in his face. Katherina kept her hands folded in her lap, listening patiently for the rest of Loki's story.

After a long sigh, he continued. "Father was inconsolable. When confronted, Hoder blamed me, said I told him to do it, that I manipulated a poor blind child into murdering his own brother. I was already at odds with my family, and this sealed my fate. Father spared my life, which the others demanded, and instead ordered that I be bound and imprisoned in a cave."

Loki turned to Katherina, staring with a frank expression. "I was married back then, to a very devoted and caring woman named Sigun. She had the biggest heart of all. To this day I still do not know what I did to deserve her, for I treated her poorly and never gave her the attention she deserved. At first I couldn't stand the sight of her. She was so annoying, and not all that pretty." He made a gesture before his face, "Really big nose, you know? But I couldn't get rid of her, and she just started to grow on you. One day, I just realized she was sort of a permanent fixture and I accepted it.

"She came to visit me every day in my prison, despite the derision and alienation she received for it. My capture and incarceration..." He absent-mindedly touched the scarring on his face. "It was a violent affair, leaving me hurt and making it necessary for her to tend my wounds, sometimes for days at a time. She never once complained." Loki's voice trailed off, and he was quiet for a while. "She was convinced I was going to perish, so she devised a plan for my escape. She located the key to the lock that held my chains to the rock. In order to get it past the guards, who searched her every time she came, she had to hide it. So, she swallowed it."

Loki began to walk in circles, slowly pounding his fist into an open palm. "Father had a special cord made to bind me to that rock. Its lock was diabolical, fashioned by wicked little dwarves with wicked little minds. Days we waited for the key to pass, and when it finally came, Sigun was acting strangely as she unlocked me, and was slow to run when we slipped past the guard at the mouth of the cave. It wasn't until we were far away, until I held up the bloody key in my hand, before I realized what was wrong."

Loki turned his back to Katherina. He looked side to side, and as he put his face in his hands, he rubbed his thumbs against the surface of his eyes. He blinked in pain, and turned back to the princess.

"You see," he continued, eyes swollen and red and brimming with tears, "the lock was so complicated, that it needed an equally complicated key. A key that was sharp and jagged and evil in design. It had cut up her entrails as it passed through her." Loki kneeled at Katherina's feet again, and with shaking hands, took hers from her lap. He looked her in the eye. "The blood! All that blood! I couldn't make it stop! I could make armies stop, but I couldn't make her bleeding go away! First her mind slipped away, then her spirit. Right before my eyes. There was nothing I could do. I didn't even have the chance to finally be a good husband. To tell her how important she was. Th-that... I loved her."

Katherina's icy demeanor fell like a portion of a glacier falling into the sea, revealing a gaze deep with empathy. She touched Loki's face.

He cradled her hand. "Do I regret not doing more to stop Balder in a way that would have avoided all this?" The question was rhetorical, and he went on, "Do I regret being arrogant and feeling superior to my adopted family? Yes, and yes. I've learned from those mistakes and have learned to live with them." He eased himself onto the fountain's edge next to Katherina, still clinging to her hands, stabbing her with his intent gaze, pressing himself against her. Her breathing was quick and her eyes were riveted to his. "The only thing I can't forgive myself is for Sigun. She died because of me, and I didn't even deserve her in the first place. I wasn't man enough at the time to tell her how I felt. I've sworn since then not to let such a thing happen again. I will always tell those whom I care for just how I feel about them."

A long moment of silence told Katherina that this was indeed the end of the story. She loosed one hand from the Viscount's grip and rubbed his back.

"My lord—Loki, I do not know what to say. It sound like you the one who need shoulder to lean on, and it make me realize that my current problem is nothing."

Loki's stormy gaze brightened, and a grin struggled to break his serious expression. He stood and spread his arms. "Then you see, I have done some good today."

Katherina grabbed at Loki's shirt and pulled him down, imploring him to sit. "You not need be so brave. I not understand why man must minimize the pain they have experienced in life. It is good to reveal it. Is there anything I can do for you?"

He lifted eyes to the sky and shrugged. "To be honest, these events are very old. Older than you. I've had time to deal with them."

"Still," Katherina said, "here I have been very frigid and all you have done is try to be friend. I feel I owe you apology."

Loki was thoughtful for a moment, then his back straightened. "Well, if you are really feeling in the giving mood..."

"What is it?"

Loki stood and paced about. "It's rather embarrassing, actually. I feel foolish for saying so, being the old man that I am."

She smiled. "What is it? Come, out with it."

Loki reclaimed his seat next to Katherina and swallowed hard. "Well, as I said, all these sad events happened a very long time ago, and after meeting you and hearing your voice, your accent, it has reminded me of those bygone years, and made me homesick. I have had very little contact with the fairer sex since that time, and I am getting on in years. I've forgotten what it is like to embrace a beautiful girl. If you would indulge me this one favor, to let me...kiss those lips...I could die and leave this earth a happy man."

Katherina's eyes narrowed a fraction. "Lord Loki..."

Loki hung his head in a semblance of shame. "If you think me a lecher, or more forgivingly, only insane, I understand. Why would you want to kiss this wretched face?"

Katherina regarded the Viscount with some amount of sadness and compassion. "I don't see any harm in it."

Loki looked up, a look of tentativeness in his eyes. "Really? This is not some sort of cruel tease is it?"

"No," Katherina murmured. "I understand what it is to want. And I certainly understand loneliness."

She cradled his face in her hands. He smiled and leaned forward.

#

Patrick briskly walked from manicured floral display to floral display. The garden was much larger than it seemed from outside and it was not difficult to become disoriented in the labyrinth of hedges and vines. He paused to adjust his cloak so that it wasn't so stifling in the noon heat, and he switched the rose into his other hand.

He was starting to think that she was not in the garden at all when he saw the color of her blue dress through some vines. He approached quickly and parted the vines to approach her.

He froze.

Through the tangle, he saw the Viscount bending over the Lady to kiss her. She did not resist. And it was not a brief touching.

A shadow enveloped him. It was a dark clawing mass that chilled him to the bone on this cloudless, hot day. His jaw clenched and his teeth ground and his brow creased so severely his multicolored eyes were nearly lost in the anger. His fist gripped the rose so tightly that the thorns bit into his hand and brought trickles of blood to the skin.

And by no trick of the light, that rose wavered and wilted. It convulsed and turned black in Patrick's grasp and more thorns grew from its stem. It broke off like ash and blew away in the breeze.

#

The Viscount Loki whistled a merry tune as he walked the bright colonnade, his boots making a clatter on the stone floor. He was in good spirits and he was finding that his delay here in Greensprings was not as bad as first he thought it might be.

He passed a doorway and from the corner of his eye saw someone leaning against the edge of the portal. He turned and smiled good-naturedly.

"Sir Patrick, how nice to see you," he said cheerfully.

The Irishman glowered. "Good afternoon, Lord Loki. How fare you?"

Loki drew in a deep breath and his smile deepened. "Wonderful!"

Patrick crossed his arms and removed himself from the doorway, stepping forward. "Oh? Any reason in particular?"

Loki's smile was almost a sneer. "I've been reaping the rewards and resources of this place. Why, I keep making so many new friends, I just don't know what to do with myself."

"You wouldn't be referring to the Lady Katherina, by any chance?"

Loki's smile faded, then reemerged. "Why yes, actually. She is quite the conversationalist, and—" he leaned forward and whispered in a conspiratorial tone—"quite passionate."

Patrick's jaw clenched and his chest tightened.

Standing closer now to the Viscount, Patrick experienced that same sensation he felt when confronted by the man in the library—an uncontrollable urge to look away, to depart. Despite the crawling sensation over his body, he resisted the urge and with an effort, maintained his focus on those swirling dark eyes that, like a snake's, didn't blink.

Loki laughed lightly and started to walk away, but stopped. "Oh, by the way. Thank you for steering me in the direction of the library, way back when. I found it very useful. It's a shame what happened to the kindly old gentleman. And what a horrible way to die. Face all contorted and his rosary all over the place. A pity, I won—" Loki's attention was suddenly lost, drawn to the ground at Patrick's feet.

Patrick, who had taken sudden interest in the Viscount's remarks on Father Benis, looked at him quizzically. "Is there something wrong, Lord Loki?"

Loki shook his head. "No. Not at all."

"What was that you were saying about the librarian?"

Loki looked away from the ground and looked upon Patrick as if seeing him for the first time. "The librarian? Oh, nothing, really."

"Really? Then I must be going. Try not to 'reap the rewards and resources' of Greensprings too much."

With that, Patrick brushed past the Viscount even though there was plenty of room to pass.

Loki stroked his goatee. "How odd," he mused to Sir Gawain's retreating figure.

In the sunlight that filled the colonnade, the Irishman was casting two shadows.

#

"Are you sure he phrased it like that?" King Mark asked. He sat at the bureau in his apartment, elbows propped up on either side of himself, chin on his joined hands. He looked tired and had dark rings under his eyes. Patrick couldn't recall when he last saw the big man smile. The chamber was filled with keep staff, all clamoring for his attention over one matter or another. Patrick had walked in during a lull in discussions concerning the spate of petty thefts. Guests were pointing fingers at one another, a few fights had even broken out, disrupting Greensprings's hallowed air of peace and cooperation.

"Yes, positive," Patrick replied.

"He specified how the beads were strewn about the room?"

Again Patrick nodded. "Am I right in worrying, Mark? I mean, last I knew it was only we Avangarde who found the body and reported it to everyone else. We kept the details confidential. How would Loki know? Maybe he had something to..."

Mark put up a hand before Patrick went too far. "I think you have a reason to be concerned, and yes I think that you did the right thing by telling me, but it would probably be wise not to mention it. One, I would hate to accuse an innocent man, and a

Guest no less; and two, if he did have something to do with Father Benis' death, then we must approach the situation with delicacy. We could cause a panic, which would have serious repercussions for the rest of Greensprings."

Patrick nodded at Mark's wisdom. There was a reason Mark was Steward, and Patrick was Reservist.

"Keep me informed, Gawain, if you hear anything else." Mark's tone was a dismissal. He was already turning toward the others in the room—toward more pressing concerns.

Patrick turned to leave, but then said, "Mark, it has also come to my attention that the Lady Katherina is spending a great deal of time with the Viscount. If it turns out that indeed he is some sort of villain, she could be in trouble. Do you think it would be wise if I tried to warn her subtly?"

Mark chewed his lower lip. "Sir Gawain, I will leave that to your discretion. I would say that depends entirely on the nature of your relationship with her."

Patrick nodded and left the chamber.

#

Sir Gawain paced back and forth across the flagstones of the keep church. He was tired and he felt sick to his stomach. The fact that Katherina was late only added to his misery. He looked about the chamber, mostly renovated since the attack on the keep, but noted that the place still cast a gloomy pallor. He moved from the shadows near the entrance to the sunlight streaming through the stained-glass dome above. This, however, only brought him close to the unsightly wood planks that covered the hole through which McFowler had pushed Sir Gregory and him during the battle. Father Hugh said that it would be some time before an artist from Paris could come and make the repair.

With a scowl, Patrick moved past the island of light, through the rows of pews, into the area just before the sanctuary.

Shadows ruled here as well. A lectern was set up before the altar, on which rested the church's one true treasure: an ornately fashioned Bible. In other cities, Patrick had seen less ornate Bibles behind barred gates. Here in Greensprings, however, the sacred scripture was accessible to anyone who wanted to read it. And even those who could not read could page through its many illustrations.

Patrick bent over the lectern and looked at the open page. His mother had taught him to read, and though he found it a difficult task, he thanked her for providing him with a skill that set him apart.

Psalm of the Thirteenth, he read, and quickly scanned down the words. He intended only to satisfy his curiosity, but about mid-scan the text started to resonate with him and he read the verses out loud: "*How long Lord? Will you utterly forget me? How long will you hide your face from me? How long must I carry sorrow in my soul, grief in my heart day after day? How long will my enemy triumph over me?*"

Patrick looked up to the cross suspended above the Sanctuary, the same cross that had crushed the hobgoblin that had slain Jason, and saw the mournful visage of the crucified Christ staring back at him.

"You know that feeling, don't you?" Patrick said to the man mounted on the cross. "'My God, my God, why have you forsaken me?'" Patrick shook his head and turned away, halfheartedly making the sign of the cross when he did. He decided he did not like the gloom here any more than the gloom on the other side of the church, and returned to the entryway where he had told Katherina to meet him. He resumed his pacing.

Finally, she entered the church. It was afternoon now and there would be no more services for the day.

"I came as soon as I could," she said, worried. "It sounded important. What is wrong?"

Patrick rubbed his hands together and sifted through everything he had planned to say. "I have come across some news that may concern your friend, Loki."

Katherina made a face but let him continue.

"We have learned that he is, perhaps, involved in nefarious activities, and may be a threat to Greensprings."

Katherina's expression was incredibly confused. "How do you know this, and how does this concern me?"

Patrick gestured with his hands, but no words came immediately. "I can't really tell you how I know this," he said. "It's an Avangarde thing. Information comes to us and we must at least investigate it. Incidentally, I'm taking a risk by telling you this. It's just that I am worried for you and thought that you should know, but you must tell no one, especially Loki."

"That make little sense, Patrick, and what make you think I am in danger?" She took her usual crossed-arm stance. Her clear blue eyes were blazing.

"Because, I know that you two are close."

"Gawain, that is..."

"I saw you two yesterday in the garden in each other's arms."

Katherina froze. The angry look on her face diffused into exasperation. "This is true. But that is neither here nor there. What am I supposed to say or do? Am I supposed to ask Loki about it? Am I supposed tell him that I won't be his friend because I heard that he may be wicked and that I heard it from a possibly jealous source?"

"I'm not jealous," Patrick snapped.

"Yes you are," Katherina returned. "This is not about protecting Greensprings. This is about protecting you."

"Is that really so surprising!" Patrick said a little louder than he intended, his eyes flashing.

"What that supposed to mean?" She placed her hands on her hips and leaned forward at him, opening her mouth to say more.

"You said you would never abandon me," said Patrick, cutting her off, "you promised, by the side of the brook where we ate." His voice was cracking, betraying the air of control he had promised himself he'd maintain.

Katherina cooled, and she put her face in her hands. "That different. I will always be you friend, Patrick, but I can't live with this agreement of ours the way it is. I don't want agreement anymore with anyone. It seem to me awfully lopsided."

Patrick sighed. "Then let's not have one anymore. Let's be together normally."

"That is not fair," she said.

Patrick frowned. "What do you mean?"

"I don't think you mean it. Either to me or to yourself. This whole fiasco between us. You are not entirely honest with me, or yourself, and especially not to that servant girl Aimeé."

"What does Aimeé have to do with this?"

"Don't tell me that. You are one to talk of seeing me in another's arms. I saw you with her in kitchen." She stabbed him in the chest with her finger.

Patrick rolled his eyes and sighed at the church ceiling. "I was only comforting her. The poor girl was raped for God's sake."

Katherina nodded once, hard. "Yes, raped because another man saw her throwing herself at you and assumed she that kind of maidservant, and so exacted tribute from her. If you had only been honest with her in beginning, and not played stupid man-game with her, maybe that wouldn't have happened."

Patrick was speechless.

"You see, Patrick, you are ship lost at sea. You are big strong ship, but you don't know where to land—or why. I can't live with that."

He chewed on the inside of his cheek and kicked at the base of the statue next to them. Finally, he shrugged. "I can't say that

I am surprised."

Katherina looked sad. "What do you mean?"

"I told you, it's the curse," he said. "I knew you would leave one way or the other. I've heard all this before."

Katherina threw her arms up into the air. "Well, if you hear all this before, then maybe I should save you trouble and leave you now."

"No," Patrick almost cried, lunging forward with hand outstretched. He caught himself short of actually grabbing the girl. "Don't. Please."

"Patrick, I'm really not going to leave you. I will still be here. I will still be your friend. Nothing has changed."

"Except that you will be spending your time with Loki instead."

Katherina didn't answer right away. "I don't know that yet."

Patrick glowered more and paced about, but couldn't think of anything to say that wouldn't send her immediately out the door. Katherina came forward and cradled his face. "What ever happen from this point on, I will be friend. Do you know how happy you made me? I know that I did not show it, but I was very homesick, very sad. I even questioned my life going on. You change that just enough so I can carry on again."

His heart was breaking, but he stood as still as the statues around them. "I'm glad that I could help. But now that you are better, you are going to leave me? Thank you very much."

Katherina appeared too sad to be angry. "Patrick, why do you make thing so difficult? I wish I could give you what you want, but I can't, and it would be wrong of me to try, if I don't feel it."

"I can't have what I want. Ever," Patrick said gloomily, thinking out loud more than anything.

Katherina had tears falling from her eyes. "Why won't you ever cry, Patrick Gawain?" She turned and left then, but at the door she turned back and asked almost timidly, "Have supper with me tonight?"

He nodded. Katherina left, and he knew that she was not the same person to him as the girl who had entered.

He outsmarted himself. He had tried erecting an impregnable steel wall around his heart to keep it from being hurt, and that wall had fallen and crushed that same heart he had tried protecting from harm in the first place.

Curse or no, he could only blame himself. And once again, the knowledge and wisdom he had garnered from this experience was no consolation. It still hurt terribly. But she had given him hope. She had insisted that they would still be close. Time would tell if the curse would be broken after all.

He headed for the church door, but stopped. Something had fallen on his shoulder. He looked and saw a wet spot. Then another appeared. Water droplets were falling on him. He looked to the ceiling and could not discern where they were coming from. He would have to tell Father Hugh about that. Moisture collecting in the rafters might cause structural damage. He left the building then.

#

Another drop landed on the flagstones where Patrick had been standing. Above it, quietly standing in the darkness was a statue of the Virgin Mary, and she was weeping.

Chapter Ten

Patrick Gawain once again skulked about.

He talked little, avoided people, and wondered why nobody would talk to him or sit with him at dinner. When he did talk, it usually was about the Viscount Loki.

"Have you ever noticed how he is always touching the girls?" he said one evening at dinner. "Especially the really young ones. Something just isn't right about him. He's always in people's business."

"If you mean the Lady Katherina," Sir McCabe said, nodding in the direction of the couple now entering the dining hall—the Viscount escorting Katherina to her seat. Patrick noted that the princess had recently taken to wearing darker colors. "I'd say she is a willing victim. If you ask me, it's a matter of the girl looking for a father-figure. I've known women to do such things."

"Or," added Sir Jon, "it's a matter of rebellion. She's deliberately and willingly spending time with an older fellow just to be contrary, to get attention. Maybe it's Loki who will end up being the victim, when her whims have changed again."

"I seriously doubt that," Patrick said, glowering.

After a while, such comments were met with silence or

rolling eyes. Even the good-natured Waylan and Corbin told him to put it to rest. Yes, the Viscount could be disagreeable, but he had broken no rules. Let it be.

Finding no support for his opinions, and feeling a little betrayed, Patrick threw himself into the task of organizing the tournament. Even that seemed to suck the life out of him; it was much more work than he had realized. Scheduling a location, coaxing the keep and village laborers into setting up the spectator seating and fencing for the competition field, organizing teams, assigning tasks to keep personnel and volunteers, and doing all this while maintaining his normal duty schedule, was next to impossible.

Though he developed a deeper respect for what the Avangarde did, especially King Mark, Patrick still found that his head remained in a fog and his gut turned every time he thought of Katherina.

And to make things worse, she ignored him: just as he knew she would. To her credit, she had truly gone out of her way to make Patrick feel comfortable at first. But the Irishman believed she had done so only to say, "I told you so." Quickly, even that faded, and she bided more and more of her time with Loki.

Patrick decided that if ignoring was the game she wanted to play, he could play, too. He neglected her, stayed away, and passed up obvious opportunities to be with her. She took notice and withdrew even more from him. That was not the result he intended.

After several weeks, he could not take it anymore. He decided to approach her, feeling that, if nothing else, he should be the one mature enough to admit fault and save a possibly failing friendship.

He found her in a side chamber, reading her Bible next to the window. Minion sat at her feet, playing with knucklebones. She absentmindedly stroked his close clipped head with one hand. Patrick stifled a shudder at the sight of her touching the ugly little man.

"Can we talk?" Patrick asked.

Katherina looked up from her book. "Of course."

Patrick looked at Minion, who was giving him a toady gaze. "Alone, perhaps."

Minion looked to Katherina for approval, then slowly stood up and waddled out.

Patrick drew a breath. "I don't understand what is happening between us. I was hoping you could elaborate for me."

Katherina closed the bible with care, but kept the page with her finger. "I'm not sure I entirely understand."

"I mean us avoiding each other. Friends don't do that. We are friends, as you said we would be, right?"

"Yes. But I don't understand this silence from you." Her icy eyes stared off at a point to his left and six feet behind him.

"Is that so surprising?" Patrick asked. "I'm a silent person in any case, you knew that, and now that you favor me less, it only becomes worse."

"Patrick, I try not to, believe me. I am just busy person. I have not much time for you any more, that's all."

Patrick wasn't quite successful in keeping the a sneer out of his voice. "You seem to have plenty of time for Loki."

"Patrick..."

"What is so special about him? What does he have that I can't offer you?"

"It not like that. It not matter of what he has compared to you."

She was attempting to trivialize the issue, and he did not feel like letting it go. "If that is the case, why is that I've seen less and less of you? Obviously he has something to offer you I don't. I can't imagine what. He is arrogant beyond contempt, abusive, a possible criminal, is old—much older than even myself, and ugly. You can't possibly find him attractive." Judging from

Katherina's countenance she was displeased with his words, but he felt better for having finally said them.

"Maybe I feel beauty is not thing of the flesh," Katherina said, crystal eyes flaring.

"Obviously."

"Nobody know him the way I do. Has it ever occurred to you that he is lonely on the inside and his outer bravado is just show to hide his loneliness? Has it ever occurred to you that he is beautiful on the inside?"

"No."

Katherina's cheeks flushed and there was a slight roll to her eyes as she looked out the window.

Patrick crossed his arms. "So you find his insides appealing? Then do you find some people's outsides pleasing, but their insides unappealing?"

"Yes, of course."

"Like me?"

"Ye—I mean no, or..." Katherina's eyes opened wide and she touched a hand to her lips.

Patrick shook his head slowly. She tried to explain herself profusely, but the damage was done. His heart felt as if it had dropped into his bowels. He had suspected all along that was how she felt about him, but did not think she would ever say it.

Patrick took a deep breath. "Katherina, my dear princess, I only wish that things could be the way they were. I don't mean like on the balcony or in the woods or in the confessional or...well, you understand...but that they could be like when we talked more, when we shared time together laughing. That is all I ask of you. You once said that I made you so happy when you couldn't have been otherwise. Can't I again?"

"Yes, of course. But ultimately we are all responsible for making ourselves happy, Patrick. I would have made myself happy again eventually."

He couldn't tell if she was adding insult to injury. "But you said you even considered taking your own life, you were so unhappy. And I helped make it better."

"I don't recall saying that." Katherina now looked puzzled.

"So those were once again just words to ease your conscience?" Katherina's eyes narrowed at the accusation. "Was I just a diversion for you? Was not even the laughter and happiness real? I really felt something for you, you know that?"

Katherina waved her arms in exasperation. "I didn't want to hear that," she all but shouted. She was a while in saying anything else. Patrick was so hurt he didn't try to fill the silence. "I can't make you believe anything. You are just going to have to believe me that it was real."

Patrick paced and ran his hands through his hair. On the one hand, he didn't necessarily like what she had to say, but on the other, the conviction in her voice made it sound as if it had been real after all.

Katherina hugged herself. She seemed to be caught between emotions, none of them positive. "Patrick, I still here talking to you. If I didn't care, I would have walked away long time ago. I still here."

Patrick nodded slowly. "I'm sorry if I am being...obsessive. I just don't want to be on my deathbed someday feeling that I hadn't at least tried."

"I understand."

A moment of silence.

"Well, would you care to spend the evening with me? A walk or something of the sort?" Patrick offered.

Katherina smiled sadly. "I can't, I promised Sister Abagail that I would help her finish a quilt. Maybe some other time?"

Patrick nodded. "Of course."

#

Sir Gawain dragged the butt of his pike along the stones on the battlements. He had no energy to carry the weapon tucked at his side, as good soldiers did.

Rain pelted him and ran down his bare face. The iron helmet he wore on duty seemed to magnify the cold, and channel it into his skull, rather than keep it out. This was the worst he had seen it rain on the Isle. And it just happened to be the night that he agreed to cover duty for Jeremiah; a favor returned.

Gusts of wind shifted anything not tied down, including Patrick's great-cloak that flapped violently about him. He was thoroughly soaked through to the skin and was generally miserable. As he did his rounds, he was finding himself spending more and more time outside the Hall for Lady Guests. At first, he thought it was his imagination, but after a few more passes on the wall by the structure, he was sure he didn't let himself gravitate in that direction. After a while, he gave in and took to pacing outside Katherina's window. Perhaps he was hoping that she would come home early from her quilt making, and then see him cold and forlorn on the wall and invite him in. Maybe he was just being an obsessed madman; victim to the whims of human behavior.

He cursed himself as he paced.

Then, a light slowly illuminated the confines of her chamber until it lit the room. The Lady Katherina hung her shawl on the wall. Patrick's heart beat a little faster with delight. She scurried about her chamber, performing routine tasks. She paused and turned as if to speak to someone who was just out of sight. Her mouth moved rapidly, and then she smiled and touched her hair. She sat at her vanity, and a dark figure came up behind her.

Patrick's heart stopped as he watched the Viscount Loki comb out her long platinum braids. His free hand wandered over the back of her neck and shoulders. Then he bent and kissed her nape. She didn't seem to mind.

When Patrick was relieved of his duties, he did not go to his warm room and bed. Instead, he went directly to Aesclinn and the pub, despite the hour.

#

The following morning the Lady Katherina strode down the corridor leading to the main hall inside the keep. It was times like this that she wished she had a lady-in-waiting to bring her breakfast in her chamber, which was a long walk from the main hall.

As she thought this, her attention was caught by the familiar sounds of leather straps creaking, as on a knight's ensemble.

She turned around and looked up. There was Sir Gawain, sitting above the entrance on the staircase. He looked dreadful.

"How did the quilt come out?" he asked. He was sprawled on the staircase. He held a goat skin flask in one hand.

"Fine," Katherina replied. She noted that he was wearing the same clothes as the day before, yet they were damp looking. Patrick was also garbed in his chain mail coat and he hadn't shaved. His eyes were sunken and he seemed to glower.

"Did it take you long to finish it? Or did you end up having much free time on your hands after all?" Patrick took a long swig of the flask. The red fluid that beaded about his mouth indicated that it was wine.

Katherina turned a lighter shade of pale. "Yes, it took most of evening."

He no longer looked at her, but focused on something in the air before him. He took another drink of the wine. "Are you sure? If you had been free, I would have been more than happy to make you laugh for the evening. Tried at least."

"I was busy entire evening, Patrick," she insisted.

Patrick shook his head. His hair hung in his eyes and Katherina could not tell whether the sounds he now was making was silent bitter laughter, or weeping.

"Tell me poem, Sir Gawain," she said, the first thing to come

391

to mind.

Patrick looked up, but his eyes were still hidden. His mouth moved into a mechanical smile.

A glittering storm had blown my way;
A foreign beauty
Whose eyes pierced like the winter sun.

At first I resisted;
I ran and denied
The grasp in which I twisted,
And wished I had died.

But then I accepted
This pale hand held out.
And for once I felt rested,
And with joy cried out.

But it was not for long.
The storm blew away,
And she was gone
With nothing to say.

My Snow Princess had become
An Ice Queen.

During his recital, he had been quite animated, but now he slumped back against the balustrade.

Katherina's chest heaved and her jaw set. She turned suddenly and left. Sir Patrick's bitter laughter followed her, interrupted only by a pause to take another drink from his flask.

#

The Viscount Loki yawned as widely as possible. He hoped

that the young Guest, William, would take the hint and stop speaking. But the boy was as oblivious as he was dull. The Viscount told himself that it wasn't much longer. A few more days and he could leave these people.

The Lady Katherina approached the table. Loki, William and Minion all stood in consideration.

"Do I interrupt?" she asked.

"No, not at all, my dear Lady. Won't you join us?" Loki elbowed Willy gently aside to make room for Katherina. She took her place and the conversation turned to other things.

Patrick entered a few minutes later, unshaven, unkempt and haggard. He looked even worse than the poor King-Steward Mark. Loki smiled to himself. Even though he had been forced to endure this place, he had had some fun. It was not unlike puppeteering. Why, there was Sir Peredur, glaring at Sir Jon who pretended not to notice; Sir Mark and Sir Gawain were hollow shadows of themselves; Sir Geoffrey still bore the faint, discolored bruises around his eyes; the maidservant Aimeé stood by with a vacant look in her eyes; and the list went on.

Katherina relaxed a bit when the Irishman took a seat—nearby, but not in her line of sight.

"You know, Lady Katherina," the Viscount whispered. "I was thinking about being naughty. How would you like to accompany me on an adventure?"

Katherina glowed. "Yes, I'd like very much."

Loki rubbed his hands together. "Splendid! How would you like to join me a week's time from now and travel to the other side of the isle?"

Minion, who had been working on a roasted chicken leg, froze.

"Isn't that against rule?" Katherina asked.

"Of course, that's why it's naughty."

"I don't know..."

Loki scowled. "Why Kat, I've never known you to back down

from an adventure. Why, I expected more from you."

Her countenance became angry and indignant. "Yes, I want to go. I just want to know what you have in mind and how you expect to get away with it."

"Well, that's more like it: I have heard tell that on a full moon's night, one can see the fairy-ghosts on the moors. Their spirit flames light up the countryside like a heavenly rainbow. Would you like to find out if there is any truth to this story?"

Katherina smiled. "Yes."

Minion hissed to the Viscount, "Master, you want to take her with us?"

Loki hissed back, over his shoulder, "Of course, fool, I have plans."

Katherina had overheard Minion's half of the exchange. "Is he going?"

Loki turned to her and murmured, "Of course, we need him to drive the carriage. How else am I supposed to divide my time between gazing out onto the moonlit moors and your eyes? I have only two eyes, you know."

Katherina's smile deepened. "Still, how do you manage to make this happen? We just can't slip out gate in middle of night with guard everywhere."

"Let me worry about that," Loki said. He noticed that Sir Gawain was leaning in their direction. "Besides, it will be no more trouble than the time we went to that little chapel you showed me," Loki said in a louder voice. "You know, when you made me tell you a story about those pictures on the wall."

Loki gently, and obviously, took the Lady Katherina's hand and kissed it.

Patrick stood and made to leave the dining hall, but caught his pant leg on the bench, stumbled, knocking over plates and falling into people, red-faced.

Before Patrick disappeared out the door, Loki raised his hands and mimed pulling on puppet strings.

Sir Corbin saw Sir Gawain leave the hall in a huff and went after him. He caught him in the corridor.

"Patrick," he called. "Could I speak to you for a moment?"

Patrick held up and wondered what he had forgotten to do. He ran his hand nervously through his hair.

Corbin looked uncomfortable. He didn't look Patrick in the eyes and sighed heavily. "We've been talking, Mark and some of the others. We think that perhaps it would be a good idea if maybe you took some time off—just for a while," Corbin added. "Until you—work things out. You seem to be under much stress right now. A distracted guard is next to a useless guard. Nothing personal, friend. It is better for everyone."

Patrick did not respond right away. He stood quietly as if pondering, or concentrating on something invisible before him. Corbin fidgeted during the silence, not sure what to say either.

At last, Patrick nodded and grunted something in acknowledgement, then said, "What of the tournament I was organizing?"

Corbin fidgeted some more, his eyes wandering. "Mark feels that the resources for such an event are best applied elsewhere at this time."

Again Patrick was silent for a moment. "When can I return to my duties?"

Corbin shrugged. "We'll let you know."

Patrick smirked. That statement held many possible meanings. He left Corbin standing there, and as he walked he ran his hands through his hair. The flush in his cheeks had not quite ever left.

"Gawain?" Corbin called.

Patrick waved him off.

Like most people, he may have wanted attention from time to time, but what he didn't want was pity.

\#

"What do you mean you're not serving Aphelon right now?" Patrick growled.

Frederique shrugged an apology. "I am sorry, monsieur, but the holiday is coming up and we need to increase our stores of the cider."

"Why, so you can increase the price as well?"

Frederique smiled. "Of course. How about some beer instead, good sir?"

"I was hoping to find myself in a drunken state as soon as possible. With beer, it will take a little longer. Not to mention more money."

Frederique shook his head. "I can give you Trub, if you are that eager to crawl into the depths of despair."

Patrick frowned. "Trub? That dark beer that if you put a fork in it, it will stand on end?"

Frederique nodded.

Patrick slapped his hand on the table. "Very well, Trub it is!"

Frederique shuddered a bit as he prepared a mug of the heavily sedimented brew for the knight.

As Patrick waited for the foam to subside, he used his last lucid thoughts to consider what led him to this chair with this drink in his hand. He knew that his actions towards Katherina bordered on obsessive, and that letting his feelings run his actions did not help his already poor image as Sir Silence. Sir Corbin's dismissal said as much.

He had known it was coming. Now that it was actually here, he was ashamed. All his work to act the part of a true Avangarde was wasted, and he was no good to Katherina, the Avangarde, or himself. So what was left? This chair, this beer—out of everyone's way. If he really felt anything for Katherina, he could do that much for her. Stay away.

Patrick took a sip of the dark brew. Actually, it was a nice change from the acidic Aphelon.

#

He spent the remainder of that night alone in the public house drinking everything he could keep down, as he did for the next many nights to come. He had nothing else to do except sit alone in the dark in his room, which was worse.

At first he tried busying himself with swordplay, but as a solo activity, it proved difficult and boring. So, inevitably, he found himself back at the Aesclinn pub. Logically, being antisocial and crawling into the bottom of a mug was the wrong thing to do, but what he knew and what he felt were different things. Drinking himself into a stupor made him feel better. Made him forget.

Oddly, however, it made the Apparition clearer. It dogged him in the halls, his room, at the pub. It followed silently, occasionally pointing with its outstretched hand, as if it were feeding off his misery. The Irishman almost became used to the thing being around. Almost.

It accompanied him one evening as he sat on the stool at the bar.

He was in rare form this evening with his hair and clothing in disarray. He no longer tried to maintain an image. He had no one to impress. Now that his days were filled with—nothing, he was slowly going mad with boredom and the dull ache of worthlessness. The madness circled about him like a dark flock of bats that obscured his good memories. At night, as he lay in his bed, if he listened hard enough, he could hear the wings of madness circling him. It sometimes made him laugh.

During the day, he lurked about the stables, the kitchens or in the basement to hide from people. It was working all too well. No one really noticed him gone. He thought, with all seriousness and chagrin, that if he were to die suddenly in his room, no one would notice until the smell alerted them.

Patrick sat bitterly at the bar and glared at the other patrons. He didn't know who perturbed him more at that moment: the silent Apparition or the loud gay patrons.

They seemed so happy. They knew each other and exchanged greetings. As far as Patrick could tell, he was invisible to them. He couldn't blame them, they were only doing what they did on a regular basis anyhow. They only did what they knew best: be themselves. Something that he wasn't entirely sure he knew how to do.

As usual, he sat by himself with a pint of Trub as his only companion—well, that and the Apparition, who sat across from him. He swirled it about, smelled it, tasted it, downed it; but it was always the same bitter drink. It dulled his senses and gave everything an unreal dreamlike quality. He couldn't dream enough or run far enough away, though, because the painful fact of reality was always there. His discomfort. His awkwardness. His sense of not fitting in.

And yes, of course, there was the Apparition adding to his malaise. Sitting across from him staring from that dark, anonymous hood that revealed nothing.

At least it wasn't pointing at him.

Instead, it seemed to shake its head in pity, as if it found Patrick too pathetic to torment any longer.

"To hell with you!" Patrick shouted. Patrons looked at him as if he were a madman. "I don't care what you are or what you think! If you have come to take me, I wish you would hurry up and do it! I tire of this game!" Men were moving away from Patrick. He didn't care. He was beyond caring.

Expelled from the Avangarde? Taken by a baleful ghost? Who cared? He just wished it would happen. Something! Anything!

So, Sir Patrick raised the glass of dark beer to the Apparition in salute. "Here's to you anyway, my only companion who stays with me through thick or thin..."

He drank deeply.

#

Avalon was famous for its apple orchards that bloomed year round in never ending cycles of blossoms and fruit. Some called it magic, some called it a miracle. To those who made Avalon their home, and whose lives revolved around the apples, they just called it a blessing and once a year they celebrated the fact. In some lands one might call it a Harvest Festival, in other lands an Oktoberfest, but in Avalon they called it Alhhard-Aphel, Apple-Day or Apple Fest.

The holiday was marked with apple pies, candied apples, apple-dunking contests, dancing, singing, bright colors, rollicking music, games, and of course large quantities of the island's signature drink, Aphelon hard cider.

Though the village put on quite a festival for the occasion, it was tacitly understood that the common folk reserved the day to let loose among themselves, and so Greensprings made arrangements for their own celebration in the keep.

Aimeé, like the rest of the staff, spent most of the day preparing for the event, which surpassed all other occasions in grandeur except for Christmas and Easter. By nightfall they finished hanging the bright streamers from the balconies and chandeliers, and setting equally festive table cloths. No sooner had they finished placing the silver and crystal, than the Guests, knights, other staff, and clergy started to filter into the hall. Until then, Aimeé had been feeling the grueling day catch up with her, but now that the room was coming alive with smiling faces and happy chatter she felt reenergized. She took her place with the other maidservants along the wall, and waited until enough seats were filled to start serving.

"It's a pity," Anna said at her side, "that we had to use some of the everyday cutlery to make up for the missing silver, crystal, and cut glass."

Aimeé frowned at the news. "They never found them?"

"Nay lass, and rumor has it that Mark may be forced to start investigatin' the servants."

Aimeé shook her head at the very idea. She just couldn't believe that any of them would steal. Where on earth could they possibly sell them? Sure, if they could somehow sneak them off the island...

She banished the thought from her mind. Today was a day to be happy.

Their rest was short-lived. The hall filled up quickly and they moved to start filling glasses and bring food-laden platters to the tables. They paused only long enough to allow King Mark to stand and greet the assembled with a short and cheery speech. After glasses were raised and clinked in a hearty response to Mark, the maidservants continued their routes about the room.

In her duties she leaned over the Lady Katherina, who was talking gaily to the Viscount Loki, and replaced an empty flagon with a full one. As she stepped back from the table, she made it a point to bump the Lady.

This did not escape Katherina's attention, who turned icy eyes on the maidservant and started to rise from her seat, mouth hardening with harsh words. But even as the Viscount Loki, with a whimsical smile on his face, reached out to halt her, she froze and looked past Aimeé, brow furrowed with concern.

Aimeé turned.

Sir Patrick, obviously drunk and disoriented, staggered into the hall. He shuffled to a corner of the room and took a hard seat next to the hearth, daring with defiant eyes for anybody to stare at him. Everyone in the room at first did stare, and pointed and turned to their companion to comment, but once he sat back against the hearth and closed his eyes, they ignored him.

Almost in a daze, Katherina sat down again. Aimeé moved across the room towards the Irishman. Halfway there, Anna stepped into her path.

"Don't do it lass, let him sleep. It's better if he stays in a harmless manner," she advised.

Aimeé withdrew her arm from Anna's grasp and said between her teeth, "He needs somebody to take care of him. Maybe I can convince him to leave or something."

She went to Patrick's side.

"Poor girl," Anna said to another maidservant, Claire. "I'm not sure who I feel more sorry for."

They both shook their heads as Aimeé tentatively approached the motionless knight.

#

Aimeé shook him awake. His eyes took a moment to focus, and it seemed that if his eyes could groan out loud, they probably would at the sight of her. Despite this, she managed a congenial smile. "Sir Gawain, you look tired, why don't you go to your room and lie down?"

Patrick scoffed. "Nonsense. I wouldn't miss this night for my life."

Aimeé looked about. King Mark had other things to brood about. The Lady Christianne, like the Lady Katherina, looked troubled by Patrick's state. Most everyone else ignored them.

She returned her gaze to the lanky Irishman sprawled in the chair. The belt about his surcoat was buckled at the wrong hole and hanging loosely, his hair was unkempt, and his boots muddy. His shirtsleeves were rolled up, exposing muscular forearms and wrists. His face was moist with perspiration, and stubble shadowed his strong jaw beneath high cheekbones. A musky aroma told her that he hadn't bathed in some time, but it wasn't an entirely unpleasant odor. Despite his attempt to be flippant, his eyes were tired and sad.

Still, Aimeé didn't want to take any chances. "Look, Patrick, if I bring you drinks on a regular basis, will you behave yourself?" she asked.

Patrick smirked, but he gave her an exaggerated salute.

"Knight's honor."

Relieved, she turned to go.

"Aimeé," Patrick said, reaching out and touching her wrist. He stared at her momentarily with those pastel colored eyes, then finally said, "Thank you." He withdrew his hand quickly, like someone realizing they were crushing the butterfly they were holding.

She swallowed hard under that gaze and something inside her melted at the timbre of his voice. She took a deep breath, then answered with a smile and a nod before leaving him.

#

She fetched him a drink, and true to his word he minded his own business, doing not much more than take sips of Aphelon and glare at people.

And true to her word, she came by regularly to refill his cup.

Back in the kitchens, she pulled Anna and Claire to a quiet corner. "Should I just bring him an entire flagon so he can fill it himself?" she said discreetly. They were older and she trusted their advice.

"No, no lass," Anna said, a little louder than was necessary to be heard over the din. "That will draw too much attention to the boy. Besides, it would be unseemly for him to be sitting there all alone with a flagon all to himself."

"Sshh, sshh!" Claire added, wavering a little where she stood. "And we don't want others demanding their very own pitcher of Aphelon. There just isn't enough to go around."

Aimeé's eyes narrowed at the two women, who were more red-faced than usual and in uncommonly high spirits. "What have you two gotten into?"

The elder maidservants started to giggle uncontrollably and produced from behind their backs the very spirits that were lifting them up.

"Sacre bleu!" Aimeé put her hands to her mouth. "Are you

mad?"

"Go on lass, take some yourself. You've earned it! You've tamed yonder beast and averted tragedy."

Aimeé first looked around carefully, then took the goblet from Claire's outstretched hand. She sipped from the brim and tasted the bittersweet hardness of Aphelon.

"That's a girl."

#

The next portion of the evening became a blur.

It was a frenzied collage of bright colors, smiling faces and raucous laughter that echoed into the night. Even the full moon seemed to beam down a cheerful smile that lit up the grounds. Nobody could tell who was enjoying the occasion more, the help or the revelers. Maidservants danced with noblemen, knights danced with nuns, Father Hugh's legs protruded from underneath a table as he slept on the bench, and Mark found it in himself to smile for the first time in a long while.

Between filling cups, serving food and being occasionally flung in a merry circle by Sir Corbin or Sir Bisch, Aimeé managed to keep Patrick's cup full, though the knight was mostly dozing.

On her last trip to fill his cup, she found him irrevocably passed out. His body was draped over the wood, mouth wide open, snoring heavily.

She shrugged and picked up the mostly full cup at his feet before he or someone else knocked it over. She returned to the kitchen, and just before entering, she looked down at the golden drink, raised it to her lips, and finished it off for him.

#

It didn't seem long before somebody was nudging him awake. When he opened his eyes, the dinner was evidently long over, all the lights save the fire place were extinguished and all the Guests were gone. And more, the fact that a headache was growing in his skull proved that he was on the road to being sober.

It was Aimeé who was kicking at his outstretched boots. She had a slight grin and at first Patrick thought it was his vision that was swaying from side to side, when in fact it was she who was unstable.

"Rosa Maria was impressed with how fast we cleaned up," Aimeé said with a hiccup, "especially since we did not wake you in the process."

Patrick squinted at the maidservant. "Have you been drinking?"

Aimeé giggled and made a small gesture with thumb and forefinger.

He shook his head, which was a mistake, then struggled to stand, but the rolling floor suggested that he wasn't as near to being sober as he thought. Aimeé offered to help. At first he declined, but then accepted when he realized he couldn't walk in a straight line.

"I thought you would be needing some help. Some of the other knights were making wagers on whether or not you had died there in that chair." She placed his arm around her neck.

"Somehow that doesn't surprise me, Avangarde humor isn't known for its subtlety," he replied.

Despite the weight difference, she held him up well. She was very strong and once they reached the outside of the keep proper, Patrick was better able to walk. The fresh air helped sober him up. The moon was setting, leaving the heavens to his brethren the stars, who twinkled with their own quiet mirth. The air was warm, but breezy. The Hall for Guests loomed ahead, beyond gently swaying branches.

Aimeé stayed at his side and insisted on accompanying him to his door.

"Probably a good idea," Patrick mumbled. "I'd probably fall

in a ditch and drown."

Achieving his door was not so difficult. Once there, Patrick leaned against it heavily, clawing at the latch to open it.

Aimeé leaned into him harder to keep him from sagging to the floor and reached for the latch herself. Patrick fell over her leaning back.

"Sir Gawain!" Patrick groaned. "Don't move, I need to rest for a moment."

Aimeé struggled to make him upright again. "You can rest all you want once I open your door." Patrick slumped again. His chin was over one of her shoulders, an arm over her other. Patrick's eyes slowly opened as he realized the nearness of her. He hair smelled faintly of honey, her dress of baked bread, and her bosom of sweat and Aphelon. Her muscles were hard from years of labor, yet it was not an unpleasant feeling and Patrick held her in his arms to upright himself. He let his hands linger on her. She too held him tighter and let him start to nuzzle her neck.

Patrick brushed his lips along her cheek and moved to her waiting mouth. Her embrace was warm and passionate and it stimulated Patrick to return the kiss intensely. She cried out in pleasure as his mouth moved again to her neck and he bit gently.

She started to run her hands over his body and he returned the gesture by cupping her bosom. She quietly cried out again. The door opened under their weight and they fell into Patrick's room.

#

Faint sunlight woke him.

His head was pounding and his mouth felt as if it had been the repository for all the waste of the world. He sat up in bed, gingerly touching his forehead, where some memory nagged at him. A sense of dread turned his stomach as he attempted to put a face to what it was that made his world feel out of place...something other than residual alcohol that made the room spin.

A subtle movement at his side jolted him to the present and the memories came flooding back—Aimeé was asleep at his side, a smile curled at the corner of her mouth.

The bottom of his stomach fell out.

He placed his face in his shaking hands, not wanting to believe what he knew all too well was true. He had committed a stupid act that he couldn't possibly explain away without totally devastating the girl. He had done the one single thing he shouldn't have done: betray Aimeé's trust.

"Patrick," a voice startled him from behind.

He jumped from the covers naked, and there standing near the bed was his mother, cowled, a profoundly sad look on her face.

"Wasn't it enough to hurt yourself?" she implored.

Patrick's heart twisted in his chest and he fell to his knees, biting his knuckles as he used to do as a child. He felt more than just naked—he felt as if his entire broken soul were laid bare.

The sad look on his mother's face turned to a leer as she stepped forward, raising an accusing finger. "Is this how I raised you?" Her countenance transformed into a hideous caricature of a woman; a crazed harpy with a skull-like face and flaming eyes.

He bolted for the door and was gone in moments, howling like a madman.

Aimeé stirred from her sleep, awakened by Patrick's cries. She sat up in bed just in time to see his naked form depart.

"Patrick!"

She looked around the empty room, pulling the sheets over her nakedness.

#

Patrick ran through the mist. He did not know how he reached the forest so quickly or how he slipped by the guards without being noticed. All he knew was that he could not run fast enough to be away from what he had left behind. He felt it was all he could do to run, run, and keep on running. He was gibbering and barely aware of the sticks and stones that he tread on in his flight, or the branches and brambles that reached up and scored his bare flesh. He staggered through stream and brook and blundered through underbrush and bounded like a deer through ferns. The mist obscured his path, but he moved deeper and deeper into the wood.

A silhouette formed in the mist—a person. His eyes widened in recognition, and he slowed to a stop.

On a grassy knoll beneath huge trees was a beautiful dark haired girl, her skin as milky white as the mist that surrounded her. She shook her head sadly, a look of eternal pity in her striking blue eyes.

Patrick fell to his knees and his breath came out in huge puffs of steam in the chill morning, his chest still heaving from exertion. The girl continued to stand and stare compassionately.

"You wanted to marry unto God?" Patrick screamed at her between gasps of breath. "Did you really? Then why did it turn out the way it did? Why!" Patrick tore up the ground in front of him and threw rocks and dirt at her, but they passed through her even as her form vanished like a reflection on the surface of moving water. Patrick let forth a scream of anguish and turned and ran further into the wood, his feet bleeding and his naked body striped with lacerations.

Ahead of him was another mist-shrouded figure, but this time no taller than his waist. She came running towards him with arms held out, a plea for help and mercy in her dark eyes. She cried in a strange language and her features were dusky, her clothing foreign. Patrick ran to meet her, no longer naked, but wearing a blood-and soot-smudged white surcoat emblazoned with a red cross. His sword dangled in one hand, a shield in the other.

To his left, a group of similarly dressed men crested the hill on horseback. Their surcoats were soaked in blood, and their tack and harnesses jangled menacingly.

They spotted the running girl and put spurs to horse and surged forward.

"No!" Patrick cried out. "Not again!"

Patrick threw sword and shield aside and raced for the girl as fast as his feet would carry him. He called to the knights and leaped to push the girl from their path, but he was too late. The mounted warriors trampled the child, kicking up mud and tossing her body about like a rag doll.

Patrick came to rest on his knees before the broken body. Bloody foam swelled from her mouth. One of the mounted knights circled back to Patrick, raising the visor of his helm to reveal a mean face and wiry gray beard.

"There are no innocents here," he stated with a sneer.

Patrick's eyes opened and he realized that he was lying on the cold ground, still naked. His head snapped in all directions, but he was all alone.

He rose to his knees and looked skyward, ripping at his hair. He longed to weep, but all that would come from him was a noise too pathetic to even be called a moan.

From the corner of his eye he glimpsed another visitor to his delirium. He turned to see the pale face of David of York. The smile lines around his mouth were set grimly as he leaned against a tree in his armor and green greatcloak, shaking his head at the Irish knight. After staring for some time, he silently turned and began to walk away without a word.

"No!" Patrick called, rising and chasing after the image in the mist. "Don't leave me again!" Patrick tackled the Englishman, only to find he was as solid as the mist. He lay on the ground for a while, in the dead leaves and dirt. Then, he started to laugh.

At first it was a mere gurgle in his throat, but then quickly turned to a full-blown guffaw and his face contorted into a twisted parody of joy. He struggled to his feet and directed his laughter to the heavens.

"Is that it?" he railed at the sky. "Is that the best you can do?"

He twirled about like an idiot, got dizzy, then stopped. He wiped his nose on his hand.

"Why must you torment me so?" he called. "Why must you send silly ghosts and demons to do your dirty work? Can't you just crush me with your thumb and be done with it? What did I do to displease you to begin with? Had I not followed you faithfully? Did I not memorize your words? Or was it that I didn't follow your word *well enough*? What! What was it?"

Patrick looked around as if expecting an answer to come out of the trees. He balled his hands into fists and screamed in frustration.

"You want to hear your words? Do you? Do you want me to repeat it to you, so you will know how dutifully I committed it to memory? Well, here is a little something King David said to you: *Because of you my friends shun me; you make me loathsome to them; Caged in, I cannot escape; my eyes grow dim from trouble.*

"*All day I call on you, Lord; I stretch out my hands to you. Do you work wonders for the dead? Do the shades arise and praise you? Selah! Is your love proclaimed in the grave, your fidelity in the tomb? Are your marvels declared in the darkness, your righteous deeds in the land of oblivion?*

"*But I cry out to you, Lord; in the morning my prayer comes before you. Why do you reject me, Lord? Why hide your face from me?*"

Patrick made a mocking bow, "I couldn't have said it better

myself! Did you answer him, I wonder? Did you!"

This last heated assertion sent his mind reeling, blinding his senses in a red rage that sent him back to pulling out his hair and spinning in circles. His head felt like it was going to explode with anger and frustration, and images of all the ghosts that came to visit him this day, plus many more, surrounded him every which way he turned. Each one was a reminder of something brutal. The images spun faster and faster until they were just a blur, leaving Patrick with only the sensation of the sound of wings surrounding him like a flock of pigeons in a madhouse.

He became nauseated and fell to his knees, clutching his ears to block out the sound. He breathed heavily, eyes shut, and waited for the vertigo to subside.

Slowly, eventually, it did—along with the mad beating of wings.

Around him, the forest was steely silent.

He carefully opened his eyes, and standing before him was the hooded Apparition, arms crossed over its chest.

"Go to hell, you cowardly thing," Patrick shouted at it. "Have you no powers but to look menacing? Am I to fear a shadow? I will not any longer! You couldn't possibly take away anything from me that hasn't already been taken. You can't hurt me! You can't touch me!"

Patrick threw a fist at it.

It caught his fist in mid air with its gloved hand. Patrick could not free his hand nor overpower the creature. It began to squeeze his knuckles with an icy grip, forcing Patrick to his knees. A sensation like creeping death traveled down his arm, causing him to fight for his breath. With a wicked twist, the Apparition threw Patrick aside by his arm. His body somersaulted to the ground, and before he could rise again, the Apparition picked him up by the throat into the air.

Patrick hung there suspended by the specter's outstretched

arm and he clawed at the gloved hand. The Apparition held up its free hand and gestured with its index finger. This it moved back and forth as if to tell the Irishman he had done a naughty thing.

Like a puff of smoke in the wind, the Apparition disappeared. Patrick fell to the ground.

He lay there for a very long time.

#

Aimeé listlessly kneaded the dough on the kitchen table, a dazed look in her eyes. For the past couple of days, it was all she could do to put her body through the motions of performing her duties. Soon Rosa Maria would catch on to her air of indifference and either scold her for it or mercilessly question her about the cause. Aimeé wanted neither to happen.

She straightened up and stared at the dough.

Moments later she sleep-walked past Anna who worked at the table next to hers, mumbled something about needing fresh air and left the room. She wandered down the maze of corridors and came to a dead end where several dust-covered barrels were stacked beneath a high window. A beam of light formed a pool on the flagstones. Dust motes floated in the air. The place whispered of sanctuary and privacy.

She sat heavily on the barrels, causing more dust to plume into the air, and she put her elbows on her knees, cradling her chin in her hands.

"What am I doing?" she mused out loud.

She thought long and hard, but could not manage to untie the knot in her stomach. A vague amount of time passed, and Anna's portly frame appeared in the hallway, and approached.

"Ah, lass, what is a matter with yea?" Anna asked, stroking her friend's tawny hair.

Aimeé embraced Anna and managed a shrug. "I've gone and done it," she lamented. "Threw myself at him foolishly, and in a drunken state he took me up on my offer. Then left me lying there."

"Well, if I recall correctly, you weren't of proper mind that night, either," Anna pointed out.

"Still, he left *screaming*, in a hurry, not even bothering to put his clothes back on. He's been gone for days now. What is it about me that would cause a man to do such a thing?"

Anna grabbed the younger woman's chin and made eye contact. "Now, you listen to me lass, that right there should tell yea somethin'. The boy has his own demons and it has nothin' to do with yea. You are a *good* person." Aimeé's face scrunched up on the verge of tears, but Anna's smiling cherubic face kept her from breaking down. "You're goin' to be all right, Aimeé dear."

"But what do I do?"

Anna shook her head. "Yea don't do nothin,' yea just take it day by day. Besides, yea haven't heard his reasonin' yet. Maybe he's been sittin' on a toilet this whole time. Anyone who drinks that much Aphelon is bound to have problems."

They laughed at the image, and it seemed the room grew a little brighter.

Anna abruptly made a face and waved her hand in front of her face. "Good Lord, what's that awful smell?"

Aimeé laughed more. "I'm sure it's just like that."

"No, truly, what's that smell?"

Once Aimeé saw that her fellow maidservant was not smiling, the smell hit her as well. She covered her mouth and nose. "Ew, it smells like something died."

#

"I'm certain it's coming from up there," Anna said, looking up the stairwell that led to the Viscount Loki's apartments. A breeze was blowing steadily from the shadows, down the hall and out the window under which she and Aimeé had been conversing.

Aimeé tilted her nose in the direction Anna was peering, and sure enough, an occasional whiff traveled to her nose from above. "There are other smells too, but there is definitely the smell of something dead."

Anna's eyes got big and she grabbed Aimeé by the arm. "Ya don't suppose he went and finally killed his little man, do yea? He was always so abusive to him, it wouldn't surprise me if he whacked him good finally and left his body to rot up there. Now that I think about it, I haven't seen the little fellow around for a while."

It was Aimeé's turn to widen her eyes. She stifled a cry with her hands, looking up the dark staircase. Finally she turned to Anna. "You don't suppose he killed Sir Patrick, do you, and that is why he's missing? There was no love lost between them on account of the Lady Katherina."

Anna's mouth dropped, and Aimeé started to climb the stairs with determination.

"What are yea doin' lass!"

"I have to know."

"Yea can't just go bargin' into a nobleman's room."

Aimeé paused, but then turned to Anna. "If it's either Patrick or Minion rotting up there, Mark should know about it."

"Exactly. That's why we should go tell him, about the smell."

"But if it turns out to be something else, we have just accused a nobleman of dastardly deeds. That just won't do. So we need to see for ourselves. If it's something else, we don't say anything."

"But what if Loki is home?"

"Then we're just two maidservants asking if he needs any cleaning done."

"What if he's not home, and he catches us in the act?"

"That's why I need you to be on lookout. Come on!"

They climbed the stairs to the door and paused.

"Now what?"

Aimeé wrung her hands, then knocked hurriedly. Some moments passed and there was not the slightest bit of sound on the other side of the door. Anna winced as Aimeé slowly turned the knob. The door swung open with a mundane creak of wood, but at the moment it sounded absolutely deafening.

"My Lord Loki?" Aimeé called out tentatively.

Anna slapped her backside. "Sshh! No need to announce our breakin' and enterin'!"

"Stay here," Aimeé said, and stepped inside.

It wasn't long before Aimeé was standing inside the room, wide-eyed and mouth agape. There were piles of forks, knives and spoons, not to mention all manner of cooking wares—taken from the kitchen and missing for some time. The hearth had been transformed into some sort of odd little cottage made of clay bricks, the sight of which prompted a memory that the crafts studio and that the groundskeeper were missing mortaring and clay-making tools.

She slowly circled the room, taking stock. In the corner was what looked like William of Monmouth's pottery wheel. Oddly, the bagpipe Jason had lent him was sticking out of the little cottage. It was then that she realized that the little cottage was meant to be a furnace, and the bagpipe a makeshift bellows.

A mirror from one of the keep's foyers was leaning against the wall, stripped of its precious metals; the metals were beaten like an old frying pan. An anvil rested near the hearth. Shards of at least one broken clay container littered the table, which was stained with some sort of sticky residue. Then there was the smell. It was almost unbearable. A breeze came through the open window, alternately stirring up smells of tempered metal, stale vinegar, and some unidentifiable chemical smell that was sharp and bit the back of her throat. It also reminded her of how the air smelled just after a lightning storm. About the only thing neat and clean in the room was the Viscount's luggage, which was neatly stacked against the wall and free of dust.

Something crunched under her feet. Glass was scattered around the table. She bent down to move the pieces around, recognizing the various colors and hues from the crystal glasses used for holiday banquets.

A fresh breeze stirred the room and she was reintroduced to the awful smell of death. It was then that something underneath the table caught her attention and she turned to look.

She cried out and jumped back. There, underneath the table, were the bodies of four bloated rats, complete with squirming maggots.

Though covering her mouth and trying not to get sick, she couldn't help but stare at the creatures out of a morbid curiosity. Unlike any rats she'd seen around the keep before, these had white fur, and their big staring eyes were colored red, blue and green. One of them had one green eye and one red eye.

"My goodness, would you look at all this," said a voice behind her.

Aimeé shrieked and jumped back to her feet.

There was Anna, who also shrieked and jumped.

"Damn you, woman! What were you thinking sneaking up behind me like that?" Aimeé all but shouted, slapping Anna on her arm.

"I heard you scream and got worried."

Anna perused the room herself while Aimeé's heart calmed down.

"Looky here," Anna said, bending over and retrieving a piece of metal from the floor. She held the slender piece of steel for Aimeé to see. Its edge was sharpened, and there was a hole at one end where a bolt dangled, and a little below that were bits of gold-colored metal clinging to the end. None of that, however, was what Anna meant for Aimeé to see. Engraved on the surface of the metal was the name Peredur.

"We have to tell Mark," Anna said.

#

"You found this where?" King Mark asked, examining what was left of the pair of scissors in his hands.

"In the Viscount Loki's apartment, m'lord," Anna replied nervously. Though Aimeé stood at her side in Mark's study, Anna took the lead, being the older maidservant. "We really wouldn't have trespassed into his rooms like that, except there was that awful smell coming from there, and well..." She started to explain the situation one more time, but Mark put up a halting hand.

"And all the other items you mentioned are still there?" he asked.

"Yes, many of the expensive items from around the keep, m'lord, but they've been broken or had all the rich parts removed. Much of the stuff was also personal belongin's like these scissors, which everyone knows that Sir Jon and Sir Peredur were always arguin' over. Come to blows almost they did. Just like Willy's pottery wheel, which he blamed Patrick for takin'."

Mark formed a steeple with his fingers and scrutinized the piece of metal.

Aimeé felt the need to say something, and added, "We don't mean to be meddlers or anything, but we thought you should know."

Mark leaned back in his chair and stared at the ceiling for some time. At last he said, "Anna, Aimeé, entering a Guest's apartment without permission is a very serious offense, but considering the circumstances, it will be overlooked. Take better care next time, and I trust that you will keep this information confidential for now. Thank you, you may go."

They bowed quickly and hurried to leave the room. On the way out, however, Aimeé paused.

"Sir Mark," she said, approaching tentatively. "There is

another matter I wish to bring to your attention."

Mark gestured for her to continue. Anna hovered at the door, looking with disapproval at the younger maidservant.

"It's Sir Patrick, he's been missing for days now. I take care of his room, and I know he hasn't been back to change his clothes or anything. Perhaps you should send someone to go looking for him..."

Mark squeezed his eyes shut briefly, his mouth forming a tight line. "Mademoiselle de la Chasse, Patrick is a grown man. He can take care of himself. I'm sure he will turn up soon enough. Right now I have more pressing matters, so, if you will excuse us."

Red faced, Aimeé bowed and left the room with Anna.

When the maidservants had gone, Corbin stepped forward from the assembled knights. "What do you think, Mark?"

Mark drummed his fingers on the bureau. "It confirms what we've known all along. Loki is a scoundrel and has been stirring up trouble—in more ways than one." He looked at Sir Geoffrey, who looked down. "But this doesn't exactly confirm him as a killer. Just a compulsory petty thief, which in my experience is a mild idiosyncrasy among nobility."

"But it does prove he could be asked to leave," Brian McCabe offered.

"But if we let him go now, then we could be losing our only opportunity to bring him to justice—if he really had anything to do with Father Benis' death," Waylan pointed out, and this brought on a loud debate among the Avangarde while Mark weighed the possibilities.

"Enough," Mark almost shouted. "We'll ask the bastard to leave."

"But Mark..."

"But nothing. Our first duty is to the safety of the Guests. If there is any chance that he is a threat, we should remove him. If we incarcerate him, and we are wrong, we run the risk of seriously offending him and the Benefactors who wrote his invitation here, and thus damaging the integrity of Greensprings. If we tell him to leave, then we still risk offending many people, but it will be nothing in comparison to locking him up. If it turns out he is responsible for the death of Father Benis, then it may be possible to apprehend him later...away from the Guests."

The Avangarde assented to Mark's wisdom in the matter.

Mark stood and strapped on his sword.

#

After their audience with Mark, Aimeé parted ways with Anna and took some time with her thoughts. The adventure in Loki's apartment had distracted her from her other problems, but she soon found herself dwelling on them again. She found herself at the stables caressing Siegfried's neck.

"What am I to do?" she asked the horse, as if expecting a more honest reply from the animal than from anyone else. "I wish you could talk, boy. Maybe you could tell me Patrick's deepest thoughts, make some sense out of him for me. You are his best friend. I heard the stories how you took care of him in the forest when he went hunting the wolf. Any other old horse probably would have run off and left him. But not you, you actually found him..." A spark lit in her eye. She looked at the big horse as if seeing him for the first time. "I bet you could find him again, couldn't you?"

Siegfried tossed his head.

Aimeé looked about, and the glimmer in her eye faded. "It's a crazy idea. There are too many people about, it's not like anybody would allow a maidservant to walk out the gate with a nobleman's horse."

Her prospects changed, however, as a commotion in the courtyard drew her attention—and everyone else's.

#

The Viscount Loki and his toady, Minion, returned home.

Loki went to his luggage, opened one of the valises and extracted a medium-sized wooden box, which he took to the table. He swept its surface clean with his sleeve.

"Minion, I know I've been spending more time with the Lady Katherina than here, but it wouldn't have hurt to spruce the place up a bit while I'm gone, and..." He paused, feeling something at his feet. He looked underneath the table and made a face. Bending over, he extracted one of the dead rats by its tail. "And to think this whole time I thought that smell was you. Do something with that, will you?" He tossed the creature at Minion.

Minion, who was distracted as usual, instinctively caught the carcass when it was flung at him, but juggled it like a hot potato when he realized what it was. He juggled it right out the window, a disgusted look on his face.

Loki rolled his eyes. "A nice surprise for whomever is walking beneath the tower. Please dispose of the others as well."

As Minion moved to obey, Loki opened the wooden box with reverence. Inside, lying in a nest of velvet, was a glass globe. This one, unlike the others they had laboriously created, held a cemetery diorama, complete with little tombstones, a dead tree, and even ravens perched on a branch. Loki lifted it from its bed and held it in a stream of afternoon sunlight. He admired it, tilted it one way, then another, letting the clear fluid inside gently stir the white flakes that covered the scene like snow. He was careful not to shake it too hard.

"What does this to them, I wonder?" Minion asked, holding the last rat out the window.

Not taking his eyes off the bauble, Loki answered, "Exposure to the primal powers of the universe."

Minion froze after tossing the rat.

"Will that happen to us?" he gulped, remembering the

colorful fire that danced on his body during the conversion of precious metals.

"Certainly," Loki said while withdrawing a cloth from his pocket. He polished the globe. "If you're a rat or some other such base creature." He looked down his nose at Minion with a grin. "I don't know about you, but I don't have anything to worry about."

Wiping his hands on his shirt, Minion came forward and peered at the bauble in his master's hand. "You never told me what this one is for. I know the other two have something to do with opening the magic door to the fairy world, though I don't understand why we need two of those."

"In order to have a bridge, you need two points, the near side, and the far side, correct?" Minion shrugged and nodded. "The other two baubles are those points, which will go on either side of the portal at the lake."

Minion scrunched one eye shut and scratched his head. "Bridge? Where are the ropes and wood that make the part you walk on?"

"In this case, it will be energy." Loki rolled his eyes when he saw that Minion didn't follow. "Very well, magic then."

Minion nodded, a dim light flickering in his eyes.

"This one," Loki said, raising the bauble in his hand, "is also a point for a bridge."

"Where will that bridge be?"

"Right here, connecting this world with the other world, to draw them together. Like a fisherman drawing his boat to land with a rope."

Minion's head-scratching turned to fierce temple rubbing and now both his eyes were squinting. "If this is one point for a bridge—or rope—where is the other bauble? We didn't make any more."

"The place we're going to, on the other side of the magic door at the lake, is its own point, its own bauble."

Minion shook his head as if trying to clear water from his ears.

Loki laughed. "Don't you worry about it. It will all be clear soon enough."

"And why did you put the little graveyard inside?"

Loki smiled and winked. "Just my own little touch. As I said, soon all things will be made clear. Speaking of which, that time is almost upon us. Start packing our things."

Minion beamed and gestured to the neatly stacked luggage. "We are ready now."

Loki nodded approvingly. "Then prepare and load the carriage. When you have finished with that, go find the Lady Katherina and inform her that our secret outing will be tomorrow."

"You still intend on bringing her?"

"Oh yes, I have special things in store for her." Loki froze, his bauble polishing coming to a stop. His long ears perked up and moved on his head. "We have some company," he said nonchalantly. He gently placed the bauble back in the box and closed the lid, then rose from his seat, crossed the room and secured the box in the valise from which it came.

No sooner had he done so, and there came a rough knock at the door. Loki looked to Minion and jerked his head towards it. Minion went to the door and turned the knob.

King Mark barreled in and knocked the little servant out of the way. The other Avangarde filed inside behind him, and stood about surveying the room, finding it just as the maidservants had described.

Mark turned to the Viscount, who returned his gaze smugly.

"And what do I owe this unexpected, but noble visit, my liege?"

Mark threw out his hand. An object spun and flashed in the air, then buried itself upright in the table. It was the suspect piece of metal that was one half of a pair of scissors.

Loki did not flinch, but gazed calmly at the taller man.

"Why thank you, but I already have a pair somewhere hereabouts," he said.

"You have been stirring up trouble the moment you arrived. You need to leave, now," Mark said.

"Well, if you insist. It's quite a coincidence actually, I was about to leave soon anyhow," Loki said foppishly. "On the morrow I will..."

"No, now."

Loki's eyes narrowed and his foppish smile faded. "I'll leave when I am good and ready, Sir Mark." He turned his back on the Steward.

Mark reached over and grabbed the Viscount by the collar, threw him against the wall, and put his face up to Loki's. "You will leave *now*."

#

Loki and Minion were frog-marched down the corridor to the courtyard. Loki's face was a fuming mask of rage. Avangarde walked before and behind them, giving them plenty of space. Keep staff formed a train behind the group, carrying the Viscount's luggage. All save one: the little valise that housed the glass bauble. On this Minion maintained a death-grip. He sweated to keep up with the long legged strides of his master and the Avangarde who escorted them. Crowds of curious Guests and staff were beginning to form as the two former Guests were steered across the courtyard to the stables.

"You will all pay dearly for this," Loki hissed under his breath, then turned to his servant. "Minion, are all the Avangarde in the keep today?"

Minion gasped as he tried to answer and jog at the same time. "N-no, Master. The Irishman, Gawain, is still missing."

This agitated the Viscount, who mused through gritted teeth, "I'd prefer all the knights be inside. Still, he shouldn't pose much of a threat." So he hoped. He wasn't entirely sure what a man who cast two shadows was capable of. Now was not the time for unknowns.

They were forced to stand outside the stables while Loki's black carriage was readied for travel. After a short delay, the stable hands finally relented to Loki's suggestion that they allow Minion to bridle the fierce black horses. During that interlude, Katherina broke through the crowd, demanding to know what was happening.

"Lady Katherina," Mark said gruffly, "an announcement will be made soon enough. Suffice to say that the Viscount is no longer welcome. So, please step away from him."

This only caused Katherina to grab Loki's hands and look into his face. "What treachery is this? Surely it is mistake."

"No mistake, my dear, they have finally decided that my oil does not mix so well with their wholesome water. It is no great loss—I was hoping to leave soon anyway. My only regret is..." He leaned closer to her and made sharp eye contact. "It is that we never had the opportunity to meet one last time at the chapel by the brook."

Understanding dawned in her eyes even as Sir Waylan gently escorted her away from Loki. She shook off the bearded knight's touch and stalked back into the crowd. Sir Waylan retracted his hand and made a face like he was handling a hissing kitten.

When the carriage was ready and the luggage loaded, Minion was lifted unceremoniously into the driver's seat by Sir Bisch, and Sir Corbin opened the door to the cabin in mock courtesy for Loki. Stiff-lipped, the Viscount entered and Corbin slammed the door, grinning.

"Don't forget to write."

The carriage pulled forward in a quick jerk and headed for the Main Gate. The crowd followed en masse and many people climbed the walls to watch the carriage ramble across the drawbridge and down the road. An almost carnivalesque atmosphere lingered in the courtyard as Guests and staff alike pressed around Mark and the Avangarde with questions. All save Katherina, who slowly backed away from the commotion and ducked into the stables. In short order, she opened a stall, entered, and led out a white steed.

#

When the storm of people had first broken into the stable, Aimeé hid herself. Stablehands dragged the Viscount's carriage out into the courtyard, then returned to wrestle with Loki's willful horses. The other horses in the stable, Siegfried included, snorted and paced nervously in their stalls. Aimeé quieted Siegfried from the shadows of his stall, and listened to the spectacle play out in the courtyard. She thought about stepping out and asking someone what was going on, but decided to save herself the trouble when she overheard just as much confusion in the stablehands' curses and chatter, especially following the Lady Katherina's exchange with the Viscount.

When the crowd moved off towards the gate, she thought about stepping out again. But before she could lift the latch on the stall, she saw the Lady Katherina entering, looking over her shoulder in a surreptitious manner. Aimeé moved deeper into the shadows of Siegfried's stall. It was from there that she watched in surprise as the princess expertly led a horse into the aisle between stalls.

What does she think she's doing? Aimeé thought. She watched the Lady Katherina climb the railing of the nearest stall like a commoner and slide sidesaddle onto the animal's bare back. Grabbing the horse's mane like a pair of reins, Katherina urged it out the rear entrance of the stables with a determined look in her eyes.

Aimeé extracted herself from her hiding place, watching Katherina's disappear in the direction of the keep's rear gate, the Back Door, disbelieving the princess would go to such lengths. After a moment's thought, however, she decided she shouldn't be so surprised. Is that not what people did for one another when they felt strongly for them?

Aimeé asked herself what she was willing to do for friendship's sake, and sighed. "Well, she does have the right idea about one thing," she said, first looking to the crowd in the courtyard, then to Siegfried, "now is the time act. What do you say, boy? Can you find him for me?"

#

It wasn't long before Aimeé herself was slipping out the Back Door with Siegfried in tow. She didn't know how to ride a horse like the Lady Katherina, but with her stout build she did manage to get the saddle, tack and harness loosely in place. She even found some other knight's saddlebags stuffed with clothing and gear, which she threw on Siegfried's back. She was certain Patrick would thank her for them.

Outside the keep, she let Siegfried root around in the apple orchard, then in the forest once she realized he was leading her in that direction, and pulling at his bridle. In the forest, Siegfried tossed his head, flicked his ears, and pulled even harder against Aimeé's grasp.

"Are you on to something?" she asked, stumbling along quickly behind him.

Siegfried jerked his head and pawed at the ground as if in response, and despite her own excitement, Aimeé lost her hold on his bridle. She cried out as the big horse trotted forward and snorted around the path.

"Hey there, mister, you come back...hey, wait!"

Siegfried took off at a gallop down the path. She ran after him as fast as she could. It wasn't long, however, before the horse was out of sight. She cursed her luck and castigated herself for not holding on tighter and for not having anticipated that this might happen in the first place. How was she going to explain this? And it was just a matter of time before her absence would be noticed at the keep.

She continued to run in the direction she last saw Siegfried, hoping that he would at least slow down to get his bearings. After what seemed like an eternity of walk-jogging, holding a cramp in her side, and getting sweaty, she still saw no sign of the animal. "Oh, dear Mary, what have I done?" she moaned in between breaths. In addition to all the reprimands she had coming to her now, she imagined Patrick's reaction if she actually did find him. Did he want to be found? And by her?

Just as she was hanging her head, thoughts running wild, she heard hoofbeats pounding on the earth. She snapped her head in that direction and started out at a run once again.

To hell with what Patrick wants, she thought with conviction, *he needs help and I'm going to make sure he gets it.*

She topped a rise in the forest and caught the glimpse of a horse moving through the trees. It wasn't Siegfried's dark flanks she saw, but the snowy white horse Katherina had taken from the stables. Aimeé also thought she heard voices hailing each other from a distance. Currently not knowing where else to go, she moved towards the voices and where she last saw the horse. If Patrick was in the vicinity, as Siegfried seemed to think, then perhaps he had caught on to the fact that Katherina was near, and was moving towards her at this moment as well.

Struggling through the brambles, she finally made her way to the edge of the wood and saw across a gurgling brook the Lady Katherina pull her horse up to the Viscount's waiting carriage. Loki was standing by a picnic blanket spread out underneath a tree near an abandoned chapel, greeting her warmly with a glass of wine. There was no sign of Patrick.

Before Aimeé had time to feel indignant at the sight of the rule-breaking princess and evicted Guest, a blast of warm air from behind almost knocked her off her feet. She turned in the direction of the wind and got a face full of dust and twigs. Her hair whipped about her head along with tree branches and bushes. Squinting, she saw the sky turn dark as roiling black and purple clouds engulfed the sun like a curtain being lowered over a lantern. The initial force of the wind dissipated and she steadied herself, but grabbed her elbows and held her arms close to her body—the gale was turning icy cold. She stared for a long time in the direction from which the wind was coming.

When no explanation readily came to mind, she turned back to Loki and Katherina, and gasped.

#

Just as she had expected, Katherina found the Lord Loki's carriage at the abandoned chapel. Since her first visit there with Patrick, the chapel had become her favorite place to escape Greensprings's stifling rules and gossip. It wasn't easy to find from the Back Door, however, and she had lost time wandering around the orchard and forest before she recognized the little creek she knew would lead her to the chapel. Here she found Loki sitting at a picnic spread, as if he didn't have a care in the world.

"Katherina," he called to her, standing with a glass of wine in his hand, white teeth flashing in a smile.

"Do you think you can help me down?" she asked.

Loki set the glass down on the edge of the carriage and raised his hands. "My pleasure. I had no idea you could ride. You are full of surprises."

"It seem today full of surprise," she responded, a hint of consternation lingering in her voice. She leaned forward and let her waist slip into his waiting hands. "What has happened?"

Loki set her on the ground. "As I said, my personal charms were starting to grate on my hosts. I guess I made one too many complaints about being treated like a child."

Katherina frowned. "That does not seem like reason to make

427

you leave."

Loki shrugged. "They are not very nice people, now are they?"

"No, they not. They very annoying," she responded, then looked around. "Where is Minion?"

"Oh, I sent him back to the keep to retrieve something." Loki waved off the absence. "Won't you help me celebrate my emancipation from that dreadful place with a toast?" Loki handed her the glass of wine and led her by the other hand back to the picnic blanket. There he picked up another glass and raised it. "Cheers," he said.

She clinked glasses with him and took a sip. "What am I to do now that you are leaving? You were only one there who let me be myself."

Loki smiled mischievously over the rim of his glass. "Why don't you come with me?"

Katherina blinked. "You can't be serious?"

"I am, very. Come away with me. You don't belong there anymore than I."

Katherina touched her chest and swallowed hard, making an awkward smile. "My Lord Loki, that very flattering, but my mother went through much trouble to make possible for me to be here, safe. I cannot take offer. Thank you."

Loki's smile wavered and a little color left his face. "What?"

Katherina took another sip and casually turned away. "That would be wrong of me to go against mother's wishes."

Loki's smile reasserted itself. "Why, that surprises me Kat, I always thought you were your own person. You did what you wanted, when you wanted."

"Precisely, and I choose to stay at Greensprings."

"But you *don't* like it there."

"Haven't you ever have mother, Lord Loki? Haven't you ever want to make her happy?"

Loki's smile was now strained and his knuckles turned a

lighter shade around the stem of the wine glass. He bent down to a box on the picnic blanket and opened it to reveal many types of bottles neatly in a row. He retrieved an open bottle of wine and held it forth, his smile once again relaxed.

"At least allow me the chance to change—" Before he could finish his sentence, the shock wave of warm air blew the picnic blanket askew.

#

Minion huffed his way up the hill, beads of perspiration on his forehead. Running errands for his master was nothing new, but running *this* far, and over fallen trees and uphill was a different matter.

Struggling over a log, he stumbled. He slid down on its far side and caught himself just before hitting the ground.

When he resumed breathing, his breath came out in a shaky rattle. Carefully he removed the little backpack he was wearing and set it on the log, and just as gingerly, removed the wooden box that held the glass globe. He slowly opened the box to reveal the glass container, and noted with a deep sigh that the floating white flakes were not all that disturbed. Loki's voice was still fresh in his mind, ardently warning him not to shake the contents, or else there would be dire consequences. Minion had only to remember the dead rats to believe it.

His nerves calmed, Minion shut the lid of the box, replaced it in the bag and donned the pack. He set out at a more cautious pace for the keep, which loomed just over the trees, and soon found a path through a thicket that would make his journey easier. Looking over his shoulder, up and down the path, and assuring himself that he was alone, he turned to finish his journey to the keep. And that was when he passed a dirty and stark-naked Sir Gawain walking in the opposite direction.

"Oh, good afternoon," Minion said pleasantly, then froze in his tracks, eyes wide.

Gulping and his heart racing, he turned back to the shambling form. The man didn't even seem to note the greeting.

"Sir Gawain?" Minion blurted out, then mentally kicked himself.

Patrick stopped. Dirt and nakedness aside, he looked a mess. His hair was in all directions and matted with twigs; several days' worth of stubble was on his chin, and there was a profoundly dazed look in his eyes.

He frowned at the little man. "You can see me?"

"Er, yes."

"Hmph," Patrick grunted, and turned to continue his wanderings.

Minion sighed and rolled his eyes. He just knew that someone was going to find Gawain, and Gawain would wonder out loud why that fellow Minion was sneaking into Greensprings.

"Sir Gawain," Minion said, eyes darting in all directions. "Where have you been? The Avangarde have looked everywhere for you."

Patrick stopped, turned, and shrugged. "It's a long story."

Minion shifted uneasily. "I...was looking for you too, actually."

Patrick managed a cynical grunt. "Does the Avangarde have better things to do? So they sent you out?"

Minion rubbed his hands nervously. "No, no. It was the Lady Katherina."

Patrick lifted his head.

"Yes. She is worried about you," Minion said. "She sent me in search of you. I am to bring you back to her, immediately."

There was a long moment of silence and Minion wasn't entirely sure if Patrick had understood him, but finally he said, "Very well, take me to her."

Patrick walked towards the little man, closing the distance between them.

Minion coughed discreetly and gestured at his nakedness. "Perhaps you should put this on first." Minion took off his cloak and handed it to the Irishman.

Patrick's face heated. "Of course. Thank you."

#

"Why must I wait here?" Patrick asked. Minion had brought him to an abandoned well at the bottom of the crevasse that served as a moat. Above and not far away was the drawbridge.

Minion sighed. "The Lady Katherina is in a hurry to see you. If you enter Greensprings looking...like this, you will cause a ruckus. I will fetch her to you in this private place, and bring some fresh clothes." With that, Minion scampered off between craggy rocks and thick brush.

Patrick pulled himself tiredly onto the edge of the well to sit. Dazed, he tried to make sense of it all. How long was he gone? Where had he been this whole time? What had he been doing? Why did Katherina suddenly want to see him? Was she sorry? How could he face Aimeé?

Eventually, he realized that it didn't matter, because soon she would be here and see him wearing Minion's little rough cloak about his waist, like a barbarian. He was going to have to face it all. In the meantime, he was afraid to let himself hope that their relationship would go back to the way it used to be.

More time passed, and still neither the princess nor the dwarf appeared, and dark thoughts started play across his mind. An elaborate joke. Minion wasn't bringing Katherina; he was bringing Loki. Others would laugh at him.

But still, he reasoned, Minion had been wandering around the forest for no other apparent reason... Before he could allow this thought to blossom into some new hope, he heard crashing in the brush and the little man burst at a dead run from around the craggy rocks. He passed Patrick.

"Oi, Minion what..."

Almost as an afterthought, Minion stopped suddenly and ran back to Patrick, whereupon he pushed him squarely in the chest. After that, he turned and ran again, not bothering to hear Patrick's shocked cry or the splash he made at the bottom of the well.

#

King Mark entered the throne room and sat. He flung one leg over the arm cavalierly, but tiredly, and sighed.

It was only a matter of time before word was out that Loki had been forced from the isle. It was quite possible that Mark's tenure at Greensprings was over with, and not just his stewardship. He would take total blame, as a good knight should. Sir Corbin would make an excellent steward, and he had an excellent staff of knights to support him.

Mark sighed again.

"Thinking about your decision?" Christianne approached the throne and took Mark's outstretched hand. Hers was tiny in his, and his grasp was strong and the warmth of it always felt good.

He smiled tiredly. "Of course."

"You did the right thing. Everyone knows it. Don't torture yourself over the matter."

"Oh, but I must," Mark replied. "I am 'King' Mark, and must analyze and fret over every matter. Banishing Loki on top of the death of Jason, the breach in the keep defenses and the inquest will most likely cause me to be stripped of...everything. Perhaps it would be best to distance yourself from me."

Christianne nuzzled and kissed his hand. "No, never."

Mark pulled her down onto his lap and hugged her. "I was hoping you would say that. I had to try, you understand?"

Christianne giggled. "I know. And now I will do my duty as queen of morale, and shall cheer you up."

She commenced to tickle him where she knew he was most

vulnerable. Mark jerked and cried out. After moments of her attack he was laughing and all his problems seemed faded. He stood up with her and threw her over one of his shoulders, and began to tickle her while she was helpless.

"Stop," she cried. "I can't breathe!" They carried on for some time, then Mark let her down.

"What's this?" she asked, bending over to pick something up from the floor next to the throne. It was a sort of jewelry box, on it was a small label that bore Mark's name.

Mark looked puzzled.

"It seems that somebody is feeling sorry for you and wants to make you feel better," she said.

"You didn't have to do this for me, Christianne."

She shrugged. "I didn't. Honest."

Mark took the package and looked it over. He shrugged himself and removed the wrappings. Inside was an ornate hinged wooden box. This he opened, and displayed the clear glass bauble inside. Christianne gasped at the sight of it.

"This is no mere gift," she said. "I've never seen such a thing. Surely it is a treasure."

They gazed at the object.

"Curious thing, isn't it?"

It appeared to be a glass orb filled with fluid. Inside was a diorama, a tiny graveyard with a dead tree and crosses.

"Oh, look," Christianne said, gently taking the thing. She shook it lightly and white flakes began to move about in the fluid like snow. Mark grunted in surprise. He took it back and shook it even harder. When he held it still in his hand to watch the miniature snow storm go into effect, however, his eyes grew big when the object levitated above his palm and jumped to the floor.

Before the gasps were out of their mouths, the bauble exploded in a silent flash that engulfed the entire keep. It spread from the throne room at the center of Greensprings to its furthest walls in a heartbeat, forming a brilliant shell of white light that pushed air before it, sending a shock wave that bent every tree and shrub in its path. A storm of dust, loose branches, and dead leaves exploded outward from the keep as if a rock had been dropped in a pond, ripples spreading in every direction.

Unlike such a splash, however, the shell of light did not collapse in on itself and dissipate, but rather solidified, becoming more distinct in shape, and darkening in color. It became a tangible object that encased the fortress under a dome.

Wispy clouds coalesced over this dome. First in barely discernible mist, then in thick cottony clouds that darkened in hue like the dome itself, from gray to angry purple, then to black. These grew in mass and began to swirl in a clockwise motion, gaining momentum. Lighting flashed in their bowels, revealing every hue of midnight. Bolts licked out in every direction, but most kissed the surface of the dome, which by now was just as dark and opaque as the clouds. Wind blew fiercely ahead of the clouds, and the clouds snuffed out the last sunlight.

As the dome lurched forward, it grew and engulfed more land. Its surface, though black, was now as scintillating as the surface of a jewel, or a star-filled winter's night. With its growth, it became more spherical, as if a ball were rising from the earth, holding Greensprings captive at its center.

As the storm raged outside of the sphere, its inside was a different story.

It was calm. Almost completely silent.

It was snowing inside the sphere, and oddly, snowing even inside the buildings. What wasn't covered with snow was sheathed in ice and frost, and a ghostly light illuminated everything like starlight reflecting off of snow. The only sound was the faintly raspy sound of snowflakes gathering.

Not a soul stirred, as every occupant of Greensprings was frozen in place like a statue—walking, sitting, working, or playing.

In the throne room, Mark was still reaching for a falling globe that was no longer there. Christianne stood behind him with hands to mouth. Both had looks of shock in their frost-covered faces.

#

"What on earth is happening?" Katherina said, rubbing her shoulders in the cold wind. Loki gazed at the gathering clouds in the sky over Greensprings, the hint of a smile on his face, but he said nothing.

Katherina fidgeted in the cold. "Do you have blanket or something?"

Loki seemed in a daze, but said distantly, "Yes, yes of course. In the carriage on the passenger seat."

As she moved to the carriage, Loki spied Minion jogging down the road to the chapel, brow glistening with sweat and wet spots ringing his neck and underarms.

"Master, I did it!" he cried in between gasps.

The Viscount gazed at the approaching storm clouds. "It would appear so. You left it in the throne room?"

Minion, bent over on knees catching his breath, nodded.

"Splendid, then Greensprings is now an anchor point. How poetic. That surpasses my wildest hopes. I'm delighted the globe exploded in the keep and not while being jostled in your pack. I honestly didn't expect you to survive the journey."

Minion blinked, but shook off the statement. "I also took care of something else that was troubling you."

Loki raised an eyebrow. "Oh?"

"The Irishman, I pushed him in a well, and if he didn't break his neck from the fall he…"

Loki caught movement from the corner of his eye and knew

the Lady Katherina was exiting the carriage. He tried to gesture for his servant to drop the subject, but it was too late.

"The Irishman? What of Sir Gawain? Did he turn up finally?" she asked. Minion fidgeted. The storm was almost on top of them, turning day into night. "Well, answer me."

Loki stepped between her and Minion. "My Lady, don't worry about it. He is of no concern to you or me. As a matter of fact, nobody in Greensprings is."

Katherina's brow furrowed in confusion. "What do you mean?"

"I'm not convinced you really want to go back there. Trust me, you are meant for bigger and better things. Those people in Greensprings had no right to tell any of us how to act, how to behave. They shouldn't be evicting anybody. They are the ones who deserve to be punished. Well, I took care of them all. Consider them...preoccupied." Loki took her hands in his. "Permit me to take you away. Let me make you a queen—my queen."

Katherina shook her hands free of the Viscount. "What do you mean 'preoccupied'? Just because I thought that place silly, does not mean I meant them harm. And I already am queen." She took a step back, as if seeing Loki for the first time, a hint of a scowl creasing her brow. "What is it with you men? You are like boy with toy." She pushed past Loki and grabbed Minion about the collar. "What of Patrick, what did you do with him?"

Loki sighed deeply and bent down to the wooden box, the one that housed many bottles. As the princess interrogated the hapless servant, Loki selected a clear bottle, unstoppered it, and upended the bottle into a napkin.

"I was hoping it wouldn't come to this, but I guess it was too much to expect everything to go according to plan."

He approached Katherina from behind and covered her mouth with the moist cloth. She struggled violently, but he hung on tight, long white fingers clutched over her face. Eventually, her eyes rolled into the back of her head and she sagged into his arms. Loki handed her limp form over to Minion, who placed her inside the carriage.

"Oh dear," Loki said, his attention suddenly drawn across the brook.

There, at the edge of the trees, stood the maidservant Aimeé. She started at the sight of Loki staring back at her and Minion putting the slack form of Katherina inside the black carriage. Then she bolted like a deer back in the direction of Greensprings.

"This is becoming absolutely ridiculous!" Loki shouted.

"What is, Master?"

Loki pointed angrily in the direction of the bounding Aimeé. Minion swallowed hard.

"She can't do anything," Minion pointed out. "She's alone now."

Loki shook his head. "I prefer to leave nothing to chance. We need as few loose ends as possible." He reached behind the chauffeur's seat and retrieved a crossbow and several bolts. These he shoved into Minion's hands. "Finish her, quickly."

Minion moaned. More running.

#

Patrick Gawain was in shock. Though from which the most, the cold water or the fact that the little bastard had pushed him in, he was not sure.

He floundered in the water and tried to orient himself in the narrow well before he drowned. He should have considered himself lucky: the well was old and abandoned but fortunately full of water. He regained his bearings and fought for the surface of the icy water.

Before he reached it, however, a bright light flashed across the surface, then the water became even colder, if that was even possible. Patrick shed the heavy cloak and swam harder.

Just when he thought he was going to break the surface of the water, his head struck an invisible barrier. Dazed, he reached out and moved his hands along a cold transparent ceiling. The more he beat on it, the more aware he became that it was a thick sheet of clear ice. He tried moving from one end of the well to the other to only find that it was completely capped.

His lung burned, and then seemed to cave in. His sight was growing dark and his vision was becoming tunneled. His senses were leaving him, moving out of reach into a din of panic.

His last blows to the ice propelled him downward and he didn't have the energy to swim up again. He continued to drift as if he already were a waterlogged corpse. He had been dead for days already anyhow. He just hadn't laid down yet.

A slight smile curled at his lips, for now he knew what it meant to have one's life flash before one's eyes. Everything, crystal clear. His mother's worried eyes, David of York's affable face, Marcus Ionus' Avangardesque smile, Waylan's good natured taunting. And Katherina. *"Patrick, no man is an island."*

His heart beat loudly in his ears. The visions and his consciousness seemed to come in flashes that corresponded with each heartbeat, and when his heart slowed, and so, too, did the visions.

Patrick's slight smile turned to sadness. Though he was content that all would soon be over with, he couldn't help but feel that he had failed. Failed just about everything, and was tricked into an icy death by a little ugly servant.

End, just let it end.

Patrick's feet touched bottom as the first of the water began to trickle into his lungs.

#

Aimeé de la Chasse scrambled through the forest towards Greensprings, wind and brush snagging at her dress.

She turned momentarily at the sound of brush breaking behind her. Minion was there and he held a crossbow level. There was a twang! and a whizzing noise, and a bolt thudded in the tree next to her. Aimeé screamed and ran twice as fast away from him.

She finally crossed the ordered rows of apple trees behind the keep. She didn't know anything about crossbows, but judging by Minion's struggle with the weapon, she imagined she could make it within sight of the gate guards before he reloaded.

She broke through the orchard to the familiar path that lay between the keep and trees, but stopped in her tracks.

The keep was engulfed by a dark sphere. The towers and some of the walls were still exposed from the surface of the phenomenon, but in the moment she stopped to gape at the sight, the sphere expanded and swallowed a little bit more of the keep.

The globe was opaque, but with an oily veneer that gave it the appearance of sparkling obsidian.

Again she heard that twanging noise and the whiz of a bolt next to her ear. She screamed again, and with heart beating and chest heaving, she ran for the Back Door, not knowing where else to go.

As she approached it, she could alternately see the outline of the Back Door and her own reflection in the sphere's surface. She stood before it tentatively, not knowing what to do. She touched it gently, and found that it was very cold, but her hand went through it. Like putting one's hand into water. She withdrew her hand and found that, though cold, it was unharmed.

Another crossbow bolt shot past her head, and it made her mind up for her. She held her breath and jumped in.

#

A warm light engulfed Sir Gawain in the darkness, and he

opened his eyes.

All was quiet. Not a sound was discernible. Not even his previously pounding heart.

Patrick approached the sourceless light. Walking or gliding—does one bother to make such a distinction in a dream or a vision? Or was he truly dead? He smiled listlessly, at ease.

No sooner had the smile come to his face, however, than the outline of a man obstructed the light. His sense of contentment turned to one of panic, then rage. It was the hooded Apparition, and what right did his worldly tormentor have being here in his afterlife, anyway? But then it occurred to him that perhaps it had been a banshee, come to guide him to the land of the dead. That would make sense.

Patrick Gawain stood before the Apparition. He did not know what to do, or what to expect. The warm light was completely blocked off from this perspective, and the dark hood was just as blank as it ever had been. Patrick reached up, and grabbed it. The Apparition did not move.

As he removed the hood, the light from behind was no longer blocked and for one brief moment, before he was blinded by the brilliance, Sir Patrick Gawain saw the man inside.

It was himself, smiling with a confident, knowing grin.

It grabbed Patrick by both of his arms, and he was hoisted heavenward.

He lost sight of his doppleganger and suddenly realized that he was once again engulfed by darkness and floating in the ice cold water. He was no longer at the bottom of the well, but was rushing towards the icy surface, lungs on the verge of bursting.

He struck the ice sheet like a missile and exploded into the crisp, life-giving air. He floundered at the surface and gasped, sucking in huge lungfuls of air.

When he had recovered enough, he made the arduous climb up the side of the well. The rocks were slick, but they were irregular and protruded enough to offer plenty of handholds.

At the top Patrick flung his leg over the rim of the well, pulled himself over the lip and landed heavily on the snow. He lay there for some time, his breath coming out in huge puffs of steam. The struggle to break through the ice, or perhaps a parting gift from the Apparition, had left his body heated. Whatever the reason, he felt the warmth leave him. After some time, he sat up and gazed in wonder at the sky, or lack thereof.

How could this be?

When he had fallen into the well, the day was a typical Avalon afternoon, full of sun and clear skies. Now it was dark as night, but with an eerie luminescence that lit up falling snow.

Snow? He reached out with his hand and let some flakes collect there and disintegrate into little moist drops. He lifted his face into the cascade. Little crystals pricked his skin. He looked to the drawbridge and saw great stalactites of ice hanging from it and the gate. All was eerily silent. Gone was the revelation of the Apparition and gone was his anger towards Minion for pushing him in. He was in shock.

After a moment of taking in the fantastical scene, he trudged through the snow to the rim of the crevasse, then to the drawbridge. And just when he thought he couldn't be anymore amazed, he paused in the entryway. There before him was the usual activity of the courtyard, except horribly frozen in place.

He slowly passed them. First were a handful of chickens and ducks standing in place like woodcarvings in a garden. Their natural colors were gone, replaced with a bluish sheen of frost and a white mantle of snow. Some appeared to have been readying to leap or scatter, their wings splayed out, but were frozen just before they could make their move. One was tipped over on its spread wing, as if it had been in mid-air at the moment of calamity.

Next was a villager herding a group of sheep, now motionless with his flock like a life-sized Nativity scene. Patrick peered closely at the man and noted his skin was blue, his eyes white like a dead person's.

Patrick backed away, a grimace on his face, and collided with the next victim.

He turned and an inexpressible sound escaped his throat when he looked up into the face of Sir Jeremiah astride his horse. In his full suit of duty armor, he looked like a war memorial. His usually smiling countenance was twisted grotesquely by obscuring ice.

Patrick looked to the keep entry and ran for it, bypassing other victims. Inside the doorway, he called out, "Hello, is there anybody there?"

Only his echo answered. He took a step inside the darkness and waited for his eyes to adjust and he soon found that here too was a strange glow, though slightly different from outdoors. He looked to the sconce on the wall; there was still a flame, but it too was impossibly frozen. It was now a glowing ice sculpture of fire, flickering from within. Snow fell on his shoulders—from the ceiling. He ventured deeper into the keep, having to high-step through snowdrifts. He passed Mother Superior, frozen in the act of handing an apple to a child.

His feet, which had been blessedly numb, were now starting to ache. Minion's wet cloak that girded his waist was also starting to stiffen and sparkle with ice. He needed shelter and clothing, and decided to make his way to the Hall for Guests and his room, but at the edge of the practice field his feet ached so sharply that he had to stop and rest at some benches. There, he found a frozen Sir Corbin and he tried to pry off his surcoat, but it shattered in his hands. Patrick stopped for fear of hurting Corbin's flesh.

He sat down on a bench and massaged his feet while staring at the eerie images of Trent and Willy flirting with two Lady Guests. He had never realized just how alive Greensprings had been. Likewise, he had never realized just how much it had become home to him, until now. Now that it was too late.

"My God, what has happened? What do I do?"

Suddenly, a sound and movement from the corner of his eye caught his attention. He stood and moved closer to the white expanse of the practice field. He lumbered through the deep, flat snow until he glimpsed a form running through the Back Door. It was a girl, crying out loudly as she ran through the snow.

Aimeé. He picked up his pace and called to her. She heard him and turned her course toward him. Patrick met her halfway, and as she approached she shouted words he didn't understand. Her face was flushed pink and her hair was loose; he put his arms out to catch her. Then suddenly, her back arched and she screamed as she fell into his arms. He hugged her limp form close to his chest and that's when he saw the crossbow bolt sticking out of her back.

"Aimeé!"

Her eyes were pleading and her mouth tried to voice words, but nothing immediately came. Patrick looked up to find the source of the bolt.

There was Minion wrestling with a crossbow, fumbling to draw back the bowstring and set a new bolt.

Patrick gently laid Aimeé down and sprinted for the little man, crying out at the top of his lungs like a berserker. The sight of the half naked crazed Irishman barreling at him caused Minion to drop the bow and run like a scared rabbit.

Patrick gave up the chase once he realized that the little man had too much of a head start and Aimeé was alone. He went back to her and cradled her head in his arms, rocking her back and forth gently.

"Patrick..." A thin ribbon of blood was running from the corner of her mouth. Patrick tried to shush her, but she grabbed his head and forced eye contact. After several false starts where she fought for air, she finally rasped out a quick summary of what she had witnessed: Loki's eviction and Katherina's abduction at the chapel.

She started to cough and shake violently. Patrick held her tightly and stroked her hair, not knowing what else to do. He had seen similar wounds a hundred times on the battlefield. He knew that there wasn't much to do.

"Aimeé, I am so sorry. I didn't see him. I didn't know he had a bow, I..." Patrick swallowed hard, the crushing realization that she was slipping away weighed down on him like a millstone. He felt as if he were in a confined space, like a coffin, helpless to move, helpless to act. "I should have tried harder."

"Patrick..." Aimeé's voice was now coming in wheezing gasps. "I am the one who is sorry. I didn't mean to be a nuisance. I only meant to make you happy."

He was shaking his head as hard as he could to stop her. "You didn't drive me away, it wasn't you. Please believe me."

Something jumped in Patrick's chest and caught in his throat. He tried to choke it down, but it still managed to escape his mouth, flaring his cheeks and spraying some spittle in the process. His eyes reddened and brimmed with moisture like water about to burst over a levee, but they could not overcome the barrier.

Aimeé's eyes were glazing over and her chest rose and fell in quicker rhythm. She clutched his arm. "Patrick, you did...at least a little bit love me? Didn't you? Please tell me that was so. Please."

Patrick's mouth opened to say something, but the only thing that would come out was a pitiful moan. Aimeé grasped his arm tighter and her chest heaved one last time, her neck relaxed, and her eyes stared into space.

Patrick's mouth was frozen open with an unformed word. An icy dagger stabbed his heart as he realized he had squandered this moment. While he wrestled with his mind and heart, the thread on the loom of fate that offered him a final chance to do one kind thing for the maidservant was snipped right before his eyes.

He stared at her lifeless form, then slowly extricated himself from her. He stood on his knees over Aimeé's body and lifted his head heavenward, forming his hands into white knuckled fists. A barrier snapped inside him and an elemental force broke loose all at once like a Biblical flood. It ran wild in a single explosion that shot forth form his lungs; a blast of anguish and frustration. The nearest icicles shattered and fell to the ground with the sound of broken wind chimes.

Once he had exhausted himself, he bent over with a sob and did something he hadn't done in a very, very long time.

He wept tears.

Chapter Eleven

Patrick sat over Aimeé's body for a long time.

He half expected her to yawn and blink her eyes open any moment, as she may have done that one morning in his room.

Snow continued to fall within the confines of the darkness that engulfed the keep at Greensprings. Yet none of it gathered any longer near Patrick and the body of the maidservant.

A tear formed in his eye and fell to the ground, making a small splash in the pool that collected there. By some magic of Avalon or miracle of God, a bubble of warmth and life clung to the tragic scene. Little by little, and almost imperceptibly, grass sprang in the moist earth around the girl's body. While Patrick rocked back and forth in misery, then rested in destitute stillness, his tears had melted the snow away in the patch of earth. It wasn't until the first colorful flower sprung up between Aimeé's fingers that he noticed what was happening. Soon, she was lying in a bed of heather, daffodils, foxglove, lavender, and clover. His heart ached too much to care. What was another enchantment of the Isle? It was not bringing Aimeé back.

He thought about what to do next, but didn't know what to do or where to go. The entirety of the authority of Avalon was frozen: Knight, noble, Church—all were rendered powerless.

The keep grounds were filling increasingly with ice and snow. The Viscount Loki was somewhere out there, with the Lady Katherina in his possession. Patrick suspected that Loki's eviction, Katherina's abduction and the storm at Greensprings were not coincidences. Somehow Loki was responsible for all this. He had brought down Greensprings and the Avangarde. Patrick burned to do something, to take action.

He bent over and stroked Aimeé's hair and kissed her forehead. He then slowly rose to his feet sniffling and staggered towards where last he saw the gate. Once leaving Aimeé's side, however, the bitter cold attacked Patrick's senses and he hugged his arms about himself. His feet pained him in the snow, and the cloak wrapped about his waist offered no warmth.

#

He crossed the drawbridge, and not very far from the gate he came to the sphere's boundary. Brow furrowed in confusion, he approached what he thought was a solid wall, but after squinting into its depths he could make out the road and trees leading to Aesclinn. Curious, he reached to it and drew a breath when his hand passed through. After briefly examining his hand, he steeled himself and stepped through the wall.

He backed away from the sphere and gave it a good look up and down, mouth hanging in wonder. He felt a brief inkling of comfort knowing that only Greensprings was afflicted, and not the entire island—but the thing swelled a little more and gobbled up a few more feet of land. That spectacle, and the streaks of lighting in the sky, filled him with new urgency.

He made his barefooted way down the trail to Aesclinn, casting an occasional look over his shoulder at the shimmering globe. It swelled forward every now and again like an advancing glacier, swallowing evergreens in its path.

He still didn't know what to do, but he hoped that seeing the village would give him an idea. Perhaps one or more of the

Avangarde escaped the tragedy. Maybe they had more information, or perhaps they needed his knowledge to make sense of the situation. In any case, the people needed to know that the dark orb was coming their way.

Patrick shielded his eyes as he made for the village.

#

When he arrived, there were many people in the town square. They were milling about like lost sheep, and sounded rather like sheep, as they argued and wailed about their condition.

When several farmers caught sight of the Irishman, they ran to his side to see if he needed their assistance. Then one of them recognized him.

"By the Almighty," a villager cried, his voice raising in hope. "It's one of the Avangarde. He'll know what to do." At that statement, the rest of the villagers gathered about Patrick and fought to be near him, crying out even more and pleading for explanation, for solace, and for help. They pulled and pushed him and he was many times nearly knocked down. A man in the crowd had the presence of mind to take off his jacket and offer it to him, which Patrick donned gladly.

Patrick grabbed his head in confusion and finally shouted at the pressing mob to be silent. Several others in the crowd took up his plea, and eventually, the cacophony subsided. Patrick hesitated at their staring faces. The pressure on him was palpable.

"Are there any Avangarde in the village?"

This inquiry was immediately followed by a negative buzz, followed by a momentary upsurge in complaints.

Patrick was urged and helped to stand on the edge of the well at the center of the town square to be better heard, and somebody in the crowd extended a pair of pants towards him. He snatched them up and stuck his legs into the holes.

"Does anybody know what has happened, and what..." He gestured at the sphere that loomed in the distance, like a new mountain. "What that is?"

"You don't know?" somebody wailed.

Again, discord ran through the crowd. The clamor rose to new levels as they shouted at him and each other. People were starting to push one another; somebody could get trampled. Patrick squeezed his eyes shut and rubbed his temples, his head throbbing.

His worst fears were confirmed. There were no Avangarde. All authority was locked in a frozen tomb up at the keep. There was only him; Sir Silence.

He opened his eyes.

"Silence!" he shouted, his voice booming with a strength he didn't realize he possessed. The crowd went silent and all eyes were on him. He glared at them like an angry parent.

"I do not know what happened," he growled. "I was absent. But I do know that that thing is coming this way, and you all must make haste to escape it. In the past hour it has spread from Greensprings to almost the edge of town, and that should give you an idea of how fast it moves. Gather only your most necessary belongings and go to the harbor." Patrick stabbed his finger at Frederique the innkeeper. "You! Warn the fishermen when you arrive and coordinate an evacuation off the island to Cornwall."

Frederique gulped and pointed at himself. "Me? Why me?"

"Because I said so."

Patrick turned his attention back to the crowd. "I cannot help you. One of the Lady Guests is missing and is in danger, and I intend on finding her. You are a smart and independent people. I have no doubt you can do this."

A woman in the crowd called out, "But you have no armor, no weapons, no horse...you are barely clothed. How will you do this?"

"I..." Patrick hesitated, his momentum wavering at the simple question. Then, propitiously, movement at the edge of the village caught his attention. A white shape bobbed at ground level. It was the swan. "I...have a plan."

#

Patrick stood on a hill watching the villagers form a caravan towards the harbor. He knelt down and adjusted the poorly fitting slippers a villager had provided for his feet, and then addressed the swan that waited patiently at his side.

"Can you take me there? To the cave?" he asked the creature.

The swan bobbed its head and honked, then slowly waddled into the forest.

#

Minion brought the carriage to stop at the edge of the lake.

He jumped down and opened the cab door for Loki, who caressed the hair of the still-dozing Lady Katherina.

"We're here, master."

Loki put finger to lips and whispered, "Excellent, fetch the valise with the other devices."

Loki slowly extricated himself from Katherina's slumbering form. He exited, and approached the lakeshore, gazing out at the pile of rocks at its center. A fine mist collected on the surface of the water like angel hair. Here at the lake, the weather was still Avalon-perfect, but a breeze was picking up and behind them, in the distance, dark clouds gathered.

He picked his way along the waterline and found what he was looking for; a small pile of stones. Here, he reached up into the air before him, facing the lake, and found what he was really looking for. His hand disappeared.

Minion joined him, carrying a leather case. "Is it as you hoped, master?"

450

Loki searched the air with both hands, finding the corners of the invisible doorway.

"Not exactly," he said at last. "It is a little bigger, but still unsatisfactory. It is not the end of the world, however, for I have come prepared." He turned to Minion, unlatched the case and opened its lid. Inside, nestled in cloth, were two more baubles like the one Minion had left at Greensprings. He gently withdrew one and positioned himself at a certain point at the water's edge.

"Now you will see what all our work was for," Loki said, and he gestured for Minion to stand in another location.

He cupped the globe with both hands and held it near his breast. Closing his eyes and tilting his head towards it, he breathed deeply and began to hum. He continued for some time, like a man at prayer. Finally, the liquid-filled sphere glowed.

Even in daylight its pulsing red light was striking. It throbbed like a beating heart. Loki opened his eyes, and satisfied at the results, replaced the bauble in the case and took out its twin.

"Rainbows are special and have power," Loki mused. "Avalon rainbows are especially powerful—direct descendants of the very first rainbow. You know what else has power?" Minion shook his head, stuck between wonder and bafflement. "Hearts. Besides having power in the poetic sense—passion, love, faith, and so on—they also hold power in a literal sense. They have a charge to them, not unlike the little shock you received from the first clay and metal capacitor I had you touch back in our room. Hardly noticeable to the untrained eye, but enough to activate our little devices here."

Loki went through the same ritual with this bauble as with the first. This time, Minion paid closer attention, and he did hear Loki's heart. The bauble flared to life and throbbed in unison with Loki's.

"There, that should do nicely," Loki said. "Minion, take that one and follow my example."

Minion retrieved the bauble from its nest and set the case down. It was warm in his hand, and not only did the light in it pulsate, but he could feel it throb like a living thing.

"Now, shake it!" Loki exclaimed, and shook his device vigorously. Minion followed suit, and ceased when Loki ceased. Flakes of the white magic powder swirled inside.

"Set it down gently, then move away with me," Loki instructed.

They moved all the way back to the carriage. The two baubles now were glaringly bright, like two fallen stars.

While they waited, Minion rubbed his hands. "Most clever, master. But the globe at Greensprings did not shine or move like these."

Loki grunted. "Yes, that one was made with a different color of the rainbow. How the powers of the rainbow manifest themselves are as varied and interesting as the different colors themselves. Each well suited to a purpose."

No sooner had he finished his sentence then the baubles exploded silently like a thousandfold glints of sunlight off the surface of water. Loki and Minion shielded themselves against the light and a howling wind.

When their vision returned, the baubles were gone, and in their place were two dancing columns of red lightning. These were rooted firmly to the earth, but they flailed and wove like willows in a storm. Then one snagged on something in the air and stopped moving, followed quickly by the other. Between them, the outline of a circle formed in the air, marking the magic door that had captured Loki's attention for so long.

The power of the columns flowed like water on the outside of the circle, then joined. When this occurred, the lightning bolts uprooted themselves from the earth and jumped wholly into the circle, crackling fiercely with an alien noise. The circle grew, widening in every direction until it was many arm spans in diameter, and its lower portion rested neatly on earth.

Then, the lightning energy seemed to exhaust itself and the circle appeared to cave in. A black nothingness filled the air.

Loki and Minion stood gaping at the spectacle that went suddenly silent. Before either one could comment, however, a whoosh exploded from the darkness like water.

They ducked, but the whoosh reached only so far before collapsing in on itself again. It left behind what looked like a shimmering pool of water—hanging in the air.

"My God!" Minion exclaimed.

"Watch your language," Loki said. He cautiously approached the shiny pool and put his face up to it. He could almost make out his reflection, and reached for the mercurial surface.

"Master, don't!" Minion cried.

Loki silenced the little man with a stern look, then slowly forced his hand into the surface. When nothing happened, he withdrew his hand and examined it. With an expressionless face, he stepped all the way through.

A moment passed and Loki reappeared, absolutely beaming.

"Come," he said. "It is time to claim my destiny."

#

Loki had instructed Minion to drive the carriage straight through the magic floating pool, and not to stop. He did just that, holding his breath and squeezing his eyes shut as he whipped the team of horses to their top speed.

He felt the difference in the air before he opened his eyes. Though the Avalon air was mild and beautiful, he felt as though a fresh breeze had blown away a mugginess. His skin felt fresh and tingly. He opened his eyes and gasped. Though he had glimpsed the landscape once before, he found the horse team and carriage racing along a flat silvery surface like that of an expensive mirror. Water kicked up and splashed him with a constant mist, telling him that they traveled over the top of a lake. Though how they kept afloat, he did not know. He glanced behind them and noted their wake left in the water, which ended at a swirling image in the air that must be the magic door.

The sky was green, and there was no sun to speak of, but all was brightly illuminated as if every part of this world contributed some sort of soft glow. The silver lake was rimmed by maroon-colored hills. All these things, however, were nothing compared to the mountain.

Straight ahead was a glass mountain. It jutted from the quicksilver lake and rose high into the air, glistening in a way that was completely unique from the maroon horizon. The mountain was made of glass—clear, dense, neither reflecting the silvery lake nor the green sky, but glinting with its own crystaline light. A path wound its way from its base to its crowning jewel: a pearl and ivory castle. Radiating from the highest spire was a column of light into the heavens.

"Make for the path to the castle!" he heard Loki call out. Loki was hanging out the window of the carriage, enjoying the scenery as much as Minion was fascinated by it.

Soon, the horses' hooves hit the beach of quartz crystal sand, then mounted the path to the castle. The roadway was composed of glass cobblestones, as thick and as heavy as their mundane counterparts, but as clear as ice. The iron shoes of the horses made a thunderous ringing, but did not fracture them.

A short trip brought the carriage to an open oval-shaped gate, surmounted by what looked like an hourglass symbol. Just as with the magic portal, Minion plowed the team through and brought the carriage to a stop in the courtyard. Here, the sound of the horses hooves were quieter.

Where the mountain was glass, the castle was pearl. No discernible stone; no brick nor mortar. Iridescent colors played over its surfaces like oil on water. The courtyard grounds melded seamlessly with the walls, all of which appeared to lean ever so slightly in one direction or another, as if they had grown there like trees.

Minion jumped down from the chauffeur's seat and opened the door for his master. Inside, Loki was gently stroking the brow of the slumbering Katherina, who had slept through all recent events.

Loki grinned. "I believe she will be a bit more even-tempered once she sees just how enchanting her new home is."

He stepped from the carriage and surveyed his surroundings.

The courtyard was enclosed by sheer walls and towers, dominated by an edifice with a single door. A staircase of cascading disks, each like the layer of a cake, spilled from this door to the carriage. Above the door was the same hourglass symbol.

"Yes, most definitely an Elohim sanctuary, or, as the locals like to call it, 'Faerie.'" Loki whispered, taking a deep breath. "Minion, take the princess and follow me."

He mounted the pearlescent stairs and opened the door to the inner sanctum. His face was alight and his smile spread wide like a child's. Inside was a large chamber, and in the darkness he could make out row upon row of columns reaching for the ceiling in the dark. He let the door swing all the way in and allowed outside light to illuminate the room and an opening on the far side. He passed through this chamber to the portal and mounted a steep winding staircase to another oblong door. Beyond, he was pleased to see, it led to a large well-lit space. Many windows opened onto a panorama.

The room, though somewhat musty, was cavernous and offered the same mind-boggling architecture as the rest of the fortress; a slanting ceiling, egg-shaped doorways, trapezoidal windows, columns that leaned, contradicting what their supporting function ought to be. It was beautiful.

He drew in a deep breath, closing his eyes, and then let it out. "Oh, at long last."

When he opened his eyes, his smile turned to a sneer. Before him were the ghostly forms of three veiled woman. They stood far apart from one another across the hall and they were all but transparent, their features all but blurs.

"You cannot enter," the foremost one declared, holding up her hand. "It is forbidden."

Loki scoffed and slapped his gloves against his other hand. He waved at the ghosts. "Be gone, shades! You have no power over me in this domain. You are no longer of this world. Not even *this* world. Now go!"

The ghosts grudgingly turned and walked away, fading as they did into nothingness. Loki laughed after them and strutted about the room. He walked before a great window. He bathed in light from the otherworldly sky and raised his arms, drawing in another deep breath. He closed his eyes.

When he opened them again, they glowed with a hint of lavender.

Minion arrived, heralded by uneven footfalls and grunts from beyond the hall. "Master," he piped. "Where should I put her?" He carried the Lady Katherina in his arms, her dress dragging along the ground.

He gestured at a long table. At one end was a huge kingly chair, and at the other was another large chair, though not quite as large. "There, put her there."

Loki traced his gloved finger along the table, noting the trail of dust he left. There were many dishes, flagons, and cups on the table, all covered in a fine film.

"I will be waking the princess soon," he said, moving to what looked like a group of cupboards and shelves against the far wall. "I would like to have a meal prepared for her. Something special, something to make her more...amenable." He opened the first cupboard and found nothing, moved to the next, and found nothing there as well. The shelves on the wall, however, held more dishes. "Also, unload the luggage from the carriage, find us rooms worthy of royalty and..." Loki froze, something catching his attention. In the center of the room past the long table was what looked like another table, but covered with a cloth. The irregular shapes underneath the cloth indicated that something was sitting on top of it.

"What do we have here?" Loki made long strides for the table and whipped the cover off, creating a cloud of dust.

Loki took a step back, eyes big.

There were two objects underneath the cloth. A rich mirror, propped up, and a very large hourglass. The mirror was held in a frame of gaudy gold workmanship, studded with magnificent clear jewels—but it did not compare to the hourglass. The glass was so clear and thin it was almost absent. A simple framework of highly polished gold rods and braces held the apparatus together. From the side, the glass chambers looked roughly heart shaped.

"What are they, master?" Minion asked.

"True treasures," Loki whispered reverently. He grabbed the hourglass with both hands and hefted it to his chest. It was almost as big as his torso, and heavy. "The likes of which I have not seen in a very long time. This is all surpassing my wildest expectations. Do the grains in the glass look familiar to you?"

Minion stood on tiptoe. After a moment's scrutiny, his eyebrows raised and he exclaimed, "Ah, the magic powder. The converted gold."

"Precisely," Loki said, and hugged the device closer to his breast.

Minion gasped when he saw the powder inside jump and collect against the glass closest to Loki's chest, like iron filaments collecting around a lodestone. The fine grains began to dance and pulse in time with Loki's heart.

"I assume you noticed that giant beam of light at the center of the castle?" Loki asked, replacing the hourglass on the table. He flipped it. The grains filling the upper chamber began to drain into the lower half.

Minion nodded.

"That is the very soul of this place, dying slowly and evaporating into the heavens." Loki smiled and laughed. "But not for much longer. This device is the heart of this place, and I just harmonized it with my own. As long as my heart beats, we have a home."

#

Remembering how long it had taken to find the wolf, Patrick believed it would take hours to find its cave again. He was wrong. The bird took less than an hour to lead him to a small hill of moss and aspen-covered granite, and then paused at a dark opening and honked at him.

Patrick paused at the entrance, and looked back the way from which he came, briefly thinking that maybe there was still somebody out there more qualified than him to get the job done. But he entered the darkness anyway.

The cave was as he remembered it. Cobwebs all but masked the sides, hiding the pictures there. He had no means of creating light, so he stumbled through the darkness. When he achieved what he believed to be the main cavern, he sat and rested his head on his knees, waiting.

Such a long time passed that he wondered if anything would happen.

Eventually, a soft glow began to illuminate the cavern until it became brilliant. Patrick did not bother looking up, but remained sitting with his head between his knees. After some time, someone spoke. It was a soft feminine voice.

"Greetings, Patrick."

Patrick looked up. It was the woman he had seen before here. Her hair was as golden and luxuriant as the cavern's treasures.

"Greetings," he responded, not knowing what else to say.

"We know why you have come, and we haven't much time," the woman said, bending over to help Patrick to his feet. Several other woman were shimmering into existence within the cavern. They approached as if coming from the walls. They all shared the same beautifully sculpted cheekbones and arched brows. Their eyes were identical—green, with starbursts at their centers. "We must prepare you."

Patrick was dazed. It seemed just being in their presence was intoxicating, dulling his senses. The maidens were reaching into the treasure and bringing forth items.

"Prepare me for what exactly?"

"Loki has broken through to the other side, and his spell is causing a cataclysm that even he is not fully aware of. He must be stopped. We cannot. As with the wolf, we cannot impede him. But you can." The nearest maiden commenced removing his clothes. Patrick did not feel ashamed in their presence, as if he were among sisters. They were wiping him down with damp towels, wiping away the grime and blood from his skin.

"A cataclysm?" Patrick let them lift his feet, foot by foot to cleanse them. His minor wounds were now miraculously gone. Once he was clean, the maidens began to place soft clothing on him, slip boots onto his feet.

"Yes," came the response, though he could not tell which one spoke. "He seeks to change the world, but it is beyond his skill. His arrogance will only accomplish to unravel the laws of nature, destroying the world."

Patrick's heart skipped a beat. "Destroy the world? I—I just want to rescue the princess."

"Be stout of heart, kinsman, we are often called to a higher purpose. Everything happens for a reason. It is up to destiny what becomes of us." They were hanging armor on him now. A finely wrought coat of golden scales. Old Celtic armor, but light and supple, and more intricate and of better craftsmanship than any he had seen anywhere else in the world.

"What am I to do?" he asked, rocking back and forth as they tugged on the straps and harness that held the armor to his body. They buckled a scabbard around his waist, and a maiden was placing a round golden shield in one of his hands, another a masked helm on his head.

"You know what to do. Go after the princess, the rest will fall into place," they replied in chorus. They were circling him and showering him with tiny silvery motes that drifted lazily onto him and chimed musically each time one struck his armor.

"I don't think that I...."

"Don't think," the tallest maiden said, placing a finger on his lips. She held out her other hand behind her and another maiden placed something in it. She presented this to Patrick. It was a sword. A beautiful work of art with a golden hilt shaped vaguely like a chalice or an hourglass, the stem of one cup forming the grip. She placed it in Patrick's palm. "Just do. It will all unfold as it should."

The sword, for all its cumbersome metalwork, was incredibly light and it seemed to hum in his hand. Patrick moved it about delicately, and found it an extension of his own arm.

"Take care how you handle that," the maiden said. "Great hands have touched it in the past, and will again in the future, should you succeed."

Patrick let the weapon droop in his arm. At her words, he suddenly felt the weight of the world on his shoulders. "Right, save the world."

The maidens took him by the elbows and led him to the mouth of the cave. They stopped short of the light.

"Go now kinsman, quickly, and remember to face your fears."

They turned then and disappeared into the darkness of the

cave. Before they were gone from sight, Patrick thought that he could see them passing into a chamber that previously was not there. A chamber filled with slumbering knights with swords lying on their breasts. Then the image was gone.

Patrick shook his head. He was only staring into darkness. He sheathed the sword and turned out to the forest.

#

The long table was dusted and set with clean dishes and silverware. A fresh flagon of wine rested within reach of Loki hand as he sat in the big chair, watching the slumbering princess. Minion placed a platter of bread on the table.

"Enough of preparations, concentrate on making something to eat," Loki said. "It is time to wake her." Minion bowed and exited. "My lady, awake, for goodness sake," Loki said in a sing-song voice, and snapped his fingers. A purplish light sparked between his fingers and faded.

The Lady Katherina's body twitched and her eyes slowly fluttered open. She woke slowly, with a huge yawn, and stretched her arms. But when she blinked the sleep from her eyes and looked around, she stood up sharply.

"Good afternoon, Lady Katherina, how art thou?" Loki chuckled.

Katherina looked about her, dumbfounded. Her eyes came to rest on Loki and recollection crossed her face. Her hand slowly came up to her mouth. "What have you done with me? Where am I?"

Her face was cross. Loki chuckled at the sight as he filled a goblet before him from the decanter. "What I have done with you," he said, "is spirit you away from Greensprings, which you never liked anyhow. As far as where you are, I believe this place was once called Castle Chariot."

Katherina stood and rushed to one of the windows. Her jaw dropped at the sight, and unbelieving bewilderment grew in her eyes.

"I know this must all be very difficult to take in," he said, joining her at the window. He held the goblet out to her. "This is not the world as you know it. To give you a simple analogy, a very simple one, this is the world from the corner of your eye. Please won't you have a drink?"

Katherina shook her head and the wonderment vanished from her face. "I want nothing you have to offer, my lord. I have not forgotten the foul smelling cloth."

Loki laughed. "Oh that, such silliness. Those crude methods embarrass me now." He bent near Katherina and held out the palm of his hand. A flame appeared there and danced about with a life of its own. Katherina gasped and backed toward the table. Loki smiled. "You see, If I wanted you to drink, I could make you. I could just as easily carve a woman from wood and make her do my bidding. But it is willingness that matters." Loki approached Katherina and stroked her chin gently. "And companionship, given freely, is much more pleasing to me."

In a daze, Katherina returned to the chair and sat down. "What do you mean to do with me?"

Loki sat on the edge of the table. "Why, whatever you want. You see, this kingdom is now yours just as much as it is mine. I want to make you as happy and comfortable as possible."

"Then let me go home."

Loki sucked air between his teeth. "Well, that poses a bit of a problem at the moment."

"Why?"

"You see, 'home' right now is going through a bit of a transformation." Katherina crossed her arms and frowned. "I don't understand. Explain."

"That's what I always liked about you. Blunt and straight to the point." When he saw that she was not amused by his charms and truly wanted an answer, he stood from the edge of the table, cleared his throat, and paced. "Well, where shall I begin?

Remember when I said this is not the world you know?"

"Yes, what do you mean by that? Where are we?" Katherina once again glanced out the window.

"You have probably heard of it called 'Faerie,' the realm of the Fair Folk, the Fey. A place separated from the normal world by invisible curtains of air, walls of illusion, a place where they could live peacefully apart from mortals. A safe haven. A sanctuary."

Katherina's brow furrowed as she digested the information. "Why did you come here?"

"Because here, I can do this..." Loki said smiling, waving his hand in the air. The cups and silverware set before Katherina levitated in the air, performed a loop, and returned to their original positions on the table in the space of a heartbeat. Katherina's eyes widened at the display, betraying a valiant attempt at maintaining an air of aloofness.

"You are sorcerer, then?"

"You might say that, but I would say a sorcerer learns his craft, whereas I was born to it."

"You are one of these 'Fair Folk?'"

"In a manner of speaking. My kind was the highest sort of Fey. Long ago, I was worshipped as a god. Myself, and others like me, thrived off the psychic energies of devoted mortals. I intend to do so again."

Katherina's concentration suddenly broke, replaced with scathing laughter. Loki stood erect, brow knitted over the bridge of his nose, the sight of which caused Katherina to go into another fit of laughter.

"What's so funny?" Loki growled.

Katherina regained her composure. "A god? I am sorry, but you never struck me as a god. I saw no god-like behavior in you until these few parlor tricks."

Loki's eyes flared lavender in color and he leaned towards her menacingly, his canine teeth revealing themselves to be sharp and pointy. Katherina's mocking laughter withered under his gaze and she withdrew deeper into the chair.

"All in good time, princess. My powers are slow to return in this place, but they are returning." He held out his hands and lightning leaped from them, scouring the walls of the chamber before fading away. "Soon, I will be as powerful as long ago! I will be a sight to behold!"

Katherina breathed shallowly, chest heaving. But she stuck out her chin in defiance. "As long as you are god in this place and not my world, I do not care. And so long as you let me go."

"Neither of which is going to happen," Loki responded, his demeanor becoming more civil. He smoothed the front of his vest. "As lovely as this place is, it just isn't big enough to content me. And, as I pointed out earlier, your world is going through a transformation. You really don't want to be there until it's all finished."

"I don't understand."

Loki smiled. "You like onions?"

Katherina seemed taken aback by the question. "No, they make breath bad."

"No matter," Loki continued. "The thing about onions is that they have many layers to them. The world, likewise, has many layers to it as well. The outer layer of an onion is dull, ugly, even dirty. Such is the world as you know it. Very simple, not the least bit extraordinary. Peel that away, however—" Loki smiled and winked—"then you have something with a little flavor to it. Avalon is such a layer of the world. In Avalon, a modicum of magic still exists, and obeys different laws of nature. Peel the next layer, and you have this..." Loki raised his hands and looked around. "This place is magic. Can't you just feel the power coursing through this place?"

Katherina looked around. She had been rubbing her shoulders and forearms, but suddenly stopped and sat on her hands. "Perhaps."

"And if you want to take it a step further," Loki continued, "peel back another layer and you have Heaven and Hell, if you believe such things."

Katherina was thoughtful, then asked, "If you are one of these Fey, then why did you ever leave in the first place?"

Loki went somber. "Believe it or not, long ago, all the world was like Avalon. That was my domain. That was where I belonged. Only the most fragile and ethereal of creatures dwelt in havens such as this." Loki turned his eyes to Katherina, a mixture of sadness and resentment in his voice. "But then the world started to change, collapsing in on itself. With every manifest event that God the Creator visited upon the earth, magic began to disappear. He drove the many gods away, until they were just shadows and memories, and mankind put more and more stock directly in *Him*, all the good it did them."

Loki paused, pouring himself a drink and taking a long sip from the cup. "The story I told you about myself, being imprisoned in a cave? That was true. I was...preoccupied for a long time. When I made good my escape, the world truly had moved on. I knew my only hope of recapturing any of my former glory was in finding one of these sanctuaries. They too, however, had mostly faded from existence."

"What happened to the Fair Folk that lived in them? Where are they?" Katherina asked, looking around.

Loki shrugged. "The Fey may be incredibly long-lived, almost immortal by human standards, but they are not immune to death. Well, they don't truly die. They grow weary of life and fade. I suspect they passed on, and without them, the havens began to fade away, too." Loki looked around. "I suspect some are still present, weak and in hiding. Yet another reason why I cannot be content to rule here only. Rule what? A ghost world?"

"But you found it, and now are here." Katherina said, noting for the first time that he now stood straighter. His shoulders were broadened and the mangy appearance of his ears and skin was gone. His features were now smooth as polished stone. Yet the pointedness of his features was more acute than ever. His ears almost stuck straight out from his head, and his eyebrows were diving blades.

"Yes. It took a very long time. It was hidden from me, but ironically I was also drawn to it like an insect to a flame. And there is a flame, so to speak. This place is fading, escaping little by little in a great shaft of light to the heavens. This place, too, would have faded soon if I hadn't come along when I did." Loki said this last while approaching the hourglass on the table, touching it reverently.

"But it is not enough for you," Katherina observed.

"No, it is not." Loki smiled wickedly. "This place will make an excellent seat for my throne, for my empire, but I intend to rule the entire world. My powers will grow, and before long all kings will bow to me."

Katherina scoffed.

This elicited a raised eyebrow from Loki. "You don't think so? This whole conversation is a result of you insisting that I send you back to Greensprings, to which I replied: now is not a good time. It is going through a conversion process. A process that has started at the keep and will, eventually, spread to the rest of the world. When it is complete, all the world will once again be as I remembered it, like Avalon. A world where my powers are complete."

Katherina's defiant gaze wavered. "I don't believe you."

"No?" said Loki, raising his eyebrows. He gently took her by the elbow and led her to the mirror on the table. Loki waved his hand over it and the polished surface began to swirl. "Incredible place, this castle. There are all kinds of fascinating devices to be found." The swirling finally coalesced into an image. It was of the opaque sphere spreading out from the Keep at Greensprings. It was almost to the edge of Aesclinn, and the villagers were leaving in droves, carrying everything with them that they could. "Once my powers are restored in Faerie, I can use them in Avalon. What you see there, that globe, is my last great spell in the outside world. Inside of it my powers will function, and it is spreading, as you can see. It neutralizes any who would stop me, then creates an appropriate environment for using my powers."

Katherina watched the scene, shaking her head. "I still can't believe it."

"Oh, believe it, my dear lady," Loki chided.

Katherina chewed her lower lip, then a spark of hope appeared in her eye. "You say you cast this spell before coming here? I thought you say your powers weak outside of Faerie. How could you cast spell that will cover world?"

"Ah, a smart one you are. I knew I picked you for a reason," Loki said, brushing aside Katherina's flicker of hope. "You are correct the mechanism I used to set the sphere in motion would not be enough alone to accomplish the task."

Loki withdrew from his pocket a silk pouch, the contents of which he emptied into his hand. He briefly looked at the couple of coins there and tossed them over his shoulder.

"Won't be needing these anymore," he said glibly, the coins bouncing noisily behind him. He shook out the cloth item before her, holding it there and passing his free hand over it like a magician prepping his audience for a trick. The pouch, however, glowed purple, which was no trick. "Imagine that the outside surface of this pouch is the world you know. The inside is this world, Faerie. My magic works inside the pouch, but not outside. Now," Loki smiled, bouncing his eyebrows, pleased with his own cleverness, "Imagine my hand approaching the mouth of the pouch is the sphere you see in the mirror." With a bit of theatrics, Loki had his free hand balled into a fist and slowly approached the pouch. He let it hover at the opening, and then without taking his eyes off of the princess, shoved his hand inside, grabbed the material, withdrew his hand and turned the pouch inside-out. "And—voila!—the inside is now the outside. Once the transforming globe comes in contact with this sanctuary's portal, then it will be supplied with enough power to transform the world." Loki placed his mouth over the opening of the purple glowing pouch and exhaled, causing it to balloon in size. "You see, I've thought of everything!"

"Yes?" Katherina reached up with both hands and squashed the balloon.

Caught off guard, Loki let the flaccid bag hang from his hand. Though perturbed, he maintained his composure and stabbed a finger at her. "*That* is not going to happen."

"I doubt God will let you rewrite his world."

Loki scoffed, returning the pouch to his pocket. "God will no more stand in my way than he stood in the way of Alexander, Caesar, Atilla, or any number of others that don't even appear in your limited history books."

Katherina scrutinized the image in the mirror, silent while she weighed all that Loki said. She frowned as a thought crossed her mind. "This started at Greensprings? What happened to the people there?"

"That is why you can't go back," Loki said, waving his hand over the mirror. The image swirled and changed to a view overlooking the courtyard of Greensprings. She recognized Willy and Trent, standing like pale erect corpses. She took a step back, gasping and covering her mouth.

Loki grimaced at her reaction. He waved his hand over the mirror once again and it returned to being just a mirror.

Katherina returned to her seat at the table, clutching her stomach as if she might be sick. "Why me? Why have you done this to me? Why did you bring me here?"

Loki cocked his head to one side. "Why? Isn't it obvious? I want you to be my queen."

Katherina's expression fell. "Q-queen?"

"Why yes. Every new kingdom must have a new king and

queen. And of course, royal children."

"Children!" Katherina exclaimed, her ice colored eyes becoming bigger yet.

"Definitely. It's a mighty big world out there to be ruling over."

"What if I refuse?"

Loki looked puzzled. "Refuse? Why would you do that? I am offering you the world on a silver platter. That is such an improvement over a kingdom on some windblown steppe, isn't it?"

Katherina's stammering turned to anger. "It sounds more like I can be your whore."

Loki pushed her gently back into her chair. "Whatever the case may be, I will get from you what I want one way or the other. How, is entirely up to you."

"You're the Devil."

Loki leaned his face into hers, his eyes again flaring lavender, his canines exposed. "If only you were so lucky."

#

Outside the cave Patrick saw the swan again, and accompanying it now was Siegfried.

He blinked. "Now, how did they manage that?" He approached Siegfried happily and hugged and stroked him. "How are you, boy? I thought you were frozen back there for sure." Patrick noticed that there were saddle and saddlebags on him, though poorly set. Puzzled, he opened the bags.

He pulled out a wrapped bundle of black cloth. This he unravelled to find a cape and an Avangarde surcoat with the white swan emblazoned on it. It smelled of Aimeé.

Everything was clear now. Aimeé had let Siegfried loose in hopes of finding him, and saddled and packed Siegfried as best she could in anticipation of his needs. Then she had gone outside of Greensprings to search, and come across Loki abducting Katherina. The maidens had nothing to do with Siegfried being here, it was just a coincidence. Though he wasn't sure anymore if there was really such a thing as a coincidence.

At the scent of the girl and the memories it invoked, he leaned heavily into Siegfried, putting his face in his hand. A knot tied in his heart, and again his confidence faltered.

No, he told himself. The time for doubts and regrets was over. Time to act. He buried his face one more time in the cloth and smelled Aimeé's scent, and then donned the surcoat over the golden armor. He felt he deserved the office after all. Today he was not a Reservist. Besides, who was there to contest him? He re-buckled his belt and mounted the great black horse. The swan honked at him. He looked over to see the bird parading next to a lance leaning against a tree. He urged Siegfried over to it and when he hoisted it, he found that it too was a work of great craftsmanship. This *was* the doing of the maidens.

After Patrick tightened up the saddle and bag on Siegfried, the swan led Patrick to the edge of the lake. The stony island at its center shimmered and seemed to warp in the air, offering glimpses of another reality, but that was now the lake's least extraordinary feature. The pool of undulating quicksilver, standing vertically, riveted his attention. Such fairy glamour caused his heart to race, but he felt fortified by the gifts he had received from the maidens.

The tracks of Loki's horses and carriage led to the edge of the magic portal, where they disappeared abruptly as if swallowed by the air.

The swan honked at Patrick, then it disappeared into the pool, just as the tracks had. Patrick's eyes widened. He did not follow. After a moment, the swan re-materialized in front of him, honking again.

"Give me a moment, will you?" Patrick said to the bird, dismounting and approaching the gate.

Drawing his sword and planting it in the ground before him,

he bent to one knee and held the weapon in front of him. During the Crusade this ritual was performed before every battle, the sword's cross-guard acting as a holy symbol. This sword's cross-guard, however, was U-shaped like a cup from which poured the silvery blade. At the opposite end of the grip, at the pommel, was its mirror image—making the hourglass shape. When Patrick held the weapon by the grip, point down and pommel up, it looked as if he were holding a communion cup before him.

There are no coincidences, he thought, crossing himself.

"My Lord God," he said, squeezing his eyes shut even harder, "I kneel before you a broken and humbled man. I have ignored you, cursed you, blamed you for what is wrong in the world, and most of all, blamed you for not intervening when I thought you should. I was...wrong, and I am sorry. I think I understand now.

"This is our world, a world you created for us and bequeathed to us. It is our responsibility to take care of it, and we should not expect you to do it for us. Just as we are to be our brother's keeper, and to love our neighbor, it is our responsibility to perpetuate good in the world, to know the difference between right and wrong, and to fight iniquity. You provide us with the courage in our hearts and the tools," Patrick raised the sword, "to accomplish this on our own. My knight's oath says protect the weak, fight for those who cannot. I have forgotten these things, and I beg your forgiveness.

"I do not expect a booming voice to answer me from the heavens. I realize your ways are often silent and mysterious. I have faith that you hear me, and I only ask that you give me the strength to do your will. To defeat the enemy, rescue the princess, save the world. If I am wrong in my assumptions, if I am not sincere enough, then do not let Katherina and those at Greensprings be punished for my shortcomings. Spare them, and do with me as you will."

A tear beaded in the corner of his eye. He heard no booming

voice; the lake water did not part before him; no angels broke out in a chorus of song. But he did feel the weight of the world melt away from his shoulders, and a warm feeling fill him from within. A comfort and confidence washed over him like the gentle caress of his mother's hand. Somehow, he found this phenomenon more extraordinary than all the magic of Avalon.

#

"I really don't see what the trouble is, Kat, most princesses would dream of having such a proposal made to them," Loki said.

Katherina looked up sharply. Her face was red and she most definitely was angry, not frightened. "What makes you think that I would appreciate such offer? Especially considering the price I must pay." She gestured to the mirror, which showed an image of Father Constant's friendly face—frozen solid at Greensprings. The image flickered to an image of the sphere engulfing the last of Aesclinn, then it flickered to another image, and then another.

"Drat!" Loki cursed, walking over to the mirror. He passed his hand over it and it returned to mirror form. "Damn thing seems to have a mind of its own sometimes."

"How could I possibly share such world with you? Especially as your concubine? How can I ever trust you again? Everything about you has been lie."

Loki's face looked hurt. He went to her side and hung there, searching her eyes. "Can't you look past this?" He gestured to the mirror. "And see my motives for what they are? I want to do this for you, too. I am not without mortal wants and needs. I chose you because I...care for you. I want you. I need someone to share this with." Katherina was starting to back up, her expression becoming more and more shocked at the prospect of what he was about to say. "Very well, maybe I was too enthusiastic about professing my intentions to you. But can't you look past that and see that I chose you for something great, to share with me because I care for you, because I lo—"

Katherina screamed and covered her ears, pacing back and forth pretending not to hear. She tried to evade his glance, but he stepped in her path every which way. Finally he grabbed her about the wrists. "Listen to me!"

"No! How can you say that? How could you also mistake what we had for love?"

Loki took a step back, pain in his face. "You mean, you never..."

"No, and even if I did, I could not, and would not agree to this...this *thing* you do to Greensprings and Avalon. I would not wed you, I would not rule an ice covered world with you, and I most definitely would not bear your children!" Katherina was almost shrieking.

Loki, the demigod, turned his hunched back to the princess, covered his face with his hands and moaned like a mortal.

"What were you thinking? Was I supposed to be impressed by your power? Was I supposed to come running like a little girl? What makes you—" Loki's face twisted into a mask of anger that made his previous caricatures pale by comparison. She took a step back, swallowing hard.

Loki approached. "You little, insolent, indignant..." His fists burst into lavender flames. "...and worthless mortal. I shall burn the flesh from your bones and decorate my mantel with your skeleton, I'll..."

"Loki, dearest, cannot you understand a little jest?" Katherina laughed nervously, smiling. She plucked at her plated hair.

Loki froze in his ranting, his head tilting to one side curiously.

"Really, you have no need of carrying on so to convince me of your powers. I just wanted to test limits of your sense of humor, and patience. Two things you will be needing if you are to rule world...and two things you will be needing if I am to be doing it with you."

Loki shrank before Katherina. His eyes returned to normal color, the flames extinguished, and his teeth seemed perfectly human. All that was left was his porcelain features, outlined by his glossy black hair and goatee. His mouth was firmly closed, his jaw muscles working beneath the skin. A barely perceptible frown creased his forehead, betraying conflicting emotions surging inside him.

"Kat, you certainly try my patience," he conceded between clenched teeth.

Katherina sauntered over to Loki and rubbed her hands over his chest. "I thought that is what you like about me most, my spiritedness?"

Loki drew in a deep breath and smiled. "Yes, you are like fire—wild and untamed. But necessary for comfort in the chill of the night."

"Yes, my lord, I am like fire, and like fire..." Katherina cradled Loki's face in her hands and looked deep into his eyes. "You can be burned by it."

She brought her knee up swiftly and struck Loki in the groin. And Loki, god or not, immortal or not, doubled over with a grunt. Katherina ran for one of the oval shaped doors and disappeared.

She came to a stairway and ran headlong down it. She rounded a corner and came across Minion who was climbing the stairs with a platter full of food and wine. He barely had time to cry out before Katherina knocked him over. He tumbled down the stairs with the clatter of metal wares, the princess stepping over and around bouncing fruits and shattered glass.

When she found the bottom, she exited another door and found herself in a courtyard underneath the green sky. Before her was a large gate that led out of the castle grounds.

She dashed for it, but when only a heartbeat away, a wall of green flames burst up before her and cut her off from escape. She fell to her knees, and all the fear and anxiety she had repressed until this moment exploded from her; the specter of fear taking control. Her body betrayed her, and she sobbed in rage and anguish.

Behind her came the inevitable sound of Loki approaching. His steps were like thunder, his howls like a storm. A shadow fell across the inner courtyard, and a thunderous footfall later, his form filled the arch. He was a giant, his eyes were not only lavender in color, but slitted and aglow with feral light. Horns curved up from his brow and fangs as big as tusks deformed his lip. Fire burned about him.

"Woman!" he howled. "Thou art betrayal!" He towered over Katherina, who covered her head and whimpered, expecting to be struck down at any moment. "God was wise in casting your kind from Eden, you take council from snakes! And it shows from daughter to daughter!" Loki stomped his foot next to Katherina's head. She cried out, broken by fear, and began to sob. The green fire plucked at her like fingers.

Loki arched his back and drew in a deep breath. He clenched his fists and released his breath slowly, and it rattled as it left him. His stature shrank and he reached down and effortlessly pulled Katherina up by her arm. He turned and dragged her in the direction of the doorway.

"I did not go through all this effort to bring you here so I could kill you in a rage." Loki growled as he climbed the stairs. The horns on his head were now gone.

"I won't do it, I won't have anything to do with you!" Katherina insisted. She cried out every time Loki yanked her arm.

They crossed the chamber with the table, and ascended another set of stairs. "It really doesn't matter what you think, I will *take* from you what I want." Now his fangs were gone, his voice smooth.

The stairs came to an abrupt end at a single door. Loki opened it and threw her in. Katherina sprawled on the floor of a small chamber with windows on all sides. It was the top story of a tower.

"You can't keep me here forever, someone will come for me!"

Loki stood in the doorway. His eyes were now their usual dark color. He looked as before; a thin, sharp man in a black cape. "My dear Lady, the nearest knight in shining armor to come to your rescue is an icicle. There will be no one coming to your aid. There are no more heroes!"

#

Patrick Gawain stood, crossed himself, and opened his eyes.

The weather was starting to change. A cold wind picked up and clouds slid toward the sun. He turned, and in the distance he could see the sphere's relentless approach, heralded by lightning.

The swan honked impatiently and dove into the gate.

"All right, already," Patrick said, mounting Siegfried and hoisting the shield and lance. He grumbled under his breath, "Stupid duck."

He stared at the shimmering pool of light, held his breath as if he were about to plunge into water, then put heels to the horse's flanks.

It was not unlike plunging into water as he passed through the air of Avalon like a thick curtain of mist and burst into a brilliant world. The swan was dashing before him and creating a trail on the silver glassy water.

Patrick was amazed. It took him a moment to find his bearings; for one moment he was in familiar Avalon; now he was on top of a horse riding on the surface of a lake as if it were solid ground. The swan half flew, half ran in front of them. It kicked up water, yet its feet also seemed to land on it as if it were solid.

He set a steady pace behind the bird. For all he knew it was the only thing keeping them afloat as they ran for a castle in the distance, their apparent destination. Siegfried charged along, snorting and whinnying with a vitality Patrick was not aware the beast had. He kicked up water like foam from crashing surf.

The swan, the horse, and the knight raced for the castle. Patrick was feeling a vitality of his own and he cried out in exhilaration, his cape snapping in the wind.

#

In the castle, Loki paced upon the flagstones. Not that they were stone at all. They had the opalescence of a mollusk shell. The entire edifice was hewn from the substance, and the mortar that bound them was as translucent as quartz. The mirror was once again flashing images of its own accord. Loki slapped the side of it, causing the images to flutter. He cursed it, but suddenly froze. He waved his hand at it for better reception.

He stood up straight. "Minion!" he bellowed.

The little man came running. "Yes, Master?"

Loki stabbed a finger at the mirror.

Puzzled, Minion gazed upon the device, then gasped.

There was Patrick Gawain charging over the lake like a hero. His shield and helm flashing, his cape billowing, and a stern look on his face. The white swan emblem blazed on his chest.

"'Don't worry Master, I took care of him,'" Loki said, his face contorting along with his voice in order to mimic Minion's. He slapped the dwarfish man several times. "I guess if you send an idiot to do a man's job, you will just end up doing it yourself!"

"But Master, I do not understand."

"Enough, silence!" He began to pace again, stopping occasionally to gaze into the mirror. He stopped the pacing and did his characteristic meditation. He drew a deep breath and looked into the mirror, his eyes flaring, and then he intoned:

Here me in the cavern darken,
and to me harken.

You vestige of the fire wyrm,
whose breath doth burn.

Rise you son of Nidhug,
and destroy this man-cub!

There was a momentary tremor throughout the castle. Loki threw back his head and laughed menacingly at the end of the command. Lightning flashed from his hands and danced throughout the chamber.

And just as suddenly as this production started, Loki ceased it and he was the image of calm.

He looked to the gaping Minion solemnly. "Was that a little much?"

#

Siegfried came to a halt and reared, pawing at the air. Patrick held on tight and watched the swan also flutter about uneasily. He had felt a tremor that reminded him of a giant's foot coming down, and evidently the animals, being more sensitive, had felt it more keenly.

Siegfried came to rest and continued to paw at the water they stood upon. They were almost to the edge of the glass mountain, yet the swan hesitated.

"Well, let's get on with it," Patrick said, and just then a ripple emanated from the glass isle, sending a small wave over the horse's hooves. "What the hell was that?"

They waited for a long moment and nothing happened. Patrick put heels to Siegfried and continued forward. The swan honked in protest, but he took no heed.

They came to the edge of the isle. It rose from a white sand beach, and a crystal silt roadway began on the other side, leading up the side of the mountain to the castle. Patrick led his horse onto the road and began to climb. The swan was still honking.

Siegfried halted, and again Patrick felt the tremor. The horse took to pawing at the ground and snorting. The hairs on the back of Patrick's neck stood on end, but nothing more happened after some moments. So he put heels to the horse again.

But before he could move on, glass exploded just above the road with the sound of a thousand crystal chalices shattering.

Siegfried bucked and whinnied, and the swan took flight. Glass was pushing up like earth before a mole, and like a mole, a creature burst forth.

"Oh my God," he mouthed.

Siegfried was evidently just as shocked, for not only was he frozen in place, but there was a *plop* followed by the unmistakable smell of manure.

The creature was huge. Three times again the size of knight and mount that stood dumfounded before it. It slithered out of the hole that produced it, indifferent to the shards of glass it dragged itself over. It scales rippled over brawny muscles. It had no wings, which Patrick thought dragons were supposed to have, but it had a sufficiently long muzzle and terrible enough teeth, and a spiny ridge that ran the length of its body. It was a rusty color, had eyes yellow and blazing around dark slits, and when it opened its mouth it revealed an evil purple tongue. It came forward, slowly and deliberately, on legs that only minimally aided its serpentine body.

It halted several body lengths from Patrick and Siegfried (the swan was nowhere to be seen) and stood on its back haunches, gazing at the would-be hero. Soon, this curious gaze turned predatory and the dragon drew in a breath.

The action could only mean one thing. Patrick swallowed

hard.

And indeed the creature did lean forward and breathe on Patrick and his mount. He instinctively put up the round shield and closed his eyes.

Elemental fire belched forth from the dragon's mouth and engulfed them in a crimson shower. Then, the dragon squeezed its eyes shut and threw back its head, letting the last of its blaze exhaust skyward, triumphant. When it looked back down, the almost human expression of satisfaction turned to surprise and disappointment at the sight of unscathed prey.

Patrick realized he wasn't dying painfully. The fire had been deflected on an invisible bubble. Patrick was sweaty, but unharmed.

The dragon drew another breath. Patrick raised his shield again.

Again the dragon breathed flame, but this time it was a thin stream of fire that shot forth like an arrow fired. This flame, so condensed it appeared to be liquid, struck the golden shield and splashed away.

Though grateful for whatever enchantment kept them safe, Patrick could tell it was not all-powerful or inexhaustible. The heat grew more intense with each attack. He had to do something, and quick, before the magical protection collapsed.

The dragon gave up on the fire, having run out of breath, and bellowed in frustration. Patrick kicked at Siegfried's sides. The horse did not have to be told twice; he shot forward, and Patrick leveled his lance.

The dragon reared up on its haunches again, pulling itself beyond the lance's reach, and swatted. The blow struck Patrick just below his shield and sent him and Siegfried hurtling.

Smart animal that he was, Siegfried used the inertia of the blow to continue forward without falling. Patrick pulled hard on the reins to turn him around for a second attack. Siegfried was more than happy to; his shod hooves made sparks on the smooth glass as he about-faced. They barreled again towards the dragon.

Again the flames engulfed them, and this time the fire was hotter and the bubble about them was closer. Patrick gritted his teeth and made a battle cry, and plunged the lance into the creature's chest.

The monster spasmed and swatted at them again. Claws struck Patrick, and he flew a long way before finally striking the glassy surface of the mountain. The wind was knocked out of him. The all-protecting shield was gone from his arm, and the lance was snapped off halfway into jagged splinters. Siegfried was nowhere. The flames were still everywhere, spraying in all directions.

Patrick struggled to his feet and made to grab his sword. The dragon thrashed in pain, its chest rent, and flame plumed out from a fiery, punctured lung. The creature tried to stand, slipped and fell down a smooth glass knoll into a ravine.

The plume from its gaping chest licked against the side of the ravine and was melting a streak of glass. Patrick tried to watch, but the heat was so unbearable he had to turn and stagger away, coughing from the fumes.

After some minutes, the flames and unearthly cries subsided. The Irishman approached, sword drawn, to the place where the dragon had gone over.

The area was leveled. Little fires burned everywhere, leaving pools of molten glass. A sulfurous stench filled the air and Patrick had to cover his face with his arm to muffle the stench of rotting eggs.

Before and below him was the dragon, caught in melted glass like an insect in amber. Patrick's helm and shield were entombed there, too. He lowered his sword.

A familiar whinny brought his attention back from the ravine. Siegfried bounded over a glass hill, mane a little singed and a gash in his neck, but otherwise healthy.

Patrick hugged the horse about the neck, as the white swan glided down from the green sky.

#

Once Katherina's heart had calmed and she realized that she was alive and largely unhurt, she set to the matters at hand: escape, survive.

She yanked on the door handle but found it secure. She kicked it, finding the action at least cathartic.

Light streamed through one of the high windows. Studying the window, she wrote it off as well. It was much too high and the wall too smooth to ascend. No matter, even if she could get to the window, there was the matter of getting to the ground. Judging from the number of stairs Loki had dragged her up, she had a long way to fall.

With that realization, she decided to inspect her prison.

It was circular, being many strides wide, and smooth all about, made from the same strange and beautiful material as the rest of the castle. A high dome capped the chamber, with six equal spaced windows just beneath it, filtering in light from the outside world. She could see aquamarine sky through them. A single door was the only means in and out.

The place was heavy with dust, and carried a musty smell that made her sneeze. There were several objects covered in cloths, which she slid aside.

The first was a pile of old chairs and a table. The next was a beautiful statue made from the same iridescent white material as the castle. It was the image of a woman in a robe, but carrying a quiver of arrows slung over her shoulder, a bow in one hand and a free arrow in the other. Katherina noted that the arrow, though a prop, was made of bronze and fitted in a hole in the hand. She admired it for a moment, but finding no use in it, moved to the next covered item.

A large mirror. It leaned against the wall, but showed her

nothing but her reflection. She used the cloth to wipe the dust off of its surface. Her hair was a mess, her bangs had come out and were falling in her face as they were apt to do, and her eyes were red and puffy from crying and from being angry.

Suddenly she gasped and jumped back a bit.

The mirror quivered and her reflection disappeared as another image came into focus. The image was not in the castle, but definitely in this world of green sky. There were three figures gathered on the slope of a mountain of glass. Katherina peered closer and she gasped anew at what she saw.

It was Sir Gawain, his warhorse, and a...duck? They were standing in a place that looked like a scene of Armageddon. It was all sparkling otherworldliness, with flames and pools of molten material. Katherina couldn't believe her eyes. She smiled and cried out in joy despite herself. Someone was coming for her after all. And Patrick of all people. She had heard last that he had disappeared. Yet there he was, looking knightly.

"Oh, Patrick. I am here. Please come get me," she cried, touching the mirror.

#

Loki tapped his temple with a finger, regarding the mirror with a blank stare. Minion didn't like it when Loki was this quiet.

"What are you going to do now, Master?"

Loki turned so quickly that his cape took a moment to catch up with him. "*I*? What am *I* going to do?"

Minion backed up, swallowing.

"As I see it, it is your responsibility, little man. You had told me that he was eliminated, along with the rest of the Avangarde."

Minion swallowed hard.

"Yet, there he is come knocking on our door with a bunch of animals. And what about the maidservant? Will she be coming along next, with an army of maids?" Loki walked over to the long table piled with supplies from the carriage. He picked up the crossbow and held it out. "Now do it right this time!"

Minion swallowed hard again.

#

Minion slipped silently off the stairs and into the huge, empty trophy chamber holding the bow before him like a holy object.

This was the only passage from the gatehouse to the castle. Sir Gawain would come eventually. Minion would wait in the dark with bow at the ready. By then, his eyes would be accustomed to the dark, the knight's would not be, and he would shoot him dead.

He moved from pillar to pillar, trying to find a good angle at the entrance.

A noise. Minion froze.

His breath became shallow, and he wiped the sweat out of his eyes. Patrick was already here. He knew it. The knight must have ridden like a madman to be inside the castle already. Yes, the Irishman was here, and he was going to gut Minion. He didn't care for Loki or the princess. He wanted to avenge his woman.

The noise again. Somebody else was definitely in the room, moving about. He moved silently from pillar to pillar, sneaking up on the noise, and stopped at the pillar closest to it.

Minion smiled. Have you now.

He jumped out from the pillar and fired. The bolt sailed off with a whistle and clicked deep in the stony darkness.

There was nobody. A rat scurried along the wall and disappeared.

Minion put a hand to his face and laughed nervously. How stupid could he be? Gawain couldn't be here already.

A shadow slid across the light, sending a chill up his spine.

He turned and his heart stopped. There, silhouetted in the doorway stood a hooded man. He moved in to the room, slipping from the light to the darkness, his appearance transforming as he did so. Changing from the hooded figure to the baleful countenance of Patrick Gawain, a sinister smile at the corners of his mouth.

#

Upstairs, from the stairway door, came a short, muffled scream.

#

Katherina wiped the mirror and shook it a bit. Physically agitating it seemed to cause images to come into better focus. She had lost sight of Patrick and the images had been changing to scenes of that bubble-thing crossing the country side. It was now on the edge of a lake with stones in the middle of it.

But now she could see Sir Gawain mounting the last flight of stairs coming from darkness. He was approaching Loki, who sat calmly in that large chair.

"Be careful, Patrick," she cried, hoping that he could hear her somehow. "He can turn into monster."

#

"Greetings and salutations, sir knight. I commend your persistence," Loki said, pouring himself a drink as Patrick appeared in the doorway.

Patrick entered quietly, sword drawn. He gazed about the room. "Where is the girl?"

"All in good time, Sir Gawain, all in good time." Loki smiled, putting his legs up on the table. "I am pleased you have made it this far. It confirms your worthiness for what I am about to offer you. Please, won't you have a drink? You look hot and thirsty."

Patrick frowned in puzzlement. "An offer from you? Why on

earth would I accept anything from you?"

Loki waved a hand theatrically. "Because I have been watching you. You are not like the rest. I believe that place, Greensprings, was misusing you, squandering your talents. They were not allowing you to realize your full potential. And most of all, as you may have surmised by now, I am more kin to the beings who once inhabited this place than to the people on the outside world—just like you."

Patrick stopped. His eyes narrowed, a hint of guarded curiosity in his eyes. He remained silent.

"I can see in your eyes the vestiges of the Fair Folk who dwelt long ago under the hills of your Green Isle," Loki continued. "They were driven there when man came, bringing their iron and their one true God. It doesn't have to be like that anymore. There are some still there. You can go back to them as a hero, releasing them from the fear of the mortals about them who multiply like a sickness. All you have to do is accept my offer."

Patrick's frown deepened, and he looked inward away from the sound of Loki's soothing voice.

Loki stood in a single smooth movement, hands held out in welcome. "You belong here, Patrick, not out there. You've always known it, haven't you? Always feeling out of place, like you didn't belong. Like you were meant for something better. It wasn't chance that brought you here to me today. I can set things right for you. I can offer you the chance of a lifetime."

Patrick felt that odd feeling come over him whenever he was in the presence of the Viscount; a disjointed discomfort, both physical and mental.

"What exactly are you talking about?"

Loki stepped forward, reaching for Patrick's weapon. "Join me, Gawain, make the world right. As we speak, that sphere you saw is engulfing the isle, and soon the world. I will be all-powerful, and I will need men like you at my side. What do you say, Irishman? Join me. We are kin, you and I. We can rule this place. Make it better. Make it the way it should be. You can have Katherina, and a thousand like her. These things will be in my power to grant you. Only say yes."

Loki almost had his hand on Patrick's sword.

Patrick shook his head and jumped back. "We are not kin," he said. He pointed the sword at Loki's chest. "If indeed I have the remnants of the same beings that are of Faerie, then we be kin as the goblin is kin to the elf."

Loki backed up, a mocking smile on his face. "You are right, Sir Gawain. We are nothing alike. You are weak, I am strong. You are gullible, I am shrewd. I am so much more than you ever will be. See..." Loki gestured at the hour glass. Only a handful of sand remained in the upper bell. "Soon the transfiguration will touch the walls of this world, and when that happens, you will witness an avalanche. Unstoppable. You will not be able to stop me."

Patrick grabbed the hour glass and pulled. It was stuck to the table as if nailed down. Loki laughed.

Patrick froze, a smile curling on his lip. "You made a mistake."

Loki laughed harder, his smile all condescension. "I doubt it."

"What you just said. You just admitted that you are currently vulnerable. That would explain much." Patrick stepped forward.

Loki took a step back, his smile wavering. "You can't bluff me."

Patrick raised his sword. "I do not think so, Viscount. The dragon? Minion? You have been stalling all along."

Loki hissed. His eyes turned lavender and lightning jumped from his hands and engulfed the Irishman, who paused in surprise. The energy veered off and dissipated harmlessly about the room. Patrick continued forward and again Loki threw a spell at him. Green flame poured from his hands and covered the knight, yet again with no effect.

Loki clutched his fists in rage. "Where did you find that armor!"

Patrick smiled, holding the hourglass-shaped hilt of the sword to his chest. "From my real kinfolk."

Loki's expression fell momentarily as he looked between the design of the weapon and the hourglass resting on the table.

"Well then," Loki said, regaining his composure and throwing off his cape, drawing his sword. "We will just have to do this the old fashioned way."

#

Katherina cursed as the bronze arrowhead snapped off in the crack of the door. She looked at the useless shaft in her hand and threw it down, and screamed in frustration. All that time wrestling the arrow free of the statue. All that time just to find that it was no match for the stout door and lock.

She paced, chewing on her thumbnail trying to think, but nothing came to mind.

Giving up, she returned to the scene unfolding in the mirror.

#

"I had no idea you were so ferocious," Loki said glibly, hopping onto the long table. He kicked the tray of goblets. Wine splashed Patrick and Loki danced to the other end of the table. "I never gave you enough credit. I always took you for a brooding has-been. The triumphant Crusader returning home with nothing but war stories. At least you got free room and board at Greensprings to show for it."

"Give it up, Loki. Your silver tongue, however offensive, will not enrage me to mistakes, nor buy you enough time." Patrick flung a half-full goblet back at Loki, splashing his shirt with blood-red wine, and hopped onto the table.

Loki leaned on his sword. "So stoic, are we? Well, if I cannot anger you, then perhaps I can—" he rushed forward, growing, bristling out "—frighten you!"

Patrick's eyes widened at the sight of the bull-horned monster barreling towards him. The thing was frightening, but no more than the dragon, the wolf, and the Apparition, so he steeled himself and slashed firmly sideways with the sword, knocking the horns aside and stopping the beast in its tracks. It bellowed in frustration, swung around with its horns again. Patrick stood his ground, grasping his sword with both hands and rained double-fisted blows on the creature. Finally, Patrick won a slash to its shoulder. The Loki-thing squealed and jumped from the table.

Its lavender slitted eyes melted back into Loki's dark ones, and it was again the man, standing there nursing a shallow cut.

"I am impressed. Stark horror does not seem to unnerve you." Loki kicked a chair across Patrick's path. "But there must be something...something that pulls the cord of panic, anger, or loss of control within you. Every mortal has one." Loki parried blows, smiling as he did. He raised his eyebrows. "I wager that I can find your cord, and play you like a church bell. Do you think?"

"The fact that you are warning me makes me think you are quite stupid." Patrick caught his breath and made a series of double-handed swings that Loki danced around.

"Well said, Irishman! But, are you sure of that? Perhaps I am that good. Maybe I am setting you up with anticipation."

Patrick wrung his hands on the hilt of the sword, alternating between a one-handed and two-handed grip. He tried to control his breathing, tried to stay calm, but his labored pants came noisily through his nose. His jaw clenched. He began to fret that these telltale signs of fear were evident to Loki, prompting the man to openly divulge his strategy in order to unnerve him. As much as he hated to admit it, it was working. Loki was toying with his mind; speaking with a maddening confidence that dug at him.

Patrick tried to sharpen his concentration.

"What of this?" Loki sneered, and his form elongated and darkened, slipped low to the ground: the wolf.

"What is wrong, manling?" it said with that chilling voice, "thought you killed me?"

Illusion! Patrick's mind screamed. The wolf leapt. He stabbed at the incarnation. Its fore claws ripped at Patrick's armor, shearing off scales. Patrick went flying and landed hard. The wolf sprang again, wet fangs aimed at his throat. He raised his sword point.

The wolf skipped to one side and yelped. Loki was again standing there, hand over a red bloom on his chest. He swiped material from the table in anger. Patrick pushed at his own ribs; still in one piece.

"Damn," Loki said. "Most fortunate ass you are."

Purple fire shot from Loki's free hand and engulfed Patrick's feet. Patrick paused, but after a brief examination that revealed no damage, he strode forth. His legs snagged on something, though, and when he looked down he saw a mass of green vines coiling up from the floor.

Loki cried out triumphantly and ran forward, sword raised.

Hesitating only briefly, Patrick hacked at the vines. Of his few choices that flashed through his mind in that split second, this must have been the most prudent, because the vines relinquished their grasp, and Patrick had just enough time to duck and catch Loki on his shoulder.

Patrick charged forward, forcing Loki against the table, between the mirror and hourglass. His and Loki's swords were locked at the hilt, and Patrick forced Loki farther over the table.

"You know what they say," Loki grunted, "if at first you don't succeed!"

He raised his free hand and purple fire danced about it.

With his own free hand, Patrick grabbed Loki's fiery wrist and forced it into the mirror.

#

In Katherina's tower prison, she watched the two combatants through her mirror. Occasionally their actions took them out of sight. She found herself shouting encouragement to Patrick and trying to warn him through the device, though it was evident he couldn't hear her. That, and she found herself helplessly chewing on her nails, ardently wishing she could do something, or that something else would happen.

No sooner had she thought this when Patrick forced Loki over the table right before her, as if this mirror were the other side of the mirror below in the hall; again giving the impression of a window. The image was so real she jumped back, fearing that Loki's back was going to be forced through the glass, spraying her with shards as they struggled.

When nothing of the sort happened, she tentatively approached the mirror again to watch, but almost immediately jumped back when this time Loki's hand did appear on this side of the mirror, gripped at the wrist by Patrick's fist. Though no glass showered her, she ducked away. Loki's hand was awash in purple flame.

The flames leaped and passed over her head. They hit the ceiling of the dome, bounced back and struck the floor next to her. His hand slipped back into the mirror and was gone, leaving a ripple effect like that on the surface of water.

"What the..." she said, putting her hands to the mirror. It was solid. "No! That isn't fair!" she cried, and beat her fist on the surface.

A sound to her right caught her attention, and she turned and gasped.

Where Loki's fire had struck the ground, vines had sprouted and were spreading towards her, their thick sinewy arms uncurling like reaching claws. Yellow buds sprung along their lengths, rising skyward and blooming into broad leafy flowers. She took a step back, but continued to watch them curiously.

Her curiosity, however, turned to horror when the centers of the flowers fully developed, revealing little faces. Faces surrounded by manes of yellow petals. Green feline eyes set above tooth filled muzzles glared at her, followed by a multitude of miniscule roars. The flower heads lunged at her, snapping their jaws.

#

Patrick and Loki exchanged blows for some minutes, in the process demolishing most furniture in the room. Eventually they leaned on their swords, staring at each other with hate and fatigue.

"The sands, Sir Gawain," Loki said between breaths, gesturing at the hourglass. "Soon, no more sword play. I will simply blast you from existence. Or, better yet, I will spellbind you, enslave you so that you can watch for a very, very long time what I do to Katherina..."

Patrick stood and wiped his brow. "I guess I better hurry, then."

Loki put a finger to his temple and closed his eyes for a moment. "I know what truly scares you, Sir Gawain. I can see it on your mind, burning like a flame." He snapped his fingers. He was the Apparition. Hooded, silent, ominous. But this Apparition held Loki's sword and it attacked. Patrick put up his sword and locked hilts.

"This image," Patrick hissed between clenched teeth. He pulled back the hood of the robe to reveal his own face, which leered with Loki's smile. "No longer frightens me!"

Loki pushed him off. "I beg to differ. Reconciliation with yourself, with your own personal demons is no easy thing." He swung hard, again and again. "It! Takes! A! Long! Time!" A shower of sparks punctuated each word. Patrick was beaten to his knees, but before Loki could bring down one final blow, Patrick tackled him at the waist and lifted him into the air. He barreled him into the ruined table. Wood and dust flew in the air. They struggled and grappled and ended up on their feet again.

Patrick stood facing himself. Loki swirled his sword in the air, tauntingly.

"I seemed to have found your cord, Irishman, despite your valiant denials. Now, how long will it take to snap that cord in half? Oh, I have an idea." He brightened, and he snapped his fingers again. Nothing changed. "How about you be me, and I you? See?" Patrick looked at his hand around the sword's hilt, and saw the narrower bones. "Is not this such a marvelous juxtaposition? You hate me, everything about me, and I dare not say that you care too much for yourself, either. And you are now me, whom you hate, and now you fight you, whom you also hate."

Patrick examined his forearms. They were Loki's thin ones. A goatee protruded from his chin.

Loki attacked. Sword stroke after sword stroke, Patrick reeled backwards. His strength was waning, the pile of sand was mounting in the bottom of the hourglass, and Loki was joyous.

"Now, how about the Lady Katherina? What would she think about our new guises? Ironically, you would be in her favor with her again, you know..." Loki's smile was victorious. "But only because you are now me."

Patrick stumbled over a broken chair and Loki's blade grazed his shoulder. Patrick cried out and scampered away.

"You did not come here for her sake, did you?" Loki paused his attack to watch Patrick's pain. "She will not love you any more for it."

Patrick growled and swung wildly, but missed and went staggering across the floor, taking another of Loki's blows with him. He was bleeding inside and out.

"You know it, yes. She is gone. Even should you defeat me, you will still just be Sir Silence, Sir Brooding. After you chased her away, your loss became my gain." Loki sent a flurry of blows at the knight, who fell underneath their weight against a pillar. Again Loki stopped to take a step back so he could survey the emotional damage he was inflicting. "How does it feel, Gawain, to chase after something that does not want you? To try to be a hero for an audience that does not care?"

Loki clicked his tongue as Patrick struggled to his feet. "But fret not, friend, I will soon put you out of your misery, and you will no longer have to worry about such things. But before I do, I want to ask you something..." He leaned closer. "Do you not find that the Lady Katherina kisses very, very well? I mean incredibly well? What do you think of those pink, soft lips? How they move passionately? How warm and moist they are...?"

Patrick threw everything he had at Loki. It was his turn to rain blow after blow, sending his doppleganger back and back while the sands drained into the bottom of the hourglass.

#

Katherina dodged the dandelions and ran to the door. There she retrieved the bronze rod and prepared to defend herself against the creeping, growing plant.

Katherina glanced over to the mirror to see how Patrick was faring and froze when she saw his image flicker and turn into that of Loki, and Loki's appearance into Patrick's.

She didn't have much time to ponder the matter because the snarling little flowers were upon her, lunging forward and snapping their teeth. She swung with the rod, missing most, but causing them to think twice about their attack. When she did make contact, a flurry of petals erupted followed by a feline hiss of dismay.

They moved to surround her, and she dashed away,

swinging wildly at her pursuers. One of the little lion heads dove through her defenses and latched onto her shoulder. The little fangs bit deeply, like multiple bee stings. She cried out and grabbed its stem, pulling it off. Backing out of range of the vine, she inspected her shoulder and noted the thumb-sized red blossom on her dress. Though not a terrible wound, she could only imagine what a hundred would feel like and all at the same time.

They creeped closer to fill the last of the space in the room, and Katherina took another look at the mirror. Patrick looked to be faltering in his struggle, or was it Loki? Their images were changing back and forth at random and she had lost track of who was who.

A snarling flower shot out at her as she pressed herself against the wall, and more were surrounding her. The lead-most flower lunged again, ducked under her swing, and wrapped itself about the rod. Katherina struggled to keep it from being ripped from her hands and she kicked at the next approaching head.

"Patrick!" she shouted at the mirror. "Hurry, I need you!"

#

Patrick reached deep inside for the last reserves of what ever he had left. Loki was wrong. There was an audience watching, and it did care. If nothing else, God was there. Perhaps that was the source of his strength.

At first Loki staggered back and struggled to keep up with Patrick's attack, but once he regained his balance, he forced Patrick back. His appearance wavered between his own and that of Patrick's, as if the spell were faltering.

"I tire of humoring you." Loki growled, his voice turning bestial. He currently wore the guise of Patrick, but with fangs. He knocked away Patrick's sword, and with his free hand he grabbed Patrick's throat and forced him over the table. "Time to go."

Loki raised his sword to make the final blow, but movement from the corner of his eye caught his attention. Cast on the floor were his and the Irishman's shadow, but a third was there, adjoined to Patrick's. It was this third shadow that was rising off the floor, growing into a hooded figure.

"What..."

The hooded figure shot forth his palm and planted it squarely in Loki's chest, sending him reeling backwards. It then reached over to Patrick's sword, which dangled from Patrick's exhausted hand, and tapped it with its finger. The sword began to vibrate, and then made an audible hum. The Apparition lifted its head. Patrick saw his own countenance peering back from the cowl, greeting him with a mischievous smile and wink.

Patrick struggled to his feet just as Loki was regaining his footing. First they looked to each other, then for the interloper, who was now gone.

"Whatever manner of trick that was, it did you no good," Loki sneered, gesturing to the hourglass. "You are too late."

There was only a pinch of grains left. With a bellow, Patrick lunged forward, closing the short distance between them. The sword in his hands now sang, shaking his arms with its voice.

He swung down hard on Loki, who met the blow with his own raised weapon. Loki's sword shattered in a shower of sparks and slivers of blade. Loki went down with a shocked expression on his face and a red gash across his chest. Patrick did not waste any more time. He stabbed Loki's torso with a double-fisted thrust.

There was an explosion of silence.

The sword ceased its singing. The grunts and cries of battle were gone.

Loki's mouth was fixed in an O, his eyes wide at the blade protruding from his chest.

Then suddenly, the silence was shattered by a wail that

came from somewhere above the chamber. Patrick thought it sounded like Katherina.

He slowly slid the blade out of Loki's body. Loki tried to stand, but lurched and fell to his knees. He managed to get up, only to fall again. He lay at the foot of the hourglass; the sands were reversing their flow. They were falling up.

A smile curled on Loki's lips, and it was then that Patrick realized that he still looked like him. Patrick looked at his own arms. He was still Loki.

Loki began to laugh, which caused blood to gurgle and foam out of his mouth. "Perhaps it is prophetic, yes?" he said, gesturing tiredly between them. His image blurred and he was once again Loki, and Patrick was Patrick.

Patrick sighed in relief.

Loki's laugh turned from a silent chuckle to an incredible guffaw.

"What is so damned funny? You are dying," Patrick said.

This caused Loki to laugh more, but when he settled down, he said, "You think this is the end of me? You think you have truly destroyed me? You have only wrested the physical from me! Had this occurred outside these walls of air, indeed I would be gone, but that is not the case. I will be back! Come when the Jotuns swallow the sun and moon at Ragnorok and the Antichrist walks the earth at Armageddon, I will be there. And where will you be, mortal, but cold in the ground. Until this day, you will know my eyes when you peer into the shadows. I will be there staring back at you, and you will hear my voice in the gurgle of the dark waters, my face in the dark of the moon, and my spirit in the shiver you feel across your spine. I am not gone."

Loki convulsed in more laughter, but a hellish light began to glow in the wound in his chest. His laughter twisted into screams. The light turned into the head of a serpent and it rose before Loki's face, hissing. Loki's expression turned to wrath and he grabbed the serpent with both hands and wrestled with it, and the serpent grew and grew, wrapping itself about the man.

Patrick took fearful steps out of the way as Loki and the snake faded. Before they winked out of existence, all Patrick could hear was Loki's angry cries.

Nothing remained but the hourglass.

#

Katherina relinquished the bronze rod and grasped two of the flowers about the stems just beneath their heads and struggled to keep them from her. Even so, vines were twining around her legs and torso and little lion heads were latching onto her flesh, stinging her. She cried out and fought harder, but the room was now completely filled with the creatures, yellow heads lining up to attach to any exposed part of her body. A growling flower hovered near her mouth, searching for an opportunity to silence her for good.

"No!"

As if by her command, the flowers suddenly halted their advance. They started to waver in place, then went limp altogether, falling from her body. The hedge of vines that filled the room collapsed in on itself. Without hesitating, Katherina danced away from them, but it wasn't necessary. Right before her eyes, they faded in color then turned to dust.

Confused, she ran to the mirror.

There she searched in its glass and screamed, backing away in horror with hands to mouth.

"No! No! It can't be!" she wailed, seeing Loki standing over Patrick's body with a sword run through it.

She turned away and slumped to the floor, sobbing.

Patrick was dead because of her, and she would be Loki's whore for the rest of her days.

She could not allow that.

She took a deep breath and stilled her sobs, wiping away the tears. Standing, she smoothed out the front of her dress. The mirror was now only a reflective surface. Her reflection was now calm, her crystal eyes glinting coldly in the light.

Footsteps scuffed on the stairs.

"No, Loki, you cannot have me," she said icily.

She bent over and retrieved the bronze rod from the floor, examined it with a detached air, then turned and struck the mirror. When the shards fell to the floor, she chose a particularly long and pointed one.

#

King Mark slowly opened and closed his hand before him.

Though the thawing was almost instantaneous, he was still a bit chilled and stiff. His clothes were soaked and water was falling everywhere in drops from the buildings. The first thing he had done was send men out in all directions to find out what had happened. Slowly the story came in from the villagers, who were still trailing in, about the magic storm that had engulfed the keep.

None of it made sense. It all had started when he dropped that bauble. Was it some sort of magic? What was its purpose? So many questions, so few answers.

Sir Corbin came trotting into the room. He too was still soaked.

"Well, is everyone accounted for?" King Mark asked.

Corbin sucked air in between his teeth. "I am afraid not, Mark. All are present except the Lady Katherina, and of course Sir Gawain, the Viscount Loki and his valet who were not present to begin with. And..." he hesitated.

"Well, what is it?"

"Perhaps you should come see for yourself."

Mark sighed heavily. Judging from Corbin's tone, it wasn't a good thing. He looked to the Lady Christianne, who sat on the throne wrapped in a blanket. He held out his hand to her.

#

The sight of the maidservant Aimeé pained him deeply.

More questions. Why Aimeé? And the bed of flowers? He sighed again. "Take her to the church, summon Father Constant and the Mother Superior, and Rosa Maria. I believe she was the closest thing the girl had to family around here."

Several Avangarde moved to do their duties and he watched them carry away Aimeé. "Damn, damn, damn."

#

Patrick bounded up the steps two at a time until he came to a single door. The top of a tower.

He tried the door, but it wouldn't budge, even after he threw back the bolt. Something was wedged between it and the frame.

Without hesitation, he threw all his weight into it and it burst open to reveal the sight of Katherina lifting a jagged piece of glass over her chest.

"No!" he cried, rushing forward. As he did, he swung the sword in a wide arc. The sword's tip caught the shard and shattered it into pieces.

Her jaw dropped and she took a step back at the sight of Patrick. "Is this another trick of yours, Loki? Are you still so cruel?"

Patrick tried to come forward but she scampered away, snapping dried old vines and flowers, kicking up dust. "It is I, Patrick, really."

"If this is so, then tell me the end of story."

Patrick frowned. "What?"

"The story, the pictures on the wall in chapel, you told me a story about them. What was the ending?"

Patrick now understood. The illusions Loki had been casting. She did not know who was who. He put down his sword and came forward, hands open.

"The knight returned home victorious," he said, a sad and pleading look on his face. "And his Lady came rushing into his arms, joyous that he still lived and that her honor was saved."

Katherina's tear-streaked face broke into a smile and she ran toward him. Patrick met her halfway and they held each other tightly. He kissed her forehead and stroked her hair.

"I was so afraid," she started to say, but he hushed her.

Then suddenly, the entire castle rocked as if by an earthquake.

"What was that?" Katherina asked, and no sooner had she then another tremor shook the foundation.

"I do not know, but I think we'd best be leaving now." Patrick took her by the hand and rushed out the door, grabbing his sword on the way out.

They ran down the stairs and passed through the demolished chamber. As they did, they did not notice that the hour glass was cracking and falling to pieces, and that the sands inside were still falling upward, now to the ceiling of the room. They ran down the second set of stairs and passed through the last room, the one that led outside. From the corner of her eye, Katherina thought she glimpsed Minion hanging upside down against a pillar, pinned there by a dozen crossbow bolts.

#

The shaft of light that emanated from the tallest point of the castle was brighter and more active than ever. Its color was vibrant and powerful, like the color of the sun. It seemed to be drawing all light through it and funneling it heavenward, draining the surroundings of color and substance.

The beam was not only drawing the light away in pulses, but the castle as well. First loose tiles and stone were sucked skyward, but then whole chunks of masonry followed by entire sections of the castle. When it was gone, the mountain began to break away like shattering crystal.

The swan cut the air ahead of the escaping party. Siegfried's hooves pounded on the water. Sir Gawain bent forward in the saddle, clutching the reins, and the Lady Katherina rode behind him, clutching his waist.

"You can make it boy, not much further now!" Patrick shouted.

The last of the glass mountain broke away. Next, the lake. It funneled skyward in a cyclone. Katherina observed the wall of destruction bearing down on them.

"Go faster!"

Patrick put his heels harder to Siegfried. Six paces in front of them, the swan disappeared into the air. Patrick smiled.

Just as the cyclone of water touched Siegfried's wake, they slipped through the curtain of air, and were gone.

#

They collapsed on the grass.

Patrick smelled of blood and sweat, his hair was sticking to his face, and his cape and surcoat were in complete disarray. Katherina did not look much better. Siegfried nuzzled through the grass for a meal and the swan was nowhere to be seen. It was a beautiful sunny day, though all was wet and dripping as if it had just rained. And the sky was blue, reflecting in a placid lake.

Patrick sat up and gazed at the stone island.

"I cannot believe that all just happened."

"You are hero. You are my hero. Thank you. I do not know how else to say that. It was not easy thing for you."

Patrick picked some wet leaves from her hair. Had he done it all for her? Did he love her? His mind and body were telling him yes, but his heart was being its characteristic silent self.

As if she were reading his thoughts, she asked, "How did it come to be you that came?"

Patrick shrugged. "I was in the wrong place at the right time. I was the only one left of the Avangarde. It had to be me."

Katherina toyed with something in the grass. "Had it been anyone else but me in there, would you still have come?"

Patrick was silent for a long moment. "Yes," he said at last. "It would have been my duty and my fate, I think, to do it. But because it was you, I had all the more reason."

Katherina had that look she got when she was trying to break something painful to him. It was then that Patrick fully knew. He had always known.

"You do not love me, do you," Patrick said.

A long silence, then Katherina slowly shook her head. "No. But that does not mean that I am not grateful or do not care for you because I do..."

Patrick put up a halting hand.

"It is all right, my dear Lady. I cannot blame you any more for not loving me than I can blame the sky for raining on me." Patrick wrung water out of his cape and laughed. "I am sorry for being an ass."

Katherina put her hand on his forearm. She looked as if she wanted to say something comforting, but didn't know what.

Patrick came closer and knelt before her. He cradled her face in his hands. "It is the good things about you that I should remember. I will never forget them, or you. I believe you are right in not loving me, for we are different people, you and I, and later on down the road, we would have parted ways and it would have hurt me a hundred times more than this. As it is, you hold a special place in my heart and I should be thankful that you came into my life at all. It was, after all, quite the adventure."

Katherina took Patrick's hands and kissed them. "Ever the romantic, you."

They hugged then, long and strongly. Patrick would never have guessed that lost love would be so pleasant.

Katherina gently broke the embrace and led him towards Siegfried by the hand. "We should be going. We will be missed. And you will return hero. Certainly now you will be Avangarde and you can pick and choose from any of the Ladies you like. Though I wager you would rather be with Aimeé..." She paused at his reaction. "Patrick? What is wrong?"

#

They rode for a long time, and during all that time Katherina was silent. Patrick veered off the beaten path into the woods.

"Where are we going?" she asked. Her face was still solemn. She had not taken the news of Aimeé's death lightly, and felt responsible. Patrick had tried arguing that point with her, but she wouldn't have it. So he let her have her misery.

"I have some unfinished business," was all he said, and she did not question him any further. They came to the mouth of the cave and he dismounted. "You will be safe here with Siegfried, even though there really is no longer anything to worry about. I dare say that if there were anything dangerous on this island, I have already killed it."

With that, Patrick slipped into the darkness.

As before, he stumbled his way to the main cavern until his feet struck the treasure pile, and there he laid the sword and scuffed armor. He waited for some time, expecting a soft glow to appear. But nothing came. He guessed that his job was done, and that the gratitude should just be understood. He couldn't be angry with them.

He turned to leave, and when he did, he knocked something over. It clinked and rolled a short ways. Without knowing why, he bent down to pick it up.

It was the chalice with which they had healed him. He hefted it in his hand, and looked upon it long and thoughtfully. He started to leave with it.

The cavern became brilliant.

"No, Kinsman, it is forbidden," boomed a female voice.

Three maidens stood before him.

"Many things are forbidden, but still done," he said.

"Do not do this, it is unnatural," she pleaded.

He gritted his teeth and looked upon the women with pain and anger. "Unnatural? *You* talk to me of what is natural and unnatural? Since I've come to this island, very little of what I have seen is natural. If God did not want me to do this, then he wouldn't have put this in my path." He shook the cup at them. "He wouldn't even have let me have knowledge of its existence, and what it can do. There are no coincidences."

The maidens were silent, yet parted before him, exposing the exit.

"You are right that this does not belong in the hands of man, and I will return it. But first, I will set things right."

Patrick left the cavern, and the glow faded away.

#

When Patrick and Katherina finally saw Greensprings, they gasped in wonderment. The walls were damp and glistening, and a majestic rainbow arched over it as if painted. The familiar keep was suddenly transformed into an enchanted fortress.

When they entered, they found it oddly empty.

"Where is everyone?" Katherina asked. "Are they all dead after all?"

Patrick shook his head. "If they were, the bodies would still be here."

They then heard singing. It came from the keep chapel, and so they followed it there.

Sure enough, the entirety of Greensprings was gathered. So many that the crowd spilled from the door onto the steps and people stood on their toes to get a better view. At first, nobody noticed the knight and the princess approaching, but when they did, they gasped and parted to offer a path.

Patrick and Katherina strode down the aisle, dirty and disheveled. At the altar were Father Constant, Mother Superior, Rosa Maria and King Mark. Laid out before them was Aimeé.

Katherina stayed at the bottom of the dais, and Patrick mounted the few stairs to the altar. Mark looked as if he were trying to voice something, but nothing came.

Patrick withdrew the chalice from his surcoat and set it on the altar next to the communion cup. He transferred the contents of the communion cup to the chalice, then brought it to Aimeé's lips. The dark liquid pooled, then disappeared into the thin gap between her lips. Nothing stirred except for a rustle of clothing as people leaned forward; a quiet murmur rippled through the congregation.

Then Aimeé's lips slowly moved, taking in more wine.

Within moments, she was coughing and fighting to sit up.

"Wh-what happened?" she murmured.

The church came alive with sound, murmurs growing into gasps of shock and joy. Everyone was pressing around them to be near. Father Hugh's eyes were wide and he crossed himself. Mother Superior had tears in her eyes, but was smiling as she pressed her hands together, mouth moving in a joyous hallelujah.

"You are alive and well, Aimeé," Patrick said softly.

She took a handful of his sleeve to steady herself. "But why?"

Patrick took her in his arms. "That is somewhat of a long story, but suffice to say that I found a treasure right under my nose, and I am not about to let it get away."

Aimeé's brow furrowed, but a smile broke out across her face like a light. She looked around in wonder.

Mark was demanding to know what had happened, Katherina was weeping with joy, Sir Waylan, the other knights, Anna, Claire, Rosa Maria and so many others were pressed around them and clapping and laughing.

Patrick was pleased to see that Sir Jon held his arm out for Katherina to take. Willy had his hand on her shoulder, and Trent stood behind, embracing all of them in his gangly arms. Patrick was confident that she was in good hands, and would not be wanting for friends.

It was going to be a long story. But there was time for it now, and there was still more to do before Patrick could do what he wanted to do most—go home, to Eire. He also knew that here was home as well. He knew that he belonged here. That he had always belonged here, he just hadn't been letting himself. Yes, first he would straighten things out on Avalon, then he would return and be an Avangarde as he rightfully would be, personality flaws and all. But first, he had a promise to keep.

"Aimeé, how would you like to meet my mother, in Eire?"

THE END

Adam Copeland was born and raised in Silverton, Oregon. He attended Southern Oregon State College (now Southern Oregon University) in Ashland, Oregon. There he studied business, chemistry and French. He spent a year study abroad in France and has ever since been passionate about traveling internationally, going to such places as diverse as Asia, Africa and Mexico. He is an avid outdoorsman, enjoying hiking, backpacking, camping, mountain trekking and scuba diving. In addition to short story and novel writing, he is a contributing writer to an online E-zine where he also makes use of his love for digital photography. Adam currently resides in Vancouver, Washington State where he is an active member of St. Joseph's Catholic Church.